PUSH

An Unexpected Forbidden Romance

NYLA K

Cover by Jada D'Lee Designs.
Stock photos by Can Stock Photo Inc., Halifax, Nova Scotia.
Formatting by Julia Scott, Evenstar Books

Paperback ISBN: 978-0-578-56364-0

PUSH (first edition) is published by Nyla K.

To any fellow authors out there who have ever been completely overtaken by a story, and compelled to write it, through the night, until your eyes are red and your fingers are cramping.

That's what this book was for me, so I dedicate it to you.

PUSH PLAYLIST

Available for download on Google Play Music!

Jump – Julia Michaels
Beautiful (feat. Camila Cabello) – Bazzi
Lucky Strike – Troye Sivan
Love Lies – Khalid & Normani
Mr. Brightside – The Killers
Delicate – Taylor Swift
Glass House – Morgan Saint
Beast of Burden – The Rolling Stones
YOUTH – Troye Sivan
bad guy – Billie Eilish
Don't Stop Me Now – Queen
Ghosts (Stripped) – Scavenger Hunt
Without Me – Halsey
Slow Dancing in a Burning Room (Acoustic) – John Mayer
LOVE FT. ZACARI – Kendrick Lamar
Lights Down Low – MAX
Better – Khalid
Sit Next to Me – Foster The People
Bad Moon Rising – Creedence Clearwater Revival
True Love Way – Kings of Leon
Somebody Else – The 1975
Habits (Stay High) – Tove Lo
I Guess That's Why They Call It The Blues – Alessia Cara
lovely – Billie Eilish & Khalid
Everything Will Be Alright – The Killers
Hide and Seek – Imogen Heap
Jump (Acoustic) – Julia Michaels

CHAPTER 1

Ben

"I'M NOT HAPPY ABOUT THIS," I grumbled, standing in the doorway with my arms crossed over my chest.

Scowling. I was literally scowling.

"Yea, so you've said," Jessica huffed, bent over the bed, spreading out fresh sheets. I could have been helping her. I *should* have been... But I was too busy brooding. "Several times already. Hand me those pillow cases."

She flicked her hand at me, motioning to the linens on my left. I glanced at them, regarding them for a moment before releasing a brusque sigh and picking them up, slowly, as if the mere act of lifting them was physically exhausting. Jessica rolled her eyes and stomped over to me, grabbing them out of my hands before heading back to her task.

I started to feel a little guilty. I was acting like a huge baby.

But this whole thing was just so... ridiculous.

I mean, honestly. *Why are we even doing this?*

"How long has she been seeing this kid, anyway?" I murmured, running my hand through my hair.

"Long enough to want to bring him home for Thanksgiving," Jessica sighed while shaking the final pillow into its clean case. She stepped back and admired the immaculately made bed, no help from me. "She's nineteen, Ben. You knew this would happen eventually."

I cringed on the inside. "She's not nineteen yet. She won't be nineteen for another two weeks," I pointed out, as if that one detail changed everything.

"Plus this isn't the first boyfriend she's introduced us to," Jessica reminded me. "She's in college now. She's an adult. Of course she's going to be dating. Lighten up."

I scoffed and squeezed my eyes shut for a moment. "*Lighten up?* Jesus, Jess... Have you forgotten where she came from? That's it. They're sleeping in separate beds." I vigorously shook my head, standing my ground.

Jessica chuckled in my direction, before leaving the room, but not without first whispering under her breath, "Good luck with that."

The doorbell rang and my heart leapt into my throat.

Jessica got up to answer it and I darted over to her side, trying to control my unsteady breathing. This was exactly the kind of impending doom I always knew would come along with having a daughter. I felt it, ever since I found out that my high school girlfriend was pregnant.

We were seventeen when we had Hailey. It was quite the scandal in our small town at the time. People have since found other things in the world to be outraged by.

But I had no concern for them, anyway. I was too busy worrying about myself; about *my* life. The birth of my child transformed me from a scared teenager who was basically shitting himself, to a grown-ass adult, with the snip of an umbilical cord.

After that I was a father. That was it. My life no longer revolved around football, installing a new sound system in my Mustang and trying to cheat on my calculus homework. My priorities had shifted in an instant. It was all about Hailey.

I would stop at nothing to protect her, to provide for her, and to love her unconditionally.

Now, you can understand why I was a little stressed out about meeting her new *college boyfriend.*

She's a sophomore, for fuck's sake. What does she need with a boyfriend?!

Jessica casually opened the door, all smiles and soft greetings, like the calm, rational parent she'd always been. I was just trying not to hulk out of my clothes next to her.

"Hi, Mom! Daddy!" Hailey squealed, leaping through the doorway to grab her mother for a tight hug. Then she moved over to me and I held my baby in my arms, unable to stop the smile on my face that she always brought, giving her a kiss on the head.

I have missed this kid.

"Hey, baby..." I crooned, releasing her and using every bit of strength in me to ignore the other human standing behind my daughter. "Missed you."

"I missed you too, Dad, but it's only been like three months," Hailey giggled, stepping back further, forcing me to follow her with my eyes.

"Still too long to be away from our princess," Jessica added, slipping her arm around my waist, mostly out of affection. Maybe ten percent out of fear that I would lunge at the dude with his hand on my daughter's waist.

"Mom, Daddy... This is Ryan," Hailey spoke, the innocent smile never once leaving her lips. She peeked up at him, and he down at her, smiling back.

Dear Lord...

"Very nice to meet you, Mr. and Mrs. Lockwood," *the boyfriend* stepped forward, taking my wife's hand and shaking it politely.

He extended his hand to me next, and I looked down at it for a moment, squinting in frustration. Jessica elbowed me and I begrudgingly took the kid's hand, shaking it with very little enthusiasm. My eyes came back up to his and I briefly looked him over. This kid was my every fear of having a daughter, realized.

My eyes bounced over to Hailey, then back to the kid as I

swallowed hard.

She's not a little girl anymore.

Of course, I already knew that. She had been away at college for over a year at that point. She wore makeup and drove a leased Volvo. She wanted to be a lawyer.

She was a woman.

But for some reason, it took her bringing home this guy–this *man*–for me to fully comprehend that fact.

Ryan wasn't much older than Hailey. He was twenty-one, Jessica already told me. But still, seeing him was like a slap in the face. The last time I had seen Hailey with a boy was before she left for college. She had been dating this little dweeb from high school. He was a nice enough boy, but that was all he was. A *boy.*

This new one, on the other hand... He was obviously full grown.

The thought made my stomach turn.

Once the awkward introductions were out of the way, the four of us sat down in the living room, doing one of those even more awkward *getting to know the parents* things where you all make uncomfortable chit-chat, trying hard to stray from topics that reminded you your daughter was most likely having sex with that guy.

I sat in silence for most of it, sipping the lemonade that Jessica brought out. She was doing most of the talking on the parents-side. But Hailey and *Ryan* seemed awfully talkative themselves.

"So, how did you two meet?" Jessica asked, and I shot an icy glare in her direction.

"We were in the library at school," Hailey smiled wide, looking up at Ryan with hearts in her eyes. I rolled mine.

"She was looking for a book for her Humanities class," Ryan continued the story. "I'd taken that class last semester, so I helped her find it."

"Then we went to lunch," Hailey finished, taking Ryan's hand. "It was very sweet."

"Sounds like it," I grumbled, and Jessica elbowed me again without even looking. *She's getting too good at that.*

"Well, we're just happy to see our little girl happy," Jessica jumped in, smiling. "Ryan, Hailey tells me you've been doing some landscaping work on weekends?"

"Yea, gotta do something to pay the bills," he chuckled, running his hand along the back of his neck. "Law school's not cheap."

"That's sort of Ben's field," Jessica told him, glancing at me. "Well, masonry contracting. But he knows a lot of that stuff."

Ryan glanced at me and nodded in interest, waiting for me to elaborate.

"It's hard work," I grunted, narrowing my gaze.

"I can handle it," he smirked. "From the looks of it, you can, too." *What...?*

"My dad played football in high school," Hailey added in a prideful tone. "But he had to give it up when my mom got pregnant." She gave Jess and I a wistful look.

"No regrets here," I grinned at her and she smiled.

"Yea, I was a little shocked when I saw Hales's pictures of you guys," Ryan chuckled, shaking his head. "You look like you could be her older siblings or something."

"A lesson to be learned for you *young and in love* couples," I grumbled, mostly in his direction. "Don't do something unless you're prepared to deal with its repercussions."

"Dad... Oh my God..." Hailey muttered, covering her face.

"Ben..." Jess scolded, but this time I dodged her elbow.

"I'm just saying..." I kept on, my eyes locked on my daughter's boyfriend as I warned him with an intimidating look.

"Understood, sir," he surprised me with a respectful nod. "Message received."

I continued my squinting at him. I couldn't figure out the guy's intentions. Was he being serious, or fucking with me?

"Alright, well, let's have lunch!" Jessica quickly changed the subject, jumping to her feet. "Hailey, can you give me a hand in the kitchen please?" Hailey nodded and stood up slowly. Jessica turned to me. "Ben, grab their bags and show Ryan up to Hailey's room."

I sighed and nodded, trying to calm myself down as I got up and followed Ryan to his car. I paused for a moment in the driveway, watching him approach his vehicle. It was a forest green BMW convertible. *How can this young kid afford that car?*

"My dad left it to me," he volunteered the information, likely picking up on my surprise. "He passed away a few years ago. Cancer."

"I'm sorry," I murmured, stepping over to the trunk and grabbing Hailey's bag.

"Thanks," he huffed, picking up his own bag and turning back to the house in silence. *Not much of a talker anymore... I hope I didn't offend him or something.*

We headed upstairs with the bags and I showed him to Hailey's bedroom, plopping everything down on the floor. It was quiet and sort of awkward, so I decided to play nice.

"Look, I don't want you to feel like you're not welcome here," I started, gripping the edge of the bedpost, thinking carefully about my words. "We're happy to have you, of course."

Ryan nodded, his gaze stuck on his shoes.

"Just know that that girl is my entire life," I continued, trying to keep my tone in check. "If she gets hurt, I will hurt whoever hurt her."

Ryan's head popped up and his eyes connected with mine. They were wide, nervous.

"I'm allowing you two to stay in this room together because I trust her. But I don't know you. So if I suspect anything going on in here that I wouldn't approve of, I'll stop it. End of story."

I witnessed Ryan swallowing hard as he nodded slowly. He was a pretty big guy. About my height, broad shoulders, long arms. It was sort of amusing to see him looking worried.

That's right, kid. Be afraid. Never mess with a man with a daughter.

"Do you understand?" I asked, raising my brow at him. I paused, waiting for him to fall in line. He was actually quiet for a moment as he stared back at me. But then he finally straightened up and nodded in agreement.

"Yes, sir. I understand completely," he said, never once breaking eye contact, or blinking for that matter.

I was pleased. He seemed like a respectful guy. *I think I got through to him.*

"Good," I smirked and patted him hard on the shoulder, before turning to leave the room, all the while smiling to myself in satisfaction.

CHAPTER 2

Ryan

"**T**HAT LUNCH WAS DELICIOUS, MRS. LOCKWOOD," I smiled politely at my girlfriend's mother, who was, by all definitions, a total hottie.

It was almost insane. Mrs. Lockwood was a MILF, for sure.

"Thank you, Ryan," she responded, grinning between Hailey and me. "And please, call me Jessica."

Hailey rubbed my back slowly, giving me a look of approval. She was happy that I was getting along with her parents. It was a big deal for me to make a good impression. We'd been dating for four months. She had already met my mother and passed that test with flying colors.

Although my mom liked everyone, so it didn't exactly say much.

Jessica got up and started clearing our plates without even saying anything. I would have offered, but she was done in a flash. I glanced out the glass sliding door to the backyard where Mr. Lockwood was mowing the lawn.

He seemed like a man full of energy all the time. He finished his lunch before the rest of us and stomped outside to do the grass. I would have offered to help with that, too, since I had some new experience in landscaping. *Maybe I still could...*

"I'm going to go see if your dad needs help," I murmured, quickly kissing Hailey on the head before darting outside.

I took the stairs of the deck two at a time, all the while watching Mr. Lockwood. He looked like your typical suburban dad mowing the lawn, minus the fact that he looked *way* too young to have an almost twenty-year-old daughter.

If the Lockwood's had Hailey in high school, then Ben Lockwood must have been about thirty-six, maybe thirty-seven, but that would be pushing it. He looked like a guy in his early thirties. Still with a full head of hair, no grays just yet–none that were visible, anyway–in shape, active... intimidating. Honestly, he scared the crap out of me just a little.

That warning in the bedroom had me on high-alert. Hailey was an overly affectionate girl sometimes. Not necessarily sexual, just touchy, lovey. I didn't want her dad getting the wrong impression and, you know... murdering me in my sleep.

Mr. Lockwood paused what he was doing and tugged his shirt over his head, tossing it behind him on the grass, before continuing with his task. I raised my brows to myself.

I hope I can still look like that at his age. It's hard enough staying in shape at twenty-one.

I stammered over to him, trying to find the right angle so as not to surprise him by sneaking up on him or anything. The mower was loud. I approached with caution, and he noticed me, looking up in expectance.

"Hey! Uh... I was wondering if you needed help with anything," I shouted over the whirring of the lawn mower engine.

Mr. Lockwood's unwavering gaze stuck on me and I began to shift my weight back and forth. He finally broke it, briefly glancing at the ground, then back up to me.

"Not much else left," he grunted, then looked behind me. "You could water the rose bushes. If you don't mind..."

"Sure, yea. No problem," I answered, repeatedly nodding my head like some kind of spazz. I decided to turn around and get started on my job before I embarrassed myself any more.

I located the hose and got everything set up, spraying the rose bushes as my landscaping mentor, Jimmy taught me. Jimmy ran the company I worked for, Heller Landscaping. I was fortunate enough that he let me work overtime in the summer, then cut back to only weekends when school started up again. Not to mention that he taught me everything there was to know about the trade. The money was good. Plus, I always liked being outside and doing physical work.

Sure, I wanted to be a lawyer someday. That was a dream that Hailey and I shared. It was what brought us together, for the most part. But still, being out in the fresh air, under the sun, using my hands... It felt good.

I glanced behind me at Mr. Lockwood, who was almost done with the lawn. He clearly did a lot of outside work himself. He had a great tan. Not a vacation tan, like the one you get when you spend a week in Aruba. This was a long-term sun-kissed look, from being outside all summer, the sun beating down on you, and frying your skin just enough to make it golden.

Glistening with a little sweat...

I shook my head and looked back at the rose bushes. I didn't know why my thoughts were running away like they were, but I ignored it and continued on spraying the roses with the hose. Sure enough, after a few minutes I was sweating. I wasn't wrong about it happening... It was just the way things went with outdoor manual labor. I was no stranger to it, working in landscaping.

Tugging my t-shirt over my head, I tucked it into the back pocket of my jeans, wiping the sweat from my brow with my arm. The sound of the mower stopped. *Hm... He must have finished with the lawn.* I kept spraying the bushes, some inexplicable curiosity swirling inside me. I saw movement out the corner of my eye and tried my hardest to ignore it.

Just watering the roses. That's it. Watering. Watering...

I glanced up to see Mr. Lockwood approaching me slowly. He said nothing, just stepped over and cupped his hands under the water pouring from the hose I was holding. He brought some water to his face and splashed it in his hair, wiping his eyes. I noticed a subtle smirk on his face as he turned to walk away.

He climbed the steps to the deck quickly. I was still watching him as he grabbed a bottle of water from a cooler up there and drank almost the whole thing in one gulp. It reminded me that my own mouth was very dry. *It's pretty damn hot out here... That water looks refreshing.*

I shook my head again, lifting the hose to my mouth and taking a quick drink, before returning to the watering. It held my attention for only another couple seconds before my eyes were sliding back up to the deck.

Mrs. Lockwood was outside now, greeting her husband with a coy smile. He pushed her up against the side rail of the deck, grinning and leaning in to whisper something in her ear. She laughed out loud and playfully slapped him in the chest. He continued to grind himself on her a little while she squealed about him being sweaty. He leaned in and ran his lips along her jaw. I swallowed hard.

Shit!

I looked down at my shoes, now fully soaked with water. I was flooding the damn bushes. *God dammit.*

I huffed out loud and tossed the hose, walking over quickly to turn it off. *That's what you get for not paying attention.*

I shook my head again, mentally scolding myself as I took my sneakers off and left them at the bottom of the steps to dry. I went back up into the house to find Hailey, ignoring the strange sensation in my chest.

Hailey instructed me to take a shower and get dressed for dinner. Apparently, her parents were having some family and friends over for a *night before Thanksgiving* dinner party of sorts. According to Hailey, it was a tradition.

I showered fast and hard. I was finding myself slightly distracted and anxious since my arrival at the Lockwood house, but I chalked it up to nerves from meeting and spending an entire weekend with my girlfriend's parents. I'd never really done this before...

I had met girls' parents before, but nothing so serious. I'd certainly never been invited to stay in their home before, that was for sure. It felt like I was being graded or something. Like everything I said and did needed to be just right.

It was sort of exhausting.

I was out of the shower, digging through my bag and wondering why I hadn't unpacked earlier, when I felt a hand on my waist. I startled and turned around fast.

"Hales, Jesus," I breathed out hard, running my hand through my wet hair.

"Hi, baby," she purred, trailing her index finger along my stomach, tracing the muscles in my abs.

"Sweetness, you can't do that here," I grumbled and stepped behind her to close the bedroom door all the way.

"Mmm... what about... here?" she grinned, her hand dropping to my crotch.

"You know what I mean..." I gasped as I inched further away.

"Why can't we fool around just a little?" she whined, following me, her fingers grazing my jaw. "I can be quiet."

"It doesn't matter, baby," I took her wrist in my hand, placing a soft kiss on her fingertip. "I'm afraid of your dad."

Hailey laughed which made me smile. She had a great laugh. And her smile was out of this world.

"My dad is so *not* scary, babe," she giggled, brushing my hair back with her fingers. "He just looks sort of badass, but he's like a big teddy bear."

"Yea, maybe for you and your mom," I said, giving her a look. "He already basically threatened me if I did anything to you in here, and I really don't feel like being castrated. Would you be able to love a man with no dick?"

She laughed out loud again, and I grinned with pride for my wittiness.

"He did not threaten you," Hailey called me out, smiling. I nodded, fully serious. "He said that if he found out we fooled around in here he would cut your dick off?" she asked while giggling up a storm.

"Okay, fine. He didn't say it outright," I mumbled, taking her by the waist. "But I read between the lines. No funny business. Not until we're back at school."

Hailey groaned, lolling her head back in frustration. "Baby! That's *so* long from now! That's like... days!"

I chuckled and tugged her closer to me. I was feeling it, too, but I couldn't admit that to her now. If I showed any sign of weakness, she would pounce, and then I wouldn't be able to resist. I wasn't sure how serious her dad was, but I wasn't about to take that chance.

Plus, I'm no sex fiend. I can go a few days without getting it on. Sure it'll be tough with this fine little piece of ass near me, but I'm up for the challenge.

Hailey settled for a couple seconds of kissing before I was pushing her out of the room so I could get dressed.

CHAPTER 3

Ben

"**W**OW, JESSICA. THAT SAUCE WAS TERRIFIC. I'm so full, I couldn't eat another bite!"

"Well, hold that thought, because there's still dessert."

Jess's brother-in-law, Greg, grumbled, holding his stomach, and we all laughed. The dinner was certainly delicious. Jess was a great cook, and she never missed an opportunity to spoil those around her with her delicious cooking. Especially at a time like this, when everyone was together.

It was a bit of a tradition for us to host a dinner party at our place the night before Thanksgiving. This year; however, we were hosting Thanksgiving dinner at our place as well. I hadn't been sure that Jessica would want to take on such a responsibility, but I guessed she was fine with it. No help from me though... I was basically useless in the kitchen. *Unless you like scrambled eggs and toast.*

Jessica and Hailey got up from the table, clearing everyone's plates. Followed by Jess's sister, Marie, and their good friend, Rachel. All of

us men just sat around staring at each other like a bunch of lazy idiots.
It was actually kind of funny.

"So, Ryan, where are you from?" Greg asked, loosening his belt,
which must have been digging into his potbelly.

"Denver, sir," Ryan replied, polite and serious. *Hm... Denver?*

"Wow! Rocky Mountains, huh?" Greg chortled.

"What made you want to come down south?" Rachel's husband,
Bill, asked.

"My um... my dad got sick," he replied, glancing down, fiddling with
his napkin as he swallowed visibly. "He and my mom split when I was
younger, and he moved to Santa Fe. I stayed with my mom in Denver,
but when he got sick, I came down..."

Everyone was quiet for a moment. I felt bad for the poor kid.
Losing parents is hard. I would know, I lost both of mine.

"Hey, why don't we go throw the pigskin around?" Greg suggested.
"You can show us if you've still got that golden arm, Lockwood."

I chuckled uncomfortably, shaking my head. "I don't know..."

"Aw come on, Benji," Bill goaded. "What are you, worried the
young blood will show you up?" He jutted his thumb in Ryan's
direction.

"Oh, uh I don't really play much..." Ryan stuttered nervously. I
smirked at him.

"Alright. Let's do it," I grunted, scooting my chair out and standing
up quick, making my way to the kitchen to kiss Jess on the cheek and
tell her what we were doing. Naturally, the ladies, other than Hailey,
looked excited to get rid of us guys for a few.

They all followed me outside to the backyard and I went to grab
the football out of the shed.

"Holy shit!" I heard Ryan's voice, and I turned to see him right
behind me. "This is freaking awesome!"

I chuckled with pride. He was obviously referring to the shed. The
word *shed* was really underselling this thing. I had remodeled the whole
place and turned it into my ultimate man-cave. This and our finished
basement were my two havens. Jess and Hailey had the rest of the
house, but the shed and basement were mine.

"You did all of this yourself?" Ryan asked, checking out the foosball table and the mini-bar.

"Mhm," I nodded, grabbing the football and turning the light off before he was even done looking at everything. I was already a few feet ahead of him before he jogged to catch up.

"The lawn looks great," he said, sincerely enough, but I still couldn't tell if he was just sucking up to me or taking a genuine interest.

"Thanks," I replied. "So do the roses. That was some first-class watering."

He stared at me for a moment, mouth hanging open, most likely unsure of whether I was fucking with him or being serious. I decided to put him out of his misery and laughed softly. His shoulders fell back, and he laughed along, still seemingly uneasy.

I was starting to feel a little guilty. I didn't want to make the poor kid feel bad. He seemed nice enough. He actually reminded me of myself at his age. Minus the five-year-old daughter, of course.

I tossed the football at him and he caught it, which was a good sign. "Show me what you got."

He looked nervously down at the ball in his hands, but then squared his shoulders and nodded at me, indicating that I needed to back up. I grinned and jogged away.

When I turned back to him and gave him the OK with my eyes, he threw the ball to me and I caught it with an *oof*, hugging it to my chest. *Damn. The kid's got an arm.*

"Check out that spiral!" Greg bellowed from behind me somewhere.

"I think All-Star Lockwood's got some competition!" Bill added, lighting a fire inside me.

I wasn't the most competitive person in the world, but there were a select few things I was damn good at, and I took pride in them.

Raising my daughter, football, remodeling, running a company, and making my wife come. Those are my skills. Oh and gardening. I don't care how girly it sounds, I can't let Jess take all the credit for those roses.

My inner high school football quarterback awoke from his nineteen-year catnap and started stretching.

"Go long, kid," I nodded at Ryan, and I saw the faintest smirk play over his lips before he started backing up.

I waited for him to get far enough away, even further than I normally would suggest because I was showing off, and I launched the ball into the air. I watched it, almost in slow motion, as it soared towards Ryan. And he actually had to run a few feet further to catch it. *Damn straight.*

He did catch it though. It was a great catch. Then he darted back up the yard, pointing to Bill and giving him another dynamite throw.

Bill played on my team in high school. Yes, I remained friends with a select few people from high school, because I'd lived in this damn town my whole life. I liked it, though. It was comforting to have all the same faces around you all the time. Still, sometimes I envied people like Hailey and Ryan for being able to pick up and move somewhere new, with no friends or family. Sure, Ryan had some family in Santa Fe, but still it must've been tough.

We played for a little while longer, just messing around. Ryan and I stuck to throwing, whereas Greg and Bill played more defense. I could hardly believe that Bill used to be in shape enough to be a tight-end. It seemed as if the new addition of his first child, baby boy William Jr., had been taking a toll on Bill.

I couldn't say that I blamed him for losing it a little. When Hailey was first born, I didn't do much in the way of working out. I was just trying to keep my sanity at that point. But still, I was a very active father. Jess always said I had a form of ADHD or some crap like that, because I could never sit still. I always had to be moving; working on a project. When Hailey was a baby, it was her toys; doll houses, Barbie dream castles with stables for horses and all that jazz. Then when she got older, I moved onto my man-caves. *All just a way of harnessing the energy, I suppose.*

I watched Ryan for a moment as he threw the ball to Greg, who nearly dropped it because he was too busy fussing with his belt again. The kid was actually pretty good. He had the arms for it, that was for sure. I noticed how fit he was earlier when he was watering the roses.

I was secure enough with myself to recognize things like that. He was a good-looking guy, no need to hide from it. If anything, it just made me more nervous. Good-looking guys always know they're good-looking. *I would know, because I'm good-looking. It's not cockiness, it's just a fact.* Before Jess got pregnant, I was in my prime. I had girls all over me nonstop.

I used to resent the fact that I had a kid and got married so young. I felt like my ending came way too soon, and I wasn't done exploring my sexual identity. But then I realized that everything happened for a reason, and if I hadn't knocked up my high school girlfriend, I probably would have gotten into bigger trouble.

It was all for the best...

But Ryan, on the other hand... He was in his prime at that moment. And he was with my daughter. Was I meant to believe that he was going to settle down with one girl at twenty-one, looking the way he did? Would I have?

All of those thoughts were silenced when I realized that a football was flying at my face. I jumped out of the way fast, before it could nail me right in the nose.

"Sorry!" Greg yelped. "Bad throw!"

"Ya think?!" I barked at him.

"Well, you were just staring off into space," Bill murmured from my left.

"No excuse to whip a ball at my face," I grumbled.

"Guys, dessert is on the table!" Hailey sung from the deck. "And there's ice cream with it, so you have to hurry before it *melts.*"

The way she said that last word sort of stung my ears. She was being flirty, and a little too sexual. I followed her gaze, which was right on Ryan, my blood starting to boil. My eyes returned to Hailey and she mimicked a kissy face before turning on her heel and scampering back into the house.

I glared at Ryan for a moment and he cleared his throat, avoiding my eye contact. He walked swiftly passed me toward the house and I huffed out of frustration. *Damn kids... All sex-crazed like a bunch of horny squirrels. Not under my roof!*

Wow... you sound OLD.

"You're in trouble with that one," Bill said, coming to stand next to me, shaking his head as we watched Ryan ascend the stairs to the deck. "That's why I'm glad I don't have a daughter."

"Yea well... you'd better get that vasectomy now then," I grumbled at him, giving him the side-eye.

"Hey, I have a daughter in high school, and I haven't had to fight off any dudes like that yet!" Greg added to the conversation, huffing as he joined us.

Bill and I shared a look. "Uh Greg... Maxine is great and everything. I love my goddaughter to death, you know that," I murmured carefully. "But let's be honest... she doesn't exactly look like Hailey."

"What's that supposed to mean?" Greg asked, sounding offended.

"I just mean that she'll find a nice boy who's smart and polite and... good at math or whatever," I answered. "And you won't have to worry about beating guys like that off of her with a stick." I nodded toward the house.

"He seems like a nice enough kid," Bill added, defending Ryan. "Quiet, respectful... Just because he's hot, doesn't mean he's a bad guy."

Greg and I gaped at one another then at Bill, raising our brows.

"Yea, I said a guy's hot. Big deal," he grunted with a shrug. "It doesn't mean I'm going to blow him or anything."

Greg gasped in horror as I scoffed out a laugh. "I'm going in now."

I was still shaking my head as I climbed the steps to the deck and went back inside for dessert.

The dinner party was over, and Ryan and I were on cleaning duty. That was Jessica's rule of the house. Whoever did the cooking was exempt from cleaning up afterward. And since I never cooked, I always wound up cleaning.

The party had gone on pretty late, as it typically did. After dessert, we broke out the drinks. Wine for the girls and scotch for the guys. Jess and I bickered for a while about whether to let Hailey have a glass of wine or not.

I wasn't stupid. Obviously she must have drank before. Her boyfriend was twenty-one, so he very well could have been buying her booze, which I certainly hoped for his sake he hadn't been. Jess thought it was fine to let Hailey have one glass, but I had to remain the bad cop and put my foot down. Hailey didn't really seem like she cared much, anyway.

She was too busy hanging on Ryan, which was irking me to no end. He seemed like he was trying to brush her off in front of me, but it was just proving my point of how all over each other they must have been when I wasn't around. Though he did politely decline the glass of scotch I offered him, which tossed a few more points to his favor.

Ryan was clearing the table while I was rinsing dishes, stuffing them into the dishwasher when Hailey swung around the corner into the room. She sidled up to Ryan, all but disregarding my presence completely, wrapping her arms around his waist.

"I'm going upstairs to bed, babe," she told him in a sort of breathy voice that sounded like an invitation. It made my jaw tick. *Clearly I've been going easy on these two...*

"Okay," Ryan muttered, and I could see him trying to slither out of her grip as he nervously glanced in my direction.

"I'll see you in a bit?" she asked sweetly, kissing his cheek.

I cleared my throat, loud.

"Yup, mhm," Ryan grunted, kissing the top of her head quick and pushing her off of him. "Goodnight, Hales."

Hailey sighed audibly and then turned to leave the room. Or so I thought. But then I felt her arms wrap around my waist as she pecked me on the cheek. Just like she used to do when she was little.

"Goodnight, Daddy," she crooned, patronizing for my benefit. But I didn't mind. I actually appreciated it.

"Goodnight, baby girl," I replied, smirking to myself as she left the room.

Ryan came up the counter with the rest of the dishes, placing everything in the sink while I was still rinsing. I glanced at him out the corner of my eye.

"I can do that, if you want..." he offered.

"It's okay," I said, my tone curt.

"Well, at least let me fill the dishwasher," he responded in a sort of command, which for some reason had me nodding and stepping aside so he could get to it.

"You're being very helpful," I spoke quietly, rinsing and handing him the dishes.

"It's the least I can do," he replied. "You and Mrs. Lockwood are letting me stay here... It's very generous."

I didn't know what else to say, so I just nodded, going on with the task at hand. I was trying not to pay too much attention to the kid, because I didn't want to make him think I liked him. The second I dropped my guard then he'd drop his and then who knew what would happen. It was better for me to keep my eye on him. Having him afraid of me was an advantage.

Still, I kept watching him with my peripheral vision, noticing how much he really reminded me of myself at that age. We actually looked sort of similar, minus the hair and eye color. Our body shapes were about the same, same height, same jawline and all that. But he had dark hair, whereas mine was light. *Dirty blonde*, was what Jessica called it. She was just a straight-up blonde, which was clearly what gave Hailey her naturally light blonde hair. And Jess and I both had blue eyes, so Hailey came out with blue eyes, too.

My blonde-haired, blue-eyed baby...

I smirked thinking about it. Ryan, on the other hand, had dark brown hair which curled a bit. And it definitely looked like he had green eyes, but then I hadn't looked at them enough to know for sure.

I shook myself out of my thoughts and finished with the dishes, drying my hands.

"Thanks," I muttered to Ryan, turning to leave. But I paused, feeling like I should be more hospitable, especially because Jess was already in bed, and I knew she would want me to check on him and Hailey before doing anything else. "Do you guys need anything?"

I turned to face him, and he stared at me for a moment, seemingly baffled by my question.

Green. Definitely green eyes.

"Uh, nope," he shrugged. "I think we have everything. Thanks... Are you uh... heading off to bed?"

I squinted at him for a moment. *Why does he want to know? Is he planning on removing my daughter's innocence or something and wants to make sure I'll be occupied?!*

"I'll probably be downstairs watching TV or something for a while," I told him. "I don't sleep much."

"Oh..." he murmured, looking like he wanted to ask a bunch of questions. But the only one he landed on was, "Downstairs?"

I grinned at him, the first unhindered, genuine smile I'd ever given him, and turned. "Follow me."

I led Ryan down the hall stairs to the basement, and flipped the light switch, illuminating my masterpiece. I stood back and admired my handiwork, crossing my arms over my chest. *If he thought the shed was cool... Check this baby out.*

"Damn..." he breathed stepping around me and admiring my digs.

Sectional leather sofa, seventy-two-inch flat screen with all the Amazon Fire TV, Alexa, voice control fixings, my work desk, complete with Mac computer setup, customized for business; pool table across the room, minibar, darts, library. The place was heaven on Earth. My own private fortress of solitude.

"This is pretty incredible," Ryan said, thoroughly studying all the intricate details of my little world.

I simply grinned and walked over to the mini-fridge, grabbing a beer from inside. "You want one?" I asked him, and he turned to stare at me for a moment.

He looked like he was waging some kind of internal war, and I wanted to tell him it wasn't that big of a deal. *It's just a beer, man.*

"Yea, sure," he finally answered, stepping over and taking it from my hand. "Thanks."

I twisted off my cap and took a big sip, letting the fizzy cool liquid quench my thirst. I glanced over at Ryan, who was doing the same. He pulled the bottle away from his lips and wiped his mouth with the back of his hand, eyeing me speculatively.

"So you did this all yourself, too?" he asked, walking around the room. I nodded slowly. He wasn't looking at me, but I think he just guessed that's what I did, because he kept on talking. "How do you find time to do all this stuff? Is running a company that easy?"

He turned to glance at me, smirking. I chuckled and shook my head.

"I wouldn't say *easy*, but it only takes up so much time," I told him, meandering over to the couch and plopping into my usual spot. "My only kid is in college, and my company is almost self-sufficient enough that I can work from home most days. Leaves me with a comfortable amount of freedom."

"That sounds like the life," he murmured, having a seat on the other end of the couch. I picked up the remote and switched on the TV, flipping through sports channels. "Did you ever think about having another kid?"

I stopped in my tracks and glared at him, blinking a few times.

"Sorry," he held his hand up, clearly trying to hide his amusement at my reaction.

I cleared my throat and brought my gaze back to the TV screen. I was quiet for a minute, absentmindedly flicking from station to station, lost in my thoughts.

"We thought about it when Hailey was in elementary school," I finally started talking again, volunteering information, though I wasn't exactly sure why. "It would've been a good time. She was a pretty low-maintenance kid. We spoiled her a lot just because we didn't have anything else to do. But ultimately... I don't know. It just didn't happen."

I took a long pull from my beer, struggling to silence my thoughts and the strange feelings of incompleteness suddenly flooding me. My pulse was increasing steadily, so I focused on channel surfing to distract myself.

"I didn't mean to pry..." Ryan spoke softly, likely picking up on my sudden weirdness, which was making the room sort of tense.

"It's fine," I jumped in, trying to prove how fine I was with everything.

We sat in silence for a few more minutes. I noticed him burrowing himself deeper into the couch and slugging back his beer. I still hadn't settled on a station, giving each one about three seconds to dazzle me before I ultimately moved on. I eventually stopped torturing the two of us and tossed the remote down on the couch, leaning back and getting more comfortable.

For some reason, I felt like Ryan was looking at me, so I tilted my face in his direction, catching him finishing off his beer. I didn't know if he had been looking at me, and just happened to look away right before I turned... But what really bothered me was that I was even thinking about whether he was looking at me or not. It was pretty strange.

This whole fucking thing is strange. I wish he would just leave...

But then he'd be going upstairs to share a bed with my daughter, which I definitely don't want. Ugh, this is an impossible situation.

"Welp, I'm gonna call it a night," he sighed, stretching his arms behind his back as he stood up.

I sat up straight. "Are you sure?" I asked, not really sure what I was doing, like, at all. "There's more beer." *Why are you trying to get the kid drunk? What is wrong with you??*

He stared blankly at me for a moment, blinking. "Uh no, thanks. I'm pretty tired. Long day..." he chuckled awkwardly. "I'll see you tomorrow. Goodnight, Mr. Lockwood."

He left quick, and I groaned inwardly thinking about what he was going to do with my daughter up there. I knew I should have made them sleep in separate rooms. *Looks like I won't be getting any sleep tonight...*

I was pacing-quietly-outside the door to the bedroom. It was almost one in the morning, and I should have been in bed in my own room, but I was too convinced that the stranger staying in my house was railing my daughter and laughing about it behind my back. So I decided against rational decisions and went upstairs to see if I could hear anything.

What did I really think I was going to do about it if I did? Burst through the door and spray cold water on them?

They were both adults. They could do whatever they wanted. I was sure they likely did when they weren't staying under my roof, so what difference did it make if they did it here?

Maybe it was even better for them to do it here, because at least it wasn't some kind of orgy or sex dungeon. At least here, they would be having regular, couple sex.

Oh God, that's my daughter. My baby that I held in my arms when she was born. I read her Curious George books to get her to sleep, and now she's being defiled by some hoodlum! I can't just stand by and–

"Ben, what the hell are you doing?" Jessica whisper-shouted at me from around the corner.

I looked up to see her coming at me, looking displeased. She stopped right in front of me and crossed her arms over her chest.

"I'm just... making sure everything is alright," I whispered back. "No funny business, that was the only rule."

"Oh my God, Ben... you're losing it," she sighed, shaking her head. "What would make you think there was funny business going on, anyway?" She asked this trying to remain serious for my whacked-out benefit, but I could tell she wanted to laugh, which made me smile.

I groaned and hung my head. "When did she grow up, Jess?" I covered my face with my hands.

She chuckled softly and wrapped her arms around my waist. "Shhh... I know, baby. It's not easy being a dad."

I let her lead me down the hall to our bedroom, where we both stripped out of our clothes like we were going to have sex, but then ended up passing out spooning. *Marriage style.*

CHAPTER 4

Ryan

THANKSGIVING AT THE LOCKWOOD RESIDENCE was quite the event. At eight in the morning the house was already full of action. I clearly hadn't come prepared for this level of holiday-party. Mrs. Lockwood was already in the kitchen starting dinner, while Mr. Lockwood set up breakfast-donuts he had bought from the local donut shop.

We were given a small window of time to eat our donuts and drink our coffee before we were instructed to take showers-separate showers, much to Hailey's disappointment-and get ready for the guests to arrive.

The guests were the same people as the day before, plus Hailey's great-grandparents, who were rather old, a few more family friends and some of their kids, and Ben's brother, Jacob, his wife and their twin girls. Hailey's house was not small by any means; it was actually pretty big. But by noon, it was brimming with people, and more noise than probably all of my family gatherings combined.

According to Hailey, her family followed the random Thanksgiving tradition of eating insanely early, so dinner was set to happen at two in the afternoon. Before that, we were given appetizers, and the guys from last night's dinner party insisted that we play some more football. Greg swore up and down that he wouldn't attempt throwing, so Mr. Lockwood reluctantly agreed.

This game of football was slightly different, because we had more players, and cheerleaders for some reason. As much as I was trying to tone down Hailey's advances toward me in front of her scary dad, she wasn't picking up on the severity of the situation. She was being more flirtatious than ever, as if she was trying to win a prize or something. During the entire game of football, every time I successfully threw or caught the ball, Hailey was jumping up and down cheering, as were her twin cousins who apparently loved to copy her every move. A few times, Hailey even skipped over and jumped into my arms, kissing my neck all over. While it felt marvelous, I could also feel her father's crippling death-stare melting the skin off my face.

She would need to stop doing things like that. I wasn't going to survive.

We were all about to sit down for dinner, and Mrs. Lockwood had asked a bunch of us *kids*-not sure when you stop being referred to as a *kid*... maybe when you have one of your own?-to help set up. Hailey and I were instructed to grab a couple six-packs of soda from the pantry and put them in the fridge.

Once she showed me where the pantry was, Hailey pushed me inside and shut the door behind us. It was a pretty tight room, basically a closet, so space was limited.

"Mmm... baby," she breathed, smooshing her body against mine, doing that thing she knew I loved, playing with my hair in the back. *That feels nice...* "I miss touching you so bad."

I swallowed hard. This whole *no sex under her parents' roof* thing was proving more difficult than I had anticipated. I think it was because it was explicitly against the rules. That *forbidden* stuff was always hot for some reason.

"Hales, we can't," I whispered, gripping the shelf behind me to stop myself from grabbing her. "Someone could hear... We have to go."

She whined out a soft noise, pressing her breasts harder against my chest as her lips found my earlobe. *Oh fuck me...*

"Hailey..." I grunted, my voice thick and husky from what she was doing. Tugging my earlobe between her teeth and sucking it gently with those sweet plump lips. It always drove me insane. I could feel the blood rushing below my waist.

"Ryan..." she purred, her hand slipping down to the front of my pants, stroking me slowly.

"Hales, you gotta stop that..." I hummed, struggling to pull away, though I really didn't want to at all.

"I want you right now, sexy," she gripped me through my jeans. "I can't wait."

"You have to wait," I grumbled, trying like hell to shut it down. "If your dad finds out..."

"Oh my God, Ryan, he's not going to find out," she pulled back and rolled her eyes at me. "He's not a detective."

"Yea well, it doesn't take a detective to hear people inside a pantry... Or to spot a boner, for that matter," I pointed out and she giggled. "I mean, come on! How am I supposed to hide this thing?"

I pointed down at my junk and she giggled some more. "I don't know, babe. That's what you get for having such a big dick."

I scoffed and rolled my eyes, shaking my head slowly. She batted her eyelashes up at my face, giving me that faux-innocent smirk. *Not amused, gorgeous girl.*

She breathed out a hard sigh. "Fine, fine fine. You win. Or rather, *my dad* wins." She fixed her hair then grabbed two six-packs of soda cans. "Must be nice to be him."

I chuckled to myself watching her as she opened the door and quickly looked around before walking down the hall. I sighed out hard to myself and glanced back down at my erection.

"What the hell am I supposed to do with you?" I muttered to my package, reaching down to adjust it, maybe flip it up under my waistband or something, when...

"Ryan?" Ben's–*Mr. Lockwood's,* dammit–voice came from right outside the door to the pantry. "Everything alright in there?"

"Uh, yea!" I replied, frantically trying to fix my stupid boner.

Next thing I knew, he was popping his head inside the pantry, giving me a positively fiery look. I purposely kept myself turned away from him, grabbing the sodas and willing my dick to deflate. Unfortunately, for reasons unbeknownst to me, it was still excited, even though the situation was anything but.

"Just grabbing these sodas for your wife... Mrs. Lockwood..." I stuttered like an idiot, holding up the cans, but not turning to fully face him.

He narrowed his gaze at me and then leaned up against the doorframe.

"Need any help?" he asked, his voice deep and crazy intimidating. I swallowed hard over my dry throat.

"No... no we're good," I replied, my own voice coming out scratchy. "I mean, Hailey just brought some out, so this should be enough."

He continued to stare at me for a few more moments, looking like he was waiting for me to turn around and leave with him, but I really couldn't. I wasn't sure if my hard-on was still visible, but I couldn't take that chance. It would have been completely mortifying.

Finally, he let me off the hook, and turned around, leaving the pantry first. "Well, come on. Dinner's about to start."

I breathed out hard and checked my pants. Nothing visible. I was good to go. I followed Ben out of the pantry, turning off the light and closing the door behind me as I tried to regain my composure.

Still feeling slightly flustered, I took my seat at the dinner table next to Hailey. One of the family friends, whose name I couldn't for the life of me remember, sat on the other side of me. He was a young guy, maybe in his early thirties, and very well-dressed. I looked around the room to see if I could remember who he'd came with, but I was starting to think maybe he was the only single guy in the group.

The dinner began and went along smoothly. The food was delicious, all praises given to Mrs. Lockwood, and then Hailey when she demanded recognition for arranging the mini-marshmallows on top of the sweet potato casserole. Between Hailey's great-grandparents and her uncles and aunts, I was being grilled a lot. It was overwhelming. I was so afraid of somehow saying or doing the wrong thing, it was making me incredibly antsy.

As was Hailey's desire to torture me at every available opportunity.

She was trying to touch me under the table, and then when that wouldn't work, she took her shoe off and started playing footsie. My eyes kept finding Mr. Lockwood's, praying that he wasn't noticing what was happening under there. He seemed like he was in a good mood, talking and laughing with his brother. But I did catch him glancing in my direction a few times.

Normally I wouldn't have minded Hailey's flirtations at all, but with her dad there it just seemed wrong. It wasn't as if he had said anything specifically, or caught us doing anything, other than the pantry earlier, but even that would have just been speculation on his part. Still, whether he'd physically witnessed anything or not, he managed to scare the crap out of me. He had this penetrating stare that really jolted me. His eyes were a bright, sparkling blue color, much more fluorescent than Hailey's.

Like the Night's King from Game of Thrones. The eyes... they were haunting.

The meal progressed from dinner to dessert seamlessly. Everyone got up to muck around, while we all helped clear the table and put out various cakes, pies and cookies. Mr. Lockwood broke out the scotch again, and on his second glass, he finally agreed to let Hailey have some wine.

"Thanks, Daddy!" she cheered, pouring herself a glass. "Are you gonna have some, babe?" she asked me.

"Uh, sure, I guess," I nodded, feeling like it was a family celebration so why not?

"No, no," Mr. Lockwood rumbled, sternly shaking his head. "If he's going to have a drink, he's going to do it right."

He smirked and grabbed a tumbler, filling it with two fingers of the fancy scotch his brother had brought over. He handed me the glass, and I accepted it, gratefully. Then he reached forward with his glass, clinking it on mine in a quick *cheers.*

I watched in fascination as he brought the glass to his lips and took a sip, eyeing me over the rim, waiting for me to do the same which I did, basically on command. I felt so cool. Like we were Mad Men, or something.

The scotch was strong, and by the bottom of the first glass, I was already sort of fuzzy. Hailey must have been feeling her red wine, giggling up a storm and dancing around with her cousins. Actually it seemed like everyone had loosened up. Even Mr. Lockwood poured me a second, and third glass of scotch, each one containing more liquor than the one before it.

We all started grabbing dessert, but no one really sat down for it. People had scattered throughout the house. Mrs. Lockwood and the ladies were upstairs, playing with the kids. Hailey was sneaking more wine when her mom wasn't looking. And Mr. Lockwood took the men and retreated to his basement man-cave for football and more drinks.

I contemplated staying with Hailey, but I secretly wanted to be a part of the guy-party downstairs. It seemed like the more Don Draper thing to do. Party and drink with the guys, then come home to your woman later, when you're nice and toasted.

Sure enough, as soon as I set foot in the basement, I knew I had made the right call.

The guys had cigars going, scotch pouring and football on the huge flat screen. It was Mantown, and I was definitely impressed. Mr. Lockwood knew how to get down.

"Hey, kid," Greg blurted out when he spotted me. "Have a seat! Make the mission complete."

Bill laughed and got up, handing me his glass of scotch. "Here, pal. This one's for you."

He dragged me over to the couch and sat me down next to Jacob.

"Take this," Jacob said, shoving a lit cigar at my face.

"Thanks..." I murmured, sipping the scotch slowly, then taking a puff of the cigar, praying like hell that I wouldn't cough.

"Look at this! We got the kid all set up," Greg went on, nudging Mr. Lockwood with his elbow. "He's part of the family now."

Mr. Lockwood glanced up at me, regarding me warily, before his gaze flitted back to the TV, like a magnet.

"So you're not from around here, huh?" the guy whose name I couldn't remember asked, scooting in next to me on the couch. He was sort of in my personal space, which was making me nervous. I took a larger sip of my drink.

"No..." I replied, and before I could say anything else, he started talking again.

"I think I would have remembered you," he grinned. There was something in the way he said it, the way he was smiling at me, that made my chest burn.

"Leave the kid alone, Tate," Jacob scolded his friend. "Meeting the family for the first time at the holidays is like a suicide mission." He chuckled and Mr. Lockwood smirked at him, laughing along.

"Well, he's a lucky guy," the man-Tate-shrugged. "Hailey's gorgeous."

"Watch it," Mr. Lockwood growled, side-eyeing him.

"Okay, okay... relax with the overprotective daddy thing," he chuckled. His eyes came back to mine as he took a sip of his drink. "I'd say Hailey's a lucky girl, too." He winked at me and I felt way drunker than I wanted to.

I should go back upstairs with Hailey. Things are getting oddly tense down here.

"So have you ever played football?" Mr. Lockwood asked, his eyes finding mine, brow raised in question. "You're pretty good."

My sudden dread retreated back to where it came from and I nodded. "I played a little in junior high."

"Why'd you stop?" he asked, giving me a fully inquisitive stare.

"My mom... um... she wouldn't sign the release forms anymore," I answered. "Said it was too dangerous."

He nodded, accepting my answer, as if he had experienced this himself.

"I don't blame her," Jacob jumped in, grabbing the cigar back from me. "Have you read the statistics on concussions in NFL players? It's staggering."

Mr. Lockwood rolled his eyes at his brother and I had to laugh.

The group of us stayed down in the basement until the game was over. At that point it was getting late and all the guys were pretty faced, myself included. Likely all of their wives would end up being designated drivers, but I didn't stick around long enough to see that shake out.

I said my *thank yous* and *goodnights* to everyone and headed upstairs to Hailey's room, where I found her passed out in her bed wearing nothing but my t-shirt. I smiled and watched her sleep for a moment, marveling at how truly beautiful she was. Her long, shiny blonde hair, angelic features, long legs and tight ass. She looked great, and I could see a lot of my favorite parts of her at the moment.

But I would have to stow those urges. I couldn't bring myself to try anything here. I just didn't want to disappoint her father. For whatever reason, he had really gotten into my head.

Who knows? I probably wouldn't be able to have sex tonight, anyway. I'm too drunk. Isn't like, whiskey dick a thing?

I shrugged to myself and changed into pajama bottoms, crawling into bed next to my girl, pulling her against me and sniffing her hair. She smelled like coconuts.

My eyes began to close as I drifted off to sleep, dreaming of tropical islands and blue eyes.

I woke with a jolt, in the middle of the night. Or at least it felt that way, since it was pitch black outside.

My head was throbbing, and my mouth was too dry. I needed water.

I slithered out of bed, trying not to wake Hailey, and made my way downstairs to get some water. The clock on the stove showed that it was almost midnight. I hadn't even been asleep that long, but apparently long enough for everyone to leave and the Lockwood's to head off to bed.

I sipped my water, treasuring the hydration. It felt great. I poured myself another glass and just stood there, drinking in the dark, reveling in the quietness of this big house.

When I was just about done with my third glass of water, I heard a noise. It sounded like it was coming from upstairs. I shrugged it off and headed back up to bed.

I reached the top of the stairs and heard the noise again. It was coming from down the hall. Rather than going straight, toward Hailey's room, my mischievous side coerced me into turning right, toward her parents' room.

The door was opened a crack. The whole upstairs was completely dark, except for some moonlight streaming in through their bedroom windows. I was about to turn back when I heard the noise again, and that time I knew exactly what it was.

"Oh my God, Ben... fuck..." Mrs. Lockwood's voice panted from inside their bedroom.

My heart started beating faster in my chest. I swallowed hard and tried to get my feet to move, but they wouldn't. I had no desire to be a creep; some kind of peeping weirdo who watches his girlfriend's parents doing it.

But let's be honest... These were no ordinary parents.

They were a young, very attractive couple. And they clearly had great chemistry. From what I saw yesterday on the deck... It was nice. They looked good together.

Mrs. Lockwood let out another quiet moan, and my gaze slid, against my will, up to the crack in the doorway.

I almost gasped out loud. I had to bite my lip to keep myself from making a noise.

It was Ben. He was fully visible in the room. His back, all those rippling muscles, leading down to his ass, exposed by the blankets, which weren't covering much of anything. And I could see Jessica's legs on either side of him, but that was about it. I couldn't see anything else of Mrs. Lockwood... Only Mr. Lockwood.

Still, it was obvious that they were fucking. The noises alone were enough to give that away. And he was thrusting... I could tell because the muscles in his back and butt were constricting.

I looked away and swallowed hard. My mouth was filling with saliva. *I should leave. This isn't right. I shouldn't watch this...*

Without my permission, my gaze made its way back up to the bed. My breathing shallowed, though my pulse was thumping in my neck. I stared with wide eyes at the scene in their bed, unable to look away. It looked... really fucking good.

Ben's broad shoulders, and his back, all of those muscles, and the glistening fine sheen of sweat covering his tanned skin... His ass. It was almost like a girl's ass. It was round and full. A very nice butt.

Wait, why am I looking at this? Why am I staring at his ass? This is bizarre.

But I couldn't bring myself to look away. I could hear more of Jessica than Ben. She was definitely doing most of the moaning. But every once in a while, I heard a gasp or a deep groan that was clearly from Ben.

He grabbed her thigh hard with his right hand, holding it while he pushed. His hands were so strong...

Okay, look away now.

"Jesus, Ben you're so deep..."

Fuck me.

I could feel the blood rapidly filling my dick. This shit was turning me on something fierce. My cock was growing harder and harder with every second I stood in front of that cracked door, watching Ben fuck his wife.

It's because they're such a good-looking couple. And, you know, the chemistry, you mentioned before. Anyone would get turned on looking at this. You're fine.

Ben's plump, firm ass looked like a peach, or something delicious like that. I physically couldn't stop staring at it. I tried to... I wanted to stop so bad, but I just couldn't. It didn't make any sense. It looked so good.

My mind was running away with me. My thoughts were swirling around my brain like a jumbled mass of dirty, devious fantasies and salacious desires.

Things that had literally never been in my brain before were suddenly there. It was confusing and overwhelming...

But also totally hot.

Ben's neck. Ben's shoulders. Ben's back. Ben's ass. In front of me. I could touch it... I could...

I gulped and watched with the widest eyes ever. The glistening, smooth skin. The muscles flexing.

"Oh God, Ben... It feels amazing... make me come, baby..."

I could be behind him, touching his ass, sliding my fingers over it... in between the cheeks.

I reached down to adjust my raging hard-on and that one slight touch brought on a wave of sensation, unlike anything I'd ever felt before.

"Oh fuck yea, baby... you feel so good..." Ben's gruff, deep voice rumbled inside the room.

And then it was in my head. And it wouldn't stop.

My hand slid over my dick again, and it throbbed in my palm.

His ass is in front of me... bent over in front of me...

Taking my dick in my hand and pressing it inside...

"Oh fuck yea, baby... you feel so good..."

Oh God. Oh Jesus.

What am I doing...?

I swallowed over and over, ignoring the tight burning in my lower stomach, spreading like wildfire up to my chest. I closed my eyes tight and shook my head.

Then I turned away from the doorway, darting back down the hall, trying to be as quiet as possible, but also knowing that I needed to get the *fuck* out of there before something bad happened.

I'm just horny. That's it. That's all this is.

I've had to go days without sex, and I'm all hot and bothered and frustrated because my girlfriend won't stop teasing me when she knows we can't do it. And then I saw a hot couple fucking... It was like porn.

That's all. Nothing wrong with that.

Forget it.

I crept back into Hailey's room, taking a deep breath. Unfortunately, I could feel blue balls already starting, and I was still so damn wound up. My dick would never go down tonight.

I closed the bedroom door tight and leaned against it, inhaling another deep pull of oxygen. I glanced up at the bed where Hailey was still passed out. Her butt was facing me, and my t-shirt had bunched up around her waist, so I could see her whole naked bottom half. I swallowed hard.

It reminded me of what I had just been watching... What I had just been looking at... Lusting over.

I stepped closer to the bed and slid my pajama pants off. I crawled in next to Hailey and pulled her closer, rubbing myself against her.

She moaned a sweet little purr of a noise and pushed her hips back, grinding her perfectly curved ass against my hard-on.

She was awake.

I slowly slid my fingers between her thighs, circling her clit a few times. She started panting, writhing around in front of me. Only a few seconds of touching and she was already wet.

She went to turn over, but I stopped her, keeping her on her stomach. I ran my hand over her ass, cupping it and squeezing.

So round... juicy, firm, luscious ass...

I bucked my hips forward, dragging the head of my cock through the wetness between her thighs.

"Mmm... Ryan..." she mewled quietly. "Don't make me wait anymore. Just fuck me, baby."

My lusts were getting the best of me. I had so many images floating around my brain... and sounds. It was all too much. There was no way I could hold out anymore.

I could absolutely *not* go all weekend without sex. Not like this.

I gripped her ass hard in both hands, bringing her hips up. I positioned myself behind her, sliding my cock between her cheeks.

"Oh fuck yea, baby... you feel so good..."

You want this dick?

My hands squeezed her ass harder.

"Oh fuck yea, baby..."

You want me deep inside you?

"Oh fuck yea, baby..."

My cock pulsed. I took it in my hand and guided it inside Hailey's pussy from behind, slowly, inch-by-inch.

She squealed softly, and I shushed her, drawing my hips back and diving in again, slow and deep. She grabbed a pillow and pressed her face into it.

"Mmm... fuck, that's good... So tight..."

I held her hips and watched that plump, peach of an ass, while my dick pumped in and out.

"Does that feel good?" I grunted, mesmerized.

"Oh fuck yea, baby... you feel so good..."

Do I...?

"... so good..."

You like when I fuck your ass?

"...fuck yea, baby..."

My pace increased with every thrust. It felt so amazing, I was out of breath. My head was fuzzy, and I felt the sweat dripping down my back and chest.

I ran my hands up Hailey's hips, then back down to her ass. I kept drilling into her, slow, but hard, thrusting my full, thick cock into her tightness. She was engulfing me, and my imagination was running wild.

"Fuck, Ryan, I'm gonna come!" she gasped.

"Come for me, baby... I want to make you come..." I hummed, closing my eyes.

All those muscles... the sweaty smooth skin...

"I'm coming!" she squealed, and I could feel her gushing on me. It almost pushed me right over the edge.

I held out until she was done quivering, then pulled out of her slowly, stroking my cock with her natural lubrication. Hailey was on the pill, but I still made it a habit never to actually come inside her. Trying to be responsible and all that...

I grabbed her ass with my left hand while I jerked with my right, spreading her ass open. Whether I closed my eyes or kept them open made no difference. I still saw the same thing...

That ass... spreading it open... pressing the head of my cock up to his tight hole...

Jesus fucking Christ...

"Jesus fucking Christ..." My hand kept sliding, up and down, kept stroking, while I exploded into orgasm, shooting my hot come all over Hailey's lower back and ass.

I released a hushed groan, letting the climax wash over me, dragging the head of my cock through the wetness I had just made all over her asshole.

Fuck...

"Fuck..." I rasped, trying to regulate my breathing. I was seeing stars.

"Wow, baby..." Hailey turned her face to peek up at me, her cheeks rosy even in the dimly lit room. "That was so hot and dirty... Where did that come from?"

I swallowed hard, reaching over to grab some tissues from the box on her nightstand.

"I don't know..." I grunted, cleaning her off. "You've just been winding me up since yesterday, you naughty girl."

She giggled, and once I was done wiping her off, tugged her t-shirt back down and flipped onto her side, reaching for me. I pulled my pajama bottoms back on and wriggled up next to her, holding her body against mine. She kissed my bare chest and nuzzled me over and over, her fingers running up and down my back. I kissed the top of her head, squeezing onto her tight.

I listened to Hailey's heartbeat for a while, as it started to synch with mine. Then her breathing became even, and I could tell she'd fallen back to sleep.

But not me.

I was wide awake. My eyes open, staring off into the darkness, wondering what in the hell just happened.

CHAPTER 5

Ben

"DID YOU HEAR SOMETHING?" I breathed out hard, my heart still hammering away in my chest.

"No..." Jessica sighed as she ran her hands through her out-of-control sex-hair.

"Are you sure?" I asked again, lying back in bed, the sheets feeling especially cool against my sweaty, stiflingly hot skin. "I thought I heard someone out there right before I exploded you into orgasm."

I grinned wickedly at my wife and she giggled, dragging her nails through the stubble along my jaw.

"You're so paranoid lately," she smirked, the nails then gliding over my throat and down my chest. "We can't even fuck without you thinking someone's watching us."

"Ha ha, you're so funny," I rolled my eyes at her, sliding the condom off and tying it before tossing it into the trash. "By the way, you know how much I hate condoms..."

"Uh yea, I know. We have a nineteen-year-old daughter, remember?" she teased, and I chuckled softly, resting my head on the pillow.

"I'm just saying... You know it feels a million times better without the latex in the way," I grabbed her waist and tugged her closer. I leaned in brushing my lips over hers. "Just let me come on your face."

She laughed out loud and smacked me in the chest, pretending to fight me off as I pulled her warmed flesh against mine, kissing her slowly.

Regardless of how long we'd been together, Jess and I just seemed to work. And sure, sometimes it was monotonous... Sleeping with the same person for almost two decades. But we made it work. It was still always good. The sex was fire, every time. And I loved her, so the passion was there.

But admit it... You came especially hard because you thought someone was watching you.

I huffed to myself and shook my head. *Shut up, brain. No one asked you.*

I kissed my wife a handful more times, then she nestled her back against my front, and we spooned. Her heartbeat slowed, rocking into me while she slept.

But I remained wide awake. I wasn't a good sleeper to begin with, and sometimes sex had the opposite effect than it should have. After I came and Jess fell asleep, I was always left alone with my thoughts.

It was never anything in particular that kept me up. My job was good. My house was great. My marriage worked. My daughter was smart and driven, and safe. My friends were morons, but they were entertaining sometimes.

Really there was nothing much to complain about.

Actually, there was nothing at all to complain about...

My life was so utterly perfect that sometimes it just set my teeth on edge.

Imagine that... Being so content that you're pissed off about it. Talk about first-world problems... Jesus.

Sure, it made no sense. But sometimes I found myself craving drama. Something to stir the pot a little.

I didn't want anything tragic... No, nothing like that. Just something... *different.* Something less ordinary than my ordinary life.

I huffed out of frustration and closed my eyes, willing myself to fall into my uneasy sleep.

Maybe someday something new will pop up... Just hang in there, you boring bastard.

The next morning I woke up kind of late. Later than usual, anyway.

By the time I came downstairs, Jess, Hailey, and Ryan were already sitting at the table having breakfast. Jess and Hailey were in conversation while Ryan sat quietly, staring at his plate.

I walked casually over to the counter and poured myself a cup of coffee.

"Good morning, family... And Ryan," I grumbled, smirking at my wife, who was grinning wide at me.

"Dad..." Hailey scolded me with her eyes, and I rolled mine.

I took a seat at the table and glanced at Ryan again. He peeked up at me then his eyes quickly fell back down to his plate.

"Good morning, Mr. Lockwood," he muttered, sounding robotic.

I squinted at him. *Jeez, what's up with him? Maybe he's hungover. Poor kid can't hang.*

I should probably tell him to call me Ben... But no. That would be too much. Mr. Lockwood is fine for now.

"Did you guys have fun last night?" Jessica asked me, and Ryan's head popped up again.

"Yea, good times," I replied, sipping my coffee. "The drinks were really flowing last night. I hope that's not a regular thing for you, Ryan... Don't become like, an alcoholic or anything."

"Dad!" Hailey whined, shooting daggers at me across the table. I chuckled to myself.

"I'm not a big drinker, sir," Ryan said. "Last night was fun, but it won't happen again."

I gave him another look, but his eyes were back on his plate. I glanced over at Jess and Hailey, who weren't paying any mind. The kid was acting strange.

Then again, I hardly knew him, so how would I know.

"Well, I have some more yardwork to do today," I went on, finishing my coffee. "You down to help me out some more?" I asked Ryan, waiting for him to zone in on what I was saying.

He was most definitely hungover, and maybe a little manual labor outside in the sweltering hot sun would put things into perspective. *You're an evil man.*

He looked up at me, his eyes wide and his face stone serious.

"Um... sure. Okay," he nodded, seeming even more nervous than he had been the past two days. It was weird, because he had loosened up a bit last night. We actually talked for a while when the whole group was in the basement.

But now he seemed like he was afraid I was going to attack him or something. I wasn't really sure where it was coming from, but I shrugged it off and got up from the table.

"Follow me, kid," I murmured, opening the door to the deck. "I'm gonna put you to work."

He stared at me, swallowing visibly, blinking about a hundred times. My brow creased, and I turned away, walking outside before I apparently terrified him any further.

I led Ryan out to the shed where we picked up the gardening tools and got everything situated. I needed to tend to the plants, prune a couple trees in the front, and whack some weeds. Normally this stuff would take all day, but with Ryan's help, we could probably bang it out in a few hours.

He was already familiar with all the tools and machinery since he'd been working in landscaping for the better part of a year now. I brought him around the yard, instructing him on what needed to be done but to my surprise, he sort of already got it. He didn't need much direction at all.

It was a super-hot day. Almost eighty and all sun. About a half hour into the work, our shirts were off, and we had to take frequent water breaks to ensure that we didn't pass out.

I was basically finished pruning my new lemon tree I had planted last year when I saw Ryan out the corner of my eye. I tilted my head in his direction and he looked at the ground.

"What's up?" I asked, confused by his awkward standing around.

"I uh... finished the weeds," he said, approaching slowly, like I was an animal who might bite him if startled.

"Good. Thanks," I replied, still focusing on my task.

"What are you doing here?" he stepped closer.

"Pruning," I answered. "You have to pluck off some of these leaves so that it'll sprout more branches as it grows."

"Hmm..." He moved in even closer, coming to stand right next to me as he examined the tree. "This will grow lemons? Like, that you can use?"

"I sure as shit hope so," I grinned at him.

He finally smiled, reaching out to run his fingers along the baby branches.

"It's cool that you have this hobby," he muttered, making eye contact and holding it this time. "I don't really have much other than school right now..."

"Is there anything that you're interested in?" I asked. "Other than school?"

"I kind of like cars..." he responded after thinking on it for a moment. "My dad had this old Mustang he was fixing up... I used to hang around and watch him do it when I was visiting. He left it to his buddy when he died. I don't think he even knew I was interested in it."

"I had a Mustang in high school," I told him. "They're great cars. I don't know shit about working on them, but I wish I did. I'd love to restore one."

He grinned, staring at me for more than a few seconds. I started to feel a little strange... He was awfully close to me.

Then he took a deep breath and stepped away. "Well, I'm gonna go grab a shower..."

"Sure. Thanks for the help," I nodded, watching as he stomped off toward the house.

That was weird.

I shook it off and went back to my tree.

"So how long are you guys staying with us?" Jessica asked Hailey and Ryan as the four of us sat down for a dinner of Thanksgiving leftovers.

"Well, Ryan had said we would leave tomorrow, right babe?" Hailey turned to Ryan, who was leaning back in his chair, eyes darting all over the place. "So we can have Sunday to rest before it's back to school."

"Um, yea. Tomorrow sounds fine," he murmured in response, picking at his food.

"Well, you know you're welcome to stay as long as you want," Jess said, and I gave her a look. *Do we really want them staying here forever? I mean, Hailey sure. This is her house. But the weird guy? I don't know...*

"I know, I'll miss the shopping with you this weekend mom," Hailey pouted.

"It's okay, dear. Maybe next time," Jess smiled at our daughter.

The rest of dinner was quiet, normal. We chatted about school stuff and sports, and all that *blah blah blah*. After dinner, Ryan and I did the dishes thing again while the girls went to go watch TV in the living room.

I was getting a weird vibe from Ryan. He seemed jumpy, or something. And I kept catching him staring at me. It was peculiar, but I honestly didn't really mind. It was something for me to complain about.

Something odd to shake up my mundane life, I suppose.

"So, you excited to get back to school?" I asked him as we finished up the dishes.

"What? Uh... yea. Mhm..." he stuttered.

"Do you do well in school?" I pressed on.

"I guess..." *Come on, kid. Give me something to work with here.*

"What's your favorite class?"

"I don't know!" he grunted, and I turned my face to stare at him in utter perplexity. He sighed out hard. "I'm sorry... I just... I didn't sleep well last night."

"Oh yea... You were too drunk or something?" I smirked.

"No, I just... couldn't sleep," he mumbled, shifting his weight back and forth. "I don't know why..."

I gaped at him again in confusion, wondering what the hell to say to something like that.

"Well, I told you, I barely sleep, so... I'm familiar with it," I told him, trying to be comforting. "You'll get used to it, I guess."

He stood there for a moment, just staring back at me. He was hard to read, and I couldn't tell if it frustrated me or intrigued me somehow. It was strange. But we ended up standing there in silence just staring at each other for a few minutes. There was no movement in the room at all, until finally I noticed Ryan's fingers twitching.

I swallowed hard and blinked. *Okay... Time to go.*

"Alright, well these are done," I rasped then cleared my throat. I couldn't think of what else to say, so I just turned and left the room, shaking my head at whatever the hell that was.

I strolled casually into the living room and plopped down onto the couch next to Jess, draping my arm around her shoulder and pulling her in close. I inhaled her hair, which always smelled so good. Like jasmine and vanilla. It was comforting.

Shortly after, Ryan wandered into the room, looking dazed. He sat down next to Hailey on the adjacent couch, pulling her in close to him. And we all sat in silence for a while, watching one of those *Avengers* movies.

I was trying to pay attention, but my mind was still elsewhere. I'm not sure exactly where it was, but it wasn't in the movie. It wasn't in the perfectly content, quiet evening with my family. It might not even have been inside the house.

My mind was somewhere else entirely, just floating around, thinking about all kinds of things. It was almost like I had completely blacked out, and the next thing I knew, the movie was over, and Jess and Hailey were yawning and saying goodnight.

Jess and I went up to our room, while Hailey and Ryan went to hers. I took my time getting ready for bed, so by the time I was tiptoeing out of the bathroom in my pajama bottoms, Jess was out like a light. I sighed and kissed her on the head, then crept out of the bedroom, making my way downstairs.

Down in the basement, I felt like I could breathe again. There I was, ready for my nighttime ritual. I rarely ever fell asleep right away with my wife at night. I usually always came down to the basement and fucked around for hours until I was tired enough to drag my sleepy ass back upstairs and pass out.

Some nights I would work, look things up on the computer. Some nights I would put on TV or a movie. Some nights I would watch porn and jerk-off. The options were endless.

Tonight felt like a turn the TV on and stare off into space kind of night.

I pulled a beer out of the fridge and opened it, taking a nice long pull. I meandered over to my couch and sat down in my spot, turning the TV on and flipping through the channels. I settled on some movie station, playing a movie that was already halfway over. I didn't care.

I just wanted to zone out.

So I did. I watched the screen, not really absorbing anything, and finished my beer in three big gulps. I got up and got another, and another, and another.

The next thing I knew I had killed an entire six pack and was feeling all loopy. I was actually giggling at something on the TV, though I had no idea why it was funny.

Then I heard a noise, from the top of the steps.

It was the basement door, opening and closing.

Oh boy. It's Jess. She's coming down to berate me about staying up and drinking all these beers. Shit...

I slinked down, hiding behind the back of the couch, peering over the edge like a fucking weirdo. Footsteps crept off the stairs and over to me.

Oh, fuck.

It was Ryan.

I let out a slow breath and sat up, meeting his eyes over the back of the couch.

"Hey," I slurred a little.

"Hey... sorry to interrupt... or whatever," he stuttered. "I just couldn't sleep again."

"Welcome to my world," I grunted, resting my head against the back of the couch. "There's more beer if you want one."

"Uh... I'm..." he started, then paused. "Okay." I heard him opening the fridge. "You want another one?"

"Yea, sure. Thanks."

He brought the beers over and sat down beside me, handing me mine. We both twisted off our caps and clinked bottles before tossing them back.

"So... what are you watching?" he asked, nestling up against the back of the couch.

"I honestly have no idea..." I chuckled. "I think these two are running away from someone... and I think that one's having an affair... Who knows."

He laughed softly and drank his beer quick. We both sat quietly, watching the stupid movie, trying to piece it all together. Ryan was picking up the plot a lot quicker than me, even though he just got there.

We talked for a bit, joking about other movies we'd seen and hated, or loved. Our tastes were pretty similar. Ryan ended up drinking two more beers, and I began to worry that I *was* in fact turning the kid into an alcoholic. But I shrugged it off. I was sick of overthinking everything. I didn't want to ruin my buzz.

Shut down your brain. Just be in the moment... Whatever the fuck that hypnotist lady was saying on YouTube the other day.

"Oh boy..." Ryan muttered through a chuckle.

"What?"

"They're finally going to have sex," he pointed out. The two characters who kept insisting they hated each other were hooking up.

I giggled out a hoarse laugh. "I knew it. Pay up!"

"Did we make a bet?" he asked.

I shrugged. The two on the screen were starting to really go at it. The dude lifted the girl up and tossed her down on the bed. It was actually sort of hot.

Out of nowhere the air in the room shifted, but I couldn't tell if it was just because I was drunk and watching two people have sex on TV, or if it really was shifting. I swallowed hard and my eyes darted to my right.

Ryan's hand was sort of close to mine. *Was he that close before? Am I imagining things?*

I moved my hand onto my thigh, feeling on edge. Another minute went by and I saw him inching closer. Now I was sure I wasn't seeing things. When he first came down, he was almost on the other side of the couch. How the hell had he ended up all the way on my side?

Oh God... This is too weird. I should go upstairs. I should go to bed. I knew this was a bad idea.

What's a bad idea? Nothing even happened. Relax, psycho.

I glanced down at the couch, and this time his hand was right next to my thigh. Almost touching me. I swallowed hard again. My mouth was as dry as a bone.

I finished the last sip of my beer and leaned forward to put the bottle down on the table. When I sat back, my head pivoted and Ryan's face was right there. Inches from mine.

I flinched, moving away as my heart pounded in my chest.

"What's wrong?" he asked, his tone making me feel like *I* was the crazy one. "Why are you so tense?"

"I... uh... I don't know..." I muttered, unable to say anything else. I just kept staring forward at the TV, trying like hell to breathe normally.

"What would help you relax?" he asked, and his hand slid casually onto my arm.

At first, I could barely even tell he had touched me. It was so gentle, I thought maybe I'd imagined it. But then I looked down and saw his hand moving on my forearm, caressing, massaging with his strong fingers.

It was then that I remembered I wasn't wearing a shirt. I was dressed in only pajama bottoms. *Because I hadn't anticipated running into anyone down here...*

And Ryan was dressed the same. We were both shirtless.

Oh God... This is uncomfortable. We're half-naked and he's touching me. I should tell him to stop...

But I didn't. I couldn't. For some reason, I just... didn't say it.

Maybe I didn't want to?

Ryan's fingers slid down my arm, covering my hand, which was gripping my own thigh for dear life. He lifted my hand and tugged it over to him. My heart was pounding so hard I could feel it rocking through my whole body.

"You're so stiff..." he spoke, his voice deep and hoarse. "You need to relax."

He took my hand and placed it on his abs. I couldn't even swallow anymore. I couldn't move, or blink. I just sat there, staring down at my hand, watching it move on his lower stomach.

It was moving. Why, I had no idea, but it was. My fingers were moving, slowly tracing the cluster of muscles, each hard divot in his abs. "You definitely need to relax," he said again in a breath, barely audible.

"How?" I asked. Again, I wasn't sure why I was entertaining this. But I asked. It was the first word that flew out of my mouth. *How can he help me relax...?*

My eyes slowly slid up his shirtless frame, over all the muscles in his torso, similar to mine, over his stubbled jaw, just like mine, and up to his eyes. Dark green and filled with part confusion and part curious mischief.

I tried to regulate my breathing as his eyes fell from mine down to my neck.

And then he leaned in, closing the few inches separating us and pressed his lips on my jaw.

My jaw clenched as a reaction to the heightened tension around us. My whole body was stiff and unmoving. He scooted in even closer and trailed his soft lips down my neck, pressing these small, delicate, hesitant kisses over my throat and my Adam's apple.

My head slowly floated back to rest against the couch as I watched, stared, in shock, at his head falling down from my neck onto my chest. His lips grazed through the blonde hair on my chest, his tongue peeking out to trace the curves of my pecs.

My chest was heaving up and down as he inched the rest of his body even closer, until he was almost sitting on my lap. He placed his hands on my thighs, fingertips gripping as his lips covered my nipple and he sucked it ever so gently. It was very subtle, but still a gasp flew from inside my throat, and his eyes met mine. My entire face and neck were on fire as I watched him, tonguing and sucking my nipple, our eyes locked the whole time.

There was no emotion on his face at all. He was completely serious. In fact, he looked just as terrified as I was.

But it felt good. I was horrified. But I didn't want him to stop.

I reclined a bit on the couch, and he moved over to the other nipple, circling it with his tongue, kissing and sucking until it was just as hard as the one he just left. My heavy breathing turned into a slight panting, and it wasn't until his hand slid coyly between my legs that I realized just how hard my dick was.

I was as hard as a fucking rock.

When he touched it, my cock jumped in his palm and he glanced down at it. Like a green light, he was on a mission.

He made his descent down my torso, still kissing and licking, down my abs, through my happy trail, until he was fully kneeling between my parted legs.

He yanked on my pajama bottoms, tugging them down to my knees, freeing my eager cock. It was so damn hard, and I couldn't tell if my heartbeat in my chest was louder or the pulse of the veins in my erection.

Still, I was more nervous than I'd ever been before. I felt like I was in some kind of dream. *This couldn't be reality, could it?*

Ryan slowly curled his fist around my shaft, and I bit my lip to stifle a moan.

"I don't think you should..." was all I could say, while trying to swallow. This was all so wrong...

But it was exciting. It was bad... *forbidden.* And I was so turned on I was shaking.

"I won't... if you don't want me to," he whispered, his voice coming out as rough and uneven as mine.

"I... I... don't..." I stuttered, not knowing what to say. *I don't want him to stop.*

He totally should. But I don't want him to.

"Not like I know how to do it anyway..." he whispered, sounding almost like he was talking to himself. His hand was still wrapped around my painfully hard cock, holding it right in front of his face. His eyes came up to mine, and I stared back at him in complete consternation.

Get up. Get out.

"You... could try..." I grunted, my voice barely scraping from my throat. "If you want..."

I saw him swallow as he looked back at my dick in his hand.

"It's really big..." he murmured with some kind of fascination in his voice.

And without any further discussion, he lowered his mouth onto the head of my cock.

"Oh fuck..." I groaned, my dick twitching between his lips. He moaned, and the vibration felt incredible.

He slipped his tongue underneath the crown, and began sucking me in further, deeper into his mouth. Slowly at first, gripping me in his fist, moving his head up and down, forward and back, sucking gently on the tip of my dick in a way that sent shivers across my whole body.

I leaned my head back against the couch and closed my eyes. It felt so fucking good... His warm, wet mouth, sucking me in and out, his tongue massaging underneath the whole time.

After a few minutes, he let go of my shaft and his hand sunk between my thighs, rubbing on my balls. I opened my eyes to look down at the insanity happening in front of me. He had seemingly found his rhythm as he worked my cock over and over and over with his mouth, dipping it all the way to the back of his throat.

I moaned and grunted, reaching out to grab his jaw like a reflex, holding his head while he sucked my dick so fucking good I could barely breathe. Our eyes locked, and I could see how turned on he was; the passion, lust, and forbidden desire just from being able to please me.

Jesus Christ... What the fuck am I doing?
This is so bad... But so good.
It feels so fucking good.
But it's wrong. My daughter's boyfriend is giving me head.
Holy fuck... I'm gonna come.

He was still sucking away, letting me fuck his mouth, his eyes locked on mine. I moved my hips gently with his tempo, his fingers squeezing and massaging my balls, pulling the orgasm right out of me.

"Ryan... fuck, I'm going to... come..." I grunted closing my eyes and releasing his head. But his mouth stayed put as my climax ripped through my loins and I blew my load into his mouth.

I gasped out loud, trying to be as quiet as possible, but it was difficult. I'd never had an orgasm like that before. It felt like it lasted an eternity. I poured every drop I had into Ryan's throat and he swallowed it all. When I opened my eyes, he dragged my still-pulsing dick out of his mouth and he looked like he had never experienced such pleasure in his life.

It was wild.

He sat back on his knees, sucking his lower lip while his chest moved up and down. My eyes drifted and I noticed that he had a raging hard-on now. It was actually huge and straining against the material of his pajama pants.

We stared at each other for a minute. My skin felt like it was on fire. I was burning up everywhere. My eyes darted between his eyes and his hard-ass dick a few times, before he slowly stood up and pulled his pajamas down, allowing his erection to bob free.

Holy shit.

He stepped closer to me, curling his fist around his long, thick cock, stroking it so slow, while he watched my reaction. My eyes were stuck on it. I had literally never seen someone else's dick in real life before. Maybe in like locker rooms or something, but I never looked, not that they were close. Or hard...

But this one was. It was right in front of me, and he was stroking it, painfully slow. The tip was glistening. That meant he was really excited. I felt my slightly deflated cock perk up at the idea.

I wonder what it would be like...

I was pretty unsure of myself. I sort of wanted to try it, but I was so nervous...

Helping me decide, he shoved it even closer to my mouth, stepping up onto the couch with one foot, to the right of my thigh. I opened my mouth and lowered my lips onto the head of his cock slowly, sucking the saltiness of his arousal, tasting him. I sucked his thick head for a bit, while he jerked himself off from base to where my lips were, milking himself into my mouth. My dick was growing harder already.

Jesus... I can't believe I'm doing this. It feels good, though. It's so bad it's good. I want more...

I moved my mouth a little further down, sucking on his solid flesh. He was panting hard, moaning and groaning and making all kinds of noises, though I couldn't tell if he was being too loud or not, because my blood was rushing in my ears.

"Oh fuck... Mr. Lockwood..." he whimpered, motivating me to take more. So I did.

I sucked his dick, more and more... Forcing him to take his hand away. He slipped his fingers under my chin, tilting my gaze up to his. His eyes were dark, filled with carnal desire, edging me to keep going; begging me not to stop.

Fuck. Yes.

Further and further I went, sliding him all the way down my throat, and I didn't even gag. I was actually proud of myself. *I'm going to make him come with my mouth... Oh God, what if he comes down my throat? What would that be like?*

I guess we'll find out.

While I was having my internal struggle, Ryan pulled his throbbing cock out of my mouth and started stroking it, faster and faster, jerking himself off hard while he gasped.

Oh fuck... he is going to come. I want to do it...

I grabbed his dick and tugged on it for him, the same way I did my own, until he burst. He shot his orgasm all over my chest, panting my name over and over. *Let me taste again...*

My chest was still heaving as I slipped the end of him between my lips again and sucked his head clean. My dick pulsed between my legs.

Holy fuck that was the hottest thing ever. He tastes good.

Wait, what the fuck just happened?!

Ryan fell down onto the couch next to me while we tried to regulate our breathing. I glanced down at the glistening come all over my chest, blinking a few times in utter shock.

I still couldn't even process what just happened. *Was that real? Was it a dream? Could that have actually happened?*

Ryan's face was flushed beet red, and he couldn't look me in the eye. Not that I could tell, because I couldn't look him in the eye either. I got up slowly, pulling my pants back up and locating some paper towels to wipe myself off. I paced around the basement for a few minutes in a state of dazed panic before coming back to the couch.

Ryan had his pants back on, and was sitting up, looking stunned and terrified. Not far off from how I was feeling.

I decided to speak first, since I was supposed to be more of the adult in this scenario. *Yea, some adult... Sucking your daughter's boyfriend's dick while she's asleep upstairs.*

I cringed and shook my head.

"Look..." I started, my voice firm and all business. "That was a mistake. We were both... drunk... or whatever, and we fucked up. But no one needs to know about it."

Ryan slowly lifted his head upward to meet my gaze. He said nothing, just blinked over wide eyes.

"It never happened," I added, clenching my jaw in fear that someone would find out the exact opposite of what I was saying.

Suddenly, the door opened at the top of the stairs. My heart leapt into my throat and Ryan instantly toppled onto his side quickly, burrowing himself behind the back of the couch to hide from view.

"Babe?" Jess's voice called from the top of the stairs.

"Yea, hun!" I croaked back, my eyes wide as I stared down at Ryan. He looked like he was going to shit himself.

"Are you coming to bed? It's late," her sleepy voice asked, and my stomach fell onto the floor. *Oh my God, I am such a piece of garbage.*

"Yea, babe... I'll be right up," I answered her, closing my eyes tight and hanging my head.

"Alright..." she murmured, leaving and closing the door behind her.

I breathed out hard, slapping my hand over my heart, feeling how aggressively it was pounding against my palm. *So this is what it feels like... the drama.*

Ryan sat up slowly, still giving me a look that I couldn't read at all.

I shook my head and walked toward the stairs, turning back to him one last time and whispering, "It never happened."

I climbed the stairs, leaving the secret behind in my getaway room, as I headed upstairs to my wife.

I crawled into bed next to her, and she wrapped her arms around me from behind, kissing my shoulder blades. I breathed out hard and closed my eyes, feeling instantly drowsy. It appeared that I had found my excitement.

And I had never felt more alive.

CHAPTER 6

Ryan

I WOKE BEFORE EVERYONE. I could tell because the whole house was quiet, and it was green like dawn outside. I took a long, hot shower, unsure of whether I was trying to scrub or burn away the memories of what happened last night, or savor them in some way.

That was the problem with what had happened. It was at two opposite ends of the spectrum. It was so good it was almost downright euphoric, and also so awful that I kept gagging for no reason.

I had absolutely no idea what to think.

I'd always been pretty in touch with myself. I could usually tell in my heart when I was feeling good about something or not. I guess I was just grounded that way.

But now my entire life view had been turned upside down. The last night literally ripped me apart, and I had no idea who I was anymore.

Am I gay?

Am I straight?

Am I bisexual?

Am I pansexual? Whatever that means.

Am I interested in Ben? Do I want to be in a relationship with him? Do I want to stay with Hailey? Do I love her?

Do I love Ben?

Am I a horrible fucking monstrous piece of shit who fucked around with his girlfriend's father? That one definitely has an answer. Yes.

I groaned to myself, resting my back against the shower tiles. *What the fuck did I do last night?*

How did that even happen??

Okay, fine. So I watched Ben fucking his wife the night before and it turned me on. And yes, I may have thought about what it would be like to sleep with him...

And then I fucked my girlfriend and got off thinking about fucking her dad. Which I obsessed about and freaked out over all damn night.

Then, yes, I woke the next morning vowing never to look at, or even think about him like that again.

But then he was being so nice to me all day. He was being kind and talkative, not scary and passive-aggressive like he was before. So yes, I thought about it more and that was why I went downstairs last night. So I did kind of want something to happen with him...

But only because I wanted to see if I would like it!

Oh well, you liked it, alright. You liked it big time.

Ugh, shut up, brain. You're not helping.

My mind was racing. There were images of me and Ben last night flashing through my brain, and I couldn't stop them.

Licking and kissing his sweet, golden skin... The look on his face right before I started blowing him... The actual sensation of having a dick in my mouth... The taste of his hot, slick orgasm as it flowed down my throat... holy fuck... oh my God.

Ben's mouth on my cock. That was crazy. I sort of slipped into sucking him off pretty easily, but I never expected him to do it back. God, his mouth felt so good. Hesitant and slow at first, and then he was chasing my orgasm the way I chased his... Coming all over his beautiful, broad chest... him sucking the rest...

I squeezed my eyes shut even tighter and banged my head against the wall of the shower.

This. Is. Fucking. Hopeless.

I already couldn't stop thinking about him, which must have meant I was gay. Or at least bi.

But that morning, when I woke up next to Hailey, I got a hard-on from feeling her soft skin, and her big tits and hard nipples pushing through the thin fabric of her tank top.

I still loved tits. I still loved pussy.

So I wasn't gay.

Ugh, God... fuck my life.

I tried thinking about another guy, to see if I would get turned on.

Hmm... who would be considered good-looking?

Umm... Ryan Gosling! No, he has the same name as me. That's weird.

How about the guy who plays Superman? Henry what's his name? Hmm... alright. Naked Henry what's his name walks in. Yea, no. Nothing.

Maybe I'm just not attracted to him. Let's try someone else.

How about... Oh! That guy Hailey's always raving about from the Fifty Shades movies. He kinda looks like Ben...

Ok, Mr. Grey walks in naked... Let's see... anything?

Nope. Ugh... this is impossible.

What if it's just Ben? What if I'm straight, but Ben is just such a strong masculine, sexual force that he drags the gay out of me?

Jesus, none of this makes sense...

What the fuck am I doing, anyway? I've been in the shower for like ninety minutes. I need to get out.

I reluctantly turned the shower off and hopped out, drying myself off, my mind floating away with my disparaging thoughts, when all of a sudden...

"Hey, baby!" Hailey chimed, slinking into the bathroom and grabbing her toothbrush. "Why are you up so early?"

"Um... I couldn't really sleep again..." I muttered, staring at her.

She was so beautiful. And I loved her, I knew I did.

We hadn't actually, officially said *I love you*, yet. We texted hearts and kissy faces, and emojis that said it. But we hadn't physically said the words to each other, out loud. And I had never been gladder about that fact.

Because when Hailey found out I messed around with her dad, she would probably go ballistic.

Ben's words from last night started to ring in my brain.

"It never happened."

Could I really pull that off? I wasn't a secret-keeper. I hated that shit.

I was a terrible liar. I couldn't even play poker because I couldn't stand the whole *bluffing* aspect. I wasn't sure that I could keep this to myself...

But then, if I didn't, Hailey would get hurt. And so would Ben, and so would Jessica. And me. Basically everyone would get hurt.

So maybe I should try? I should try to keep this secret to spare everyone getting hurt...

Plus, there was another teeny, tiny, itsy, bitsy issue remaining...

I wanted to hook up with him again.

It was bad. So completely wrong. And I didn't *want* to want it.

But I did.

"Baby!" Hailey snapped her fingers in front of my face, spitting her toothpaste into the sink.

"What? Huh?" I grunted, blinking.

"Did you hear what I said? My mom wants to know if we can stay another day so I can go shopping with her tonight. It's a tradition. We always do it," Hailey explained.

The rational part of my brain wanted to tell her no. We had to leave today so that I could get the hell away from Ben and leave this whole mess behind me.

But then the other part... the fun part... knew that staying another day meant another chance to have a repeat of last night.

God, I want that...

"Okay," I answered fast. "We can stay."

Well, so much for that rational thing...

"Thank you, baby! Thank you so much!" she squealed, hugging onto me and squirming around. I swallowed hard and pulled her against me, suddenly feeling violently ill.

When we eventually made our way downstairs, I was scared shitless. I looked around every corner for some sign of Ben, but I didn't see him anywhere. I felt like I could breathe for a moment.

That is, until he came downstairs, shirtless and wet, clearly having just come out of the shower.

I gulped, feeling instantly nauseous again.

When Ben swung around the corner and saw me, he stopped dead in his tracks, his eyes widening briefly in a look of sheer panic, which lasted only a split second before he stuffed it down and plastered on a fake smile.

"Good morning," he grumbled, breezing past us, refusing to make eye contact with anyone.

"Morning!" Hailey chirped. "Where's Mom?"

"Still getting ready... something about you guys shopping or... something," Ben stuttered, pouring himself coffee.

"Yea, Ryan and I are staying another night so Mom and I can go shopping today like we always do," Hailey cheered.

I saw Ben freeze, even though his back was to us. When he finally turned around, his brow was furrowed and his mouth was hanging open.

"You're staying another day...?" he asked, his eyes darting frantically between Hailey and me. I nodded slowly while Hailey jumped up and down. "Are you sure that's a good idea...?"

I shrugged impassively, while Hailey gasped, "Why wouldn't it be?"

Ben looked nervous. More than nervous, he looked... disturbed. I knew because I was feeling the same way.

But for some reason, seeing the look on him made me angry.

Why is he so upset? Is it because he doesn't want to hook up with me again? Maybe he was really saying it never happened last night because he's ashamed.

He's probably some completely homophobic guy who always secretly wanted a dick in his mouth, but now that he's had it, he can't live with himself and he's going to stuff it down and never talk about it again.

Jeez... what a nightmare.

I stared at him for a moment, raising my brow. He squinted at me, clenching his jaw. I had no idea what that look meant, but before I could obsess about it anymore, Jessica came downstairs, looking as radiant as ever.

"Good morning!" she sang. "So, have you decided?" She looked to Hailey and me. I nodded, putting on a fake smile.

"Yes! Ryan said we can stay!" Hailey whooped again, her and her mom dancing around the kitchen. I wasn't sure what kind of shopping they were going to do, but they were certainly amped over it.

More amped than Ben is about being alone with me again, that's for sure.

"Okay, so we're going to leave for the outlets in a couple hours, maybe after lunch," Jessica said, then turned to Ben. "But, baby, will you and Ryan please clean out that section of the garage with all the junk we sorted? The guy is coming to pick it up in an hour."

Ben and I shared a desperate look, said nothing, and walked silently toward the garage.

Being in a confined space with Ben was difficult. I just wanted to ignore the tension between us, but it was so hard because every time I looked at him all I could see was his giant cock in my mouth. It was making me crazy.

I'm a straight guy with cock on the brain... That's great. I love my life.

Ben was being very broody. He was lifting things and tossing them on the ground in such an aggressive manner that after a while, I just stopped what I was doing and stared at him, waiting for him to sort out whatever meltdown he was having.

He slammed one last box down right next to my feet, then huffed and ran his hand through his hair.

"There. Done," he grunted, pushing past me. "Bring those out to the street."

Uh, excuse me? My patience was wearing thin.

"Please..." I muttered under my breath. He stopped dead in his tracks.

"What did you just say to me?" he grumbled, his tone downright chilling.

"I said, *please*. Because that's what you say when you're asking someone to do something," I hissed, narrowing my gaze at his back. "You don't just bark orders at them, like some kind of drill sergeant. You say fucking please."

He spun around slowly and then stalked up to me. He got very close; so close that I could feel the warmth radiating off of him onto me. I could smell him... like freshly washed clothes and that Dove for Men soap that I like. I swallowed hard, trying not to waver as my eyes met his, crossing the less than an inch that separated us in height.

"I don't need to say anything to you, Ryan," he spoke, eerily quiet, his blue eyes cutting through me. "I don't need to speak to you anymore. Just do what the fuck I say so we can move the fuck on and get the fuck away from each other."

"Oh, is that fucking right?" I snarled, stepping even closer to him, until our faces were inches apart.

"Yes, that's fucking right," he growled, his breath warming my lips. I wasn't sure if we were about to fight, or kiss...

All I knew was that I could have just backed down. It would have been so easy...

But instead I stood my ground. I squared my shoulders, clenched my jaw, and said, "Make me."

Ben's blue eyes turned into a blazing inferno and he placed his hands on my chest, shoving me backward, hard, against the wall of the garage. My back connected with the drywall and I coughed. But before I could step forward to lay him the fuck out, his hands were on my neck and his lips were on mine.

I felt like something exploded inside me. I was scared and angry and turned on all at once.

Ben groaned into my mouth, tugging at my lips with his, sliding his tongue inside to meet mine. I was still shocked, but it felt so good that I had no choice but to kiss him back. I grabbed his ass and pulled him toward me, causing our hips to crash together. He was so fucking hard, and so was I.

I had never felt another erection rubbing up on mine before... It honestly felt sublime.

"Fuck, you're driving me insane," he gasped, pulling me closer to him by my hair, sucking and biting my bottom lip. "We can't do this..."

"No... we... can... not..." I panted in between the most hungry, needy kisses of my entire life. Every time his tongue touched mine, I felt a tremor in my cock.

My hands slid down over his strong chest, soft skin covering rock-hard muscles. The same chest I had blew my load all over last night. The memory made my dick throb against his.

"Oh my God, was last night real?" he hummed, grinding himself on me. "Did we really do that?"

"I think so..." I whimpered.

"I'm so fucking hard right now..." he moaned while dragging his crotch in one long fluid motion along mine.

"Yea... I know," I huffed, kissing him softer, sucking his lips and tonguing his tongue. *This feels too good for real life...*

"Okay... let's stop on three..." he breathed, and I burst out laughing. "You stopped already..." he grinned. "I said on three."

I shook my head and rolled my eyes. *He's so fucking bossy, but in a sexy and kind of adorable way...*

We both backed off of each other and tried to compose ourselves. Luckily, we were securely inside the garage with the doors closed so no one could see us.

"Alright now I'm serious..." he grunted, running his hand along his jaw. "No more. Never happened... Not happening again. The whole shebang."

"Okay, fine," I muttered, crossing my arms over my chest. "I think I should go shopping with the girls then."

"Why? Because you can't resist me, and you know that being alone in the house with me for hours will turn you into a raging sex fiend again?" Ben smirked that cocky grin that made my blood boil and my dick stir.

I narrowed my gaze at him. "Uh no. Actually I was thinking that about you."

"Excuse me?" he huffed.

"You can't keep your hands off me... clearly," I motioned in the air regarding what just happened.

"Are you serious?"

"Dead serious."

"Well, that's not at all the case. In fact, I'm totally fine," Ben chirped, looking smug. "So if you want to stay here while the girls go out, I'm cool with it. I'll stay downstairs and you can stay upstairs."

"Fine by me," I replied. "We won't even have to cross paths."

"Good."

"Great!"

"Wonderful!"

We both scowled at each other for a moment, each of us remaining stubborn and standing our ground. I took a deep breath, looking him over but keeping it brief, so as not to give him the satisfaction. He did the same, then bit his lip.

"I mean..." he started, his eyes sparkling. "They will be gone for hours..."

"True," I nodded. "We'll have the house to ourselves."

"Mhm... So there's probably no harm in... hanging out. Just watching some TV or whatever." I could already see the wheels turning in his mind, which sent a shiver of excitement through me.

"Totally. It's just TV," I confirmed, my voice already hoarse with anticipation.

"Exactly," he grinned.

"Sounds perfect." My eyes lit up.

I watched anxiously from the front window as Jessica's car pulled out of the driveway, she and Hailey driving up the street and far away from the house.

They were going shopping at the outlets for some Black Friday weekend sale. According to Hailey it was a tradition, and sometimes they were out until midnight.

It was only five in the evening.

Plenty of time to explore...

I heard Ben rustling around in the kitchen. I wasn't sure what he was doing, but since our bizarre, sexually charged moment in the garage, we'd been trying hard to avoid one another at all costs.

Lunch was odd. We had all sat down together, making mundane small talk while eating sandwiches. Ben and I didn't really talk, but every time I felt him watching me, I would look up to catch the very end of an incredibly intense blue stare. It made me so nervous I started to feel nauseous, while simultaneously filling my whole body with tingles of excitement and impatience.

I had been counting the minutes until the girls left, even though I wasn't sure why. It wasn't like I knew what I was going to do with Ben once we were alone...

He was just so intimidating. I suppose that was what captivated me the most and made him sort of irresistible. He was strong and quiet and sort of scary. It still blew me away how gently he touched and kissed... and gave head.

I found myself wondering what would happen if we went further than third base... If we actually... *fucked*. I couldn't stop thinking about it, the whole duration of our awkward lunch, and the hour or so before and after. I was so curious about what Ben would want to do... About what he would like.

Obviously neither of us had ever been with another guy before... And before the other night, such curiosities had never so much as crossed my mind. But for Ben, clearly my boundaries and inhibitions went out the window.

Would I let him fuck me? Would he let me fuck him?

Sure, I had been fantasizing about it since the night I spent drooling over his perfect ass while he fucked his wife. I wanted to know how it felt, to fuck someone like him. Someone so masculine and in-control. It was like a high. I was fiending for it.

I wasn't sure what we would do now that we had the whole house to ourselves for hours, but the possibilities were endless. And incredibly worrying.

After all, this was my *girlfriend's* house. The house where she grew up. I was just a guest here. I had been here less than three whole days and I was already messing around with her dad. *What the hell kind of person am I?!*

I needed to get away. I needed to think for a minute.

I had no idea where Ben was, but I knew he was going to come looking for me at some point now that the girls were gone.

And then we were going to hook up.

I was still so excited I was nervous. Or I was so nervous I was excited. One or the other.

I slinked upstairs, slowly, making my way into Hailey's room to get some air. But as soon as I was inside, I felt even more suffocated, so I left and walked down the hall, peeking into Ben's room. Nope, not in there either. *Jesus, this whole house is off limits. It just goes to show how wrong this is...*

I gulped to myself, making my way all the way down the other end of the hall to the guestroom. My hands were shaking a little as I stepped inside, taking a deep breath.

Ah, that's better. Here I can breathe. It's neutral territory.

Before I could get too comfortable, I heard Ben's footsteps coming down the hall and I swallowed hard. My stomach was in my throat.

He appeared in the doorway looking flustered. Probably the same way I was looking.

"What are you doing in here?" he asked, glancing around the room.

I shrugged, unable to speak actual words.

He walked up to me slowly and cocked his head to the side, regarding me with a look of quiet contemplation. I wasn't sure what he was thinking but then again, I wasn't really sure what I was thinking either. My brain was completely cloudy.

He's hot... so I guess there's that. And he's a good kisser, better than most of the girls I've kissed before. And he definitely gives better blow jobs than most girls. But maybe that was just because it was new and different...

Who knows... but you need to stop thinking.

I took another deep breath and shut my brain off completely. I silenced all of my loud, anxious, nagging thoughts of guilt and uncertainty, locking them away in my mind for another time. And I focused on the being standing in front of me. I disregarded the fact that he wasn't ever what I thought I'd wanted prior to two days ago and ripped up any labels my mind wanted to create. And I just looked at him.

He was gorgeous, there was no denying it. He was tall and strong, and built. He had a pretty face, and delicate features that were a sharp contrast to how strikingly handsome he was. He had a big body, firm everywhere; strong hands and soft lips. Hooking up with him last night was fun, and I wanted more fun.

So that was it. In deciding whether to be good or bad, I chose bad. And didn't look back.

While I was watching Ben, Ben was also watching me, though he still looked nervous, as if he hadn't fully made his choice yet. So I decided to help him out.

I reached up slowly, tugging his face to mine and kissed him, soft but impatient and ready. I knew we didn't need to rush, but for some reason I felt like an addict who was withdrawing. It was like I was on the outside, looking in. Watching the events unfold like a movie. And I desperately wanted to see what happened next.

We kissed slowly for a bit, lust moving through our bodies like electricity. We spent a few minutes getting used to each other, finding a rhythm together. It was still so new and foreign, kissing a guy. I could feel his stubble rubbing on mine, and it was actually turning me on a lot. I savored the slight burn as our tongues swirled; while we sucked and licked and bit until our lips were swollen.

I grasped the hem of Ben's t-shirt and slid it up his torso, removing it and tossing it somewhere. Then he did the same to mine. Our hands were everywhere, roaming, touching, exploring. I ran my fingers up and down his strong back and wide shoulders, reveling in how similar our bodies were. It was so unexpected to be hooking up with someone just like me. And it was surprisingly hot as hell.

Plus, he had the softest skin. When his lips moved down to my neck, my hands glided down his chest and stomach, feeling how strong and hard his body was until I got to the waist of his jeans. I unbuttoned and unzipped, pushing them down fast.

He pulled back to look at me, blinking slowly, completely serious. I couldn't tell what he was thinking, but from the look in his eyes, I could tell he was turned on by me taking charge. Ben was used to control, and I was sure the same could be said for his sex life. Maybe he wanted me to take him over... To just have my way with him. The thought of it had my erection desperate to escape my pants.

Reading my mind, he unbuttoned and unzipped my pants, pushing them down, leaving us both in our boxer briefs. We wore the exact the same ones, Calvin Klein's, which I refused to comment on at the moment, though it was pretty amazing. And we both had visible hard-ons.

Ben pushed himself against me, kissing me again, slow and deep, while he ground every inch of his hardness on mine. I stepped back and pulled him onto the guest bed, where he climbed on top of me, growling and panting while we kissed so hard and furious, I thought we both might burst into flames.

This was so much more intense than last night. This time we were in a bed, getting naked together. That could mean only one thing...

I wasted no time sliding his boxers down, allowing his erection to flop out onto my stomach. He kicked them off the rest of the way, then pulled mine down, all the way off my legs, tossing across the room.

Ben gazed down at me for a moment, his eyes hooded with frantic desire. I licked my lips, my heart hammering inside my ribcage with anticipation for what would come next. I felt desperate for him, which wasn't something I could ever remember feeling before. He moved in and kissed me again, capturing my lips with his, rubbing his long, hard cock against mine.

It was almost amusing how similar our dicks looked. They were basically the same size, girth and all. I grabbed them both in my hand at once and jerked them off together.

"Fuck... Ryan, that feels good," he grunted, moving his kisses down my neck again, this time onto my chest, licking and sucking all over my pecs and my nipples. It felt divine. *No wonder he got so hard from this last night...*

He took his time kissing and nipping a trail down my body, and it became apparent that he was figuring out what he liked. What he liked with *me*. *This is about exploration, I suppose. He wants to try things. Mmm... That sounds like fun.*

Ben made a fist around my cock with his rough hand. A man's

hand. And he watched it closely as he began jerking me, slow and steady, from my balls all the way up. He glanced up at me, keeping his eyes on mine while he slid the head of my cock into his mouth and started sucking.

It was like the night before only so much better. He was naked, on top of me, and I was naked beneath him, and he was sucking me so so good... I could barely control myself.

"Fuck, Ben!" I gasped out loud, my cock twinging in his mouth.

"You should probably be sort of quiet..." he grinned. "Just in case."

"Sorry..." I murmured, breathing out hard and unsteady.

He worked my dick over and over in his mouth, so warm and wet, swirling his tongue around on the crown, then hoovered it between his lips like a damn lollipop. My eyes rolled back in my head and I groaned, my hips bucking forward with his movements.

He tugged his mouth off me and continued stroking with his hand while he moved his mouth down to my balls, alternating between tonguing and kissing them. It was a fantastic feeling. The only problem was that I could definitely come soon, and I didn't want to yet. It was all so exciting. It reminded me of the time I lost my virginity, and I couldn't let that happen. I needed to make this one count.

"Ben," I gulped his name, watching his head bob in front of me.

"Mhm..." he grunted with me in his mouth.

"Don't make me come..." I panted, my face and neck heating like an oven.

His eyes met mine and they sparkled. He really liked the fact that he was making me feel so good, that much was clear.

He let my cock spring from his mouth, then scooted back up to me on the bed, laying on his side. He placed his hand gently on my waist and pulled me flush against him, kissing my lips so soft I was melting.

Ben flicked his hips, dragging his erection against mine, then whispered, "Touch me."

My dick pulsed at his words, a fire slowly spreading throughout my insides.

I rolled on top of him, pinning him to the mattress, grinding our dicks together, building friction that felt so good, I couldn't stop the noises from escaping me. I held his jaw, kissing him harder, seeking out his tongue until he began to squirm.

My hands leisurely traveled down his chest, across his firm pecs and hardened nipples, which made him hum. *That's a good sound.*

Further down they went, touching his abs, tracing all the defined muscles, before sinking lower, my fingertips grazing his balls, making him shudder.

"Do you want my mouth... here?" I asked in a whisper over his lips and he let out a gasp of the word *yes* that had my cock twitching against his.

So my next mission was to work down his body the way he had done to mine, licking, kissing and nipping everywhere while he moaned softly. I arrived at his large luscious dick and sucked the length of it between my lips, letting him fuck my mouth until the tip grazed the back of my throat. His fingers were in my hair, holding my head in place for him. It was so dirty, and so fucking hot I couldn't even be bothered not to grind my cock on his leg.

Ben began to spread his legs and my curiosity got the best of me. I left his dick wet and moved onto his balls, licking them until he spread his legs wider, making enough room for me to do what I was starting to think he wanted next.

I grabbed his ass with my hands and squeezed, panting out swift breaths, giving away how fucking bad I was lusting. My thumb subtly grazed his crack and I heard him whimper. *He's destroying me right now... Jesus.*

Ben was writhing, lifting his hips to my mouth, clearly wanting so much all at once. It was one of the hottest things I had ever experienced.

"I should... uhh... should I get... something...?" he rambled, pulling my hair as I teased the head of his cock with my tongue some more, letting my fingers roam again.

I wasn't sure what he meant, or if he even knew himself. *Does he want to get lube? Or a condom? What does he want? I'll give him literally whatever he wants right now...*

"Mmm... don't stop," he growled, changing his mind. *Okay so no condom... Or lube...*

"I'll make it wet," I breathed, my voice so rough I could barely recognize myself. *I think I'm blushing.*

But to my surprise, he nodded fast and said, "Make it wet. Make it wet and touch me there... I want to see how it feels."

I swear to God I'm about to come all over this bed.

With shaky hands I gripped Ben's ass hard, spreading him open and wasting no time sliding my tongue over his tight hole. He gasped out loud, and I could feel him tightening up, but I started stroking his dick with my hand again and he seemed to succumb to feeling, allowing me to eat him the way I was used to eating pussy.

Stop. That. Train. Of. Thought.

This was by far the naughtiest, dirtiest thing I had ever done. The fact that I wasn't supposed to be doing it was never far in my mind, and for some reason it just served to turn me on more. I licked him there over and over, probing him with the tip of my tongue until my own dick was so hard it was ready to break off.

"Jesus fucking Christ," he choked out. "Fuck, your tongue feels good... "

I used his words as motivation for my devious activities, kissing and licking his ass in between sucking my finger, tracing his rim through the new lubrication. I decided to just go for it, since he had already told me to before, and pushed said finger into his hole, fighting against the resistance.

He hummed, then moaned, biting his lip as he glanced down at me.

"Do you like it?" I asked, not waiting for him to answer me before I was thrusting it in further.

"Fuck!" he gasped, his head falling back on the bed. "Oh God..." *I think that's a yes.*

I fingered him slow yet dedicated, trying to find that infamous spot everyone's always raving about. I knew it was in there... *Maybe I should use another one.*

Ben was grinding against my hand, and when I took my finger back he made this sexy as fuck whining noise that fueled me even more. I slid two fingers inside him and I must have hit something because his whole body tremored.

"Ryan," he grunted, his chest heaving. "Fuck *yes...*"

"Is this good?" I fisted his cock while my other hand was knuckle deep in his ass, pushing and pulling. His ass looked even more incredible now than the other night.

God, I want to replace my fingers with my dick right now. Is that bad?

Can't go down that road right now... No thinking.

"So fucking good..." he rasped, licking his lips. "More..."

I paused and blinked hard, sitting back to look down at him. I had sort of expected him to freak out about this stuff, but apparently he was completely game. Honestly, I thought he would want to fuck me, which I would have been alright with, too. Maybe... depending on what he did first.

But instead he lied there on the bed, his broad chest moving with his rapid breaths, legs spread, knees bent, and his hard, monstrosity of a cock twinging on his stomach. I pulled my hand away and inched up to him, closer, until I could glide my erection between his wet cheeks.

Fuck... this is what I was fantasizing about the other night... And now it's happening. Oh Ben Lockwood... I will make us both come so good, I promise.

"You want this?" I asked through a hoarse growl, sliding the head of my cock over his asshole.

He groaned softly, his cheeks flushing as he grabbed his dick, jerking himself slowly. "Yes."

I licked my palm and stroked my cock with it, momentarily feeling like I was in a porno. It was completely crazy. And so fucking hot I was burning alive.

"Do you want me to fuck you, Mr. Lockwood?" I asked again, probing him with the head of my cock, pleading with my eyes.

"Put your dick inside me," his deep, sexy voice rumbled up at me. "Slowly... at first..."

Anything you want, Ben. Anything for you.

I took my cock in my hand and pressed the tip into him, pushing gently, moving my head around in the wetness. It was so tight, his body struggled against me, though Ben clearly wanted it. He was panting and whimpering out some of the hottest noises I had ever heard.

I swallowed hard, my eyes moving back and forth between the downright lethal look on his face, and the entrance to him.

"Relax for me," I gave him a gentle command, pushing harder, forcing my thick head. He breathed out slowly and nodded, visibly relaxing a bit. I used my left hand to grip his thigh, massaging up to his hip while I continued to push.

Finally, after some work, my head slid inside his opening, and we both groaned out loud. It felt so good neither of us gave a fuck who was listening.

"I'm gonna move in more, baby," I grunted, my voice so hoarse I sounded like pure sex.

"Yes... please..." he mumbled. *God, that's hot as fuck...* I pushed in further and he groaned again. It was the tightest thing that had ever squeezed my dick in my whole life.

One more push and I broke through another ring of muscle. Now about half of my dick was inside him. This time I pulled back slightly and then pushed back in, working some of the lubrication. I pulled and pushed again, grunting as I went, removing an inch, then thrusting another... deeper and deeper until I was up to my nuts in him and it felt so good, I wanted to scream.

"Fuck me, Ryan..." he growled, gripping the comforter on both sides. "Fuck my ass."

"Oh *Jesus*... you feel so fucking good, Ben," I told him, drawing my hips back then thrusting deeper, fucking him slow and deep and hard, making sure to hit his spot. More than anything I just wanted to see his dick come from me fucking him. I was chasing it.

I grabbed his hard, thick cock, veins throbbing in my hands, and I jerked him while I fucked him. I met every thrust with a stroke of his big, juicy cock, pumping myself into his tight ass over and over while he cried out my name.

"Fuck Ryan... I'm gonna... come..." he told me, out of breath and raw. *I want that...*

"Good... come for me," I commanded, lifting his hips and leaning down enough to get his cock by my mouth. "I'm going to swallow you while I'm fucking you... because you taste so fucking good."

He yelped out a string of curses while I shoved my aching cock all the way inside him, and he erupted like a volcano. I slid my lips over his head just in time to catch his hot load in my mouth, swallowing it all, setting me off into my own orgasm.

"Fuck, Ben... Mr.... Lockwood... *Fuck!*"

My dick burst inside him, pulsing over and over, emptying my climax deep in his perfect ass. I couldn't move... couldn't speak. There were no words.

Just the best sex I'd ever had in my entire existence. We were both breathing so heavy, panting and gasping for air, our bodies covered in glistening sweat.

I pulled out of Ben quickly, yet gentle so as not to hurt him. He hummed and stretched his legs out long, squeezing his eyes shut, while I fell down on the bed next to him. My heart was beating like a drum inside me as I stared up at the ceiling.

Holy... fuck...

We laid in silence for a while, side-by-side, just staring at nothing. I wasn't sure if there were words to be said right now, but if there were, I certainly didn't know which ones to use.

I just fucked him. We just fucked.

I put my dick inside a guy. A guy I'm not supposed to have. And it felt like fireworks.

Finally, I rolled onto my side, checking on my new fuck buddy. You know, to make sure he was okay.

"Ben..." I whispered his name, unsure of what I wanted his response to be... or what I would say if he did respond.

He grunted himself into movement and rolled onto his side, facing me.

"Ryan..." he replied, his face serious and his tone stern.

"It doesn't have to... be weird or anything," I murmured, watching his gorgeous face closely. "It's just physical, so... you know... It's fun. Right?"

He squinted at me, remaining quiet for a moment. He looked like he wanted to make some kind of typical smug Ben comment. But then he breathed out slowly and his eyes softened.

"It was fun," he squirmed closer to me, and to my surprise, he pulled me flush against him and kissed my lips, softer than he ever had before. I practically melted. *Okay, maybe I really did...* "I can't wait to do it again."

He grinned on my lips, and it was definitely contagious. I couldn't fight the smile.

"Come on! While the water's still warm!" Ben shouted at me from inside the shower of the master bathroom.

"Okay, okay... Jeez, you're bossy," I huffed, opening the glass door to the shower stall and stepping inside.

It was actually much more than a shower stall. More like a *shower enclosure*. The thing was massive. It looked like it could fit at least five people. There were dual shower-heads, though Ben left only one on, so I was forced to get close to him. I knew his game. I wasn't stupid.

After I popped Ben's cherry, we just lied in the bed for a while, touching and kissing. And because it was us, it eventually turned into more, and we ended up sixty-nineing and swallowing each other's dicks like fucking come fiends. It was insanely hot.

I'm getting hard again just thinking about it...

Once that exciting romp was over, we were so sweaty and covered in... stuff... that Ben suggested taking a shower. He got in first, but I kept getting paranoid, needing to check that the girls hadn't come home yet before I could enter a sexy shower with Ben.

I could only imagine what would happen if his wife and daughter came home while we were in the shower together. I cringed just thinking about it.

Ben lathered up shampoo on his head, then did mine, which I thought was pretty sweet. Though he did it like a total dude, being all serious and domineering the whole time. It was still odd to me that he seemed to be like that in all aspects of his life, except when I was balls deep in his sweet ass.

"Ryan..." Ben grunted, rinsing his hair and giving me a look.

"What?" I asked, looking around for whatever he was about to scold me for.

"You're getting hard again," he muttered, fully serious, glancing down at my dick, which was inflating, poking him in the hip.

"Mmm... so I am," I grinned, grabbing his hand and moving it around my cock.

"Oh, I see. So every time I'm naked around you, you're gonna want to fuck me?" he rasped, looking like he wanted to be serious, though the beginning of a dimple was peeking through.

I laughed softly. "Well, why would you be naked around me if I weren't going to fuck you?"

"Um right now, for example," he raised his brows. "We're showering."

"Hmm, okay," I rolled my eyes at him. "If we're just showering then why didn't you turn on the other shower-head?"

He pursed his lips, which made him look devastatingly sexy. "It's a waste of water."

"Oh is that right?" I chuckled, and he laughed back.

"Okay... fine," he grabbed my waist, pulling me closer. "Maybe I did want to take full advantage of this alone time..."

"Mmm... yea?" I smirked, kissing his perfectly pouted bottom lip.

"Yea," he gasped and kissed me back, sliding his sweet, warm tongue into my mouth, making me hum with desire.

I couldn't believe it was possible to be getting this many erections in such a short span of time. But I was already rock-solid again, and Ben's delicious footlong of a cock felt like steel.

I spun him around using the soap to wash his sexy muscular back, taking the opportunity to really covet his ass. It was so fucking nice. I grabbed the cheeks, massaging, caressing and squeezing them, pushing my erection between them and sliding it up and down over his asshole.

I kissed his neck and shoulders all over, pressing him up against the wall of the shower while I knelt down and worshipped his ass just a little, kissing, licking and nipping all over it.

"You have... the best ass... I've ever fucking seen or touched," I growled at him from behind, stroking my cock in my right hand, gripping his ass with my left. "Or fucked."

He moaned, his deep voice echoing off the bathroom walls.

"Are you still sore, or can you take this dick again?" I asked him, running my fingers over him and feeling him pucker.

"I can handle it," he rumbled, popping his butt out for me. I grinned wickedly.

"Good. Bend over, please," I commanded, in a nice way, and he did as I asked without question, bending his sweet, perfectly plump and firm ass over right in front of me. I growled again looking at it, touching it, giving it a little smack.

"Oh fuck you..." he whimpered, sounding like it was taking everything in him to let me control him like this, which made me smile.

"Mmmm... fuck you," I whispered then spread him wide and guided my throbbing cock into him.

It went in much easier this time, because he was more relaxed, and already lubed up from the shower, but it was still so tight, squeezing my dick like a vice. I started out slow, but just seeing him bent over in front of me was my first fantasy of him come to fruition. His hands gripped the wall while I slammed my cock into him, pulling almost all the way out then thrusting back in nice and deep.

"Jesus, Ben... your tight ass feels so good stroking my cock," I panted to him, holding his hips and drilling into him hard and fast.

"Give it to me, Ryan... I want that big dick."

"You like that don't you?" I hissed, making him mine, pushing him against the wall, taking note of his strong, veined arms holding up both of our weight.

"Yes... Oh God yes... I'm already used to it," he drawled, grunting with my thrusts. "It feels so good... Right... there..."

"Fuck... I wish I could always fuck you," I murmured, not really knowing what I was saying, getting lost in my rhythm. *I'm going to come soon... again.*

"You can," he whimpered then groaned out loud, moving one of his hands between his legs, grabbing his fat cock. "Fuck, Ryan, I'm so close... Harder."

I was fucking him so hard and fast, my balls were smacking against his skin, his perfect ass turning pink before my eyes.

"Oh God, Ben... you're fucking perfect... I don't want to leave you," I grunted, feeling my orgasm coming on. I was right at the brink.

"You can have me whenever you want... All you have to do is ask," he gasped, pushing his hips back against mine. "Oh God... I'm fucking... coming!"

"Come for me, baby," I wrapped my arm around his waist, holding him against me as I kissed and bit his neck, watching him orgasm from over his shoulder.

"Come inside me," he pleaded. *Oh... Ben... Fuck.*

I groaned out loud, releasing my climax, holding his hips tight as I poured it so deep inside him, trying like hell to make him mine.

The realization that he wasn't came on quick, dumping ice-cold water all over my post-orgasm high.

No, Ben Lockwood was most definitely *not* mine. He was Jessica's. *Jessica Lockwood.* His wife. My girlfriend's mother.

Hailey.

Oh my God, fuck me. What am I doing?? I can't do this!

I pulled out of him fast and leaned up against the shower wall, struggling to catch my breath, though it was difficult. I was having some kind of panic attack.

I think I like him...

This is bad. I have to stop. We have to.

I glanced up at Ben and he was regarding me with a look similar to what I was feeling. Like he was regretting what we had just said to each other.

He cleared his throat and stepped back under the water, letting it wash over his smooth, golden skin. I was just standing there, looking sort of hopeless, wondering how I had gone from blissful-serendipitous, even–to completely lost in seconds flat.

Ben finished washing himself off in even less time, pressing a chaste kiss on my jaw before jumping out of the shower like it was about to explode. I blinked a few times, standing under the cascading waterfall shower-head.

I wanted to turn back time, just a few minutes... Maybe an hour. I just wanted to go back and freeze it. I wanted to stay in that bed with him and forget everything and everyone else.

But that wasn't going to happen. I didn't have a time-machine, and I knew Ben didn't either. There was no way this could go any further than this strange, fucked up, life-changing weekend. Hailey and I would leave tomorrow, and drive back to school, far away from Ben and the memories of all this... craziness.

I couldn't tell if I was relieved or sick.

I got out of the shower slowly and of course Ben was already gone. I had no idea where he was, but I couldn't know. I shoved him out of my mind as much as possible and grabbed a towel, drying off and picking up my clothes, taking them back to Hailey's room.

I sat on the edge of her bed, and my head fell into my hands.

Well, shit.

CHAPTER 7

Ben

THE SUN WAS JUST SETTING. It actually looked really beautiful. If I were able to stop for a second and look at it, I'm sure it would have been very relaxing.

Unfortunately, *stopping* was not an option. Ever.

Stopping led to thinking. And thinking led to mental breakdowns. So I would just have to make sure I kept moving and busy at all times for the rest of my life. No big deal.

If Jess thought I had ADHA before, she's going to be in for a treat...

I stomped through the backyard, grumbling to myself about how fast the weeds were growing, as I made my way to the shed. I opened the door slowly and turned on the light, taking a deep breath as I looked over my surroundings.

What was it about these *man-caves* that relaxed me so much as opposed to, say, everywhere else in the world? Was it because they were my own personal spaces? They were slightly secluded, I suppose. And they were all mine.

Sure, I had people over all the time, and invited them to hang out in the basement, or in the shed, playing games, watching TV, and drinking heavily. But still, they *belonged* to me. They were mine because *I* made them. So many other things in my life were decided for me. Or decided on by me, but not *for* me. I decided on things that would benefit my family, and our financial situation. And yet, I barely ever did anything for me.

Until today.

I closed my eyes tight again. I really had to stop thinking about what had happened with Ryan. And how it happened, where it happened, how many times it happened... How good it felt when it happened.

I had seriously thought last night could have been a fluke. Like a mistake or something. We just got our wires crossed for a second, but it was fine. People were entitled to slip-up and do crazy things sometimes. We're all human.

But then that idea went right out the window when I was kissing him in the garage and my dick was so hard, I thought it was going to rocket off my body. It felt so good, and so wrong.

I knew in that moment that things were going to happen when the girls left to go shopping. I tried to fight it in my mind, though. The entire rest of the day, I was actively forbidding myself from thinking about him in any sort of way at all, which in hindsight probably just made the desires all the more powerful.

Who are we kidding? Forbidden stuff is always the best.

Like getting fucked in the ass, for example. I mean, really, God. If you want people to not do something, maybe don't make it feel so good.

I swallowed hard over my rapidly-drying throat. I almost still couldn't believe I did that...

I had never done any butt stuff before. I wasn't one of those guys who was always asking his wife to slip a finger in there while she sucked him off. But if I had known how good it would feel, maybe I would have been. Honestly, the thought had never so much as crossed my mind.

Until I was naked in a bed with my daughter's boyfriend between my legs... *Jesus, it was so hot. So dirty, and naughty, and bad. So so very bad... And the best orgasm of my life.*

I had openly admitted to myself that Ryan was good-looking. I knew it, and I wasn't afraid of it. *He's hot. Okay, fine. Great.* There were tons of hot guys out there.

If it was really about experimenting with a dude, then why couldn't I have just done that?

Jess and I had been married for nineteen years. If I asked her to have a threesome with me and some hot guy, she probably wouldn't even bat an eye. Jess was cool like that. She was open-minded and fun, and kinky when she wanted to be.

So why did it have to be Ryan? Why, of all the people on this big, giant planet, did I have to have sex with my daughter's boyfriend? Seriously... *Am I psychotic or something?!?*

I huffed out hard and stammered over to my gardening tools, looking for the pruning shears. I needed to distract myself from the fact that the girls were still out, and the only other person in the house was the one I needed to stay away from. So I was going to fuck with the rose bushes a little.

If I could just locate those damn shears...

I heard movement behind me, and I looked over my shoulder fast. I saw Ryan, approaching me hesitantly. He looked worried and nervous, his eyes wide and his strong jaw clenched.

I stood up slowly, ignoring the weird thump in my chest. I needed to not be affected by him the way I had been. We needed to shut this whole thing down, and quick. My wife and daughter could be home any minute, and while I already made sure that every single piece of evidence from our sordid affair was properly disposed of inside the house, there couldn't be even an ounce of sexual tension between us when they came back.

"Hey..." he spoke first, shifting his weight back and forth as he stared at me from across the room.

"Hey," I grunted in a brusque tone, blinking a few times. "Are they..."

"Home yet?" he finished my question. "No. Hailey just texted that they're leaving the outlets now..."

I nodded slowly, glancing down at the gardening tools by my feet. The outlets were about a forty-five-minute drive from home, so we had some time to sort our shit out before they got back.

"I'm gonna ask Hailey if we can drive back tonight," Ryan muttered, his face fully serious.

My eyes popped back up to his and my brow creased. "Really? Why?" He gave me an obvious look. "I mean, it's so late..."

I was so confused by what I was feeling; it was almost making me sick. I wasn't sure how it was possible to feel relieved and upset at the same time.

"Yea, I know, it's just..." he paused and sighed, shrugging as his eyes fell to the floor. "I don't think I should be here anymore."

"Ryan..." I grumbled, running a hand through my hair. "No, you probably shouldn't, but I don't want you to drive all night just to get away from me. You can leave in the morning..."

His eyes darted back up to mine, and he looked momentarily crushed, which confused the shit out of me even more. I didn't want to hurt him, but we had to think rationally here.

I was married. And it wasn't like some kind of loveless marriage or anything. I was still very much in love with my wife. I wanted to be with her for the rest of my life, and I knew that wouldn't change. If it hadn't changed in nineteen years, it wasn't going to, even after this.

This thing with Ryan was exciting, and different. I had been looking for something to shake up my boring life, and I sure as fuck found it. But it didn't mean that I didn't love Jess. The two almost had nothing to do with each other.

Except that they did, because Jess would be crushed if she found out I cheated...

And Hailey would be devastated if she found out it was with Ryan. *God dammit... what the fuck did I do?? How did everything get so complicated in one fucking day?!*

"So... you do want me to leave?" Ryan asked, his voice almost nonexistent.

"Ryan, it's not about what I *want*," I scoffed, shaking my head. "You *have* to leave. You're going back to school. With Hailey. That's where you belong. Today was fun... It was... fucking fantastic, but it was a mistake." I paused to collect my thoughts. "I love my wife... And you love Hailey."

"Hailey and I are still young..." he shook his head, looking down again. "We have our whole lives to be serious."

"So you're saying you were just stringing her along?" My eyes hardened at him. "She's my daughter, Ryan. I told you what would happen if you hurt her..."

"Me?" he let out a condescending laugh. "What about you? I'm pretty sure sleeping with her boyfriend constitutes hurting."

My jaw clenched, as did my fists by my side as my blood began to boil. I took a step closer.

"Don't you dare fucking talk to me like that," I snarled, staring daggers at him. "It takes two to fuck, kid. Yes, I accept my part in this, but I didn't force you into anything. You can try to paint me as the devil, but your hands are just as dirty as mine."

His chest was heaving a little, nostrils flaring in obvious anger. It reminded me of the garage earlier... And how hot it was to fight with him. All that raging testosterone... It was clouding both of us from thinking rationally.

I had to stop it. I was still pissed, but I needed to focus.

Ryan seemed to be making the same realization, because I saw him swallow hard, and his eyes yet again fell away from mine.

"So that's it then?" he asked, sounding despondent. "We just pretend it never happened?"

"You got a better idea?" I sighed. My temples were throbbing. I felt a swift migraine coming on.

Ryan shrugged and started walking toward me. My pulse instantly quickened. As he approached me, I backed up, but he still kept coming.

"Ryan..." I pleaded with my eyes, begging him to stay back. I obviously couldn't help myself where he was concerned, and I needed him to keep away before something bad happened again.

"I just want to say goodbye..." he murmured, only a few inches from my face. "We won't get to when the girls are here."

I swallowed hard and nodded. "It's for the best."

He nodded back, his gaze dropping to my lips. *He just wants to say goodbye... It's fine.*

He leaned in slowly and I met him in the middle, our lips pressing together softly. I couldn't help the involuntary moan that slipped out of my mouth into his as his lips parted, and he slid his tongue in to meet mine. I reached up and grabbed his jaw, kissing him harder, sucking tenderly on his plump bottom lip.

It just felt so good, the next thing I knew he had backed me up against a wall and we were making out, furiously. I spun him around and pushed him against the wall, my hands running all over the place. He grabbed my ass, and I ground my hips against his, feeling his erection and letting him feel mine.

Minutes passed and still no sign of slowing. The goodbye aspect of the kissing was long gone and was replaced by a burning need. Gasping and panting, grunting and moaning, kissing, sucking, licking, biting. It was all so *necessary*. I was fearing that I wouldn't be able to just sweep this indiscretion under the rug. This feeling was too good not to have all the time.

I was beginning to sympathize with drug addicts. *Maybe I should take up heroin or something... It's gotta be safer than this.*

Another few minutes and Ryan was unzipping my pants and dropping to his knees.

"Ryan... we really can't..." I whimpered as he pulled my aching dick out of my pants, stroking it with his slightly rough hand.

"Shhh... it's okay, baby," he purred, gazing hungrily at my erection, a look that made it pulse in anticipation. "We have time."

"No, I know, but... We were supposed to be done..." I tried to protest, but then his lips wrapped around the head of my cock and my eyelids drooped.

I lolled my head back against the wall as his head bobbed in front of me, sucking and sucking and sucking until I was breathless and dizzy.

"Fuck... why are you doing this to me?" I rasped, my lips quivering through the intense pleasure. His mouth was so warm and his lips so soft. It felt like every molecule in my body was vibrating in electric shock. "How am I supposed to..."

He started palming my balls, shoving me into the back of his throat until I felt the orgasm looming, burning from my loins all the way up to my chest. He hummed with my cock sliding in and out, over and over until I exploded into a fully debilitating climax.

"Fuck Ryan... good God, *fuck*..." I gasped as my dick pulsed into his mouth. I hadn't even noticed that he was gripping my hand in his, squeezing it tight. I had never experienced a blow job that gave the blowing party so much pleasure. He was as high as I was, which was crippling.

I was coming down for so long I barely realized that he had stood up and was holding onto my body, panting and grinding his erection on my waist. Then he kissed me, shoving his tongue in my mouth so I could taste myself. I grabbed his face and kissed him harder, sucking his lips and tongue, trying to get everything I possibly could from him.

"Dad! Ryan!"

My fear jolted in my chest, and we pulled apart so fast we both almost toppled over. I whipped my pants up while Ryan inched over to the shed door, which still happened to be wide the fuck open. *Fucking morons...* My whole body was shaking as I stared over at him, time moving in slow motion.

He breathed out a hard sigh and rolled back against the doorway, leaning on it to prop himself up. I gaped at him waiting impatiently for an explanation as to what was happening.

"They're home," Ryan breathed in disappointment that was palpable.

"Oh... shit," I sighed out of relief after having the complete crap scared out of me. "Is she coming out here?"

"Probably," he shrugged, running a hand through his hair. "She was on the deck."

"Alright," I huffed, straightening myself up a bit, stepping in front of him. "Are you okay?"

"Mhm," he grunted, refusing to look at me before he turned and left the shed.

I stood there frozen for a moment until I heard his voice greeting my daughter.

"Hey, Hales! We're in here!"

I walked out of the shed slowly and faltered at the sight of my daughter hugging her boyfriend tight. The same boyfriend that I had just spent an entire sex-filled afternoon with; whose mouth I had just come in not two minutes earlier.

So no surprise that when Hailey went for a kiss, he dodged it and kissed her cheek. He glanced at me briefly, making it seem like he didn't want to kiss her in front of me, but I couldn't tell for what purpose anymore.

I'm so fucking lost right now.

"Hi, Daddy!" Hailey chirped, prancing over and kissing my cheek.

"Hi, baby," I murmured, trying to shove down all my disparaging thoughts and fake a smile. "You guys have fun shopping?"

"Yea, we did," she answered, taking my hand and pulling me toward the house, Ryan following along, hands shoved into his pockets, looking pretty damn distraught. I didn't enjoy seeing him like that, but there wasn't much to be done about it now. "Did you guys do any bonding today?" Hailey grinned up at me.

I flinched and almost stumbled over my own feet.

"Uh... we just did more yardwork," I muttered, trying to keep my tone even.

"Well, we stopped at Pizza Hut. Are you guys hungry?"

She glanced behind us at Ryan who shrugged. She seemed unaffected by his poor mood, peeking up at me as I gave her a half-smile and a nod.

I was absolutely not hungry, but I didn't want to make the situation any more tense or awkward than it already was.

Hailey dragged us back into the house where Jessica was getting the food setup on the table. She glanced up at me and smiled, to which I blinked and swallowed hard. Just seeing her face was smashing through me. I felt like the biggest piece of shit in history at the moment and I needed to get away fast before I slipped into a panic attack.

Jess rounded the table and wrapped her arms around my waist, pressing a kiss on my chest through my t-shirt. My breathing was picking up by the second.

"Baby, are you okay?" my wife asked, her brow furrowing as she looked me over. "You feel really warm." She lifted her hand to my forehead, but I pulled away.

"Fine," I rumbled, kissing her hair. "Excuse me for a sec."

I rushed out of the room toward the downstairs bathroom, whipping the door open and slipping inside, closing it tight behind me. I backed up against the door and squeezed my eyes shut, taking a deep breath, trying to steady my pulse.

I really couldn't do this. I couldn't sit down for another meal with the three of them, knowing what had happened... What was just happening. It was all too much.

My mind was screaming at me.

You wanted this. You asked for it.

I cringed and stepped up to the sink, turning on the water and splashing some on my face. When I finally opened my eyes and looked in the mirror, I barely recognized myself. And I couldn't tell if that was good or bad.

I paced the bathroom for another ten minutes or so before I decided I finally had to leave. When I peered into the dining room, Hailey, Ryan, and Jess were all sitting down with plates of pizza in front of them. Hailey was whining about how gross pepperoni was, picking them off her slice and tossing them onto Ryan's plate. He just laughed softly, shaking his head.

"I was a vegetarian for two months," Hailey pointed out with a prideful grin. "The meat industry is basically Auschwitz."

Jess coughed into her drink.

"Are Big Macs vegetarian?" Ryan teased her. "Because I'm pretty sure you took down two of them that night after The Killers concert."

She gasped in feigned outrage and elbowed him hard in the side. He grunted and faux-pouted at her, trying hard not to laugh. Jessica was watching the two of them in amusement.

I gulped and blinked a few times. I loved these people... I never wanted to hurt them.

Hailey and Ryan looked good together. They were a sweet, loving, playful couple. It made my bones ache to watch them together like that. I found myself wondering if the whole time he had been here, Ryan was unable to be himself because of me...

Things between us had been tense since day one. The whole time I assumed it was because he was dating my daughter, but maybe it was because of this weird attraction. I clearly intimidated him, but I could tell he was attracted to me. After all, he had made the first move. But still, I never stopped him. It had seemed like I was the one with the control at first... Maybe I started all of this.

Did I really do that to him? Did *I* fuck this whole weekend up? Was this all *my* fault?

I knew that whatever happened, I had to protect these people at all costs. I just had no idea how I would protect them from me...

I finally forced my feet to move and stepped into the room, taking my seat next to Jess, unable to keep the seriousness off my face. Jess looked up at me, regarding me with concern.

"Are you okay?" she asked softly. I stared into her eyes for a second, feeling the weight of everything pouring down on me like a waterfall.

I need booze.

"Yup," I grunted, kissing her on the nose before abruptly standing again, rushing to my bottle of scotch on the shelf and pouring a big glass. I took a generous sip before I even sat down, then took my seat again, sipping a few more times, letting the warmth burn through me. It was a welcomed distraction.

Jessica raised her brow at me. "Are we getting lit tonight?" She smirked.

"Oh my God, Mom, please don't say *lit*," Hailey groaned, which made me laugh a little. I was already starting to feel swimmy.

"Come on, sweetie! I'm still young," Jess cheered. "I know the lingo!"

"I hate having young parents..." Hailey grumbled, picking at her pizza.

"Lighten up, Hales," Ryan barely grinned, draping his arm around her shoulder, pulling her in closer to him. He seemed a bit more relaxed now, but his face was still mostly serious.

"Yea, baby. Some people like it," I smirked, unable to keep my eyes from quickly darting to Ryan's. His face froze, and he glanced down at his plate.

I downed the rest of my scotch quick, almost gagging but silently praising the buzz it was bringing on. I got up and grabbed the bottle and another glass, bringing them back to the table. I poured myself another drink, then poured some into the second glass, sliding it over to Ryan.

"Drink up, kid," I rumbled, eyeing him cautiously. *Fuck the whole alcoholic thing. He needs this as much as I do.*

He paused for a moment before taking the glass and sipping it much slower than I was. Hailey and Jess giggled.

"Well, if you guys are getting lit, then I'm getting in on the action, too," Jess sneered at me and prepared to stand, but I grabbed her arm gently.

"I'll get it," I murmured, standing once again to grab a bottle of wine for Jess.

I could feel Ryan's eyes on me as I moved toward the kitchen, opening the bottle with the wine opener, and pouring two glasses; a regular one for Jess and a mini one for Hailey. *She deserves it.*

"You guys have no idea how annoying it was having you as parents," I heard Hailey griping from the table. "All my friends had crushes on Dad!"

I shook my head as I brought their drinks back over to the table. Hailey tried not to look too excited about hers, taking a small sip and giving me an appreciate smile as I sat back down next to my wife.

"Yea right," I scoffed at her, sipping my drink again.

"No, Dad. I'm being fully serious," she went on, rolling her eyes. "Stacey, Maggie, Beth... Jennifer Finley!" she squealed. "They were all *obsessed* with you. Just like all my guy friends were obsessed with Mom! Freddy and Kevin? Never stopped talking about how hot she was. And then there was Tony Harrison, the boy I was crushing on junior year, who was always staring at Mom every time he came over!"

I chuckled softly while Hailey did the gun to her head thing. I glanced at Jess, her face flushing up a storm.

"Sorry, sweetie... Your mom's a MILF," I rasped wearing a wicked smirk, wrapping my arm around Jess's waist and pulling her closer to me.

Jess giggled, sipping her wine slowly. "Then you're a DILF," she purred, batting her eyelashes at me. I gazed at her for a moment, tugging at my lip with my teeth.

Then my eyes briefly darted across the table at Ryan. He was giving me some kind of look I really couldn't read. I swallowed hard.

"You guys are so gross," Hailey pretended to gag, taking a petulant bite of her pizza before nestling up at Ryan's side. His eyes softened as he brought his glass to his lips.

"And I hate to break this to you, honey, but your friend Tony wasn't interested in me," Jess shook her head slowly, her sympathetic gaze aimed at Hailey. "He was into your dad, too."

Ryan choked on his drink and started coughing hysterically, which would have been my reaction, too, except that my glass was already empty.

I glared at him for a moment while Hailey rubbed his back. Jess laughed to herself.

"Are you serious?" Hailey squealed, wide eyes aimed at her parents. My mouth hung open, and I shrugged awkwardly. I certainly hadn't been aware that her high school crush, one of several boys who used to come over after school under strict supervision, all of their faces since blending together, had been looking at me.

Although now, given the events of this weekend, I would need to start paying much more attention to whatever vibe I was giving off.

"Yea," Jess sighed through her laughter, running her fingers up and down my arm. "The poor boy was probably a little confused. But then, who could blame him? Your father is kind of irresistible."

Jessica was giving me googly eyes, biting her lip, and I was trying so hard not to look at Ryan, although I could smell the awkward tension radiating from the two of us like a pheromone. My face and neck were so warm, I was sweating a little.

"Ew, Mom. Please stop," Hailey closed her eyes, shaking her head.

"Yes, can we please change the subject?" I grumbled, pouring myself another drink. "There has to be something else we can talk about..."

Jessica rolled her eyes at me, picking up her slice and taking a bite. I tried to make it subtle while I glanced at Ryan quickly. I wasn't at all surprised to see him killing his drink.

After that dreadful experience, the conversation moved on to lighter subjects. But Jessica was clearly getting a little tipsy off the wine, and she wouldn't stop talking about how much she would miss having Hailey and Ryan in the house, and how they could come visit any time they wanted.

I kept quiet, and kept on drinking, as did Ryan. He didn't even look to me for permission to pour himself drinks anymore. He just kept doing it, which was making me nervous and frustrating me at the same time. He obviously wasn't afraid of me anymore, that was for sure. *Can you really be afraid of someone you've fucked in the ass?* I mentally scolded myself and shook my head. *Stop that.* My mind was drifting all over the place. I had no idea what I was feeling anymore. I was refusing to acknowledge the fact that Ryan was on my mind throughout the whole dinner. The fact that he would be leaving tomorrow never left my brain, and I still wasn't sure how I would react when he was gone.

Will I miss him? Will I be relieved? Will I forget about this whole ordeal and just go back to my normal life? Will I see him again? No, absolutely not. That one-hundred-and-fifty-million percent could *not* happen. *Once he leaves it's over. For good.*

A pit settled in my stomach, so I dumped more scotch on it.

When we were done with the food, Hailey went upstairs to shower and change or something like that. Ryan volunteered to clean up, and while I wanted to help him, I figured I needed to give him some space. The air in the house was almost stifling.

I stepped outside onto the deck and leaned against the railing, gazing up at the stars. The sky was pretty clear, like a black and blue sheet speckled with glitter. I watched it for a while, silently praying for a shooting star. I wanted to see one; something to let me know there was a reason for all of this. Something to restore my faith in life... In myself.

I felt Jessica's presence before I saw her, and it instantly warmed me, as much as the alcohol had. She walked over quietly, wrapping her arms around my waist and smooshing her small body against my big one. We really fit together so well; like two puzzle pieces.

She rested her head on my chest and I leaned down, burying my nose and lips in her hair, inhaling deep and letting her smell consume me. Jess was like a drug to me, too, but with a different high. If Ryan was like ecstasy, then Jess was like valium, or something. She made me calm and content. And happy.

Suddenly I felt tears pushing behind my eyes at the thought that I had ever been even remotely unsatisfied with my life the way it was. My life was wonderful, because I had this beautiful, smart, caring woman who loved me unconditionally.

All she ever did was take care of me, and worry about me, and support me.

And what did I do? I cheated. I lied. I fucked someone else. *You don't deserve her. You don't deserve either of them.*

"Mmm... you're so warm," Jessica murmured, trailing her fingers up and down my back, gliding them slowly down to my hip; my ticklish spot. It was a turn-on.

I pulled my face back and gazed down at her, brushing her soft blonde hair back with my fingers. She bit her lip, her slightly glassy eyes connected with mine.

"Hi, gorgeous," I whispered, my lips curling into a slight smirk.

"Hi, sexy," she mewled, giving me that look that said *I really want to be naked with you right now.*

I loved her looking at me like that, but right now more than anything it was making me uneasy. I couldn't fuck her tonight, could I? I had sex with someone else earlier... It wasn't right.

I growled to myself, silencing my nagging thoughts and leaned in to kiss her gently. She whimpered between my lips and I grabbed her ass, hard, causing her to moan.

Suddenly there was a crash from inside the house.

I glanced up through the sliding glass door and caught the end of Ryan glaring at me. He looked pretty pissed off. I raised my brow at him, and he turned away, picking up dishes and slamming them forcefully into the dishwasher, making an awful lot of noise.

I sighed to myself, closing my eyes tight for a second.

"Is everything okay in there?" Jess asked, turning over her shoulder.

"I should go help the kid out," I forced a chuckle, releasing my wife with a pat on the ass. "Will you wait upstairs for me, baby?"

"Mmmm..." she grinned, grazing her nails over my stomach as she reluctantly pulled away. "If you take too long, I might start without you." She winked at me, and my heart thudded in my chest.

My wife was horny... Or maybe just drunk. But usually they were one in the same. I watched her with a pained expression as she slipped back inside, saying goodnight to a sulking Ryan before she disappeared out of sight.

I breathed out hard and stepped inside, approaching Ryan slowly. He was still putting things away, banging them around, throwing some kind of temper tantrum. I stood there looking stupid for all too long. *I'm so out of my element here...*

"Hey..." I muttered, moving an inch closer.

"Sup..." he grunted without making eye contact.

"You need help with that?" I asked softly, tilting my head to the side.

"Nope," he grumbled, slamming the dishwasher shut, causing everything inside to clank around. "All done."

"Kid, take a walk with me," I commanded, gently. "Let's get some air."

He stared at me for a moment, his moss-colored eyes cold and hard, his jaw clenched. He looked like he wanted to resist, but in weighing his options, going outside with me was probably a lot less depressing than staying inside this house. So he huffed out loud and turned toward the door.

"Fine. Let's fucking go then," he spoke quietly, walking out the door fast, crossing the deck even faster.

He practically jumped down the steps and kept on speed-walking across the backyard, around the side of the house to where the lemon tree was. I wasn't sure how he knew that was where I would suggest walking, but I had to assume he knew it was the only part of the backyard where there was little to no view from the house.

I stomped along behind him, rushing to keep up, but he was basically running, fuming several feet ahead of me. It wasn't much of a walk. It was more like he was running away, and I was chasing him.

"Kid, slow down..." I grunted, trying to reason with him, though he ignored me. "Ryan... Ryan, come on, will you just..."

I jogged up to him and grabbed him by the arm, in an attempt to tug him to halt. He finally stopped, spinning around to face me.

"Don't fucking touch me!" he barked, yanking his arm out of my grasp. His eyes were wide with rage, mouth set in a hard line, his jaw uncompromising.

I pulled my hands back and held them up. "Okay, okay. I'm not touching."

He huffed and rolled his eyes, pacing around the lemon tree, shaking his head over and over while he mumbled to himself.

"This is so fucking stupid..." he grumbled, running a hand aggressively through his hair.

"What is?" I asked, my voice deep and steady, yet calm and comforting. I was starting to feel really fucking bad for stressing the kid out, but I didn't know what to do to fix it. I could barely process my own feelings, let alone help him with his.

"This! This whole fucking thing..." he replied, finally stopping to look at me again. "I don't want this... I don't want *you.*"

His words stung, but I would never admit it.

"Alright," I shrugged, blinking a few times. I tried to hold his gaze as long as possible, but after a few seconds, my eyes fell to the ground.

"None of this makes any sense, you know?" he breathed, sounding a little less angry now, but just frustrated. "I didn't plan on... I never thought I would..." He stopped and exhaled rough, shaking his head.

"I know," I whispered, making an impromptu decision to step closer to him. Surprisingly, he didn't back away. "Neither did I."

He was quiet for a moment, just staring at me, his broad chest moving up and down with his breaths. I wasn't sure if I should say anything else, so I just stared back.

"I like pussy, Ben," he said, fully serious. "And tits. I love them, actually..."

"Okay, watch it," I hissed, narrowing my gaze at him. "You're dating my daughter."

He chuckled and rolled his eyes, and I couldn't help but laugh softly myself.

"But yea... me too," I sighed, smiling at him with my eyes.

"So... what the fuck does this mean?" he asked, looking helpless, like he really needed an answer that I just didn't have.

"I don't know," I replied, shaking my head slowly.

"I'm leaving tomorrow..." he said, still staring directly into my eyes. The eye contact between us was always so intense. It felt stronger than other eye contact.

I nodded slowly. "Yea..."

"Will I see you again?" he asked, stepping even closer to me, until we were only about a foot apart.

I shrugged. "I'm not sure..."

"Do you want to see me again?" he raised his brows at me.

"Ryan, I told you. It's not about what I want..." I huffed.

"Yes, it is, Ben," he jumped in, his tone firm. "That's exactly what this is about. What do *you* want?"

I froze. I had no idea what I wanted anymore.

Well, of course I *knew.* But they were conflicting things, so it didn't make sense. I wanted to see Ryan again. I wanted to be with my wife. I wanted Hailey to always love and respect me. I wanted everyone to be happy.

It sounded so corny and immature in my mind, I couldn't even think about saying it out loud.

So instead of saying something stupid, I said what my heart wanted me to say, right now, without a second thought.

"Meet me in the shed after the girls go to sleep."

Ryan stared back at me for what felt like an eternity. His face was covered in so many different emotions, I would never have been able to detect them all. For a moment, I actually thought he was going to say no... He was quiet for so long.

But after searching my face for some kind of guidance, he finally took a deep breath and nodded. I mirrored his expression, and reached out, subtly running my fingers over his arm, down to his hand. He slid his fingers in between mine, and I could already feel it again...

The fire; the passion; the lust.

Maybe tonight was the end...

Maybe it was just the beginning.

When I finally made my way up to my bedroom, I was in a bit of a trance. I couldn't tell if I didn't recognize myself anymore, or if I was discovering the real me. I didn't exactly feel different, but different things were happening around me. I was doing different things... Did that make me different? Or had I just changed–evolved–as a person?

I focused on what I had to do as I crept inside my bedroom, closing the door mostly all the way. I didn't mind leaving it open a crack because I knew for a fact that Hailey was in her room, tucked away in bed. I could almost hear her snoring from down the hall, so she wasn't an issue at the moment.

Plus, I couldn't be concerned with anything else other than my current mission. I had some business to handle...

The room was dark, all the lights off and only some moonlight streaming in through the partially drawn curtains. The advantages of having a bedroom on a higher floor... We had a great view, and great lighting.

My wife was already in bed, wearing nothing but a pale pink silk nightgown that she looked completely flawless in. She was writhing around in the sheets, giving me those bright, sparkling eyes as I stared back at her, my face fully serious.

I tugged my t-shirt over my head and tossed it on the floor, then slid my pants down, with my boxers, leaving them behind as well. I crawled onto the bed, grabbing my wife by her calves and yanking her toward me fast. She squealed and giggled as I grinned up at her, spreading her legs wide and positioning myself between her thighs.

I moved up to kiss her softly, gliding my tongue over her bottom lip, then yanked the lacy top of her nightgown down, exposing her breasts. Her nipples perked up in the cool air and I took the opportunity to suck and nibble at them a little bit.

She started panting softly, combing her fingers through my hair while I licked, kissed and sucked all over her gorgeous tits. Then I moved down to the apex of her thighs and began pressing soft, warm kisses all over her inner thighs, making a path up to her sweet spot.

She whimpered out a plea for me to kiss her there, so I did, kissing her pussy gently, slow and torturous, running my bottom lip over her clit. I took it between my lips and sucked, causing her to moan out a little louder, the pleasure she was feeling evident.

It was then that I heard the noise I had been expecting. Jess was too distracted by my tongue slipping inside her to hear it...

My gaze darted to the crack in the doorway, and our eyes met.

I knew it. He was watching.

Mmm... that's so hot. Let's give him a show then.
I turned myself ever-so slightly so that I could keep my eyes on
Ryan's while I gripped Jess's thighs hard in my hands, swirling my
tongue around on her soaking wet flesh. She tasted so sweet... She
always did. My dick was so hard it was throbbing.

Ryan cocked his head to the side, sliding his hand down to his
erection as he started to touch himself over his sweatpants. I could see
the outline of his giant dick all the way from there. I slowly reached my
left hand up to Jess's tit, grabbing it, squeezing and pinching her nipple
just enough to make her groan. My right hand gripped my own cock in
a tight fist, stroking myself painfully slow while I continued to eat my
wife's pussy like a fucking fiend.

It was so damn hot, I was about to burst. Seeing Ryan out there
turned me on like crazy, and I just wished that he could come in and
join us. It would be the best of both worlds...

*Would Jess ever want that? Would she care if I wanted this young,
strong, sexy guy to rail me in the ass while I ate her pussy so good, she
went cross-eyed?*
It was something we could explore someday, but I would have to
approach with caution.

On a less cautious note, Ryan's hand was in his pants and he was
jerking himself off, his eyes still stuck on my mouth and what I was
doing to my wife. He loved pussy, and tits. He had told me so when we
were outside. I also happened to know he loved my dick and fucking
me, so I imagined this whole thing was working to destroy him just as
much.

Jessica's hips lifted off the bed to meet my hungry mouth, and I
stuck my tongue inside her sweet opening, fucking her with it a little,
before taking her clit between my lips and sucking so hard that she
exploded into a whirlwind orgasm, squeezing her thighs on my head
while she screamed my name over and over.

I let her ride it out, and by the time I was coming up for air, I was
looking to the doorway to warn Ryan to take off before we were busted.
But he was already gone.

I sighed out hard and let go of my rock-solid dick, breathing deep
over my wild pulse. I wasn't going to come just yet. After all, I had plans

for my dick later.

I wrapped Jess in my arms, kissing her softly for a minute, but she was fast asleep within seconds, which was exactly what I knew would happen. *I may not be perfect, but I know how to make my wife come so hard she immediately lapses into a mini coma.* I got up and quietly stepped back into my clothes. I briefly considered mouthwash but decided against it. I wanted to see how kinky the kid really was.

I left the bedroom and made my way downstairs, trying to be as quiet as possible as I tip-toed out onto the deck then down into the backyard. I was basically running toward the shed at that point. I was so excited; the anticipation bubbling over.

I opened the door to the shed and slowly stepped inside, closing and locking it behind me. It was dark inside, except for one lit candle on the far side, by the couch. I meandered over and found Ryan lying down, reclined against the arm in only his boxers, looking casual and seductive and so fucking sexy. I took a moment to look him over, the contours of his muscular body illuminated by the dimmed glow of the candlelight.

His eyes met mine, and we watched each other, the excitement so real and raw, with also a hint of familiarity. We knew each other's bodies pretty well at that point, even though it had only been one day. But we definitely knew what the other liked. And what he wanted.

I ripped my t-shirt off and did away with my pants, climbing on top of him in only boxers. He grabbed my jaw and pulled me down to his lips, kissing me hard, his tongue seeking out mine. He groaned between my lips as I pressed my hands down on his chest, gripping and squeezing his pecs while I rubbed my erection on his.

"Mmmm... baby, you taste like pussy," he hummed, his cock throbbing against mine.

"You like it?" I grinned as our tongues flicked.

"Mhm," he grunted, moving his hands down to my ass, palming me hard. "You were so hot in there..."

"I wanted you to come in..." I gasped, reaching inside the waistband of his boxers, feeling up his solid flesh in my fist.

"I wanted to..." he breathed, his lips trailing along my jaw.

"I want you to fuck me while I fuck her..." I told him, my thoughts exciting me to a whole new level. I had seriously never been harder. "I want to fuck you while you fuck her..."

He groaned, sliding my boxers down. I kicked them off then removed his. We made out for a while, naked, our heated flesh moving together on the couch while the candle's flame flickered.

My lips swept down his neck and I whispered on his sweet skin, "Let me fuck you."

"*Mmm... so bossy, Mr. Lockwood*," he teased with an aroused grin, then closed his eyes and leaned his head back, making himself more comfortable.

I grinned back and ran my tongue over every inch of him, landing on his big, thick cock. I took him in my mouth and got lost in blowing him. I sucked him hard and deep, drawing out some of the sexiest sounds I had ever heard anyone make. I moved my mouth onto his balls, kissing and tonguing them before he spread his legs beneath me, opening himself up.

Fuck, I can't believe I'm doing this... How do I even...?

I took Ryan's full ass in my hands and spread his cheeks, slowly lowering my mouth between them. I flattened my tongue and licked his hole over and over, thrusting it inside and fucking him with it, the same way I'd done to Jess's pussy earlier. He started panting and whimpering, his whole body relaxing in front of me. I could feel that he was ready. And fuck, so was I.

I left him nice and wet before sitting up and stroking my cock a few times as I looked down at him. His eyes were drooping in complete arousal, his lips moist and swollen, his big, hard dick resting on his stomach while he waited anxiously for me to take him. I grabbed his ass in my left hand, taking my aching cock in my right and pressing it up to his asshole.

"I want to push inside you so bad," I hummed, shoving the fat head of my cock in his backside. He was resisting a little, likely because he was nervous. So I reached out and ran my fingers up and down his dick slowly, over his balls, caressing him in a very sensual manner. "Relax, Ryan."

"I'm trying..." he whispered, his Adam's apple bobbing in his throat. "I can't stop thinking about the fact that this is our last night together."

I breathed out slowly and cocked my head to the side. "Shh. Don't think about that right now, baby. I just want to make you feel good..."

"Fuck... I want you to..." he breathed, his eyelids drooping shut while I pushed into him again, slow and gentle. I could tell he liked the feeling already. Touching the outside was an obvious sort of pleasure. The first push was a shock, but a good shock. It set your nerve-endings on fire. I wanted to do that for him. I wanted him to know how good it could be...

"Let me inside you, Ryan... please," I moaned, pushing again. I could feel him relaxing. "I need to know how you feel."

I flicked my hips once more and my head slid inside him. He gasped out loud, and I whimpered, biting my lip and thrusting in further. It was so fucking tight I couldn't even comprehend the feeling.

"Oh God," Ryan's voice rumbled from inside his chest. "Your cock is actually inside me..."

"Mmm... it feels better than I imagined," I growled, pumping into him slowly, tugging back just a bit before sliding in more.

He was gasping and groaning and reaching for my hips as I worked up a rhythm, fucking him deep, with everything I had. My cock was stretching him, and it was so tight I had to actively stop myself from coming too soon.

Ryan was loving it, as I knew he would. It only took a second to get used to it, and the next thing I knew, he was saying things like, "Fuck me harder, Ben. I love how you fuck my ass... Your big cock feels so good in me."

Jesus, I love when he dirty talks... Especially when I'm inside him so deep. Holy fuck, I'm up to my balls. Oh God... fuck me. Fuck fucking me this feels sublime.

"Ryan... I want you on top," I pleaded, my voice cracking. I was right on the edge.

I reclined slowly, pulling him on top of me, my cock inside him the whole time. He looked briefly startled, placing his palms flat on my chest. I ran my hands up the sides of his ass, gripping his hips tight. I began to move my hips slowly, pushing upward then pulling back, guiding him with my strokes.

He gazed down at me, his eyes sparkling as he licked his lips and started to move with me. We found a rhythm together almost right away, and before I knew it, Ryan was riding my cock like nothing I had ever experienced before.

He was swiveling his hips, rocking them forward and back, moving his tight ass all the way up my cock then back down. It felt divine. I could barely breathe right.

"Ryan, fuck me," I grunted, digging my fingertips into his waist, watching his hard dick bob up and down.

"Mmm... Ben... Your dick feels amazing," he leaned down, kissing my lips softly.

I squeezed his ass hard with both hands and pounded into him over and over, the sounds of us fucking echoing off the walls.

"I'm so close, baby," I told him, nipping at his bottom lip with my teeth.

"Me too..." he gasped, shoving his tight hole down on my cock over and over until we were both sweating and raw. "I want to come with you."

"Come with me... Please, baby," I whispered, and I kissed him, burrowing every inch of myself inside him until my dick exploded into orgasm.

He cried out in my mouth, finding his own release, his big cock throbbing as he came all over both of us, while my own cock pulsed, emptying every last drop deep inside his ass. We were both panting so hard, sticky with sweat and all kinds of stuff, our voices hoarse from crying out in the throes of passion. I doubted that anyone would hear us all the way up in the house, but I hadn't really thought about if the neighbors could hear.

Damn... That would be a hard one to explain...

Ryan pulled off of me, curling up at my side. I turned to face him, wrapping my arm around his waist and pulling him close to me. I kissed him gently for a bit, until we finally peeled off each other and I felt my eyelids drooping. The last thing I remembered before passing out was that I'd finally found something to help me sleep...

My eyes crept open, and I blinked a few times past my grogginess. It was very dark around me and it took a moment before I remembered where I was.

Oh, fuck... I'm still in the shed. We fell asleep in here. Not good... I registered the sleeping form next to me, his head resting on my shoulder and his sculpted arm draped around my waist while he breathed soft, warm breaths that tickled my skin. I watched his face for a moment while he slept peacefully, reaching out to push his silky hair back with my fingers.

I was feeling a new level of calm at the moment, and my chest ached with the desire to stay here with him for as long as possible.

Unfortunately, that wasn't an option. We had to get up immediately before my wife or daughter realized we were gone.

"Ryan..." I whispered, trailing my fingers along his angled jaw. "Wake up. We have to go, baby."

He grumbled, eyes still shut, tugging me closer to him and pressing tender kisses on my chest. I chuckled softly, leaning in and kissing his lips so gently that I made myself hum.

"I'm serious," I said, giving him a little smack on the ass before I started to sit up. "We shouldn't have fallen asleep. The girls could wake up any minute and come looking."

Even thinking about Jess, or Hailey, finding us like this caused my pulse to quicken with dread.

Ryan's eyes opened slowly, and he stretched out a little, yawning and gazing up at me.

"How long did we sleep for?" he asked in a raspy, sleepy voice that was completely hot.

"Mmm not sure," I rumbled. He sat up slowly and winced.

"My ass is sore," he whined, pouting at me which made me laugh.

"You get used to it," I murmured, turning to grab my clothes.

"Yea well... I don't think it'll be happening again since, you know... I'm leaving soon," he gulped, sounding slightly despondent.

I stood up, pulling on my pants as I watched him move in slow motion.

"Do you think you would... find another guy... or something?" I asked hesitantly, then pulled my shirt over my head. "Like someone at school...?" I had no idea why I was asking him this. It was none of my business.

"Probably not," he muttered, wriggling into his boxers before standing up in front of me. "After you, no one could live up to that." I wanted to smile, but I couldn't. Both of our faces were so serious. We just stared at one another, eyes locked, registering the feelings between us. It wasn't just about sex. This weekend was different for us. I liked him... And I knew he liked me, too.

I swallowed hard and looked down first, stepping away to grab his clothes for him. I handed them over and he continued dressing, watching me out the corner of his eye.

"Would you?" he asked, and I raised my brows. "Find another guy to hook up with?"

I shook my head slowly. "I'm married..."

"Yea, but you know..." he breathed, eyes wide. "You obviously like it."

I like it with you.

I almost said the words, but I stopped myself just in time. I had to bite my tongue, swallowing them back down before they could get out. I couldn't tell him that. I couldn't *say* that. This was supposed to be a fling; a fling we would soon forget about after he left. I couldn't admit that I was feeling him more than just a fuck-buddy. I couldn't admit it to myself either.

I'm just overtired. It's been a long weekend. I need to sleep on it. We can talk a little before he leaves.

"That was fun, kid," I forced a grin, kissing him quick before turning to leave the shed. "I've gotta get some rest... You should, too."

I glanced at him one last time before opening the shed door. He was standing there, gazing back at me, his eyes sparkling.

"Sure thing, Mr. Lockwood," Ryan's lips curled, showing me a dimple.

I winked at him and left the shed, heading back up to the house. The sky was already starting to turn light green, meaning it must have been super early in the morning. *Damn, we fell asleep for a while...*

I moved through the house as quietly as possible, creeping upstairs to my bedroom. I took off my pants and t-shirt, climbing into bed in just my boxers and pulling Jessica's body against mine. She purred out a soft little sigh of contentment as I burrowed our joined bodies beneath the comforter, kissing her temple before drifting back to sleep.

"Daddy..." Hailey's voice whispered to me while I slept. "I love you."

"I love you too, baby girl," I murmured. *Am I dreaming?*

"I'll see you in two weeks..." her sweet angelic voice rung through my mind. I could see her in my dream...

Golden blonde hair, ocean blue eyes, that gorgeous innocent smile. It reminded me of when she was little, and I used to push her on the swings. Her infectious girly giggle, the way she would squeal as her hair whipped around her face and she shrieked, "Higher, Daddy! Higher!"

I could still smell the crisp winter air. I could see the rays of sunshine, illuminating her beautiful face, cheeks a rosy blush. She was the most magnificent thing I had ever done. My whole entire life.

My daughter.

And suddenly she was gone. I felt my chest hollow as I looked for her everywhere but couldn't find her. She had disappeared. I ran around frantically, my heart hammering in my chest as I tried to find her... But it was too late. She was gone.

"I'm so sorry, Hailey..." I breathed, tears fighting from behind my eyes. "Please forgive me..."

I gasped out loud and jolted upright, my eyes flinging open. I panted out my heavy breaths as I looked around the room, reacquainting myself with my surroundings.

I was in bed, in my bedroom. I sighed out loud and closed my eyes tight, grating my fingers over my face. *It was just a dream...*

I reopened my eyes and looked around the room again, trying to calm down. Jess wasn't there. The morning sun was shining through the windows. I glanced at the clock on the nightstand. It was just after eight.

She must have already gotten up to make everyone breakfast.

I stumbled out of bed on relatively shaky legs, heading to the bathroom. I brushed my teeth then hopped in the shower right away, scrubbing off the sweat and sex. The water felt good on my skin, washing away all the uncertainties from last night. *And from that dream...*

It left me feeling sort of empty, which was odd. I had a strange sinking feeling that I just couldn't shake. I needed to go downstairs and see my family. I needed to make sure everyone was okay.

I dressed quickly and darted down the stairs, expecting to see Hailey and Ryan at the table eating, Jess in the kitchen doting on them.

But instead when I got there, the kitchen was empty. As was the dining room.

I saw Jessica sitting outside at the deck table with a cup of tea and a book. I slid open the glass door, and she looked up at me as I approached her, with clear confusion on my face.

"Morning, baby," she chirped, smiling before returning to her book.

"Morning. Where's Hailey?" I cut right to the chase, looking around the backyard, hoping to see her and Ryan out there somewhere.

"She and Ryan left already," she answered, glancing up at me through a bemused expression. "They said they wanted to get back and settled before school tomorrow."

My stomach dropped. It fell right smack onto the floor.

"They... left...?" I breathed, my brow furrowing hard. Jess simply stared up at me, likely wondering why I was reacting this way. I tried to correct my face, attempting to look a little less shattered. "I mean, she couldn't even say goodbye?"

"She did," Jess murmured, giving me a sympathetic look. "She went into the bedroom and kissed you goodbye."

The dream... It was real. At least, her voice was.

But what about Ryan....?

I swallowed hard, my jaw clenching in aggrieved confusion. *He couldn't have at least waited until I woke up....? I mean, Jesus. I didn't think he would just leave like that. Fuck...*

"Oh, baby..." Jess pouted at me, chuckling and grabbing my hand. "Don't worry, we'll see her in two weeks for her birthday. You're such a sweet father, you always have been. And Hailey is Daddy's little girl. That will never change."

I glanced down at her, my lips quirking up slightly in appreciation for her trying to cheer me up. I pulled out the chair next to hers and sat down, locking our fingers and bringing our joined hands up to my mouth, kissing her knuckles.

I was feeling so many emotions; I didn't even know where to begin. I just couldn't believe how much I actually missed having my daughter in the house all the time. She had already spent an entire school year away last year, and this was her second one. Her being away wasn't new.

But for some reason, after everything that had happened this past weekend, I just felt like I was going to lose her. Like she would slip through my fingers or something.

I didn't want to admit it to myself, but I knew it was guilt. I was filled with a morbid sense of guilt for what I had done to my daughter, stinging my stomach like acid.

I had sworn to protect that girl from anything that meant to cause her harm. I just never knew that it would be me who hurt her.

CHAPTER 8

Ryan

I WAS DRIVING, CRUISING, DOWN THE HIGHWAY in my BMW, with Hailey in the passenger seat, singing along to the radio. We had already been driving for almost three hours and had another two to go. But we were making good time. Leaving early in the morning was a good idea... for more reasons than one.

Hailey had been talking at me the whole ride on and off, and I'd been attempting to remain engaged, but my mind was definitely elsewhere. I was barely holding myself together at the moment, trying like hell to hang onto my sanity by ignoring any and all urges to think about what happened over the past forty-eight hours. It wasn't easy. I was feeling incredibly stressed, and I just wanted to be home. I had to keep reminding myself not to speed. I needed to get us there safely and in one piece.

Hailey was in the middle of yapping about her friend Britney getting them tickets to some concert for her birthday when her phone started ringing.

"It's my dad," she sighed, and my heart went crashing into my stomach. *This is entirely ridiculous.* My hands were instantly sweating as she answered the phone. "Hi, Daddy."

"Hey, baby," Ben's deep, rough voice came over the speakerphone. *Ugh, God... Why did she have to put him on speaker?* "I just got up and realized you were gone..."

"Yea, Ryan wanted to get on the road early so we could be home and settled before school," Hailey told him, gazing out the window. "We both have eight a.m. classes tomorrow."

"Oh... alright," Ben grumbled, and I could picture the look on his face. It did some very confusing things to my stomach. "That's fine. I just wished you could have stuck around to say goodbye..."

"I made sure to kiss you goodbye, Father," Hailey giggled. "I'm not going away forever. You'll see me in two weeks."

I inhaled a deep breath and held onto it. This was now the third time Hailey had mentioned her birthday in two weeks. Apparently, her parents had plans to drive up and take her to dinner. I was already thinking of ways to get out of it.

"I know, I know," Ben sighed hard into the phone. "How's the drive so far?" The concern in his voice made my chest hurt.

"Good," Hailey chirped. "Ryan's doing most of the driving. Okay... *all* of the driving." She giggled and glanced over at me, grinning. I struggled to smile back.

"Okay... good," Ben huffed, and I could all but see him in my mind, pacing and biting his lip. The images in my head were making me feel weak. "He's... you know... being safe?"

I bit the inside of my cheek, trying hard not to react, though it was killing me to hear his voice and not talk to him. I fucking missed him already, and I needed to not. It had only been a few hours. I would never survive the rest of my life without him...

Buck up, man. Seriously.

"Yes, Daddy," Hailey replied in a patronizing voice, grinning while she rolled her eyes at her phone.

"Good... good," Ben breathed. "Well, I just wanted to say I love you, and it was so good having you home this weekend."

I wasn't sure if Ben sounded so vulnerable because he was talking to his daughter and didn't know he was on speaker. Or maybe–just maybe–because he was affected by me being gone, too.

Don't be delusional. You saw his face last night. This was a fling and nothing more... He *has zero feelings for you other than an empathic love for the feeling of your cock anywhere near his body. Stop kidding yourself.*

"It was good seeing you too, Dad," Hailey told him. "We had a great time."

"And... you can tell Ryan that..." Ben's gruff voice stuttered then paused. "That it was good meeting him. He's... he's a great guy."

I tightened my grip on the steering wheel, my heart thudding hard in my chest. I held my breath and refused to let it go, for fear that I would yell out something to make myself known.

I wanted to tell him I had the most amazing weekend of my entire life, and that no matter what my brain was telling me, I could never forget about it. Sure, meeting and hooking up with Ben changed my world and confused me down to my core, making me question everything I ever thought I knew about my sexuality and the way I love. But that wasn't necessarily a bad thing. He brought out a side of me I didn't know existed. I had never felt more alive than I did with Ben, and while it was seriously fucked up what we had done, in so many ways, it was also pretty fucking wonderful.

It was selfish, irresponsible and downright stupid. But it was real, and raw, and honest. There was a part of me that wanted him to know that.

But I wasn't a fool. There was no way I could tell him any of it, especially now.

So I bit my tongue and swallowed my emotions, stared straight at the road ahead of me, and focused on driving. Moving forward. It was all I could do.

"Aww, thanks, Daddy," Hailey swooned, peeking over at me with a smile, though I refused to look at her. I just couldn't. "That means a lot. And Ryan loved meeting you and Mom, too. He's super appreciative of you both for letting him stay. And I am too, of course. You guys are the best parents ever."

Ben was quiet for a moment, and I heard him take a deep breath.

"Anything for you, princess," he rasped, sounding all too serious.

"You know that."

"I know, Dad," Hailey replied, nodding out the window. "I love you so much."

"Love you forever, Hailey bug," Ben crooned, and my chest felt tight. "Be good."

"Always. Bye, Daddy dearest," Hailey murmured. "Talk to you soon! Tell Mom I love her too!"

"Will do. Bye, baby girl," Ben grunted, and Hailey hung up her phone, breathing out a sigh.

"He's so overprotective," Hailey told me. "I'm actually kind of amazed he liked you so much."

I swallowed hard and peeked at her quickly out the corner of my eye.

"Not that he wouldn't like you," she giggled, reaching out to trail her fingers along my shoulder, up to my neck, toiling them in my hair. "You're pretty charming, after all. But you're the first guy I've actually brought home... I was a little scared for you."

She giggled again, moving her hand down over my chest. I forced another smile, though it felt like work, trying to figure out what to say. I was still shaken from hearing Ben's voice like that. I just wanted to sit in silence with my thoughts for a little while, but obviously that wasn't going to happen, what with the endless chattiness of my passenger.

"Your dad's a good guy..." I rumbled, instantly over-analyzing my words in my head to make sure I hadn't said it in an overly affectionate tone. "He loves you so much it's almost... unfathomable. Your parents are really great... opening up their home to me like that. I'm just glad I was able to make a decent impression."

Hailey was suddenly quiet, which made me nervous. I glanced at her again and she was staring out the window, deep in some kind of thought. I wasn't sure if she'd even heard what I said, but I decided to go back to not talking. I listened to the song playing on the radio, tuned out my thoughts, and just drove.

Roughly two hours later, Hailey and I were five minutes from our exit. It was morning, but I was so tired I just wanted to go home and take a nap. *Is this what depression feels like?*

"Baby, do you mind if I drop you at your place?" I asked Hailey in a hesitant tone. "I just wanna go home and get some rest... Plus, I think I still have some reading to finish for Litigation."

"Yea, that's fine," Hailey responded softly, sounding just as tired as I felt. She had actually fallen asleep for the past hour, which was good for me. The silence was helping ease my overworked mind.

"Thanks, baby," I sighed, pulling off the highway.

I drove through the city streets, feeling slightly more comfortable now that I was home. Or at least, in the city I considered my home now. It was only about an hour drive from where I had lived with my dad prior, before he died. But I moved out my freshman year of college and got my own apartment, where I had lived for the past three years with my roommate and best friend, Alec.

Alec's girlfriend moved in with us last year, so now I was in a sort of third-wheel living situation, but I didn't mind. The two of them were quiet, clean and respectful. Plus, because they were a couple living there, and I wasn't, they spent most of their time in their room, giving me free rein over the rest of the apartment. I wondered to myself if they had even come out the whole weekend while I was gone.

I pulled up in the driveway of Hailey's building and turned off the engine, hopping out to grab her bag. I followed her upstairs with her things and got her settled inside, eager to drop her off and get home. I was almost on auto-pilot at the moment. It was weird. I was like a vacant zombie.

"Thank you for coming with me this weekend, baby," Hailey sighed, stepping up to me as I stood in the doorway, all too ready to say goodbye. She slid her hands up my chest, wrapping her arms around my shoulders and holding on tight. "I'm glad you got to meet my parents. They obviously liked you a lot."

"Thank you for inviting me, sweetness," I rasped, resting my hands on her lower back, tugging her closer until the fronts of our bodies melded together. I leaned in, gently resting my forehead on hers while I gazed into her sparkling blue eyes.

I love this girl. I really do... In so many ways we're perfect for each other. But is that enough? Could I really be with her forever? Make her happy... forever? Or would I just ultimately hurt her, like everyone hurts everyone, because we're all just self-serving narcissistic pieces of shit?

I cringed at my agonizing thoughts, taking one last look into my girl's eyes before closing mine and pressing a sweet, soft kiss on her lips. She hummed out a delicate breath that tickled my lips, parting hers and sliding her tongue in to meet mine. I felt her warmth filling me as I deepened the kiss, trying hard to take in as much of her goodness as possible.

We continued to make out in the doorway for a few minutes before a throat clearing brought me out of my trance. Hailey and I pulled apart, steadying our breathing as we moved out of the way for her roommate who had clearly just come home from the gym or something, standing behind us in the hall in her yoga pants, crop top and disapproving stare.

Hailey's roommate, Ramona, was a decent enough roommate, I guess. She was also quiet, clean and respectful, like my roommates, except that she had a mean resting-bitch-face and was the kind of girl you knew was most likely always talking shit about you as soon as you left a room.

Maybe it was just me... And the fact that we had made out at a party last year and I never called her or reciprocated her desire to date me.

Ramona brushed past us, scowling, and I took that as my cue to bounce. I kissed Hailey once more on the lips, then once on the forehead for good measure, taking her face in my hands.

"Bye, Hales," I whispered, making eye contact, committing that gorgeous blue to memory. "I'll call you."

She nodded quickly, giving me that killer smile that crippled me even more now than it had prior to this past fucked up weekend. I let her go and left the apartment quick, turning back once before I got to the hall stairs, giving her a smile. She blew me a kiss, and I caught it, turning away again and racing back to my car.

Once I was settled back inside the BMW, I could breathe a bit more. I was alone. This was good. I needed to be alone for a while.

I drove the fifteen-minutes it took to get to my place from Hailey's, parking in my usual spot and bringing my stuff inside. Every ounce of strength I had left was used to get inside my apartment. When I was in, I dropped my bag on the floor and fell flat onto the couch on my stomach.

"Fuck my life," I grumbled with my face smashed in the fabric.

"Rough weekend?"

I lifted my face and saw Alec and Kayla, his girlfriend, sitting at the breakfast bar in the kitchen eating cereal. I literally hadn't even noticed them. Alec raised his brows at me.

"No, it was great," I muttered sarcastically, resting my head back down on the couch, staring at the coffee table.

"So... meeting the parents went well then?" Alec asked, continuing to probe me for information.

"It was fine," I huffed, succumbing to the hollowness in my chest. "Exhausting... A complete and total mind-fuck of a weekend. But... fine."

Kayla giggled softly. "Poor, Ry-bear. Hailey's an only child to parents who had her when they were teenagers. I told you it wasn't going to be easy."

"Yea, well, they liked me," I pointed out, struggling not to say any more.

"That's good, man," Alec crooned. "I'm happy for you."

I dragged my tired ass up off the couch and took my bag, heading toward my room.

"Well, you guys can have your privacy for a little while longer," I grunted, sounding completely wiped. "I'm gonna go to sleep... til next year."

The last thing I saw was a sympathetic smile on Alec's face before I shut myself inside my bedroom and didn't come out again until the next morning.

I had just left the gym, exhausted and sweaty, and was jogging back to my apartment. It was Saturday night; almost one week since Hailey and I left her parents after that insane weekend.

I listened to the music blaring in my ears through my headphones as my feet pounded the pavement. I worked out at the school gym, and since my apartment was less than three miles from school, I usually always ran to and from the gym, rather than driving. That way I could get my cardio in and dedicate all my gym-time to lifting and calisthenics. I had been working out a lot over the past week. Basically any time I wasn't in class or doing homework in the library, I was at the gym. I made it a point to wear myself out, to sleep easier. It was still a challenge getting even a few hours at night, but I took what I could get.

I hadn't seen Hailey at all since I dropped her off Sunday. We talked on the phone every day to check-in, and before bed to say goodnight, but we were both super busy with school at the moment, so there wasn't much time to hang out.

Okay, that was bullshit.

I easily could have made time for her if I wanted to. But the truth was I was afraid to see her.

I was still feeling monumentally guilty over what had happened, and I was starting to think I would never be able to forget it and move on. At least, not with Hailey.

I loved her a lot, but I realized that my feelings for her were more of a *treasuring* kind of love, not a passionate, can't-live-without-you love. I truly cherished her. In my eyes, she was like an angel, or a goddess or something. And I was just a fucked up monster who hurt her... without her knowing about it, of course.

I had briefly considered telling Hailey what had happened between me and her dad. But I ultimately decided against it. I couldn't do that to their family. To Hailey and Jessica... and Ben. I had no desire to hurt them like that. It would have to remain a secret forever. Which could only mean one thing for our relationship...

I stammered up the steps to my place, out of breath and sticky, dragging myself inside and immediately making my way to my bathroom. I got into the shower fast and began lathering up, washing away the sweat from yet another strenuous workout. I was becoming a pretty boring person lately, what with basically living at school. Sure, I was in the best shape of my life, but none of my friends–other than Alec and Kayla–had seen me in weeks.

I continued washing off, my mind sneakily drifting to last weekend. To the shower with Ben...

How fucking good he looked, naked and wet... The adorably bossy way he washed my hair. Touching him... kissing him... fucking him.

Pushing his hard body up against the wall and sliding my cock in and out of his tight ass...

I gulped and squeezed my eyes shut. I reopened them and glanced down at my dick, which was so hard I could almost see it throbbing. I sighed to myself and pushed all the memories away, rinsing off and hopping out of the shower.

I had been trying not to think about Ben... Trying not to remember everything we did together, and how wonderful and dirty and wrong it was. I was distracting myself with school and the gym, attempting to keep myself busy, but at the end of the day, that was all it was. A distraction. A means to an end.

My dick was still hard as I dried off and stepped into my boxers. I peered down at my cock again and raised my brow, silently scolding him.

You need to stop it. Go away with your devious, lustful thoughts. I'm just trying to move on, okay?

I could almost hear my dick responding... *You miss it. I know you do. You fucking loved what you and Ben did together. You're craving it, like an addict.*

I knew on some level, my brain below my waist was right. If I couldn't have Ben, maybe I could look for someone else...

As if right on cue, because my life was that fucking ridiculous, my phone started ringing. And, of course, it was Hailey.

I cringed internally, the guilt and shame inside making me sweat as I answered the phone.

"Hey, Hales," I murmured, forcing a smile out of my voice. "How's it going, beautiful girl?"

"Good, baby," she chirped, sounding her usual, outgoing, happy self. She always sounded like that, even when she was upset. It was sort of mesmerizing. "Missing you a little. What are you up to?"

"Nothing much. Just got home from the gym," I told her, pulling some jeans on and putting her on speaker before tugging a t-shirt over my head. "I was just going to chill at home tonight... I have reading to do." I silently prayed that she wouldn't ask to come over.

"Cool," she replied, unaffected by the fact that we wouldn't see each other again tonight. "I'm meeting up with Brit and Holly in a little bit.

We're going to dinner then maybe out."

"Oh, alright. Sounds fun," I said, unsure of whether or not I should feel offended that she already had plans that didn't include me. I wasn't, so I guess that sorted it.

"Do you think we could have dinner tomorrow, baby?" Hailey asked. "I need to see you."

I swallowed hard. My first instinct was to say I was busy with homework, or make up some excuse, but I couldn't do it. I couldn't put this off any longer. I needed to see her, too.

"Sure, baby," I nodded to myself. "Let's go to Suki or something."

"Okay, sounds good," she murmured, a little more serious than usual. Maybe it was in my head... "I'll meet you there at eight."

I gulped, my stomach knotting at her not wanting me to pick her up. My brain was working overtime, and I actively had to stop it, silencing all of my nagging thoughts.

"It's a date, sweetness," I told her, my voice low and uncertain.

"I gotta go, baby. I'll see you tomorrow," Hailey said, too ready to let me go.

"See you then, Hales. Have fun tonight."

"You too, Ryan."

We both hung up, and I started to feel sick. I could still barely comprehend how different everything felt after last weekend. My entire world had somehow changed, and I felt like I was struggling to hold it all together.

I definitely couldn't sit inside my apartment again tonight, alone, wallowing in a pit of self-loathing and despair. I needed to do something to get my mind off it all.

I should go out... Maybe see some friends. Get drunk. Forget about my fucked up problems for a night.

I shook my head and decided against it. I didn't feel like seeing my friends right now. I actually didn't feel like seeing anyone I knew at the moment. *Well, maybe one person...*

No. I couldn't think about him. He was the last person I needed to be thinking about. Yes, maybe he had helped me discover this whole other part of myself. But it couldn't have just been about him, could it? There was no way Benjamin Lockwood was that powerful.

That's what I need to do. I need to prove that this whole thing was just about sex, and that Ben had nothing to do with it. He just so happened to be the person who was there when these new revelations came about. But there's no way it was because of him. It was purely coincidental.

I finished getting ready and grabbed my car keys, heading out the door. I hopped into the BMW, and the next thing I knew I was driving. I drove for a while, almost an hour, away from my city, heading up north, toward a new city. A different city. Where I knew no one, and no one knew me.

Once I got there, I settled on a bar along a strip. I didn't know the area well–it had been years since I'd been there–but I figured this spot was as good as any to get a drink.

When I stepped inside, I immediately began to feel self-conscious. It was a pretty small, pretty divey bar. Most of the people looked like they were probably regulars. It didn't have any of the frills, specialty cocktails and trendy menu items that most of the bars we went to near school did. This place was full of middle-aged alcoholics, one bartender serving from one shelf of booze, and a jukebox playing the greatest hits of Creedence Clearwater Revival.

Where the hell am I?

I took a seat on a stool at the very end of the bar, keeping my eyes to myself so as not to piss off any of the angry biker-looking dudes currently inhabiting the establishment. The bartender, a girl who may have been pretty a few kids and a couple stints in rehab ago, came over to take my order.

"What can I get for ya, handsome?" she rasped, sounding like she had already finished several packs of cigarettes tonight.

"Scotch on the rocks, please," I muttered.

She turned away to get my drink, and I took a deep breath, looking around behind me. It was very dark in the place, which was obviously done for a reason. There was a pool table on the far side of the room where a few scary guys with lots of tattoos were playing, one of them pressing a blonde girl in a shorter-than-short skirt up against it while she fingered his belt buckle and whispered in his ear.

There was an open door that looked like it led to a back patio which was clearly where all the smoke was billowing inside from, some cigarette and some very much *not* cigarette. There were a few girls bobbing over by the jukebox, touching each other while some creeps watched with eager looks on their faces. There was another group of people trying to look inconspicuous in the back, and I began to wonder how in the hell, out of all the bars in the city, I had happened upon the most dangerous one.

Another coincidence?

The bartender dropped my drink off and walked away without even telling me how much it was, sashaying her way to the other end of the bar and leaning over to greet two guys in suits who looked like businessmen. I blinked a few times and looked down at my drink, taking a big sip, letting the warmth of the alcohol run through me.

I had absolutely no idea what I was doing in this place. If I wanted to get drunk, I could have easily done it somewhere closer to home. Some place where I was less likely to contract hepatitis or get knifed in the parking lot.

I finished my drink in record time and ordered two more, tossing cash down on the bar. I finished the second even quicker, so by the time I was working on the third, I was feeling pretty nice. I noticed a few eyes on me, but I really tried not to engage anyone. All the girls seemed to be spoken for, not that I would have ever dreamed of hooking up with some random chick in a place like this.

Still, the tipsier I became, the more my mind began to wander.

There had to have been a reason why I'd come all the way out there. My subconscious wanted me to do something that my brain refused to acknowledge, and I needed the alcohol to keep the two parts of me from starting a brawl with one another.

You came to forget about Ben.

I blinked slowly, mentally scolding myself for allowing his name to enter my thoughts, although I really just couldn't help it. I wondered what he was doing; if he was thinking about me; if he was drinking scotch in his basement or in the shed, desperately trying to forget about me too.

It was exhausting trying to pretend I didn't care.

"Wait a minute... I know you."

I looked up and saw one of the businessmen approaching me slowly with a wicked smirk on his face. I squinted at him, trying to process who he was through the dim light and alcohol flowing in my bloodstream. He looked awfully familiar... But I couldn't put a name to his face in my currently hazy state.

"Tate Eckhart," he grinned, leaning up on the bar in front of me. "I met you last weekend at Ben Lockwood's for Thanksgiving. Your Hailey's man, right?"

I swallowed hard, slowly piecing it all together. *Yea, that's right. He was the only single guy there... Friends with Ben's brother. This is too weird...*

"Ryan Harper," I nodded slowly, looking him over quick. He was wearing what looked to be an expensive suit, collar opened, his hair slightly more mussed up than the last time I saw him.

"Yea, that's right. Ryan," he spoke my name in a strange tone, his eyes staying on mine. "Never expected to see you here."

"I could say the same," I raised my brow at him.

He chuckled and pulled out the stool next to me, plopping down on it while still facing me. He was very close, his knees almost touching mine, which instantly reminded me of the basement last weekend. He was one of those guys who liked to be in your personal space. I wasn't sure how to feel about it.

"I'm in town on business," he rumbled. "Just tonight." His eyes squinted slightly, that bizarre smirk still playing over his lips.

My mouth became suddenly dry. I felt like I should probably leave. I didn't know what the hell I was doing there, but I was almost positive that no good could come of it and leaving would be the smart thing to do.

But for some reason, I couldn't bring myself to do it.

Instead I brought my drink to my lips and killed the last of it, glancing down the bar at the other businessman, who was less concerned with what his friend was doing than he was with staring down the bartender's shirt.

My eyes came back to Tate's, his head cocked slightly to the side, as if he was waiting for me to make some kind of decision. I wasn't sure how to do that when I didn't know what the options were.

"What kind of business?" I asked quietly.

He grinned slowly, showing off some very straight white teeth. "Buy me a drink, and I'll tell you all about it."

"You cheated."

"No, I didn't! How would I even do that?"

"I don't know, but you did."

"Fine, best two out of three," I slurred, grinning and trying to line up the next round of shot glasses.

I took my quarters in my hand and bounced the first one off the bar, landing it directly in the first shot glass. I glanced at Tate and sneered. He squinted at me, wearing that evil smirk that I was realizing was how he looked about ninety-eight percent of the time.

I tossed the next quarter down again, and it went directly into the second shot glass. I grinned and bit my lip, narrowing my gaze, which was getting blurrier by the minute, and flicked the third quarter, popping it into the third shot glass without even the slightest hesitation.

I threw my arms up and raised the roof in celebration while Tate scowled and shook his head, pursing his lips to keep from smiling.

"Uhh... you were saying?" I teased, my eyes darting back and forth between his and the shots, lined up and ready.

"You're a fucking prick," he grunted, picking up the first shot glass and tossing it back, wincing a bit. This was already our third round of shots, following too many glasses of scotch to even count.

He pulled the quarter out from between his lips and set it down on the bar in front of me, then grabbed the second shot glass, taking that one quick. Before he could get to the third, I grabbed it.

"I'll do this one... Ya know, give you a break before you pass the fuck out on the bar," I smirked and gulped it back, barely feeling the burn anymore. It was just going down smooth at that point, but I was far from sober. I had no idea how I was getting home tonight.

I pulled the quarter out of my mouth and flung it at him, then leaned up against the side of the bar, mirroring his stance. He was still close to me, but now that I was drunk, I didn't really mind.

Tate actually wasn't that bad of a guy. We ended up talking for a while, about work and school and stuff like that. He was an investment banker and he drove a Maserati. He clearly thought he was the shit.

But still he seemed pretty impressed that I was Pre-Law, and asked all kinds of questions about what I was studying, how much more school I had, and when I would take the bar, if all went according to plan. He was cocky, but interesting, charming and funny.

He was also very attractive, but I was trying to keep that fact in the back of my mind, only to be thought about later when I wasn't so drunk. For all I knew, I could have had beer goggles on. Or scotch goggles...

Yea, but you noticed him at Thanksgiving dinner, and you weren't drunk then. Well, not at first, anyway. It doesn't matter that he's hot. Who cares? You spent all last weekend fucking a guy, so admitting one is attractive won't exactly demolish your self-image.

Still, Tate liked to be close, which I remembered from last weekend, too. And being close meant that I could smell him. He wore cologne that was very subtle. I wasn't sure what it was, but it was pretty masculine and musky. I kind of liked it. Plus, that mixed with the sweetness of the booze and smoke in the air was a very heady combination. It wasn't stuff I was used to being around, and it was sparking a flame inside me.

Something that was different, and bad. Something wild.

Tate reached over to grab the quarters in front of me. He had ditched his suit jacket shortly after we started drinking, and now he was in just his white button-down, collar undone, showing his clavicle and the very beginning of some light chest hair; his sleeves were rolled up his forearms, and I couldn't help but notice that he had strong arms, with veins sort of bulging out a bit.

He was obviously in shape. Not as big as Ben, or me, for that matter. But I could tell that his suit was tailored to fit his broad shoulders and chest, narrow waist and tight ass.

I barely even recognized that I was checking him out so hard until the sound of the quarter smacking against the bar snapped me out of my wandering thoughts. My eyes bounced back up to the game. He had missed... again.

"You're really not good at this," I sighed, nodding at the bartender to signal more drinks. I wasn't sure if she would bring shots or scotch, but I didn't really care. I was getting fucked up. On what didn't exactly matter.

"Yea well... I have other skills," he rumbled, leaning in for his next shot, but this time steadying himself with a hand on my thigh.

I glanced down at his hand, then back up at his face. He was concentrating on the empty shot glass, but his eyes briefly flicked over to mine and he winked, before going back to his task. This time he made it.

"Yea, bitch," he grinned with pride, leaning back, but leaving his hand on my leg.

"Hmm... congratulations," I smirked, raising my eyebrow at him.

The waitress came back with two more shots of something different this time, and we each picked one up, clinking then tossing them back.

"Mmm... fuck me," he grunted, slamming the glass down on the bar.

I squinted at him, licking my bottom lip and tugging it between my teeth as the alcohol warmed my throat.

"So, what I still haven't managed to figure out, Ryan Harper, is why you're all the way out here, instead of drinking with your college buddies back at school. Or, you know... your girlfriend." He tilted his head, his dark eyes glassy and sparkling as he slid his hand slowly off my leg, but not without first letting it trail awfully close to my crotch. My dick twitched.

"I wanted to get away for a night," I shrugged, revealing nothing as I placed my glass down next to his.

He leaned in closer to my face and whispered, "How far away do you want to get?"

I moved my face in front of his. "Depends... How far can you take me?"

Tate breathed out slowly, his chest moving up and down as his eyes fell to my mouth. Then he abruptly stood up before me, glancing down to watch my eyes.

"Meet me in the bathroom in five minutes," he growled. Then he turned and stalked away from me, heading toward the back of the bar which I guessed was where the bathrooms were.

I took a deep breath and closed my eyes. What the fuck was I doing? I didn't want to hook up with some strange dude in the bathroom of this sleazy bar.

My hands were actually shaking, and I was getting a little sweaty. I wanted to order another drink to calm my nerves more, but then alcohol had gotten me into this mess in the first place. *Yea, I think you're calm enough already, bro.*

I stood up fast, getting ready to take the fuck off and never look back, but I froze in my tracks. I swallowed hard and looked around. This place was chock full of all the most lascivious activities. Everyone was drunk. Literally everyone, even the bartender. Girls were flashing their tits to guys playing pool, people basically dry humping in the corner. I had seen tons of people coming and going from the bathrooms all night, meaning they were either fucking in there, or doing drugs, or both.

It was clear that these were the kinds of things that went down in a place like this, and that was why my subconscious had brought me here. No one was paying attention to me, nor would they give the tiniest fuck if I went into that bathroom right now to hook up with a guy.

And honestly, I was sort of desperate to find out if hooking up with Tate would be like hooking up with Ben. They were very different people. And sure, Tate didn't make me feel the way Ben did just by looking at me. But that wasn't his fault. It was mine.

I had been beginning to think that maybe I romanticized the whole thing with Ben in my mind, building it up into some salacious affair that would go down in history as the single most influential sexual moment of my life. But I was only twenty-one. I had plenty of time to make other great sexual memories. I had plenty of time to figure out what I wanted, and to be young and stupid before I had to settle down and think about my future.

I mean, fuck, I'm going to be a lawyer soon. I need to do this now while I still can.

And more than anything, I wanted to take Ben off that damn pedestal in my mind. He was just a man, after all. Not a fucking god.

I huffed and shook my head, stomping toward the back of the bar.

I was on a mission.

There were three bathrooms, and none of them had markings for men's, women's, or even unisex, which was weird. There were just three doors, one right beside the next. I gulped, trying the first handle, jiggling it gently. It was locked. I moved on to the next one, and before I could try the handle, two girls and a guy burst out of the third bathroom, all giggling up a storm, hanging all over each other.

I took another deep breath and turned the handle to the middle door, which was unlocked. I pushed the door open a crack and peeked inside. Tate was in there, leaning up against the wall, staring at me with that damn smirk on his face again.

"What are you doing?" he chuckled, stepping forward and grabbing me by the arm, dragging me inside the bathroom, and locking the door behind me.

"I wasn't sure... which one you were in," I breathed, feeling much more drunk now that I was up and moving around.

The bathroom was a full-room stall situation, so there was just a toilet, a sink and a trash can. It was a decent amount of space, and not as gross as I would've thought from seeing what the rest of the bar looked like. Still, it was a weird vibe in there.

Graffiti and drawings all over the walls, one fluorescent light above our heads, flickering. Being in there was making me more nervous.

Tate stood in front of me, close, his fingers lacing with mine as his eyes stuck to mine like glue. His smirk was gone now, and he appeared fully serious.

"Well, you found me," he grunted. "What are you going to do?"

Before I could over-think any more, I grabbed his face and pulled his lips to mine, kissing him hard. He groaned softly between my lips, pressing his hips into mine, pinning me to the door, his hands immediately running over my chest and stomach, feeling up my muscles through my t-shirt. I parted my lips and slid my tongue into his mouth, flicking it along his in gentle strokes, sucking on his bottom lip.

"Mmmm... fuck, Ryan," Tate gasped in between heated, slippery kisses, his hand gliding inside the waist of my jeans to rub up on me over my boxers. "Jesus, you have a big dick."

I closed my eyes tight for a second. I wasn't sure why, but Ben popped into my mind. It was probably just because I was hooking up with a guy, and Ben was the only other guy I'd ever hooked up with... So naturally I would compare the two.

But still, I had this strange guilty feeling in my gut. Not even for Hailey, my fucking *girlfriend* whom I was cheating on, yet again. No, I was feeling guilty because I didn't want to hurt Ben. Which was insane.

"Ben can't ever find out about this," I whispered on Tate's lips. He tugged his hand back and started unbuttoning and unzipping my pants.

"Why would I ever tell him?" he breathed, breaking our kiss briefly to give me a look and tug my pants down just below my ass.

"I don't know... I'm not saying you would tell *him*," I huffed, while he took my dick out of my boxers and started stroking me. I grunted, breathing out a steady breath. His hands were softer than Ben's... "But you might tell someone else, who could tell someone, who could... ya know..." My voice trailed off and I kissed his bottom lip, sucking and biting it. He had really nice lips.

"Yea, I get it," he grinned as I kissed along his jaw, unbuttoning his dress shirt slowly. "Don't worry, your secret's safe with me. I'm not trying to out anyone."

I moved back and stared at him for a moment, mouth hanging open. He wasn't understanding what I was saying...

Wait, am I more worried about people finding out I like to hook up with guys, or about Ben finding out I hooked up with someone who isn't him?

I didn't have the time or energy to obsess over that right now. It would have to wait until later.

I slid my hands inside his open shirt, running my fingers over the definition in his chest, tugging his shirt to untuck it from his pants. Then I undid his belt, slowly, keeping my eyes on his. It was hot, and my dick was definitely hard, but mostly just because this was all so new. It wasn't at all the same as it had been with Ben.

Stop thinking about him. Jesus.

I kissed Tate again, reaching inside his boxers to grab his dick. I stroked it a few times, then he grabbed me by my ass and pulled me closer, grinding his erection on mine. He pulled his mouth away, leaving me hungry for more kisses from his soft, plump lips, and kneeled down in front of me. He palmed my cock, jerking it a few times before he wrapped those luscious lips around me and started sucking.

"Mm... *fuck*..." I whimpered, closing my eyes and leaning my head back against the door.

Tate sucking my dick was a completely different experience than with Ben. Even on our last night together, Ben was still so gentle and hesitant. It was clear that he had never done it before me. Tate, on the other hand... Well, let's just say he was definitely experienced. He sucked my dick like a pro.

I opened my eyes and watched him go, fascinated by how good his lips looked sliding up and down on my solid flesh. I ran my fingers through his hair and held his head while he worked me over. It felt really fucking good.

"Tate... your mouth feels fucking awesome..." I drawled, watching him stuff me all the way down his throat without flinching. "Suck my fucking dick... God, fuck, I just... didn't want Ben to find out about us, you know? He can't know I hooked up with you..."

Why are you talking, crazy? Shut the hell up!

I had no idea why those words were coming out of my mouth, but I couldn't have stopped them even if I wanted to. *Maybe I'm just drunk...*

Tate made eye contact, yanking his mouth off my cock and standing up in front of me.

"Oh my God..." he grinned, breathless, his cheeks flushed and his lips moist. "You're so fucking into him."

"What?" I gasped, and he took both of our dicks in his hand, stroking them together.

"Don't feel bad about it, Ryan," he kept on, kissing me gently. "We're all into Ben Lockwood. He could make even the straightest guy drop to his knees." He chuckled, reaching into his pocket and pulling out a condom.

Wait, what? They're all into Ben? Who's "they"?? Have they hooked up with Ben? Was he lying about me being his first guy?

My mind was racing. Ben had never technically said that I was the first guy he'd ever been with. But I just assumed because of how nervous he was that night in the basement... *Maybe he was just nervous because you're his daughter's boyfriend... Jesus Christ, what the fuck!?*

"Have you ever hooked up with him?" I asked, my voice deep and hoarse with jealous rage as he tore open the condom wrapper with his teeth and slid it over my erection, causing my dick to jerk in his hand. *So I guess I'm fucking him...*

"No," Tate laughed softly, eyeing me like I was crazy for a second. "Only in my dreams..." I breathed out of relief, trying not to be obvious. "No, as far as I know, Ben Lockwood is all about pussy. But I mean, alpha personality, that body, those smoldering stares... He's a fucking wet dream, that man."

I tried to control my breathing, but my heart was thudding like crazy just from talking about Ben, while of course having my dick handled by this other hot guy. I couldn't process anything that was happening at the moment. So I shut it all down and kissed Tate hard, tonguing his tongue, pulling his fat bottom lip between my teeth.

I turned him around and shoved him against the door, yanking his hips back so that his ass was right in front of my crotch. I pushed his pants and boxers down around his ankles and spread his cheeks, gliding my thumb over his hole. I moved in and kissed his neck all over, turning his face to kiss his lips, while I dragged the head of my cock between his full ass cheeks.

"Fuck me, Ryan..." Tate panted, breathless and so fucking ready for my dick. "Imagine you're fucking Ben... And I'll imagine his cock is filling up my ass."

I growled, grabbing him hard by the hips, and closed my eyes. I didn't want him to be right... I didn't want to be thinking about Ben... But I was. I couldn't stop.

And Tate was giving me the green light to imagine myself fucking Ben's tight ass, which was all I wanted in the whole world. It was so much more confusing than just being a theoretically straight guy with a girlfriend who was fucking a random dude in the bathroom of a bar.

Fuck this... I want Ben so bad.

I took my cock in my hand and pressed it into Tate's asshole slowly. He relaxed easily, allowing me in. I gave him a good, hard thrust, shoving my entire aching cock inside him, inch by agonizing inch. He was so tight as I broke through each ridge until I was up to my balls. I stared down at his firm behind in front of me, remembering Ben's. The time in the shower... Or our first time. When he was lying beneath me, legs wide open, sweet ass spread out before me, waiting to receive my cock.

He was so nervous... And so was I. I didn't even need to ask him if he'd been with another guy before. I could tell because of the obvious anxiousness, moving between us. We were both nervous, but also excited. More excited than we ever had been.

Just thinking about Ben and our first time had me fucking Tate hard and deep, stroking every inch of myself in his ass, pounding him against the door. He was moaning and grunting, quietly enough, but also probably not really caring if any drunk degenerates heard us. I got lost in my rhythm, and my memories, and the feelings. I was all sensation at the moment, pounding into a miscellaneous man, having drunk, gay sex while I fantasized about my girlfriend's father until I exploded into orgasm, coming hard in his ass.

I was so dazed that as soon as my cock was done blowing my load in the condom, I was pulling out and turning Tate around so I could suck the come out of him, all the while remembering the look on Ben's face in his basement last weekend. It made my heart heavy when I came to and realized he wasn't really there.

Tate and I exchanged numbers and said our goodbyes after that. I slept in my car for three hours to sober up, before waking at five in the morning to drive the hour back home.

Back to reality.

I stayed in bed all day on Sunday, recovering from my ravaging hangover.

Alec came in a few times to check on me and make sure I wasn't dead, which I appreciated. Kayla made me French toast and bacon, which revived me enough to haul my booze-soaked ass into the shower at six-thirty to get ready for dinner with Hailey.

Last night was sort of a train wreck, and I knew tonight wouldn't be much better.

I got dressed in something decent and left my apartment early, eager to get this whole thing over with. I was a big ball of restless nerves when I arrived at the restaurant. I was twenty-minutes early, so I sat at the bar while I waited for my girlfriend.

Suki was Hailey and my favorite sushi spot. It was where we had come for our first official date. Dinner, anyway. Our real first date was the lunch date we went on after I met her in the library at school almost five months ago.

I had seen Hailey before around school, but never worked up the nerve to talk to her until that day in the library. I had broken up with my girlfriend of nine months a few weeks earlier when I found out she was cheating on me. Against all of my better judgements I had been swept up in a relationship in college with a party girl, knowing that it would have made more sense to stay single, and save my heart the inevitable trauma.

My then-girlfriend, Dahlia, hypnotized me with her sass and confidence, and her big eyes and even bigger tits. Being with her was like being on a rollercoaster for nine months straight. It was a tortuous debacle, and when it finally came to an end—with me catching her at a party having a threesome with two guys I had almost considered friends—I was understandably fine with going back to being single.

My friends had a nickname for me that started freshman year and really accentuated itself after Dahlia and I broke up—*Heartthrob Harper.* I was enjoying being single again, just living it up, hooking up with girls and not giving a fuck. Until the first time I saw Hailey...

It was right before spring break. The sun was shining, and there was a nice breeze blowing through the courtyard which chilled off the heat. I was with Alec and a few of my friends, standing around, talking shit before class. Hailey was a freshman, so when I saw a new face I didn't recognize, I immediately took notice.

She was walking with one of her friends, and they were rushing—like freshman usually were—most likely running late for a class across campus. Hailey's shoelaces on her Converse sneakers were untied, so she had to stop to tie them. She waved her friend off, telling her to go on, and not to wait. She crouched down, setting all her things down on the ground to tie her shoe. She had a bunch of books, and an apple she had been holding. When she put everything down, her apple started rolling away, and she had to walk over and pick it up when she finished. It was such a stupid thing to pay attention to, but for some reason I couldn't stop staring at her. Even now, I could still feel the smile that kept taking over my lips all day every time I remembered her apple rolling off, and her adorable, frustrated face when she went to pick it up, carrying all of her big, heavy books in her arms.

I had desperately wanted to help her carry them, but I didn't feel like being berated by my friends. Plus, I was nervous. Deep down, I'd always been a shy guy. I was never exactly sure where I got the nickname *Heartthrob Harper*, but I certainly didn't feel like a heartthrob then. I still didn't.

I saw Hailey a few more times around campus after that day, and it took us winding up alone in a certain section of the library together before I could work up the courage to talk to her. And it was the best thing I had ever done.

I felt high the first time I made her smile. When she looked up at me with those staggering blue eyes, I felt like I was home. I think I fell in love with her that day.

I would always love Hailey. She was such an amazing person. She wasn't like Dahlia. She was sweet, and kind and so damn funny. And she was beautiful. Gorgeous, flawless and classic, like a work of art.

Regardless of what happened tonight, or in the future, I knew I would always love Hailey Lockwood. Part of me wondered what the hell I was doing...

I felt her presence before I saw her, and I glanced up to see her approaching me slowly, all smiling and vibrant. I couldn't help but smile back, the first genuine smile I'd given anything in days. I stood up and took her by the waist, leaning down to kiss her on the cheek, and inhale her magnificent scent. My heart thumped in my chest, and I was a nervous wreck all over again.

"Hey, Hales," I whispered to her, taking her hand.

"Hi, baby," Hailey replied, gazing up at me with her forehead lined in some kind of uncertainty that made me feel physically ill.

The hostess brought us to our table, and I wanted to just turn around and leave. I didn't want to sit down at the table. I didn't want whatever was about to happen to happen.

We got settled at our table and just stared at each other for a moment. I hadn't seen her in so long... It was weird going from seeing her just about every day to not seeing her for a whole week. It made this whole thing feel so much heavier. The weight of it all was on my shoulders, and I felt like I was being crushed.

Finally, we decided to speak.

"So... Did you have fun last night?" I asked her, glancing down at my menu, pretending to look it over when really, I was just scared.

"I did," Hailey gave me a small smile, cocking her head to the side. *Oh, God... this is so terrible.*

"Hales..." I sighed, putting down my stupid menu and closing my eyes tight for a moment. "Listen, we have to..."

"Ryan, wait," Hailey stopped me, and I looked up. "I know what you're going to say... And before you do, I have something to say to you..."

I swallowed hard and nodded while Hailey took my hands on top of the table.

CHAPTER 9

Ben

OKAY, *HERE GOES...*
I clicked on the video on my computer, waiting for it to load while sitting at my desk downstairs in the basement. It was late, almost three in the morning at that point, and naturally I couldn't sleep.

Jessica had passed the fuck out immediately after she got home from dinner with Rachel. Apparently, they had gotten sort of drunk so when Jess came home, she was all hot-and-bothered, basically dragging me upstairs for some playtime. Unfortunately, by the time I had finished taking a thirty-second piss, she was already snoring, face down, ass up in bed, with her pants half off.

I laughed softly to myself, because she was adorable. But I was still horny as fuck, and she clearly wasn't waking up anytime soon. I waited for about an hour to see if she would, but no such luck. Hence the computer...

I went to my usual porn site to find some quick jerk-off material but got a little side-tracked.

See, the thing is...

I saw a video with a guy who looked an awful lot like Ryan. And that reminded me of Ryan... and our exciting weekend together two weeks ago. Once my mind was going in that direction, I started looking up other things.

Despite the fling with Ryan, I had still never watched gay porn before. I had thought a lot about our little tryst over the past two weeks. I told myself repeatedly that I wasn't going to, but he kept creeping into my mind at odd times. So now that I was horny and using the internet and my hand as my girlfriend for the night, of course I was itching to check it out for the first time.

That and I kind of wanted to see if it interested me at all, or if the thing with Ryan was more of an isolated incident. I hadn't been able to tell if I was so attracted to Ryan that I needed to have sex with him, or if I was just bored and looking to experiment with a guy, and Ryan happened to be there at a coincidental time.

This was what I was hoping to figure out with my little video here...

The video began to play, and I turned the volume all the way down, watching the screen with wide, curious eyes.

From what I was picking up on after the first couple minutes, there was a guy who had a fight with his wife and came over to talk it through with his friend, after which the two friends started to experiment. It seemed corny so far, but the one guy definitely looked like Ryan. He was big, tall and defined everywhere, with dark hair.

The other guy was tall and built, too, which was why I had decided on this video. It was seemingly what I liked... *Clearly.* Both those guys had tattoos, which I was also cool with. I didn't personally have any, but I wasn't opposed to it. *Definitely looks good on these guys.*

The video was finally getting interesting when the guys started kissing. They were making out on a couch, grinding on each other. It reminded me of Ryan and me in the guestroom... And in the shed. *Okay, stop. You weren't supposed to think about him the whole time! Otherwise what's the point?*

The guys started getting naked, which was inflating my cock just a little. And then the Ryan-looking one started sucking the other guy's dick. My own dick was getting harder and harder while I watched, reaching inside my pajama bottoms and stroking myself softly. It looked good, but I was acutely aware of how fake the whole storyline was.

Like, with Ryan and me, for example... *Oh God, here we go...* When we sucked each other off for the first time, we were so hesitant; nervous and almost demure about it, because we were shocked by what was happening. It was so arousing because it was unexpected, and dirty, and built-up. If these guys wanted to sell the story, they needed to go slower; make it more passionate and sensual. Instead they were just sucking and deep-throating, and it was so obvious that they had done it a million times before.

I sighed in slight disappointment, continuing to stroke my erection, which was hard, but not anywhere near as hard as it was when you-know-who was down here with me...

The next thing I knew, the one guy was sliding his big cock inside the other dude's ass and pumping away. It was sort of hot to watch, but I was completely out of the story. It was mostly just hot now because of how much the dark-haired guy looked like Ryan. I closed my eyes and leaned my head back, jerking off to my own porn collection...

Mmm... Ryan's sweet, soft lips. Kissing me; sucking on my bottom lip then biting it. His warm, wet, hot mouth trailing down my body, licking and sucking along the curves of my muscles, my nipples... Then sucking my cock into his mouth, moving up and down on me, over and over... Oh God, yes. Ryan... suck my dick, baby.

My hand began stroking faster the more excitement coursed through me.

His tongue in my ass, getting me wet... His big, long, thick cock pushing inside my hole, filling me up so deep. Fuck, it was such a shock at first, but it didn't hurt the way I thought it would, even though his dick is huge. No, it felt incredible... Stroking, between my legs, penetrating me, fucking me... It was so bad, so wrong. Illicit. His long dick, so far inside my body, grazing that sensitive spot deep... so deep...

I was grunting and panting, jerking my hard dick from my balls all the way up then back, remembering the way Ryan had sucked the head of my cock while he was still inside me, swallowing all of my come until he exploded inside my ass. I felt the orgasm sneak up on me and the next thing I knew, I was coming on my own stomach, whimpering out the name I wasn't supposed to be thinking.

Fuck me. So much for that whole idea.

I sat there dazed for a while, before I finally picked myself up slowly. I cleaned up and turned off the stupid video that I wasn't even watching. I powered off my computer, yawning as I made my way back upstairs to my bedroom, grabbing my drunk wife and cuddling up with her warm body. By the time I fell into an uneasy sleep, the sky was as pale as dawn.

"Jessica! Are you almost ready to go?" I shouted at my wife from the living room, checking my watch again for the third time in the last fifteen minutes. "We're only going for one day! Jesus, why are you packing your entire life?"

"I'm coming, Ben! My God, relax..." she yelped at me from upstairs. I rolled my eyes and continued pacing.

I wanted to get on the road. It was a five-hour drive to Hailey's school, and we needed to get there, check into our hotel and get freshened up before our dinner reservations at eight. I was super excited to see my baby girl for her birthday. I had picked out a gift that I knew she would love, specifically from me–it was a tradition for Jess and me to each buy her our own gift, because she was an only child and spoiled to holy hell. I just couldn't wait to see her and hear about how school was going.

That being said, I was also more nervous than I had been in a while, almost to the point of physical sickness. Our dinner reservation tonight was for four. Me. Jessica. Hailey. And a fourth. We all knew who the fourth was...

Oh God, this is too much. I can't see him. I shouldn't see him. I want to see him...

I was going into this weekend knowing full well that under no circumstances was I allowed to so much as flirt with Ryan. I wasn't allowed to touch him, unless I was shaking his hand hello, or goodbye. I wasn't allowed to talk to him, unless I was asking him about school, or work. I wasn't allowed to look at him, unless he was speaking directly to me. Absolutely no funny business.

Don't think I'm not seeing the irony here.

Jessica finally trotted down the stairs, dragging an unnecessarily large bag behind her. I scoffed and shook my head, walking over to grab it for her.

"What the hell do you have in here? Ten-kilos of Bolivian fish-scale?" I scolded her with my snarky tone and my snarky look. I was all snark at the moment.

"Stop staying up all night watching *Narcos*," she grumbled with a grin, following behind me, locking up the house on our way out.

I tossed her heavy-ass bag into the trunk and got settled in the driver's seat, turning on the engine and buckling up, preparing for this little road trip.

"Did you remember to feed the cat?" I asked while backing out of the driveway.

"We don't have a cat, darling," Jess sneered and began fiddling with the radio.

"Good. One less mouth to feed," I muttered, driving buoyantly down the street, away from our neighborhood, and toward Hailey.

"You're exceptionally funny today," she hummed. "Might I guess why..."

I gave her the side-eye. "First of all, I'm always funny." I barely let a grin slip while she laughed to my right. "Second of all, tease if you will, but I'm a dorky dad. Have been since we were seventeen. It's not changing anytime soon."

"Mmm... thank God for that," Jess purred, leaning over the console to feel me up a little.

I jerked the wheel on purpose, causing her to shriek and fling right in her seat. "Oh, Jesus! Sorry... I almost hit a raccoon." I grinned wide, and she smacked me in the chest, laughing through her rattled sigh. "No distracting the driver, little Mrs. Unless it's with road head."

"You're the most obnoxious person on Earth..." she huffed, tugging her book out of her purse on the floor and flopping back in her seat.

"Hey, you married me," I sighed. "That's on you." I winked at her, and she smiled big.

Five long hours and only six pee breaks later, we arrived at our hotel. It was in the happening part of downtown, walking distance to

Hailey's school and her apartment. Hailey was very bright, and I was insanely proud of how well we'd raised her. She liked to hang out with friends and goof around like any other kid her age, but she had always taken her studies seriously.

She received scholarships and grants to help her with her tuition but still, most of her schooling was being paid for by yours truly. It was alright though. I had been preparing for it since she was six and declared that she wanted to be an astronaut. And then seven when she changed it to rainforest biologist. And then nine when she changed it to heart surgeon.

Hailey had many declarations for her future over the years, so I had figured I might as well start saving for school early. When she finally landed on lawyer, I was ready. And I had needed that mental preparation, too. I almost had a heart attack when I received her first tuition bill from UNM.

But it was all good, because Hailey was following her dream. She was smart, dedicated, motivated and driven.

And she was an only child. Thank God for that.

Jess and I left the car and our bags to the valet, checking in at the front desk and making our way up to our room. I had booked us a suite, figuring that we could make this a nice little overnight getaway. We had been meaning to start taking more trips together now that Hailey was in school, but I often got sucked into work and procrastinated. It was all part of my boring, ordinary married guy lifestyle. Boring married guys didn't go anywhere. Well, maybe somewhere cliché like Cancun or Aruba. But never anywhere fun.

Maybe I should book a surprise trip somewhere cool for Jess and me... Like, Tokyo, or Ireland, or Croatia. Somewhere none of our friends have ever even thought to go. After all, I'm not just a boring, ordinary married guy anymore...

I shook the miscellaneous thoughts out of my head as we opened the door to our suite, eyes widening in excitement while we looked around. The room was huge. It had all kinds of awesome amenities, and we spent a solid fifteen minutes exploring before we found ourselves at the minibar.

"Champagne, my love?" I asked Jess, popping open a bottle.

"Alright, calm down, moneybags," my wife scolded me, though she snatched the glass of Moet out of my hand the second I finished pouring it. "Do you know how overpriced this stuff is?"

"We're celebrating," I grinned, holding up my glass in front of hers. "Nineteen years ago, you said two words to me that... well, first scared the fucking shit out of me," I chuckled and Jess grinned, biting her lip. "But then forever changed my life for the better. Baby, knocking you up was the best thing that's ever happened to me." Jess pouted at me, looking like she was about to tear up. "Cheers to another awesome year raising the best kid in the world with you."

"Cheers," Jess whimpered, and we clinked our glasses, toasting to our daughter's birthday. We both sipped at the same time, eyeing each other over the rims of our glasses.

She placed her glass down first on the bar, while I chugged mine until it was empty. She smiled up at me, waiting for me to set my glass down before launching herself at me, attacking me with a flurry of kissing and sucking and biting.

In less than thirty seconds we were naked and fucking on the floor of our fancy hotel suite.

Jessica and I decided to walk to the restaurant since everything was so close and we were probably going to drink at dinner. We could always Uber it back if we didn't feel like walking later. We got there early to make sure we had everything ready when Hailey and Ryan showed up.

Sitting at the table, I was so nervous I was ready to crawl out of my skin. I was excited to see Hailey. I couldn't wait to give her my birthday gift. And even though I would never let myself admit it, I was excited to see Ryan.

I was so anxious I felt like I might vomit. But still excited, nonetheless.

So you can imagine my surprise and confusion when Hailey walked up to the table alone.

Jess and I stood up, greeting our daughter with hugs and kisses and loving warmth, murmuring *happy birthday* to our darling girl. And I tried to remain subtle while I looked around, waiting for him to come in from parking the car or something.

Hailey took one of the empty seats across from her mother and I, smiling in contentment at us. Jessica and I shared a bemused look, before turning back to Hailey. I wouldn't be the one to ask about him, but it was actively killing me not to.

"Where's Ryan?" Jess asked calmly, and I felt a twisting sensation in my gut as I awaited her response. *He's in the bathroom... He's running late... He'll be here in a few minutes...*

Hailey paused for a moment, glancing down at the table. "He's not coming."

My pulse quickened as my heart sank a little. *Oh God, I hope he's okay. Did something happen to him? Oh, fuck... maybe he decided not to come because of me. He's avoiding me. Wow... that hurts more than it should.*

"Oh... Why not?" Jess replied, her brow furrowed in concern. I was grateful that she was the one asking all these questions, because I couldn't bear to speak at the moment.

Hailey was quiet again, taking a deep breath. "We broke up."

My stomach turned, and I felt my mouth filling with saliva, like I was going to throw up or something. I blinked over and over at Hailey, watching her face for some sign of devastation or tears, or distress, but I just didn't see it. She looked fine. Slightly disappointed, but more guilty than anything. Like she was afraid we would be mad at her.

"Oh, sweetie," Jess whispered, cocking her head to the side in that comforting motherly way. "What happened?"

"Nothing, really..." Hailey shrugged, her forehead lined as she stared back at us. "It just didn't work out."

"What do you mean it didn't work out?" my voice finally escaped my throat, sounding gruff and stern. "Did he... do something?" I clenched my fist under the table, praying she wasn't going to tell us he had cheated on her or something.

Of course I realized how hypocritical that was. I was the last person who could ever pass judgement in this case, especially where Ryan was concerned. But I secretly wanted to know if he had hooked up with someone else... I didn't want Hailey to have to go through that. Or me... *Jesus, get ahold of yourself. This isn't about you, asshole!*

"No, no! Nothing like that," Hailey replied, coming to Ryan's defense. "It was mutual. If anything, I kind of... initiated it." She breathed out softly, glancing down at the table again, fiddling with her silverware. "I really care about him, but I realized after I brought him home that we're both so young. I don't want to be tied down at nineteen."

She glanced back up at us, her eyes widening. "Not that what happened with you guys is bad or anything. It's amazing! You've been together since you were kids and you're still in love... It's crazy. But obviously that doesn't happen to everyone, and Ryan and me still have a lot of our lives to figure out."

I swallowed hard and took Jess's hand under the table, squeezing it tight. I wasn't sure why, I just felt like I had to.

The waiter came over, pouring us water and asking about drinks, but I shooed him away. I couldn't even think about that right now.

"I'm so sorry..." Hailey frowned, staring down at her empty plate again. "I know how much you guys liked him..."

Jess huffed and shook her head, taking Hailey's hand on top of the table.

"Sweetie... sure we liked him. He was really a nice boy, but you don't have to worry about us. We just want you to be happy."

"Thanks, Mom," Hailey smiled softly. "This is the right decision. For both of us."

"Are you sure?" I asked quietly, Hailey's eyes flicking over to mine. "You're sure this is... what you want?"

For some reason I felt like she was breaking up with me. I had no idea why I felt so sick over this, but I just did. I had sympathy pangs in my gut for Ryan. She said it was mutual, and I believed her, but still... I couldn't help feeling like this was somehow my fault. Like if she had never brought him home, they would still be together.

"Yes, Daddy," Hailey nodded, her eyes wide and shining blue right at me. "It's for the best. We agreed to stay friends. Completely amicable." She grinned, and I almost couldn't believe how mature and grown-up she sounded.

"Amicable..." I grumbled, shaking my head and scoffing at the table.

"Sorry, Daddy... I know you guys bonded," she apologized again, causing my eyes to shoot back up to hers. "I didn't mean to get you attached to someone and then take him away."

She giggled quietly, most likely out of some teasing amusement, but I was actually shaking. This topic was making me uneasy.

"I promise I'll find another guy to bring home for you," Hailey continued giggling, glancing at Jess, the two of them laughing up a storm.

My eyes were so wide, ready to burst out of my skull. My heart was racing, and I felt like I was having an out-of-body experience.

"Baby, she's kidding," Jess cooed to me, rubbing my arm gently. "Hailey, please tell him you're kidding before he has a coronary."

Hailey sighed out her giggles, wiping her eyes. "Daddy, I'm joking! Sheesh, don't blow a gasket. I'm going to stay single for a little bit. But not, like, in a slutty way, so don't freak out! I'm just going to focus on school and friends and college. Relationships can wait."

"That's very mature of you, muffin," Jess murmured, supportively.

I think I'm going to pass out.

I took a couple deep breaths, trying to comprehend everything that had just happened. I was glad that Hailey was happy, and that she had such a well-adjusted head on her shoulders. But I couldn't help feeling slightly bummed.

Putting aside the secret aspect of our relationship, Hailey was right about me bonding with Ryan. I got along well with him. I thought he was a great kid. Smart, funny, loyal, strong, good-looking... the whole package. Did Hailey really want to give that up just to be single? After all, if dating was the game, wasn't falling in love the winning trophy?

Okay, who are you more concerned for, your daughter or yourself? If she doesn't love him enough to want to be with him, then it's good that she realized it now, rather than waiting until after they're married with children, and ending up divorced.

I sighed out hard, trying to steady my whirlwind thoughts, while Hailey and Jess continued talking about the break-up, and how everything had worked itself out. I was still trying to wrap my head around it. And while I was feeling sort of uneasy about the whole thing,

I couldn't help but notice the intense wave of relief that washed over me. It had been a growing fear of mine that Hailey and Ryan would stay together, get married, and have kids someday. And then I would be forced to see him all the time at holidays and family gatherings, knowing we had fucked each other that first Thanksgiving weekend. Realistically, I knew on some level they had to break up. No one could put themselves through that. It was where most of my guilt had come from.

I worried that Ryan was being forced to give up a potential lifetime of happiness with my daughter just because I was too irresponsible to keep my hands, and other body parts, to myself.

I was suddenly struck with an overwhelming urge to talk to Ryan. I needed to know that this wasn't my fault.

Of course Hailey would say it was mutual. She didn't know the truth. But Ryan did. He would tell me what really went down.

I waited until after we ordered our food to excuse myself. I made my way to the bathroom and once I was locked securely inside the stall, I pulled my phone out of my pocket. I didn't have Ryan's number, but I had another way of contacting him...

Much to Hailey's dismay, I had an Instagram account. Not that I used it often. Social media wasn't really my thing. But one of its few advantages was that it allowed one to secretly stalk a party of his or her choosing.

I happened upon Ryan's Instagram account last week, during one of my late nights in the man-cave. He didn't seem to use his much either. Still, there were a few pictures on there that I had enjoyed looking at when I was acting like I didn't miss him, and not fooling myself one bit.

So this was my in. I pulled up my Instagram account on my phone and searched for Ryan. I opened a direct-message to him, and started typing, pressing send before I had time to second-guess myself.

Me: Hey...

I breathed out hard and closed my eyes. I really hoped he saw it right away and responded. I could've said more... But I wanted to see if he would even answer first before I dove right in.

I waited a minute, chewing on my lower lip while I stared at my phone screen hard, my hands trembling with impatience. Then the little icon appeared under my message, indicating that he had seen it.

I gulped and held my breath, watching the word *typing* next to his name, telling me he was writing a response. It came up for a second, then disappeared. Then popped up. Then disappeared again. This went on a few times, still with no response coming up, and my brow furrowed in confusion. *Damn... Is he writing a fucking novel?? What the fuck is going on?*

Finally, his response came through, and I rolled my eyes at my phone.

Ryan: Hey.

That's it?! It took him three minutes to write the same fucking word I wrote in one second?

I huffed and typed out another message.

Me: We need to talk
Ryan: About what...?
Me: You know what.

It took him another minute before he responded to that one.

Ryan: Everything is fine Ben. Don't worry about it.
Me: Bullshit. I need to see you.
Ryan: That's not a good idea...
Me: Yea I know. I'll message you when I get back to my hotel

Another long pause. This kid was frustrating me. I needed to get back to the table.

Ryan: I wish you wouldn't

Rejection burned through my chest.

Me: Really?
Ryan: You're making this really hard on me Ben
Me: I'm not trying to... I just want to talk
Ryan: Then fucking call me or something... I mean Jesus Christ...

Now I was getting pissed. He was being such a stubborn bitch. I held my breath and stood my ground.

Me: Not good enough. I need to see you.

No response.

Me: Please...
Ryan: Fine. I'll come by. Just message me when you're ready and let me know where you are.
Me: Thank you

I exhaled swiftly and shoved my phone back into my pocket, scurrying out of the bathroom and back to our table. The waiter was just dropping off bread and drinks.

"Everything okay?" Jessica asked as I took my seat.

"Fine," I gave her a tight smile, then turned back to my daughter. "So, what's new at school?"

We had just finished singing happy birthday to Hailey, and the waiter was serving up the custom-made cake we had ordered specially for her. Chocolate black cherry cake with pink vanilla buttercream frosting and intricate little roses all over it. The thing was very impressive, and Hailey was in heaven.

Jess went first with her gift—a Pandora charm bracelet, complete with five charms of all different varieties. Then it was my turn. Hailey's eyes bugged out of her skull when she opened the box and tore back the tissue paper to find the exact Fendi wallet she had been lusting over for months. I knew almost nothing about fashion, or designer labels. But I knew when my baby girl liked something. That I paid attention to.

"Oh my God, Daddy! I love it!" she squealed, jumping out of her seat like it was on fire and circling the table, hugging me so hard I almost fell back in my chair. "Thank you thank you thank you!"

"You're welcome, you spoiled brat," I chuckled and kissed her head.

"And thank you, Mom," Hailey whimpered, breaking free from me to hug Jess. "Seriously, you guys are the best parents ever. Just the fact that you drove all the way out here for a birthday dinner was enough for me."

"So you don't want the wallet?" I teased. "Because your mother's had her eye on it since I brought it home..."

"No!" Hailey barked. "No no. That's mine. And the bracelet. No takesies-backsies."

I grinned and sipped my drink, feeling pretty proud of myself.

We stayed in the restaurant for almost another hour, eating cake and chatting. I was so glad that I had a kid who actually enjoyed spending time with her parents. True, maybe it was because she didn't see us every day. But it still felt nice to hang out with her and Jess, and just enjoy each other's company.

By the time we were leaving, Jess and I were both tipsy, and as I predicted, she wasn't nearly as amped about walking as she had been on the way there. So we called an Uber and got back to the big, fancy hotel room for the night.

It was almost one in the morning, and while my wife seemed exhausted, she was determined not to waste a night in our expensive luxury suite. So she decided to take a relaxing bubble bath in the giant bathtub.

For a second, I considered joining her. The tub was so big, it could have easily fit three people comfortably.

But I also had something very important to do, and I was growing more and more impatient with every second that ticked by while I waited to do the thing I had to do.

Once Jess settled in the tub with the lights dimmed, a glass of wine and her book, I decided it was the perfect opportunity to slip out for a minute.

I messaged Ryan again, telling him to come by the hotel parking lot. He responded almost immediately, letting me know he would be there in ten minutes. *Okay, good. Now I just need to think of something to tell Jess about where I'm going. I shouldn't be gone long, so...*

"Baby?" I called from outside the bathroom, trying to keep the hesitation and uncertainty out of my voice. "I forgot something in the car... I'm gonna run down."

"Okay, babe," Jess replied, already sounding heavily sedated.

I left the room quick, making my way downstairs to the parking lot. I paced through guest parking, all the way to the back of the visitor's lot, instantly spotting the green BMW. My heart was already in my throat. It happened so fast; it was like the ground had been ripped out from under me.

Wow, okay. Remain calm. He's just here to talk. Nothing else.

I just need to hear about the break-up from him. I need to know it wasn't my fault.

I ambled over to his car, trying to seem casual, all the while shaking so hard my teeth were almost chattering. I had never been more nervous in my life. I couldn't tell if I was excited, scared, anxious, or guilty... *D, All of the above.*

I couldn't see anything through the car's tinted windows, which was freaking me out even more for some reason. I finally approached the passenger door, slowly tugging on the handle. As soon as the door opened, the interior of the car filled with a dim light, and I could see Ryan. He was just sitting there in the driver's seat, leaning back, trying to look casual himself, though his knee was bouncing rapidly in place.

I slinked inside the vehicle, nestling up in the cozy leather seat and closing the door behind me. Everything felt like it was moving in slow motion. The first thing I noticed was the smell. The car still had that new car, leather smell to the interior. But because it was Ryan's car, it also smelled like him. The whole inside was filled with the sweet, slightly musky scent of him, and it brought on a wave of memories, like rushing water flowing through me. I couldn't believe how much my body reacted to the sense.

I turned in my seat to face him, and I felt like I was being drop-kicked in the chest.

He looked so painfully good; I didn't even know what to do with myself. He was wearing gray sweatpants, not fully fitted, but still just tight enough to look really fucking good on him, and a white t-shirt that hugged his muscular frame in the absolute best way possible. His dark hair was slightly mussed up and damp, like he had just gotten out of the shower not too long ago, which accounted for the hint of soap I was smelling on his skin.

He obviously hadn't shaved since I last saw him, and was sporting a bit of a beard which made him look older, and devastatingly sexy. And his green eyes were wide, staring back at me in some kind of apprehension. I couldn't help but notice that he looked tired. He had slight circles under his eyes, and I hoped he hadn't been staying out partying, or losing sleep over some asshole. *Me.*

"Hey..." Ryan spoke first, staring at me hard with a look I couldn't read.

"Hey," I mumbled back, running my hands up and down my thighs to distract myself from everything I was feeling.

"How've you been?" he asked, sounding concerned, which made me warm everywhere.

"Good. You?" I asked in return, my eyes darting all over the interior of his car.

"Good. Can't complain..." he muttered, reaching forward to rest his hands on the steering wheel.

After that it was quiet inside the car. Silent. Neither of us said a word for what felt like an eternity, and the only thing I could hear was the sound of my blood rushing in my ears. I took a deep breath, and opened my mouth to say something, but nothing would come out.

"So... you wanted to see me?" Ryan finally spoke, fully turning in his seat to face me, giving me his undivided attention.

And I couldn't at all remember what the fuck I wanted to talk to him about.

My mind shut down and my body took control, forcing my hand to reach out and grab his. He looked startled for a moment, but it didn't change the fact that his fingers instantly threaded through mine, squeezing my hand tight with his.

I leaned in closer, sealing the gap between us, taking his jaw with my other hand and pulling his face closer, forcing him to lean over the center console. He whimpered and closed his eyes for a moment while my fingers trailed through the scruff along his sexy jawline. He breathed out softly and reopened his eyes, locking me down with that powerful stare.

"I *needed* to see you," I whispered, my eyes darting to his full, soft lips.

"Why?" he asked, his voice barely audible. My hand slid down to rest on his shoulder.

"I need to ask you..." I grunted then stopped, swallowing hard. "I needed to know... if it was my fault."

He stared back at me for a moment, blinking a few times, his fingers slowly caressing mine.

"No," he rasped and shook his head. "It wasn't."

I let out a hard breath. "Are you sure?"

He nodded slowly. "If anything, you helped me realize it wasn't going to work. I love Hailey... I always will. But it wasn't meant to be."

I took a deep breath, watching his face closely. "Are you okay?"

"I still don't really know..." he murmured, chewing on his bottom lip as his eyes fell to our joined hands. "It's weird. Sometimes I miss her, but then when I do, it doesn't feel right... Nothing ever... fucking feels right."

He huffed and shook his head. He looked sort of sad, which made my heart heavy.

"I feel like I fucked up your whole life," I told him, my forehead lined with regret.

He chuckled softly, his eyes coming back up to mine. "Jeez... Someone's a little cocky."

I laughed quietly, allowing myself to smile just a little, because he was, and it looked so fucking good on him.

"You know what I mean," I grumbled, cocking my head to the side. "I feel like if it weren't for me, you could have stayed with Hailey and been happy."

"Ben, listen to me," he commanded, so I did. "Yes, what happened with us was fucked up and wrong. But it changed nothing about Hailey and me. It just made me realize that there are parts of me I never even knew about before... Parts that are stronger and more passionate. And real. You didn't ruin me, Ben Lockwood. If anything, you made me better."

My heart thumped in my chest as my breathing shallowed. I blinked a few times, biting my lip to keep it from quivering with my nerves. It must have caught Ryan's attention, because his eyes dropped to my mouth for a second, then slid back up to my eyes.

I did the same thing, casually glancing at his lips, watching them part as he breathed in a quick gasp. The air inside the car was thick and warm. I felt like my whole body was buzzing.

That was it. I couldn't hold back anymore.

I tugged him by the nape of his neck to me and our mouths clashed as I kissed him hard. So hard that simultaneous groans flew out of us and into each other while our lips locked. Fireworks were exploding inside me as I kissed his sweet, soft lips over and over, swallowing up his moans like my favorite treats.

It felt different kissing him when he had the beard. It was rough, yet soft at the same time. It was hot, and I parted my lips, gliding my tongue between his to taste him. All of his hesitations disappeared the moment our tongues met in the middle. And after that he was basically climbing over the center console trying to get as close to me as possible in the confined space of his coupe.

"Mmm... baby..." I panted, licking and sucking and nipping at his luscious lips while my hands roamed all over his front. "I missed you."

"Don't do that..." he whimpered, sliding his tongue over my bottom lip then tugging it between his teeth in that way he knew I loved. "It's not even fair how much I missed you."

"Did you?" I hummed, sliding my hands up under his shirt, my fingers desperate to take in the feeling of him.

"Yea..." he whispered, combing his fingers through my hair, tugging me closer so we could kiss so fucking deep.

"Yea?" I rasped, admiring how deliciously hard his torso was.

"Yea," he growled, breathing warm over my lips, making my cock throb.

"Jesus, Ryan... You have no idea what you do to me..." I told him, moving my lips through his beard and over to his earlobe, licking and sucking it gently.

"What do I do to you, Ben?" he asked in the most arousing tone I had ever heard. I still could barely believe I was here with him now, kissing and touching. It felt so right... It felt like this was where I was supposed to be.

Even though that was absolutely not the case.

There was a war waging inside me, between my brain and my dick. On the one hand, I knew I had to get the fuck out of there, because my wife was upstairs in the hotel room. But on the other hand, I wanted to tease Ryan, and turn him on. I wanted to make him tremble.

That would be more fun than worrying about stuff.

I decided to go with the fun option. You know, the stupid one.

"You make my dick hard, Ryan," I whispered in his ear, tugging the lobe gently between my lips.

"Mmmm... do I?" he groaned, sliding his hand between my legs.

"Mhmm," I hummed, cupping his pecs, circling his hard nipples with my thumbs. "So *fucking* hard."

"Did you miss me taking care of your dick?" he asked softly, stroking up and down on my hard-on through my pants.

"So bad, baby," I said, my voice hoarse with arousal. "Just like I miss taking care of yours."

He whined out loud and pulled my face back to his, kissing my lips raw.

"Fuck, I want you," he snarled, sucking my bottom lip over and over. "Where can we go? How can we do this?" He was desperate, and it was burning me from the inside out.

I tore my mouth off of his fast, trying hard to compose myself. We definitely needed to stop. We couldn't fool around in a car in the hotel parking lot.

"Can we go to your place?" I asked hesitantly, not even fully aware of what I was saying. *Does he even have a place? Does he live in some shack, or a studio with four roommates? Could I actually go somewhere with him? It seems like a really bad idea to leave Jess here...*

"Yea, but..." he nodded then paused. "What about... your wife?" I closed my eyes for a minute, trying to calm down and think. Maybe I could text Jess and make something up... But what? "I know," I told him, attempting to pull my phone out of my pocket while maneuvering it around my raging hard-on. "I'll just tell her I'm going for a walk. She knows I can't sleep at night... She won't even think twice."

"Are you sure?" he asked, appearing worried and uneasy.

"Yea. But we have to make it quick," I said, giving him a slightly warning look, raising my brow as I texted my wife.

"Mm... Typical Bossy Ben..." he grumbled, trying and failing to hide his smile as he turned the car on and started driving away.

I texted Jess that I was wired and restless, and that I needed to go for a walk, promising I would be back very soon. I didn't get a response in the ten minutes it took to drive to Ryan's apartment, but I just figured she had already passed out.

It would be okay. It had to be.

I was just going to spend a few minutes with Ryan, getting my fix because I was a literal addict, and then I would go back to Jess and everything would be great. *Desperately reaching...*

Ryan brought me inside his apartment, which was actually insanely nice. Not at all the cramped studio I was imagining. He warned me to be quiet because he had a roommate who lived there with his girlfriend and apparently he had no desire to explain to them why he was sneaking a *giant dude*, as he described me, into his room at two in the morning.

Once we were securely tucked inside his bedroom with the door locked, I was itching to get him naked. I just wanted to touch and kiss him everywhere. It was almost insane. I needed to slow my roll...

Except that I couldn't. There was a timer on this little excursion, and I probably wouldn't be seeing him again after tonight, the thought of which bummed me out more than I wanted to think about. I needed to make this count.

I grasped Ryan's face and kissed him softly, making him whimper out this sexy little noise which hardened my cock something fierce. We made out for a minute, sucking and tugging at one another's lips in desperation while I shoved him toward his bed, causing him to stumble backward until he was sitting. I knelt between his legs and began yanking down his sweatpants to the tops of his thighs.

He wasn't wearing boxers. *Well, fuck me.*

"God, Ryan..." I grunted, grabbing his long, hard dick in my hand and stroking it slowly, licking my lips. "You don't even know how many times I thought about this in the past two weeks."

"Really?" he murmured, his voice soft and slightly hesitant. He reached out and trailed his fingers along my jaw. My eyes bounced up to his, and I nodded.

"Yea... I missed sucking your dick," I rasped, slipping my tongue under the fat, smooth head of his perfect cock, tonguing it nice and slow.

He groaned and bit his lip, most likely to quiet himself, gripping the comforter in his fist. I ran my tongue up and down the sides of his shaft, licking him like some kind of delicious Popsicle, before gliding him between my parted lips, sucking hard.

"Uhh... Ben... Jesus Christ..." he panted, flicking his hips forward, pushing himself deeper down my throat.

I grinned–almost... as much as I could, anyway–and sucked him harder; slow but steady; really working him over good. He was clearly loving it, moaning out all kinds of noises. I glanced up at him to watch his face. His eyes were closed; his lips moist and trembling. He looked so good, I couldn't even stand it.

"I missed your mouth..." he whispered, fucking my face slowly.

I tugged my lips off for long enough to tell him, "I missed you..."

Then I was back to sucking again, massaging his balls with my curious fingers.

"Ben... I wasn't going to tell you this, because I wasn't sure if you'd want to know..." he hummed, his eyes rolling back in his head.

I wasn't really paying much attention to what he was saying. Sometimes Ryan got a little chatty when we were hooking up. I thought it was cute. He wasn't a big talker in day-to-day life, but for some reason when I had his cock in my mouth he liked to gab.

I hummed with said perfect dick sliding in between my parted lips and he groaned.

"I fucked Tate Eckhart..." he mumbled, his voice quiet and

reserved.

I paused for a moment, glancing back up at his face. His eyes were still closed, and his brow was furrowed in duress. I watched as he swallowed hard, his Adam's apple bobbing in his sexy throat. I tugged my lips off his cock and stroked him slow but firm with my hand.

"If this is your weird version of some kinky role-playing game, I would say it needs work. But A+ for effort," I raised my brow, jerking him off and tonguing his head some more. He was so hard, it was almost unbelievable.

"No, Ben... I'm being serious," Ryan huffed, peeking down at me. I looked at him again, my hand stopping its movements.

"I'm sorry... Serious about what now?" I asked, fully confused by what he was trying to do here.

"I... I fucked Tate Eckhart," he said it again and this time the world around me froze.

I sat back on my knees and just gaped up at him; this beautiful, sexy young guy, hard dick all out and covered in my saliva. We were supposed to be fucking right now, not talking about... whatever he was trying to talk about.

"I don't understand..." I started, then paused. "How would you fuck Tate Eckhart? You don't even know him. You just met him at my house two weeks ago."

"I ran into him at some sleazy dive bar in Santa Fe," Ryan spoke slowly, his face so serious it was making me sick. "He said he was there on business..."

"Wait, hold on. I'm so confused right now," I grunted, raking my hand through my hair. "Are you being serious?"

"Yes, I'm being serious..." he rumbled.

"Ryan, don't fuck with me," I growled at him, my eyes hardening as my blood began to boil. *If he's trying to make a joke right now, I might just punch him.*

"I'm not fucking with you, Ben!" he breathed, dropping his head into his hands for a moment. "I wasn't sure if I should tell you, because it's not like you really need to know... But I just... I didn't want you to..." He paused his stuttering and took a deep breath.

"Holy fuck, you're serious..." I said in a robotic tone as I watched him. He looked like he was struggling. My stomach was twisting like someone was wringing out a wet cloth, and my chest was burning and tight with jealous rage. *What is this...?*

"Yes, Ben! Jesus, I said I was serious," he barked at me, trying to keep his voice down, still unable to look at me. "Why would I lie about something like that?"

"Oh my God... What the fuck?!" I snarled, standing up fast and pacing around his room. "Tate Eckhart?! You don't know him, Ryan... Why would you...?"

I was so confused I felt like I might fall down. I could barely comprehend what he was even saying, my mind struggling to process this revelation. And my reaction wasn't making any sense. Ryan was a grown-up. He could do whatever, or whoever, he wanted. It wasn't my business.

But for some reason the idea of any other guy—more specifically *Tate* fucking *Eckhart*-touching him and kissing him made me feel murderous.

"Yea, well, I barely knew you when we first hooked up," he pointed out, his face finally turning back up to mine.

"That's different..." I scoffed and shook my head.

"How? How is it different?" he asked, folding his arms over his chest.

I stared daggers at him, then my eyes fell down to his still-hard cock before coming back to his face. He tugged his pants up to cover it.

"It just is," I grumbled, frustrated at being unable to express how I was feeling.

"Okay, Ben..." he sighed, defeated.

"I can't believe what I'm hearing right now..." I resumed my pacing. "Why...? Why would you fuck him?? I need to know why."

I stopped in front of him, looking down into his dark eyes, searching them for some kind of solace that I wasn't getting. It was making me uneasy.

"I just wanted to forget about you..." he murmured, standing up, only about a foot of distance separating us. "I was missing you so bad, and I didn't want to be. And then everything with Hailey..." he paused and sighed again. "It was too much. I felt like I was drowning. So I went somewhere far away, where I didn't know anyone, and got drunk. Then he showed up... and it just happened."

"Ryan..." I whispered, then cleared my throat, trying hard to stow my intense vulnerability. "That *sucks.*"

"Why, Ben?" he asked, moving in closer, placing his hands on my hips. "Is it because you're jealous?"

"I'm not jealous of that little prick..." I swallowed hard. *Liar.*

"No?" he tilted his head to the side, reaching out to push my hair back with his fingers. I closed my eyes briefly and exhaled a slow breath. "Then why are you so mad?"

"Because!" I growled, my brows pushing together as our eyes locked in one of those powerful staring contests. "You're... mine." I whispered the word, so low that it was almost nothing more than a breath slipping from between my lips.

Ryan gaped at me in awe. He blinked a few times over wide eyes, appearing fully stunned.

"I'm... *yours?*" he asked, his voice deep and gravelly. I nodded slowly.

"I don't want him touching you..." I commanded with my eyes and my scary tone, as my hands grabbed his ass hard, pulling him into me until I could feel his erection on mine. He gasped. "I don't want him to have you... at all."

"Ben... I..." he stuttered, nervously, shaking his head a little.

"Did you kiss him?" I asked, stepping forward with him, my eyes dropping to his lips.

He stumbled backward onto his bed, and I crawled on top of him. I raised my brow, waiting for him to answer me. My heart was hammering in my chest.

I didn't know why I was torturing myself by thinking about what they had done together. But I wanted to hear him say it. I wanted to see how scared he was to tell me. It made me feel... empowered, dominant. It made me feel in control, rather than spinning out. *I want him to know he's mine.*

"Yes," he finally answered, nodding slowly.

"How did it feel?" I asked, hovering over him, straddling his thigh, my hands on either side of his broad shoulders, holding me up while I looked down at him.

"It was... okay..." he flinched, eyeing me cautiously.

"Did he kiss you... like this?" I moved my face in slowly, brushing my lips over his, parting mine over his pouted bottom lip, giving it a sweet, soft kiss.

He moaned out a breathy noise and shook his head.

"Did it feel good when he touched you?" I kept on pushing, grinding my aching cock on his thigh through my jeans.

"Not like this..." Ryan panted while I grasped the hem of his t-shirt, slowly dragging it up his torso, revealing all of that rippling muscle definition which made my mouth water. "Not like you..."

"Did he suck your dick?" I growled, kissing down his neck, slowly, onto his chest, licking all over, taking his sweet little nipple between my lips and sucking it hard. He groaned out loud and bit his lip to shut himself up. He nodded quick, opening his eyes to look down at me with a purely guilty expression on his face.

I gulped hard, attempting to swallow down the jealousy burning my esophagus.

"Did he make you come?" I asked with clear hesitation, though my voice was still deep and intimidating.

"Ben, I was trying to forget about you..." he whispered, reaching for my face, but I pulled away.

"Why would you want to do that?" I squinted at him.

"Because I couldn't have you," he mumbled, regretfully. "I still can't..."

"You can," I huffed, moving my face back up in line with his. "I told you, all you have to do is ask."

"You know that's not true," he pointed out, his plump bottom lip jutting out slightly in this little pout that made me sort of crazy.

This whole thing was insane. It had gotten so out of hand.

What am I doing here? What am I doing with this kid?

My mind was telling me to go before I dug myself any deeper, but my heart physically wouldn't let me. It was controlling my actions and leaving clearly wasn't an option.

"I want you..." I whispered, kissing him so tender and sensual that

I felt like I was melting all over the place.

"I want you," Ryan rasped back to me, reaching for my face again, though this time I let him.

He held my jaw in his hand while parting his lips, sliding his tongue in to meet mine. It felt so good... He tasted like cinnamon and chocolate. I was in agony as we kissed harder and deeper, my crotch grinding on him as I built up some friction which was threatening to unravel me completely.

"Did he fuck you...?" I asked, my heart lodged in my throat. *Please say no... Good God, I won't be able to handle it. I'll go on a killing spree.*

"No," he answered fast, his fingers moving to the buttons on my shirt, undoing one slow button at a time.

"You fucked him?" I asked in a growl. I needed the clarification.

"Mhm..." he grunted, moving his hands inside my now open shirt, pushing it off my shoulders. "I told you, Ben. I was trying to forget you..."

"By putting your dick inside that stuck-up little bitch?" I hissed, my jaw clenching from the unwanted images rattling around in my brain.

"Stop," Ryan demanded, grabbing my face and forcing me to look at him. I gulped and blinked. "It was just sex. It meant nothing. I had to imagine I was fucking you anyway..."

My stomach flipped, and a small smile tugged at my lips. "You did?"

"Yes, Ben," he smirked an aroused little grin that made my cock twitch. "I told you, no one can live up to you."

"You imagined you were fucking me when you were fucking him?" my voice rumbled from inside my chest.

"I had to," he nodded, reaching for the waist of my jeans, unbuttoning and unzipping them. "I missed you so much..."

I gasped, warmth flowing through me as we stared at each other. It was the most erotic thing ever, the way our eyes connected. It made me feel like we were fucking, even when we weren't.

Ryan yanked my pants and boxers down below my ass, and I slithered out of them the rest of the way. He took his sweatpants back off, and we rolled around in his bed, naked, kissing and touching everywhere, our heated bare flesh pressing together. Everything was blurry, the air in the room was a haze of sexual tension and lust.

"Fuck me, Ryan..." I pleaded, taking his hands in mine while I sucked his bottom lip. "I need you to fuck me."

"I want to..." he whimpered, dragging his cock against mine.

I rolled onto my stomach, lifting my hips and rubbing my ass on his erection. I heard him gasp, which brought a lazy smile to my swollen lips. I couldn't even comprehend how badly I wanted his big, long dick all the way inside my ass. I was craving it so hard I was dizzy.

Ryan sprawled out on the bed behind me, running his hands down my back to squeeze my ass in two handfuls. He massaged me, caressing my cheeks with his strong hands. And then I felt his lips and his breath on me, kissing and nipping my flesh. He sucked hard on my ass cheek, biting me a little until I gasped out loud. Then he spread me open and licked my hole over and over, long feathering strokes that made me shudder.

I groaned, pressing my face down into the comforter, surrendering to the feeling of his tongue in my ass, teasing me and making me wet. His mouth moved down to my balls, and I had to bite my lip to keep quiet. He was so gentle, yet rough and impatient. I could feel how aroused he was in his actions, and it made my knees buckle.

His tongue dove inside me a few more times before he sat back up, and I could hear him panting. I was ready to feel his cock probe me from behind, but instead he grabbed my hips hard and flipped me onto my back, pushing my thighs open so he could kneel between them. He moved on top of me, gliding his hands up my hips.

"I want to see you," he whispered, grinding his cock on mine. He was so hard I could feel him pulsing against me. "I want to watch your face while I fuck you."

I nodded slowly and his eyes moved to my lips, coveting my mouth. I could tell he wanted to kiss me, but wasn't sure if I wanted it, being that his mouth was just all up in my butt. I had zero reservations about anything at the moment, so I pulled his face down to mine and kissed him deep, our tongues pressing together in full-on passion.

Ryan grabbed his cock in his hand and looked in between our writhing bodies, pressing himself up to me. I breathed out a steady breath, calming myself and relaxing every muscle in my body enough to let him in.

He guided the head of his dick inside me, slow and gentle, giving it that first push. He was so big, there was always some initial shock, but I welcomed it. I wanted him inside me where no one else had ever been before. I wanted us to be *one.*

The head of his cock slid inside and we both groaned out loud, then shushed each other and laughed softly. Staying quiet would be a challenge. We weren't used to being shy with our sounds of appreciation during sex.

Ryan kissed my lips as he pushed in further, filling my ass up, inch by delicious inch. I felt so completely full of him it was almost unbearable. But it was amazing, and when I relaxed enough to let him stroke in me, I became unhinged.

He pulled back and drove in more and more, developing that punishing rhythm that stole every ounce of breath from inside my lungs. Although we had done this before, it still never ceased to amaze me how overpowering it was. It was so bad; naughty, dirty... Downright lethal. And the best high of my entire life.

"Fuck me, baby..." I croaked, my voice coming out shaky and hoarse. "Fuck my ass."

"I'm fucking your tight ass, Ben," Ryan moaned, holding my hip with his left hand, his fingers digging into my flesh while he thrust inside me, over and over and over again. "My hard dick is filling you up."

Our bodies were covered in sweat, skin glistening and gliding together while we fucked. I spread my legs wide, wrapping around him and holding him close to me. He was up to his balls in my backside... I could feel them pressing against the beginning of me, which made me wild. I hadn't even touched my dick yet, and I felt like I could come any minute.

Ryan and I must have had the same thought, because we both reached for my cock, which was twinging on my abs, ready to explode. Both of our hands rubbed up on my firm flesh while Ryan pumped in my ass harder and faster. We were both grunting and panting, trying so hard to be quiet. It was like work. I just wanted to scream his name out loud because what he was doing felt so goddamn good.

"You fuck so good, baby," I told him, kissing his soft lips. "You're gonna make me come..."

"I'm gonna come hard and deep in your perfect ass, Ben..." he purred, pressing his chest against mine, our skin slipping and sliding from the sweat. Our nipples were rubbing together, and it felt divine. *God, I'm going to come so hard for him. I love his perfect dick inside me...*

"Make me yours, Ryan..." I whimpered, holding him tight, gripping his back as I stood at the edge of the precipice.

"You're mine, Benjamin Lockwood," he grumbled, his hips working overtime, thrusting in me so deep, I could feel his cock hitting every nerve up and down.

Each time his big dick touched my spot, it was like unbearable euphoria. I was about to break. I couldn't even control my volume anymore.

"Ryan... oh fuck... Ryan... baby... fuck me... *fuck... me...*"

"Ben, I'm gonna come in your ass," he gasped, pushing and pulling and pushing, stretching my tight hole to fit his engorged erection until I couldn't hold back anymore. "Oh... *fuck*, Ben!"

I could feel Ryan release inside me, and it sent me right over the edge. I started coming so hard; it was like I was diving head-first off Niagara Falls.

My orgasm rocked through my loins, hot, slick come shooting out of my dick, all over the both of us, while he emptied deep in my ass. My balls were throbbing through the contractions while Ryan's name fell out of my mouth repeatedly, my voice strained.

His hips came to a slow and gradual halt, while he sang my praises. "Ben... God, you're amazing... How do you make me come like that? I've never come so hard in my entire life... You're so perfect. Your ass is so tight... and you're... just... so... *fucking...* perfect."

We were both sweaty and sticky, our voices raucous as we tried to catch our breath. I was coming down from the high for a while, even after Ryan pulled out of me and fell onto his back by my side. It was fucking fantastic. The best sex I'd ever had.

Quite the reunion.

We recovered for a bit, staring up at the ceiling, questioning our entire existence and everything we had ever done. Well, that was what I was doing. I wasn't sure about Ryan...

Eventually he rolled onto his side, wrapping his arms around my waist, pressing soft, sweet kisses all along my neck and shoulder. I turned to him, looking over his face, brushing his silky dark hair back with my fingers.

"I have come all over me..." I murmured softly. "And inside me."

Ryan giggled, kissing my lips quick. "Let's go get cleaned up."

"Okay, but I don't have time to take a shower," I sighed, watching Ryan roll off the bed and stumble toward his bathroom, admiring his physique as he went.

His body is out of control... Has he been working out more?

I sat up slowly, wincing over the intense soreness happening in all of my muscles, especially the ones below the waist. I carefully scooted myself off the bed, walking sort of funny across the room. Before I joined Ryan in the bathroom, I checked my phone for a potential response from Jessica.

Hm... Still nothing. That's weird, right? Shouldn't she have at least asked when I was coming back?

I pushed my uneasy thoughts out of my brain long enough to go clean off. Ryan was already in the shower.

"Baby, I can't take a full shower," I told him again, stepping inside the shower, making sure the water only hit my body, not my head. "My hair can't get wet because Jess will know something else happened."

Ryan stared at me for a second, running his hands through his wet hair. Then he nodded quickly.

"Okay..." he muttered, stepping out of the way.

I moved under the warm water, letting it rinse away all the sweat and sticky stuff. I spun around to wash the rest of me, and when I turned back toward Ryan again, he was making a face.

"What?" I asked, confused by his reaction to my backside. "Is there something on me?"

"Umm... I'm so sorry..." he breathed, slightly remorseful, his lips curling into a timid smile.

"What...?" I asked again, my brows pushing together.

"There's a... um... hickey. On your ass..." he mumbled, chuckling softly.

"Are you fucking serious?" I gasped, turning over my shoulder, trying hard to see my own butt. I couldn't see anything. "You gave me a hickey on my ass?! Ryan!"

He giggled quietly, biting his lip to stop himself in case I wasn't in the mood for laughing, which I kind of wasn't, although I couldn't stop the grin from pulling at my mouth. I wasn't sure if I should have been worried or not.

"Is it big?" I asked, turning and pushing my butt at him. He grinned wide and took my ass in both his hands, looking it over closely. He ran his thumb over one spot for a second, and I instantly had goosebumps. His touch was so gentle... His hands were strong and big, manly, but he touched so sensually. It sort of blew me away.

"I think you'll be alright," Ryan chirped, patting me on the ass. I turned back to face him.

"Is it... obvious that it's a hickey?" I asked seriously. I was still slightly concerned that it might be something I'd have to explain to my wife.

"I don't think so," he shrugged, his lackadaisical attitude toward this whole thing both calming me down and pissing me off at the same time. "Just say it's a bruise... if she asks, I mean."

He was clearly referring to Jess, commenting on my unspoken thought, which creeped me out a little. *How did he do that...?*

"Ryan, this is serious," I scolded him, because my feelings were overwhelming me, and my default setting was to get defensive for no reason. "I can't just walk around with hickeys on my ass." Ryan chuckled softly, covering his lips with his fingers so as not to blatantly laugh in my face. "Is this funny to you?" I glared at him.

"Yea, Ben..." he sighed, his eyes sympathetic toward my frustrations. "It's a little funny." He stepped in closer and grabbed me by the waist, pulling me into him while I pouted like a brooding teenager. "Come here."

He held onto me, our wet bodies pressing together as he stared deep into my eyes, like he was trying to figure me out. It was completely terrifying... because I wanted him to. He kissed my lips softly and I finally let go of my fake anger and stopped fighting, allowing myself to relax and kiss him back.

"I'm sorry about the hickey..." he whispered, his breath warm on my lips. I nodded quickly, my eyes closed tight as I struggled through my erratic heartbeat. I had no idea what was going on inside me, but it was becoming crystal clear that this thing with Ryan was anything but casual. "I didn't mean to do that. It was an accident. I guess I just got carried away..."

"It's okay," I mumbled, swallowing hard. *What the fuck am I doing? What are we doing?*

"You said... I was *yours*..." Ryan breathed, and I opened my eyes to look at him. "It just... made me go a little crazy for a second."

"I'm sorry I said that," I blurted out, instantly regretting it.

Ryan's eyes widened, and he gave me a slightly wounded look.

"I just mean... I shouldn't have said it," I grumbled, shaking my head. "I shouldn't have reacted that way to the thing with you and Tate. You're a single guy. You should be able to do whatever... with whoever..."

"So, that's what you want?" he huffed, raising his brows in confusion. "You want me to see other guys...? Because that's not what you said..."

"No, Ryan, of course I don't want you to see other guys," I rolled my eyes at him, tugging myself out of his grip. "But what am I supposed to do? I'm married... I love my wife. Yes, you're single now, and the mainly fucked up aspect of this thing has been slightly resolved, but it doesn't change the fact that I'm still cheating. I'm still fucking everything up, and the last thing I need to do is drag you down with me. You should get out now and save yourself before it's too late."

I whipped the shower curtain back and hopped out of the shower, reaching for a towel. My hands were shaking. I was so tense and frightened I felt like I might have a panic attack. I dried myself off, covering my face with the towel, trying to take deep breaths and calm the hell down.

I needed to get the fuck out of there. I had been gone way too long.

I heard the shower stop, but I left the bathroom before Ryan got out. I rushed toward my clothes, dressing quick, all the while mentally scolding myself for doing this. Sure, I had been thinking about Ryan nonstop since he left two weeks ago. And yes, being with him now felt like a broken piece of me had been restored. But I couldn't allow this to happen. I couldn't stand to hurt Jessica. I couldn't possibly break my wife's heart.

I had to stop this, even though I desperately wanted it to never stop.

"So you're just leaving then?" Ryan's voice came from behind me. I closed my eyes briefly and exhaled hard before turning to face him.

"I have to," I breathed, sounding, and probably looking, so damned desperate.

Ryan nodded, swallowing visibly and glancing at the ground.

"Will I see you again?" he asked quietly, still looking away.

"I don't know..." I answered, truthfully, because I didn't. I knew I *shouldn't* see him again. But honestly, I found it nearly impossible to stay away from him.

Even after he left two weeks ago, I knew that I would see him again this weekend, when we came for Hailey's birthday. And sure, I told myself that I was forbidden from hooking up with him. But in the back of my mind, there had still been a glimmer of hope; a longing to somehow get him alone, and be with him again, the way we had, reminiscent of that weekend. It was that small voice, the one I had attempted to silence during the entire past two weeks, over and over, that drove me to this moment.

I had tried hard to fool myself into thinking I would be strong, and leave that weekend in the past, as a fond memory. But in my heart, I knew my attempts were futile. Knowing I would see him again kept me going over the past two weeks.

And it would keep me going again, until the next time.

I stammered up to Ryan, taking in the look on his gorgeous face. He looked upset, but with that same sparkle that I was feeling in his eyes. As if he knew as well that no matter what, we would definitely see each other again, regardless of how much we said no.

I held his face in my hands, savoring the feeling of his beard beneath my fingers, and kissed his lips, soft yet rough enough for him to groan into my mouth. He gripped my hips hard, pulling me closer while we kissed slow and deep, telling each other everything the other needed to hear without words.

When I finally pulled back, we were both breathless. I rested my forehead on his, watching his bottom lip tremble with his uneven breaths. I couldn't help myself. I pressed one more kiss on his lips. Then another. And then another, which made him smile, and made me smile back.

Jesus, you're both so corny. Why don't you fucking marry him already... sheesh.

"Do you want me to drive you back?" he asked, quiet and inquisitive.

"I would love to have ten more minutes with you..." I told him, locking my blue eyes on his dark green ones. "But I should probably just get an Uber." He pursed his lips, clearly not enthused by this idea, but nodded anyway in reluctant acceptance. "Plus, it's late. You should get some sleep."

"Look at you, worrying," he grinned, looking awfully pleased with himself. "Benjamin Lockwood *likes me.*" He wiggled his eyebrows in a teasing fashion that made me squint at him.

"Watch it, kid," I growled, though a wicked smirk was playing on my lips. Then I smacked him on the ass, and he yelped.

"I'm too wired to sleep now, anyway," he sighed, watching as I pulled my phone out of my pocket, opening the Uber app. "And all the sex made me hungry. You want some cereal before you go?"

"Cereal?" I raised my brow at him in between entering his address.

"Mhm. Captain Crunch," he murmured, then leaned in closer to my face. "With berries." He pressed a quick kiss on my chin then darted out of his bedroom.

I huffed a laugh, shaking my head as Uber informed me it was locating a nearby driver. It was taking forever, and I wondered if maybe I had bad service. I went to the doorway of his room and peeked around the corner. I was afraid his roommates would be out there walking around, and I didn't feel like having to answer questions about the nature of our relationship, or forcing Ryan to.

Although, why would they need to know anything? We could just say we're friends or whatever... We were out drinking, clubbing... whatever the fuck kids do these days, and I came over to have some cereal before I went home. See? Perfectly normal.

I stepped out of the room slowly, trying to tip-toe as I made my way to the kitchen. Ryan was sitting at the breakfast bar, joyfully demolishing a huge bowl of Cap'n Crunch Berries in nothing but his grey sweatpants. He looked so fucking good it was almost unfair. The kid could easily have been a model or something.

I shook myself out of my thoughts, ignoring the fact that I was a straight, married man in his thirties ogling his daughter's twenty-one-year-old ex-boyfriend, with whom I had engaged in several naked, sweaty, come-filled encounters, and stalked over to Ryan, leaning up against where he was sitting.

"You get a ride yet?" he asked with a mouth full of cereal. I shook my head slowly, resisting the urge to kiss him. I had no idea why I was suddenly finding it impossible not to be all over him constantly, but I needed to leave now before I ended up just moving the fuck in. "There's probably no one around at this time of night. Just let me drive you."

"But your cereal," I teased, smirking as he laughed.

He shoveled a few more bites into his mouth, standing up to bring the bowl to the sink when we heard a door opening. My heart leapt into my throat and I considered hiding. It was an overreaction, of course, but I glanced at Ryan quickly to see if he wanted to push me under the table or something.

He was watching the doorway closely as a pretty, young girl with dark hair came out, wearing nothing but an oversized t-shirt. She was yawning and rubbing her eyes, padding her bare feet right toward us, though it didn't appear that she had even opened her eyes yet.

When she finally did, she stopped dead in her tracks, her sleepy eyes widening and bouncing from Ryan to me, to Ryan to me, to Ryan, and then landing on me and staying there for a moment.

"Um..." she rasped, looking confused.

"Kayla, this is my friend Ben," Ryan said with a confident grin. "Ben, this is Kayla. My best friend, Alec's girlfriend."

I nodded slowly, looking back over at the girl, giving her a quick smile.

"Hi there," she muttered, resuming her walking, scooting past us and going for the fridge. "Just getting a drink..."

She pulled a carton of orange juice out of the fridge, then opened one of the cupboards, reaching up to grab a glass. She was very short, probably only about five-two, so when she reached up, the t-shirt she was wearing lifted slightly, showing off the curve of what appeared to be a very delicious-looking ass. I could almost feel myself drooling at the sight of her short, toned legs leading up to that perfectly round booty. *Damn... that's hot.*

I hadn't even noticed how hard I was staring until I felt Ryan's elbow jam into my ribcage. I quickly snapped out of it, swallowing hard and glancing at Ryan who was giving me an arrogantly teasing look, smirking like he had it all figured out. Kayla finished pouring her drink, heading briskly back toward her room.

"Nice meeting you," she turned to smile at me, cheeks slightly flushed, before she scurried back into her room and closed the door.

"Likewise..." I was left whispering, while Ryan laughed quietly, dumping his bowl into the sink.

"Down, boy," he crooned, slipping on a t-shirt quickly then grabbing me by the arm and tugging me with him.

"What?" I shrugged as we left his house, hopping into the passenger side of the BMW. "She seemed nice."

Ryan laughed again, settling into the driver's seat, starting up the engine and giving me a knowing look while he buckled his seatbelt.

"Oh yea? You got that impression from her butt cheeks, did you?" he sneered, pulling out of his driveway.

"Hmm... Look who's jealous now," I hummed, leaning back in my seat.

"I'm not jealous of that," he grumbled, his brow furrowing as he focused on the road, cruising us down the street, back to my hotel.

"No?" I raised my brows as I watched him.

"No. I know you like girls," he said, peeking at me out the corner of his eye. "You're married to one, after all."

"Yea," I sighed wistfully. "And my wife's a tasty piece, for sure."

"No arguments here," he rumbled. I turned slightly in my seat.

"You think Jess is hot?" I asked, curiosity lacing my tone.

"Um fuck yea," he nodded. "Your wife is bangin."

"Yea, she is..." I muttered, gulping at the recollection that I hadn't yet heard from her, and it was after three in the morning. *I hope she's okay...*

"You're not jealous of me liking girls?" Ryan asked, bringing my attention back to the driver.

I paused to think for a second. "No."

"Only other guys..." he murmured. It was supposed to be a question, but it came out more like a statement, because we both already knew the answer.

"So it would seem..." I hummed, running my fingers over the stubble along my jaw.

"Can I ask you something?" he asked, his tone hesitant. I nodded, and though he couldn't see me, he kept going. "Where would you want this to go?" He glanced over at me quickly. "I mean, if you could have it any way you wanted... What would you choose?"

I stared at him for a moment, considering his question. The truth was that I had no idea what I wanted to happen. All I knew was that I wanted to stay with Jess, and I also wanted to keep seeing Ryan. I wanted to have my cake and eat it, too. It wasn't at all realistic. *But he said any way you wanted...*

"I want to be with Jess... and you," I spoke softly, running my hand along the back of my neck. "I know that doesn't make any sense... But I just... I don't know," I huffed and shrugged out of frustration. "I know I have no claim on you or anything. And I have no right to tell you who you can and can't see... But I hate the idea of you being with... well... anyone who isn't me, okay?"

I breathed out hard and slouched back in my seat, crossing my arms over my chest.

It was quiet in the car for a second, while we drove through the streets, getting closer and closer to goodbye.

I finally let my eyes drift back over to Ryan, and he was smiling a sweet, shy smile, tugging his bottom lip with his teeth, trying to stifle it.

"You're loving this, aren't you?" I grunted at him, narrowing my gaze in his direction.

"Yea, kind of," he replied with a cocky little grin, showing me a side-dimple that I just wanted to lick. *Jesus, I'm in trouble.*

"Whatever. I just definitely don't want you seeing that arrogant twat

Tate Eckhart again," I growled in a very stern, domineering tone. Ryan glanced at me and raised his brow. "Please."

"There ya go," he chirped, pulling into the visitor's parking lot of the hotel. "Was that so hard?"

I gave him a warning smile, and he laughed out loud.

He pulled into the same spot where he picked me up earlier and turned off the ignition. We both unbuckled our seatbelts at the same time, turning to face each other. There was a mirroring downhearted look on both of our faces, each of us sharing the same depressing thought.

Our time was up.

"Thanks for meeting me," I murmured, reaching over to grab his hand.

"Thanks for coming over," Ryan smiled softly, lacing our fingers.

"I like your place," I told him, and leaned in.

"Maybe you can come over again soon..." he grinned, moving in closer still, until his lips were hovering over mine.

"Mmm... I'd like that," I whispered, kissing him gently. He whimpered between my lips as we kissed, slow and passionate, saying our goodbyes without words.

"I'll miss you, baby..." his voice vibrated out of him onto my mouth.

"I'll miss you more..." I breathed, running my hands down his shoulders, onto his chest.

"I wish we could have just stayed in bed," he pulled back, leaving his eyes closed.

"I know, babe," I pouted, grabbing his chin and forcing him to look at me. His green eyes locked on mine as we gazed at each other. "But I've gotta go. I don't even know what I'm going to say to Jess..."

He nodded slowly. "Good luck. Message me if you can..."

"I will." I kissed him a couple more times, then gave him a smile, trying to lighten the mood before I hopped out of the car.

I struggled not to look back as I made my way out of the parking lot and into the hotel. I was rushing a little, through the lobby and into the elevator. Once I was securely inside, I leaned my back up against the wall and breathed out hard.

My God... What in the fuck just happened?!

It seemed like every encounter I'd had with Ryan since that first night in the basement had been more intense than the last. Each time we said we were done, we came crashing back together like an explosion of intense chemistry. We were drawn to each other, like magnets. And I didn't understand how I could move forward from here.

The elevator dinged, snapping me out of my thoughts and forcing me to move my feet. I anxiously made my way down the hall toward our suite. I took a deep breath before swiping my key card in the door, opening it carefully, trying to be quiet as I slowly entered the room.

I expected the whole place to be dark, which it was mostly, except for one dim light, coming from the bedroom. It was completely quiet, and I could feel my pulse steadily increasing as I kicked off my shoes and walked into the bedroom.

I just wanted to crawl into bed next to my wife and fall asleep, putting all the drama out of my mind, tucking it away for another time. Unfortunately, when I stepped through the doorway to our room, I saw Jess, sitting up in the bed, staring at me.

Her eyes were wide, and she looked tired, her mouth set in a grim line. I gulped, looking away as I tried like hell to act normal, unbuttoning my shirt and shrugging it off.

"Hey, babe," I muttered quietly, tossing my shirt onto a nearby chair, then stepping out of my jeans. "Sorry I was gone for so long... I went for a really long walk, just checking out the area, and then I got lost..." I lied, grabbing my pajama pants out of my bag and pulling them on over my boxer briefs. I normally would never wear pajamas over my boxers, but I couldn't risk revealing the hickey right now.

Jess still hadn't said a word, but I was afraid to look her in the eye while I lied to her face. So instead I just meandered over to my side of the bed, crawling in next to her. The air in the room seemed tense, and I couldn't tell if it was all in my head or not.

I bit the bullet and finally looked up at my wife. She was watching me closely, her face still. It didn't even look like she was breathing. My mouth was so dry I could barely swallow.

"Is everything okay?" I asked, feeling the sweat bead on the back of my neck.

She remained silent, staring back at me. My nerves were rattling inside my body.

"Jess...?" I muttered, cocking my head to the side.

"How's Ryan doing?" she asked, her voice steady and serious, her face remaining cold as stone.

I froze for a second, my heart plummeting into my stomach. But I recovered quickly enough, squinting at her.

"What do you mean?" My forehead creased as I struggled to fabricate a look of startled confusion.

"Well, you went to his house, right?" she raised her brow, tilting her head in question.

"Why...?" I huffed, blinking a few times. *Oh, God... Dear God, sweet Jesus...* "Why would I go to Ryan's house...?"

"I don't know, Ben. You tell me," she grumbled, narrowing her gaze.

I gaped at her with wide eyes, unable to move, speak, or blink. I felt the bile rising.

Okay, calm down. There's no way she knows anything. How would she? Just act natural.

My brain was in panic-mode, rushing over any and all possible scenarios in which she could have figured out what I was doing. But I kept coming up blank. I was too startled to think clearly, so I just stared at her; an utter, vacant look of helplessness.

Finally, she sighed out hard and rolled her eyes.

"I went down to the parking lot looking for you," Jessica muttered, speaking slow and somber. My stomach tightened, and I really felt like I might be sick. "You said you were going to get something from the car, but you didn't even bring the keys with you. And you were acting weird, so I went after you. But when I got to the car, you weren't there. Instead, I saw you getting into a green BMW."

She stopped and took a deep breath, exhaling slowly. My hands were shaking so hard, I had to make them into fists to stop them. Fear was clutching my windpipe, making it hard to breathe. *She saw us in the car. She saw us...*

"I recognized it as Ryan's, and I wanted to know what he would have been doing here, so I got into our car and waited to see where you guys were going. You sat in the car for a while... Not sure why. But I waited... and waited. And *waited*," she hissed, her voice still so eerily quiet, her eyes dark and hardened.

Okay, so maybe she didn't see us. The windows are tinted, so...

"And then you finally started driving away," she grumbled through a visibly clenched jaw. "So I followed you." My heart dropped again.

Fuck.

"You *followed* me...?" My gruff voice flew from inside my throat.

Fuck. My. Life.

"Mhm," she hummed, glaring at me. "That's how I knew for sure you were with Ryan. I saw the two of you get out of the car and go into his house. I mean, I'm guessing that was his house, right...?" She raised her brow at me, her eyes calling me the fuck out and making me weak, every fiber of my being completely shattered.

I didn't want to answer her. I tried desperately to think of something to say that would save me; to turn it around in my favor. But there was nothing.

Where else would Ryan and I be going together other than his house? Think, dammit! Make something up!

"Ben, there's really no point in lying right now," her face showed only anger and disapproval. "I know it was his place. What I don't know is what you could have possibly been doing in there for so long."

I gulped. "How long did you..."

"An hour," she cut me off. My jaw hung open and my brows raised. *An hour?!* "I sat outside in the car... for *an hour* waiting for you to come back outside. Finally, I gave up and drove back here. I actually wasn't sure if you would come back at all..."

"Of course I was coming back..." I whispered, trying to force my voice out in more than a distressed squeak from inside my throat.

"Yea?" She cocked her eyebrow again. "You were in there for a long time, Ben. What were you doing...?" Her face was less severe now. It had changed suddenly to one much more vulnerable; she looked terrified. "What could you, and Ryan, possibly have been doing in his house for hours at two in the morning?"

My bottom lip started to quiver, and I bit it, glancing down at my hands, my head shaking subtly over and over.

Oh my God, I can't do this. What am I supposed to do? I can't hurt her... She can't know.

But I can't lie to her either. She's my wife... Holy fuck, she's going to leave me. She'll divorce me if she finds out. Oh my God, I'm losing my shit!

"Ben!" she shouted my name, causing my eyes to fling back up to hers. My breathing was out of control. "Just answer me, goddammit! Tell me what the fuck you were doing. No lies... No bullshit stories. Just tell me the truth."

"I... I was... *We* were..." I stuttered, and my voice gave out. I hummed out a desperate sound and flopped back against the headboard. "Okay... so... the thing is..."

I swallowed hard, rubbing my sweaty palms on my pajama pants. *Just tell her. Fuck it. You can't lie to her... Anyone else in the world, but not her.*

"Ben..." she growled, and I glanced at her again.

"Alright, just promise to hear me out. Just... don't leave. Please?" I begged her, my eyes wide with duress.

She gaped at me, eyes bugging out, mouth hanging open.

"Don't give me a reason to," she squeaked, looking petrified of what I might be about to say. I could almost see her mind flashing through all the horrible possibilities.

I sat up straight and took a deep breath, closing my eyes while I let it out. I couldn't believe this was happening. I was on the verge of a huge freak-out. On some level I knew this day would come. I just didn't think it would happen so soon.

I reopened my eyes, locking them on my wife's while I turned my whole body to face hers.

"Jessica, I love you," I whispered. "Just know that no matter what I'm about to say, I love you so fucking much, and I have for nineteen years. You're everything in the world to me..."

"Jesus Christ..." she whimpered, already looking like she might burst into tears. "Ben, what did you do...?"

"I... I fucked up," I breathed, my heart breaking inside my chest. "I'm so fucking sorry, baby. I fucked up..." I paused, and my head dropped into my hands. "I... we... Ryan and I... we were together..."

I took another breath, trying to calm down. I wasn't making any sense. I needed to get ahold of myself.

"Together...?" she asked, her voice soft and high. I nodded slowly. My face still covered by my sweaty palms. "Like, as in... what? *Together* doing what?" She ripped my hands away from my face. "Ben, tell me exactly what the fuck happened!"

"I slept with him!" I huffed through my gravelly voice. Jess gasped, her face paralyzed in pain, as if I had just slapped her. "We... had sex."

The room was filled with stifling silence. It was so quiet it was physically painful. I just wanted to her say *something.* Scream at me or hit me... Anything. The silence was making me suicidal.

"How..." Jess finally let out a breathless squeal. "How did this happen?"

I shrugged and shook my head. I didn't want to tell her anymore. I just wanted to leave it at that and never talk to her about it again. This conversation was destroying me, and it hadn't even gotten started yet.

"Ben..." she murmured, moving her face in front of mine, forcing me to look into her eyes. "You slept with our daughter's ex-boyfriend tonight. There are so many questions... I can't even... Jesus fucking Christ. Start fucking talking before I leave you here and never come back."

At mere mention of her leaving, my heart lurched in my chest and I started shaking more.

"No... please don't," I shook my head over and over. "It's just... I don't even know where to begin."

"How about begin with how the *fuck* this even happened!" she shouted at me, her voice cracking.

"It started... the night after Thanksgiving..." I rumbled, running my hand through my hair.

"What the fuck?! Are you fucking kidding me??" she cried, leaping out of the bed like it was on fire.

"Where are you going?" I scrambled onto my knees on the bed, ready to tackle her if she tried to leave.

"Benjamin Michael Lockwood!" she gasped, full-naming the shit out of me. I cringed. "You're telling me you *had sex* with our daughter's *boyfriend* while they were staying in our house?! How could you do that? To her... To me?!"

She was up and pacing around the bedroom. I watched her, wracking my brain with potential ways to fix this, but I kept coming up blank. There was absolutely nothing I could say or do to save this situation. I just needed to tell her the truth and pray to God she would forgive me.

"I'm sorry..." I whispered, and she turned to face me, her nostrils flaring, eyes filled with flames of hatred. *Wrong answer.* I knew she was going to attack me before she even moved, so I just braced myself for the impending beat-down.

Jessica stalked over to me and climbed back onto the bed, pushing me until I fell backward. She jumped on top of me, knocking the wind out of me with her knee in my stomach, then pinned me down to the bed and started slapping and punching me all over, grumbling and cursing my name repeatedly.

"You. Are. Such. A. Fucking. Selfish. Piece. Of. Shit. You. Asshole!"

The rest was all *fuck yous* and *I hate you* and *bastard asshole monster* so-on and so-forth. I just tried to cover my face with my arms and fend her off.

"Jess, please!" I growled, finally grabbing her by the arms and holding her up on top of me while she heaved and shook out of anger. "I know I fucked up! I'm sorry, okay?! Nothing I can say or do will take back what happened... Just let me explain."

"What is there to explain?" she grunted, ripping her hands out of my grip. "You cheated on me. You *broke* our wedding vows... And with a fucking *guy*?! So what... are you gay now??"

"No..." I scoffed, shaking my head. "I'm not *gay*. I love you, Jessica. I still love you and I want to be with you forever. I told you that will never change."

"Then why..." she whimpered, her voice coming in and out while she sniffled. I could see her trying to blink back the tears, which was crushing me down to my soul. "Why would you cheat?"

"I don't know, baby..." I answered, holding onto her waist while she sat on top of me.

"Don't fucking *baby* me, Benjamin," she snarled. "You fucked up. You fucked up so fucking bad I can't even look at you right now!"

"Well, you have to look at me," I commanded, blinking up at her. "I'm your husband, and I'm here trying to tell you about how bad I fucked up, and how sorry I am. I'm not letting you give up on us."

"Ben, I would never give up on us," she said, the softness in her voice smashing my heart to pieces. "You're my forever... I just don't know why you would do this. Are you... sick of me or something?"

"No! What? Why would you even say that?" I grumbled.

"Um, because you're telling me you've been fucking our daughter's twenty-one-year-old boyfriend!" she hissed. "Obviously you must have been looking for something else... God, I'm so stupid."

"Stop that," I seethed, gripping her flesh tight. "This is so *not* your fault, at all. I promise you, I wasn't out looking for anything. I didn't plan this... It just... happened."

"It just happened?" she sneered, rolling her eyes. "You mean you tripped and fell onto his dick?"

"Jessica, please," I shook my head. "I never in a million years would have predicted this. I never thought I would ever..." My voice trailed off, and I breathed out hard, closing my eyes.

"Our daughter's boyfriend..." she muttered in a disapproving tone. "Did they break up because of you, Ben? Was this your doing?"

"No," I answered quick. "That was the reason I saw him tonight... I had to ask him. I had to know if it was my fault. But what Hailey told us was right. It was mutual, and Ryan says it's for the best."

She scoffed and rolled her eyes again. "So is *Ryan* like your boyfriend now?"

"Jess, I don't have a boyfriend," I tried to assure her with my gentle tone. "I only have a wife, and I love her."

"But you weren't thinking about your wife when you were sleeping with a guy..." she glared at me, her deep blue eyes shooting daggers at me.

"Of course I thought about you..." I whispered, the knot of guilt settling in my stomach. "I thought about how much I was betraying you, and how much this could hurt you... I never wanted that, Jess."

"Then why would you do it?" she whimpered as a tear rolled down her cheek. "If you wanted to experiment, I'm game, you know that. Just be honest with me. This is a marriage, Ben. If we can't communicate, it'll never work. I always thought we had the most open, honest relationship of anyone I've ever known. But now... you're making me question whether I really know you at all."

My heart felt like it was being stabbed repeatedly with a jagged knife. *Jesus, this hurts so bad. Why the fuck did I do this to her? Maybe she should just leave me...*

No. I can't accept that. I love her too much to let her go. I will fight for this woman until the day I die.

"Jessica, don't say that," I pleaded. "You know me. Of course you do. This was such a... fucked up situation. It made no sense. It just came out of nowhere, like I was hit by a fucking Mack truck or something. One day I'm just living my life, everything normal... and the next thing I know my whole world is upside down."

My wife stared at me for what felt like an eternity, saying nothing. Just sitting on top of me, her hands resting flat on my chest while she straddled my waist. She glanced down at her hand for a moment, I'm guessing because she could feel how hard my heart was beating. She pressed her palm down harder over my pulse, her eyes coming back up to mine.

"How did it happen?" she asked, her voice switching to less angry, and more curious.

"I don't even know, babe..." I rasped, still shaking my head. "I wish I had an answer for you."

"But like... how did it start?" she mewled softly, gaping at me with wide eyes. "Did he... kiss you or something?"

I blinked a few times, gazing up at her in confusion. Did she really want me to give her the details? Would it just make her angrier? Or could it help her understand...?

"No..." I answered quietly.

"Tell me... please," she whispered. "I need to know."

I swallowed hard. "He... came down to the basement. The night after Thanksgiving. We were drinking and the next thing I knew he was..." I paused and cringed, praying that she wouldn't make me continue.

Much to my surprise, she didn't look as stunned as she had before. And she didn't appear disgusted or creeped out.

She looked fascinated.

Jess raised her brows, silently telling me to keep going, though I was still hesitating.

"You know... like..." I stuttered, giving her a look, trying to get her to read my mind, so I didn't have to say it out loud.

"He was what, Ben...?" she asked again, standing her ground. I sighed and blinked.

"Sucking my dick," I grunted, swallowing hard again.

I heard her gasp quietly, then she bit her lip. "Did you...?"

I nodded slowly, and her eyes widened.

"How many times were you two together... in our house?" she asked, her quivering voice sounding rather throaty.

"The whole time you guys were out shopping..." I told her, feeling a wave of guilt wash over me. "And that night..."

"So you fooled around with me and then left to go be with him...?" she asked, blinking at me.

I nodded again. "Only because I knew he was leaving..."

"Wow, Ben..." she shook her head. "I don't even know what to say..."

"Just say you forgive me," I begged with my voice and my eyes. I took her hand in mine and squeezed it. "Tell me you still love me..."

She breathed out hard and collapsed, curling up on top of me, resting her head on my chest. The room was silent again while we just laid there, listening to each other breathe.

"Do you love him?" she asked quietly.

I froze and waited to see if my initial answer changed the more I fought against it. But it didn't. My stomach clenched, and I bit the inside of my cheek.

"I don't know..." I whispered. "I love you."

"I love you too, Ben..." she hummed. "This is just... too much."

"I'm sorry..."

"I know."

We laid there for hours. Jess fell asleep first, and when I could see the light streaming in the windows from the rising sun, I finally drifted into an uneasy sleep, clutching onto my wife as hard as I could.

My eyes slowly crept open. I blinked a few times, pushing past my grogginess as I flipped over on my back, stretching out my arms. I felt like I'd been through some kind of marathon, and my brain was aching as much as my body.

I rolled onto my side to check the massive hotel bed for my sleeping wife. But she wasn't there.

Memories of last night came flooding back to my now fully awakened mind.

Ryan... his house... us together...

Jessica. She knows. She knows everything.

I shot up fast, looking frantically around the room. She was nowhere in sight.

I jumped out of the bed, stumbling to my feet as I darted all over the suite, panic spreading through me like wildfire.

I checked the bathroom, the living room, kitchen, and finally the balcony. She was gone.

My heart started beating faster and faster, dread rising from my stomach like bile.

She left me. She left.

I grabbed my phone and started calling her, praying that I could somehow convince her to change her mind and come back to me.

I heard a phone ringing. It was coming from the kitchen.

I followed the ringtone, and my phone dropped away from my ear, slipping out of my hand and onto the floor.

Jess's phone was sitting on the counter. She left it there.

She left her phone... Why?

I meandered back into the bedroom, noting the fact that all her things were still there. It gave me slight peace of mind. She wouldn't have left without her things, and her phone...

I called down to the valet stand to ask if our car was still here. The manager informed me that Mrs. Lockwood had taken the car about an hour ago.

I gulped and hung up, saying nothing else, plopping down onto the couch.

My wife left me in our hotel suite, and took the car, but not her phone. That probably meant that she didn't want me to contact her... *But why? Where would she go?* I took a deep breath and tried to relax. She probably just needed some space to think. She would be back. She had to.

I leaned back on the couch, resting my head as I stared up at the ceiling. My entire life was coming crashing down around me. I needed to stay strong and try to hold it together, but the truth was that I had never felt more scared and alone.

You wanted this.

I cringed and closed my eyes, praying for my wife to forgive me and come back.

CHAPTER 10

Ryan

I WOKE UP FEELING LIKE SOMETHING TERRIBLE HAD HAPPENED. I wasn't exactly sure why. I had slept pretty well last night. After I dropped Ben off at his hotel, I came home and passed out the second I hit my mattress. I guess all the activities had really worn me out.

I still could barely comprehend everything that happened last night. It was almost insane that I had gone from completely miserable to utterly blissful in just a matter of minutes.

Even though the break-up between Hailey and I had been mutual, it still hurt like a bitch. Sure, I had gone to dinner that night last week knowing in my heart that I had to end it. But when she told me she thought we should see other people and live our lives while we were young, I couldn't help but feel like I was being stabbed in the heart.

I knew it was selfish and immature, and some macho guy thing, but I couldn't help it. It was a different story when I was the one ending it. But when I found out she wanted it too, I really felt the sting of pain. Like rubbing salt in a wound.

Still, we handled it like adults. We said we would remain friends, and she came over the next day so we could exchange stuff. She gave me back all my clothes she had been hoarding, and I gave her back the keys to her place. It was sort of heartbreaking, and I wouldn't admit it to anyone, but I stayed in my room all day after that listening to break-up songs and deleting pictures of her off my phone.

It was stupid. I had wanted it, too. We couldn't be together, not after what happened with Ben. But I still had to respect the process.

I moped around for the rest of the week, losing myself in school and the gym, trying to keep up my routine. Boredom was the enemy. But still every night I felt more and more lonely. I had even contemplated calling Tate, but thankfully I had talked myself out of it. That wasn't what I wanted... Or rather, he wasn't *who* I wanted.

Saturday was rough, because I knew all day that Ben was coming to town for the birthday dinner that I was supposed to attend. It was like work actively trying to keep myself from driving over to the restaurant where they were just so I could watch them from outside like some kind of pathetic ex stalker dude. I was able to talk myself out of doing that, too. Instead, I forced myself to stay at home and watch movies with Alec and Kayla, third-wheeling it up and really wallowing in self-pity.

Until Ben messaged me.

I had tried hard to resist that one more than anything else. I wanted so badly not to respond to him, and just be the bigger person. But even over Instagram DM's the guy was so demanding and irresistible. I didn't stand a chance.

And now that I thought back on it, I was almost giddy. Last night was one of the best nights I'd ever had. Not only because of the sex, but because of what we'd said to each other.

What we admitted to each other.

I had no idea what would happen with Ben and I in the future. And I knew for a fact it would probably get really rough and completely fuck with all of our lives. But I couldn't deny the fact that I was starting to like him more than I'd liked anyone else in a long time. It was scary as fuck, but exciting and real. Our connection was so powerful. I would have had to be someone much stronger than I was to resist it.

My doorbell rang, and I sighed out hard, pulling myself off the couch. I was home alone at the moment. Alec and Kayla were out grocery shopping for the week; their Sunday afternoon ritual. Hailey and I used to tag along from time to time, like the grocery store was a fun place to double-date. I guess everything is fun when you're in an actual relationship that doesn't have to be hidden from the world due to infidelity and the general awkwardness of how it came to be...

I stalked over to the door, expecting an Amazon delivery, since Kayla was addicted to online shopping. I opened the door fast, and my heart stopped beating.

"Hi, Ryan..." Jessica Lockwood greeted me in her usual soft, sweet tone, though her face was missing the smile I was used to seeing there.

"Jess... er... Mrs. Lockwood..." I grunted, my eyes wide and unblinking. "Hi."

"Sorry to just show up like this..." she murmured as she glanced at the ground, playing with her blonde hair. "Can I come in for a minute?"

"Uh... yea," I nodded, unable to stop my voice from sputtering a little. "Sure. Of course."

I stepped out of the way, motioning for her to come inside, quickly peeking behind her to see if I spotted Ben anywhere. I didn't, so I closed the door.

Jessica was looking around my apartment, checking the place out, as if she was investigating for clues or something. I walked toward the living room, trying to guide her that way. My heart was beating so fast I could hear it, and my palms were sweating.

Oh my God... What is she doing here? What the hell... I'm freaking out. Whatever this is, it can't be good.

"Would you... like something to drink?" I offered, trying to be a nice, polite host, and distract myself from the fact that last night I fucked her husband less than fifteen feet from where she was standing. "I have juice, coffee, tea, water..." My voice trailed off.

"Um, no thank you," she gave me a curt smile and sat down on the couch.

I nodded awkwardly and sat down in the love seat, adjacent to where she was sitting. I sat up straight and folded my hands on my lap in an attempt to appear as normal as possible, when really I could feel the secret radiating from my entire body like a pheromone.

Jessica stared at me for a moment, her eyes bright and inquisitive. She was looking at me like she was studying me and it was making me even more paranoid than I already was. *Just act normal. You can do this. She doesn't know anything. Just relax.*

"So... to what do I owe the pleasure?" I asked, going for casual and upbeat, but in my mind I just sounded like a fucking weirdo. A *guilty* fucking weirdo.

She took a deep breath and glanced down at her lap for a moment. I swallowed hard over the bile trying to rise from my stomach.

"Ryan..." she whispered my name, her eyes slowly coming back up to mine. They were so blue, but a darker shade than Ben's. Her eyes looked more like Hailey's. Actually, she looked so much like Hailey it was a little alarming.

I waited for her to continue but unfortunately, she said nothing else. So I replied, "Yes?"

"I know this is... kind of strange..." she breathed, her forehead lined with unease. "It's actually just... so fucking bizarre..." She paused and exhaled a shaky breath.

I didn't understand what was going on, but I was fairly certain I was going to pass out.

"What is...?" I asked, my chest heaving up and down with my rapid breaths.

"I know," she whispered, tilting her head to the side.

Oh, God... "Know... what?" I swallowed hard again.

"About you and Ben," she spoke in a soft, timid voice.

The world stopped spinning and my whole body broke into a cold sweat. I didn't know what to say or do, so I just stared back at her with my mouth hanging open.

"He told me last night..." she went on, fiddling with her rings on her left hand. "After... I kind of found out something was up..." she huffed and shook her head. "It's a long story, but regardless, he finally told me the truth. So... I know."

I shook my head slowly, unable to form thoughts let alone words to speak. I felt like I could vomit.

"Ryan..." she said my name in a pleading tone, looking at me like she wanted me to say something to comfort her, but there was no way

I could do that. *I* was responsible for her current state of angst. I couldn't fix it. It was my fault.

"Jessica... I am *so* sorry," I whimpered, closing my eyes and covering my face with my hands. "Jesus Christ... I'm so sorry. I don't know what I was thinking." Words started spewing from my mouth and I couldn't stop them. "I just... it just... happened. And then there was no taking it back. But I wish I could because I would never want to hurt you... You're such an amazing woman. You were so nice to me that weekend, and I just... I fucked it all up. I'm so sorry... Please forgive me..."

I exhaled a hard breath, trying to correct my breathing before I had a panic attack. Then I felt the couch shift next to me, and I opened my eyes, turning to see Jessica sitting by my side with a look of sympathy on her beautiful face.

She reached out and brushed my hair back with her fingers. "Shh... it's okay, Ryan. Just breathe. It'll be alright."

I nodded quick and tried to breathe, my heart jumping against my ribcage. She wrapped her arms around my waist and hugged onto me, resting her head on my shoulder, rocking me slightly, trying to calm me down.

"You really have no idea how sorry I am..." I rasped, shaking my head.

She took my hand in hers. It was so soft and small, and delicate. It was comforting. Really everything about her was. She had such a calming presence.

"I know you're sorry for hurting me, Ryan..." she breathed. "But you're not sorry for what happened. And neither is Ben."

My head popped up, and I gaped at her.

"Look, I don't know anything about what's been going on between you guys... other than the very few details I got out of Ben last night," she spoke, calmly and rationally. Her voice was so soothing, like honey or smooth jazz. "But I know my husband. And I know that he loves me with all of his heart."

I nodded. "He does."

"So for him to do something like this... outside of our marriage... It must be pretty overpowering." She gazed up at me, holding my hand tightly in hers. Our fingers instinctively threaded together, and it reminded me of how Ben and I always held hands.

I blinked a few times at her.

"So... Where do we go from here?" she asked, her eyes locked on mine.

I paused. "Does... Ben know you're here?"

She shook her head in response, and I swallowed hard over my increasingly dry throat.

"I just think... maybe you should talk it out some more," I grumbled, shrugging and breaking our intense eye contact. "I think you guys can talk through anything. You're like, the most amazing couple..."

"Ryan..." she sighed my name, slightly patronizing, but also warm and nurturing. "I don't want you to feel guilty. And I don't want you to hurt. You're a great guy. Hailey only had the best things to say about you, even after the break-up."

"I just... don't know what to do with myself anymore," my head fell forward in my free hand as I rubbed my eyes. "I feel like I just keep making the worst possible decisions."

Jessica wrapped her arms around me again, even tighter this time. I could feel her breasts pressing into my side, and I forced my brain not to acknowledge how good it felt. She moved her face in closer to mine as her soft, warm breath tickled my neck. My heart was beating so hard, I was afraid she could feel it.

Her lips touched my neck, so gently, it was like a butterfly had landed on me or something. I bit my lip and squeezed my eyes shut. *Jesus, what am I doing...?*

"Don't worry about it, Ryan," she whispered, close to my ear, making me warm everywhere. "Just give us a little time... Just let me think for a bit. We'll figure something out."

My pulse was racing. Before I could turn to look at her again, she was standing up and walking toward the door. I wanted to call out to her; to ask her what she meant, or what she wanted me to do. But she was already gone.

I huffed out hard, listening to the sound of her car leaving my driveway, while I sat there in stunned silence. I had absolutely no idea what had just happened. All I knew was that I was breathless, and for some reason, unbeknownst to me, I had a painfully stiff erection. I glanced down at my dick and shook my head. What the hell was wrong with me? Honestly, it was like I had no clue who I was anymore. I had spent the last two weeks of my life fucking guys, when before that point I had considered myself to be a fully straight man. And now, I was sitting here, rocking a confusing hard-on, courtesy of the wife of my potential-boyfriend-fuck-buddy-whatever-you-call-him. Seriously, were my mind and body that fucked up? All Jessica did was hold my hand and hug me a little... And kiss my neck.

But still, it wasn't sexual. *Was it?*

I shook my head and reached for my phone on the coffee table. I needed to message Ben and let him know what happened. He deserved to know that she came by.

I pulled up my Instagram DM's and selected Ben. I was just about to type out a message, but I stopped myself.

Jessica had said that Ben didn't know she was here. That meant that she didn't tell him on purpose, because she didn't want to. And that was her prerogative. It definitely wasn't my place to blow up her spot like that. She would talk to Ben when she was ready, and when she did, it would be between the two of them. I had nothing to do with their business. I wasn't a part of their relationship. I was just the other man... *The home-wrecker.*

I growled out of frustration and stood up, pacing around the living room. My life was becoming more and more complicated every day. The visit from Jessica was another mind-fuck to add to the nice little collection I was gathering. She came over to tell me she'd found out about me fucking her husband, and yet she didn't really seem all that pissed off. Actually, she didn't seem upset at all. Maybe a little confused, but that was to be expected. Shit, I was confused as fuck, and I'd been living with this shit for two weeks.

Still, I would expect a woman who found out her husband had been cheating to be a bit more... put-off. I had seen those *Cheaters* shows before. Usually the chick would run up and smack a bitch in the face; the *bitch* in this case being me. But Jessica came here and ended up hugging me.

Maybe she had already kicked the shit out of Ben last night. Maybe she stabbed him... Maybe she had him tied up somewhere and was going to murder him and bury his body in the dessert.

Okay, dial back the crazy, bro.

There was absolutely no way that Jessica Lockwood would ever do anything like that. She was one of the kindest people I had ever met. She was sweet and joyful and loving. Just like Hailey. That must have been where Hailey got it from. Plus, she was clearly dedicated to her husband, and their marriage. I had admired the chemistry between her and Ben when I first met them. I remembered thinking it was what I wanted to have someday.

It had honestly made me a little jealous. I mean, sure, Hailey and I had great chemistry. But it was more like a friendly, playful kind of new-relationship interaction. It was the kind of teasing flirtations you'd see in high school students. We were like kids playing house.

But Ben and Jessica, on the other hand... They had a real, strong, meaningful relationship. I imagined that having a baby together before your eighteenth birthday would do that to you. It allowed them to form this unshakable bond together. They were connected by something so deep, it was a part of them. Just thinking about it set a longing in my chest.

Jessica Lockwood was so dedicated to her man that she didn't react with anger or jealousy when learning about his infidelities. Instead, she came over here to talk to me, and ended up comforting *me* about the affair.

Oh, God... Is that really what it was? An affair?? I hate that word. It sounds so dirty and sordid. Although, I suppose that's exactly how it was. At least, that's how it started.

Ben's wife had every right to be angry and hurt. But she just didn't seem like she was. I couldn't put my finger on exactly what was off about our conversation, but more than anything it seemed like she was accepting, and slightly curious.

And what the hell did she mean by that whole "let me think", "we'll figure something out" thing?? Figure what out? What did she need to think about?

My mind was racing with the need for information. I just prayed that she wasn't thinking about leaving Ben. If the thing she needed to *figure out* had anything to do with divorcing him, I'm sure I would throw myself off a bridge out of guilt.

Suddenly the front door flew open and Alec and Kayla came stomping inside, carrying bags of groceries. I stowed my worrisome thoughts and tossed my phone down on the couch.

"Oh, hey!" Alec grunted in my direction, bringing everything to the kitchen. "Look who's up."

"You missed some killer grocery shopping," Kayla smirked, following behind Alec, setting bags down on the counter. "Avocados three for five bucks! *And* a sale on Cinnamon Toast Crunch."

"Sounds thrilling," I teased, jaunting over to the door. "More bags for me to bring in?"

"Yes, please," they both answered at the same time, and I was already out the door.

I grabbed the rest of the bags from Alec's car, fumbling to carry all eight of them, so as not to have to make a second trip. I brought everything inside the house, dumping them all on the kitchen floor while Alec and Kayla were already putting stuff away.

"You know, just because you and Hailey broke up, it doesn't mean you're not allowed to come shopping with us anymore," Kayla said, stocking the freezer with ice cream, frozen burgers and, my personal favorite, Hot Pockets.

"Kale, as much as I love listening to you guys bicker over whether to get whole milk or two percent, I hardly think it makes sense for me to tag along with you for couple activities," I grumbled, leaning against the counter. "It's bad enough I live with a couple now that I'm single again. I'm not going to be a third-wheel, always hanging around, butting in on your time together."

"Don't be such a tool, man," Alec grinned, handing Kayla things while she stuffed them into drawers in the fridge. "We don't see you as a third-wheel. You're my best friend, and we love you."

"Yea, there's a difference between us all hanging out together and you latching onto our relationship," Kayla pointed out. "I mean, let's be clear. I'm not asking you to date us or anything." She giggled which made me smile. "But of course you can still do errands with us. Especially because you live here too... And you can afford the good cheese."

"Babe, there is literally no difference between Kraft and the store brand," Alec huffed, and Kayla rolled her eyes.

"Oh boy, here we go again..." she muttered, and I laughed out loud.

"I'm just saying, you're paying for a label," he kept on. Kayla and I shared a look, both of us snickering at his expense.

The three of us continued putting the groceries away, laughing and joking about various food-related topics. As much as I always tried to resist feeling like a third-wheel, they were my best friends and I loved hanging out with them. Plus, the light-hearted nature of our friendship was working to take my mind off the chaos happening in my life.

That is, until Alec brought up a new topic.

"So, I heard you had a friend over last night," he said while getting all the ingredients together for lunch. Kayla elbowed him in the side and shot him a look.

I narrowed my gaze at them. "Yea... I went out for a few with my friend Ben..." I was trying my absolute hardest to sound and act normal, like I was talking about an actual friend, not a dude I was secretly banging. I kept my eyes focused on the breakfast bar, flipping through one of those grocery store coupon booklets, as if I really cared how much I could potentially save on four two-liters of Pepsi.

"Hm. That's cool," Alec said, his tone unreadable. I refused to look up at his face for fear that he might instantly know I was lying. "I've never heard of any *Ben* before. Is he a new friend?"

"Yup," I nodded as my heart rate spiked.

"Well, Kayla here seems to find him rather swoony," he hummed, and I finally glanced up, watching him give her a teasing look. She rolled her eyes, dutifully arranging slices of cheese on slices of bread for our grilled cheese sandwiches. "She blushes every time she thinks about him."

"Oh my God, I do not!" she squealed in defense, though her cheeks were suddenly reddening up a storm. "Jealous much?"

"I'm not at all jealous of Ry-bear's new *friend*," Alec rumbled at her, then stuck his tongue out.

"Why did you say it like that?" I asked, furrowing my brow at them. "He *is* my friend. I just met him a couple weeks ago, and... we hung out last night. It's no big deal."

"Oh yea. We know *all* about the *deal*," Alec snickered, and Kayla's eyes widened at him, making another face.

"What the hell are you talking about?" I sighed, trying to remain calm and aloof when in actuality my stomach was twisting, and I had to stow my guilt by tapping my foot rapidly against the chair.

"Ryan..." Alec turned to face me, leaning on his elbows on the breakfast bar. "It's totally cool if you brought a *friend* over to *get busy* last night. You know me... I don't judge."

My heart started hammering in my chest and I felt a cold sweat break out all over my body.

"Babe... leave him alone," Kayla whispered, shooting a quick worrisome look at me.

"What do you mean...? I have no idea what you're talking about..." I gulped. Now my whole leg was bouncing under the table.

"Dude, we share a bedroom wall," Alec said, his eyes lit up with amusement. "You weren't exactly being quiet."

"Jesus fucking Christ..." I breathed, dropping my head into my hands so I could rub my temples. My face and neck were burning up and I could feel a swift, unshakable migraine coming on. I couldn't actually believe this was happening. I felt like I was in some kind of nightmare.

"Ryan, it's fine," Kayla jumped in, sounding supportive and sweet, which just made me want to blow my brains out even more. "You know we don't care who you see... We just love you. No matter what, right babe?" I heard Alec grunt which meant she must have elbowed him again.

Holy fucking shit... What is wrong with my life? Can't I just catch a break for one fucking day?!

"Of course. Shit, he knows that," Alec rasped. "I'm sorry, bro. I'm just messing with you. You're single now. Do you. You're my best friend on Earth. Like I said, I don't judge."

"Yea... And I mean... he is *really* fucking hot," Kayla murmured, and this time Alec elbowed her. "What?! I'm just saying... It's almost unbelievable how hot he is..."

"He's Hailey's dad..." I mumbled under my breath, my hands

running through my hair in severe angst.

Might as well tell them... This secret is starting to seriously fuck with me. Plus, they're my best friends. I know they won't judge or tell anyone.

"What?" Alec gasped, sounding thoroughly shocked.

"Oh my God..." Kayla shrieked. "Ryan! Are you serious?" I nodded slowly, still too ashamed to look at them. My face was so red I could feel it. I might have been breaking out into stress-hives.

"Bro... tell me you're fucking with us," Alec pleaded.

I finally lifted my face enough to see them gawking at me, fully stunned.

"Do I look like I'm fucking with you?" I sighed out of anguish. My temples were officially throbbing.

"Well, that explains why he looks like he's in his thirties..." Kayla broke the silence first.

"Kayla... Jesus. Enough drooling over the guy," Alec scolded her. "He's Hailey's *dad.*"

"Ryan... How did this happen?" Kayla asked me, ignoring her boyfriend, who clearly was getting a little jealous.

"I still don't even really know..." I huffed, swallowing hard. "I was there for Thanksgiving. Everything seemed normal, at first. He was just your typical, overprotective, scary dad. I mean, he's *gorgeous*, but still. That didn't mean anything. I was just there for Hailey and it was all going fine. Then, I don't know, something just flipped. I started looking at him differently and the next thing I know, we were hooking up and I just couldn't fucking stand not being near him."

I stopped and took a breath, shaking my head slowly. "You guys know me... I've always been strictly into girls. I love them, for fuck's sake. Maybe a little too much... Until I met Ben, I was so comfortable with who I was. Never a doubt in my mind. And then, he comes along... and the whole planet just shifts on its axis. Now I think about him constantly... What's he doing? What's he thinking? Is he happy? Is he thinking about me?" I dropped my head onto the table. "It's exhausting feeling like this."

The room was quiet for a few minutes while I rested my forehead on the cool marble of the breakfast bar, questioning reality and my entire existence. I didn't understand how it had come to this, but I was in way over my head, and there was no digging myself out.

I think I'm falling for him...

"Wow, Ry..." Alec whispered. "I'm so sorry you're going through this. I wish you would've told me sooner."

"I couldn't," I grunted. "This is my mess, and I have to deal with it on my own."

Suddenly, I felt arms wrapping around me. Kayla's first, and then Alec's. They group hugged onto me hard, and I chuckled softly because if I didn't I would burst into tears.

"We're here for you," Kayla squeaked, kissing my cheek. "Always. No matter what."

"Yea, bro," Alec added. "Besties for life."

"Thanks, guys," I sighed, fighting against the tears that wanted to push from behind my eyes. "I love you both."

"We love you, too," they said in unison, which made me laugh again.

When they finally peeled off me, I felt better. It was a huge weight off my shoulders, having finally told someone what was going on. I hadn't realized how much it was weighing on me. Now that Jessica knew, and my friends, the reality was becoming slightly easier to bear.

However, it was also now one-hundred percent real, which was a staggering thought.

"Let me make you some lunch," Kayla hummed in an almost motherly way. "Grilled cheese is my Ry-bear's favorite."

I smiled at her, the first genuine smile I'd given anyone since I dropped Ben off last night.

"So, what are you gonna do?" Alec asked, his face still serious as he sat down next to me.

"I'm not sure," I shrugged, chewing on my lower lip. "His wife knows. She found out last night."

"Really?!" Kayla shrilled, dropping the pan hard against the stove.

"Yea... She came by right before you guys got back," I told them, the memory of Jess being here still fresh in my mind.

"And you're still alive... I would say that's a good sign," Alec almost grinned.

"She actually wasn't nearly as upset as you would think," I murmured, feeling fidgety again. "She doesn't hate me... She didn't scream at me, or cry, or call me names. It was almost like she was sympathizing with me. Like, she knows how much of a force her husband is, and she understands what I'm going through..." My voice trailed off and I shook my head. "Whatever. It doesn't make any sense."

"So they're staying together, then...?" Alec asked, looking slightly bummed for me. "Are you gonna be okay with that?"

"Yea... I have to be," I grumbled, feeling a wave of fatigue wash over me. "I don't really have a choice."

"Well, you never know," Kayla chirped in an optimistic tone. "I think it will all work out."

"Thanks, Kale," I muttered, forcing a smile at her back while she fried up some grilled cheese sandwiches.

When they were done, we all sat down to eat together. I was hungry, but at the same time the mere act of eating seemed impossible. It was very frustrating.

"Hey, you know what would go good with these grilled cheeses?" Alec said, noting the dismal look on my face, jumping up from his seat. I slowly lifted my chin to see what he was doing. He reached into one of the cabinets and pulled out a bottle. "Tequila."

CHAPTER 11

Ben

I WAS SITTING OUTSIDE ON THE BALCONY OF THE HOTEL SUITE, staring at the surface of the table which was now covered in five little empty bottles. I had killed one nip of each kind of liquor in the mini bar; one for every hour that had gone by since my wife left me.

We were supposed to check out of the hotel and go home today. But since I woke up to Jessica having taken off, with my car, it became clear that we weren't making it for the extended noon check-out time. So I had to plead with them to give us another night. Thankfully, most people checked out on Sundays, so the room was available... For the last-minute price of eight-hundred dollars a night.

I had been worrying myself sick for the past five hours, wondering where the hell my wife was, if she was okay, praying that she would eventually come back to me. The alcohol was the only thing keeping me from throwing myself off the damn balcony.

I had briefly considered going out to look for her. But without a car, and limited knowledge of the area, I wasn't sure exactly where or how to even go about looking. I thought about calling Hailey, but the last thing I wanted was to explain to her that her mother had walked out on me without her phone. Then I thought about calling Ryan but dismissed that idea fast. I couldn't drag him into this. I had already fucked with his life enough. The best thing for him would be to forget about me and move on.

I was like a tornado, or cancer. Wreaking havoc on everyone and everything that crossed my path. I had seriously never felt lower in my entire life. I just wanted to go to sleep and never wake up.

Suddenly I heard a noise. The sound of the hotel room door opening and closing.

I jumped up fast, stumbling to my feet, the alcohol swimming through my bloodstream making me dizzy as I wobbled, staggering back inside. I dashed through the living room and saw Jessica, kicking off her shoes and making her way over to the minibar. She didn't look at me, completely disregarding my presence while I stood there looking dumbfounded.

I was so relieved that she was back in one piece. Even though she was clearly still upset with me, I felt a weight off my shoulders as my worries about her being in danger faded. She looked so small and sweet and delicate, I just wanted to wrap her up in my arms and beg her to never leave me again.

Jessica grabbed a bottle of water from inside the fridge, opening it and taking a long sip. The silence in the room was excruciating, the air thick and heavy with tension. Most of it was coming from me, because Jessica seemed fine. Just thirsty.

She finished her bottle of water and finally turned to face me, her eyes sliding over me quickly before landing on mine. My forehead creased so hard, I was giving myself a headache. I couldn't stand it anymore. I needed to talk to her. We needed to talk through this... To figure it all out. Together.

I slowly stepped up to my wife, fearing that she would run away from me. Fortunately, she didn't. She stayed standing there, stock still, while I moved in closer, gazing down at her with wide eyes. My chest was heaving, and I reached out to touch her, almost expecting her to flinch. Of course she didn't. So I ran my fingers along her cheek, savoring the soft, warm feeling of her flesh.

She simply stared up at me, chewing on her lower lip, her eyes seeking out something in me that I just couldn't comprehend. My patience finally ran dry, and I grabbed her by the nape of her neck in one hand, the other taking her by the waist as I pulled her into me. She collapsed against my body, wrapping her arms around my waist, hugging onto me tight as I held her just as hard. I buried her face in my chest, trying so hard not to suffocate her, while I kissed her hair over and over, breathing in her scent and letting it calm me down, like it always did.

Jess whimpered in my arms, and I could tell she was crying because she was trembling, and her tears were soaking through my t-shirt. My heart was being ripped to shreds as I held her, rocking her gently, and whispering to ease her pain.

"Shhh... baby, it's okay," my lips moved in her hair, by her ear, my eyes squeezing shut tight. "I'm here. I have you, and I will never ever *ever* let you go... I promise you, Jessica, I will breathe my last breath on this Earth loving you with every single bit of myself."

"Ben... I'm s-sorry I left..." she sniffled, her whole body shivering against mine.

"Baby, please don't apologize to me," I grumbled, pulling her face back and holding it in my hands while I kissed her tear-stained cheeks. "You have *nothing* to be sorry for. I'm the asshole here, not you. I love you so much, Jess... God, I just... I'm so sorry. I love you..."

I trailed my lips down her jaw, whispering my apologies on every surface of her while she gripped my back, squeezing onto me. Her hands slid around to my front, then she dragged her nails across my abs, which made my dick twitch.

The air between us was now stiflingly hot, and I was panting, kissing her jaw and her neck and her face. And then her lips. Soft, gentle, but urgent. She purred, parting her lips enough for me to suck on them.

"Fuck... Jess... I'm sorry, baby..." I grunted, my right hand slipping down to her butt as I gripped it hard, pulling her into me as close as possible. "You're so goddamned perfect. I fucking love you..."

"Ben..." she mewled, grinding her tight little body against mine, pressing her breasts onto my chest. "I don't even know... I'm so confused..."

"Me too..." I breathed, sliding my tongue between her lips, touching hers gently, which made her whimper into my mouth. "Everything is so fucked up... But you're the only thing that holds it all together. I need you, baby."

"I need you too, Ben," she told me, her hand gliding down to my crotch. "I need you now."

"Now?" I asked hesitantly, unsure of whether she really wanted to get physical with me after everything that had happened.

"Yes. Right fucking now," she murmured and tugged my lower lip between her teeth.

"Fuck..." I rasped, my cock throbbing against my thigh.

I lifted her up quick, holding her by the ass as I carried her quickly to the bedroom, all the while with her lips teasing my neck and jaw. Once we were there, we both became frantic. I tossed her down on the bed, crawling on top of her and yanking her shirt off, then my own. I slid her pants off fast, with her panties, then rid myself of mine, moving in between her parted thighs.

We kept kissing, hard, our lips raw as our warmed flesh melded together and I dragged my rock-hard cock through her wetness. Our movements were desperate, hands everywhere, touching, feeling one another, our bodies grinding together in the purest passion. I had no idea what we were doing, or how this would solve anything, but it was just so *necessary*. I wanted to make love to my wife and prove to her that I would always need her.

I wanted her to feel how much I loved her; I wanted to make her come a thousand times to make up for ever making her think I didn't.

I reached my hand between our writhing bodies, gliding my fingers through her arousal. She moaned at my touch, and my dick was aching. I loved how much I affected her; I loved that we could still burn each other up, even after all this time.

I grazed my thumb over her clit a few times, feeling her tremor from the sensation. Then I took my cock in my hand, pressing it slowly inside her, my head pushing through the tight, wet, warmth of her insides.

"Oh, God... Ben..." she gasped, her fingers tugging at my hair while I forced myself in deeper. "Fuck I forgot how good you feel bare..."

"Baby, your pussy is magic," I growled, drawing my hips back a bit then thrusting inside her again, deeper, past the halfway point. "Jesus, I love how you feel around me..."

"Your cock is so big," she cried, licking and sucking and biting all over my neck and throat. "Fuck me, Benjamin Lockwood... Fuck me so good with your big, perfect cock."

"Holy *fuck*, I love you..." I hummed, my dick responding to my wife's praises, straight up throbbing inside her.

She wrapped her legs around my waist, hitching her ankles at the top of my ass while I pumped into her, deeper and deeper until my balls were pressing against her entrance, soaking wet with her delicious juices. I just wanted to taste her... But that would have to wait.

I kept on thrusting, hard and deep, fucking my wife with everything I had. We were both glistening with sweat as I ran my hand up to her tits, massaging and caressing, taking her nipple between my fingers and squeezing it until she groaned, her pussy clenching around my cock. I worked my dick in her so good, so deep that I felt my orgasm building in my loins. My balls were tight, almost ready to explode, and I had to focus on not coming until she was ready.

Fortunately for me, I felt her legs stiffening around me, her panting becoming uneven, a telltale sign that she was about to come. My hips bucked into her, feeling every single ridge of her insides sliding up and down on my hard dick as she began to tremble.

"Ben... fuck me, Ben..." she squealed out loud, scoring her nails across my chest. "I'm coming... Oh my God, I'm coming!"

"Come on my cock, baby," I growled, my voice hoarse as I let go.

"I'm coming on your cock..." she drawled, and I felt her walls contracting over and over, so fucking tight, squeezing me while her pussy gushed all over my dick.

I gasped out loud, holding her small body in my arms while my dick exploded, pulsing and shooting my orgasm deep inside her. Her name fell from my lips repeatedly while my hips slowed, and I collapsed on top of her, trying hard not to crush her while my chest heaved, and I tried to catch my breath.

"Holy shit..." her voice creaked, fingers trailing up and down my back.

"I know..." I hummed, lifting myself up enough to kiss her soft, sweet lips. "That was fucking amazing."

"Fuck yea it was," she giggled, out of breath. I chuckled back, gazing down at her, marveling at her flushed cheeks, swollen lips and sparkling blue eyes. She was a goddamned revelation, this woman.

How in the fuck did I get so lucky?

"I am so in love with you," I whispered, staring at her with hearts in my eyes.

"You really are, aren't you?" she breathed, less of a question, and more of a statement. She had some dazed wonder in her voice, as if she had questioned that fact for a moment, but I had managed to reaffirm her faith in us.

"I am, Jess..." My face turned serious. "No matter what happened... Or what does happen... My love for you is here to stay. And so am I. I'm not going anywhere. Ever. You're stuck with me, Mrs. Lockwood."

"Thank God for that," she grinned, biting her lip. And this time she had the hearts in her eyes.

I slowly pulled out of her, kissing down her neck and chest, licking and sucking her gorgeous tits while her fingers burrowed in my hair.

"Mmmm... Ben... What are you doing to me?" she panted, sounding worn out and oh-so-sexy.

"I'm going to make you come over and over and fucking over until you can't walk for the rest of the day," I rasped with a wicked smirk, nipping down her toned stomach, nestling my face between her thighs.

I extended my tongue, slowly lapping her up like a delicious ice cream cone, tasting our collective orgasms mixed together. It was so fucking kinky and hot, I could already feel my dick inflating again.

I ate my beautiful wife's pussy for only a few moments before she exploded into another orgasm. And then I let her rest for a minute before I did it again.

"Mmm... that feels so good..."

"Does it?"

"Yes..."

"Should I kiss it?" I grinned.

"Um, not unless you want to get kicked in the face," Jess giggled, wiggling her toes in my hand.

I laughed softly and continued massaging her foot, soft yet firm, pressing my thumb into her arch and making her head loll, eyes rolling back in her head. I was beaming with pride at being able to make her feel so good. I never wanted to disappoint her again, and knowing that I excelled in the physical stuff, I was using my powers to my advantage.

It was evening again. The sun had set on another crazy day, and it was safe to say that we had turned it around.

Jess and I had spent hours in bed. I made her come so many times I lost count after a while, and true to my promise, she remained horizontal for the rest of the night, until I eventually carried her into the bathroom to the giant, lavender-scented bubble bath we were currently enjoying. Prior to the bath, we had ordered room service–one of everything from the menu, since we were ravenously hungry from all the sex–and ate in bed while watching TV, chatting and laughing, and truly enjoying one another's company, more than we had in quite some time.

Jessica and I always had fun together. As much as I used to whine, we really weren't a *boring married couple*. Sure, sometimes the monotony overtook us, but that was a part of any marriage. It was about being comfortable together, and Jess was my best friend. So of course I was comfortable with her. I hadn't gone a day without speaking to her since I was seventeen years old.

That being said, the thing with Ryan really shook things up. And for whatever reason, it seemed to have brought Jess and I even closer together. We hadn't had a nonstop fuckfest like that since our honeymoon, and I couldn't remember the last time we took a bath together. We both agreed that all the fun we were having together was well worth the extra night in the city and the additional eight-hundred dollars.

The only issue was that we hadn't yet spoken a word about Ryan, the affair, or where she disappeared to for five hours today. We were really just having a wonderful night–one of the best we'd had in a long time–and I didn't want to ruin it. It was like we'd had a big fight earlier, made up, and now we were reveling in the post-fight bliss.

But the thing with Ryan wasn't just a regular old fight. It was a serious marital hiccup.

Ryan had popped into my head a few times over the course of the evening. It wasn't unusual. It had been happening since I met him. The only difference now was that I wasn't feeling guilty about it or scolding myself internally every time it happened. It almost seemed as if Jess being here now, laughing with me and playing with me like we always did, meant that she had fully forgiven me for the affair, and was accepting of it. The impression I was getting was that she was okay with it, and that made thinking about Ryan while I was with my wife okay.

Unfortunately, that was just speculation from my optimistic mind. There was no way for me to know if Jess really was okay with it unless I talked to her about everything. And I really didn't want to be a buzzkill.

You know you'll have to buck up and mention it sooner or later. You might as well pick sooner. After all, how long do you think you'll be able to stay in this bubble of undying happiness before you start to miss him....?

"Baby?" Jess's voice penetrated my thoughts, and I glanced up at her gorgeous blushed face.

"Yes, my love?" I replied, still rubbing her foot as we reclined in the giant Jacuzzi tub, with so much space that we could both sit, facing each other, with ample leg room.

"I need to tell you where I went today..." she murmured, her face serious, her big eyes wide and glistening at me.

My heart instantly started racing as I stared back at her, nodding hesitantly, bracing myself for something that might upset me. It had been secretly driving me crazy all day, wondering where she had been earlier. I wanted to know, although part of me was terrified to hear it.

"Well, first I just went driving around the city," she breathed, looking down at her fingers as they moved through the bubbles. "I was just thinking and driving... I drove past Hailey's apartment and considered stopping in to see her. But then I didn't want to lie to her about why you weren't with me, and I didn't want to worry her. So I drove past her school a bunch of times, past the stadium... I left the radio off the whole time. I just needed time alone with my thoughts."

I breathed out a sigh of relief, cocking my head to the side as I watched her. Something told me my relief was premature.

"And then... I ended up at Ryan's," she said, calmly, her eyes sliding up to mine and staying there.

My hand stopped moving, and I gaped at her in shock.

"You went... to Ryan's...?" I asked, raising my brow at her.

She nodded slowly, then bit her lip. "Yea. I don't even really know why... I just... wanted to see him. I had this strange urge to see him and talk to him, and let him know about everything."

My face was frozen as I stared back at my wife. She was so calm talking about this. Someone on the outside would have had no idea that we were talking about a person I cheated on her with.

I had a bizarre gut reaction to this news. I was inexplicably upset with Ryan for not telling me that my wife had been to see him. I knew it didn't make any sense, but for some reason I saw Ryan as a party loyal to me. If my wife had gone to see him, he should have let me know right away, rather than keeping her secret.

Don't be stupid. He can do whatever he wants. You're still the asshole in all this, don't forget that.

"So... did you?" I finally spoke, my voice quiet and reserved. "Did you... talk to him?"

Jessica nodded slowly, her face giving nothing away. I raised my brows again, waiting for her to elaborate.

"It wasn't anything serious," she mumbled, the words coming out slightly defensive. "I just told him you told me about you two. I just wanted him to know that I know... you know?"

My eyes squinted slightly. This wasn't making a whole lot of sense. Something wasn't adding up.

She went all the way over to his place just to tell him she knows about us? Couldn't she just have called him or something? Maybe there's more to this than she's letting on...

"What did he say?" I asked, my voice deep and questioning.

"He was very apologetic," she answered, sounding pleased by this fact. "He seemed really troubled by the whole thing. I think he's struggling, Ben. He clearly has feelings for you."

I ignored the thump in my chest at hearing that, and focused on what she was saying. The way she was talking about Ryan, it almost sounded as if she was standing up for him. She wasn't at all acting like this was the person I slept with outside of our marriage. She was treating it like I had harmed him in some way, and she felt bad. Like we were kids, and I had pushed Ryan down in the playground, and now she wanted me to apologize and play nice.

It was all very strange. Don't get me wrong, I was glad she wasn't pissed off. I was more relieved than I could even comprehend that she hadn't gone over to Ryan's house and stabbed him or something. It could definitely have been worse...

But still, the whole situation was bordering on ludicrous. I didn't know what to think, let alone how to respond to what she was saying. I simply watched her closely, biting the inside of my cheek.

"So... that's it?" I asked quietly. "You just went over and... what? Consoled him?"

She shrugged. "I mean, I guess, a little. Look, baby, I know it doesn't make any sense. You cheated on me with him. I should probably be angry..."

I huffed and pursed my lips. *Well... yea.*

"I don't know, maybe it's just because he's a man," she shook her head. "I guess if it was some hot young girl you cheated with, I would be more upset..."

"You think?" I asked, seriously wondering, though it seemed like it should be obvious. *None of this makes any sense, really.*

"Maybe," she shrugged again. "But in no way am I condoning you going out and fucking a girl for the sake of the argument!"

I chuckled softly and warned her with my eyes. She grinned back at me and bit her lip.

"I still wish you would have talked to me before just doing it..." she sighed, pouting a little.

"You mean, talked to you before hooking up with him?" I asked, even more confused by where this conversation was going. She nodded, peeking up at me. "Well, like I said, I didn't exactly plan on it happening... It wasn't anticipated, baby."

"I know..." she murmured. "I get it."

I paused for a moment, curiosity rippling inside me.

"If I had talked to you first..." I started, and her eyes widened. "What would you have said?"

"You mean, if you came to me and said you wanted to try hooking up with a guy?" she asked quietly.

"No, not just any guy," I shook my head. "Ryan."

She gaped at me for a moment, tugging her bottom lip between her teeth. My eyes darkened and blazed through her as I awaited her answer, though I already knew what it was.

She was quiet for a moment, and I could see her breathing picking up, her breasts moving up and down beneath the bubbles. She had a wicked look of mischievous arousal on her beautiful face, giving her a youthful glow, her cheeks rosy as she slid her tongue slowly over her lower lip. My eyes darted to her mouth for a second, and I swallowed hard.

"I would have been into it," she whispered, her eyes locked on mine, the look in them sending blood straight to my dick.

An electric chill ran through me, thrilling me inside and giving me a fresh sense of excitement. *This is new...*

Just when I thought I had tapped out on the new, adventurous side of Ben Lockwood... Mrs. Lockwood stepped up to bat.

CHAPTER 12

Ryan

I AM SLIGHTLY DRUNK.

My body was swaying as I stumbled toward my bedroom.

"Hey, you gonna make it, buddy?" Alec's drunk voice slurred at me from across the room. "Don't fall and bust your pretty face open." Kayla started giggling.

"Hardy har har... you're so damn funny," I rolled my eyes as I tried to make it into my room without walking into the wall. "I just need to get my phone..."

"Wait... why is he getting his phone?" I heard Kayla whisper to Alec. "Ry-bear... why do you need your phone?"

"I just wanna make a call..." I drunkenly muttered, feeling around in the dark for my phone, which was supposed to be resting on my dresser where I left it. Although I was pretty damn drunk. I could have moved it after my tenth tequila shot, and certainly would not have remembered.

"Call who?" Alec shouted from the living room. "You better not say Ben... Cause if you do, I'll have to smack you around a little."

I snorted out a laugh. "Aww... It's sweet that you think you could."
My hand finally slid over my phone. *Gotcha!*

I turned to leave my bedroom and jumped when I saw Kayla
standing right outside my bedroom door with her hands on her hips.
She was so much smaller than me; it was like I was being scolded by a
garden gnome.

"Friends don't let friends drink and dial," she said pointedly,
holding out her hand.

"You look like Tinker Bell with dark hair..." I mumbled, blinking
slowly as I swayed back and forth in my drunken stupor.

Kayla smiled wide and tilted her head. "Thank you. But seriously,
Ry. Give me your phone. I'm not letting you torture yourself by calling
him."

"But he deserves to know how I feel..." I huffed, pouting down at
her face.

"Yea, maybe. But you can tell him when you're sober," she said
firmly. "And it'll probably make more sense, and you won't regret it."

"Fine. I have a better idea anyway," I grumbled, leaning against the
doorframe. "Will you drive me to him? I'll tell him in person."

Kayla giggled, taking me by the arm and slowly walking me back
over to the living room.

"Aww, Ry-bear, you're so sweet when you're in love," she sneered,
and I scrunched my face at her.

"I'm not *in love*," I pretended to gag. "I just... I don't know..." I
shrugged. "He makes me feel things in my stomach. Like, twisty things.
And he's so bossy and scary but like in a cute way. And... he's just so
pretty to look at." I pouted again. All this Ben talk was making me want
to see him... And touch him and kiss him.

And maybe put his big dick in my mouth... Or my butt.

Wait, what were we talking about again?

Kayla smiled and sighed, her cheeks flushing a little. "Yea... he is
really pretty to look at..."

"You should see him naked," I whispered and winked at her. Her
face lit up like Christmas.

"Alright, you drunken fools!" Alec yelled at us. "I'm starting the
next episode right now, whether your asses are on this couch or not!"

"Come on," Kayla locked her arm in mine, walking me back over to the couch. "I'm not missing *Orange is the New Black* just because you want to drunk-dial your hot older married boyfriend."

I sighed and flopped down onto the couch next to Alec, then he shoved me out of the way to make room for Kayla. The three of us sat together, binge-watching the new season of *OITNB* on Netflix, and taking a shot every time Piper said *"Alex"*.

We were all completely shit-faced.

My friends had decided early that the only way to keep me from obsessing about the disparaging state of my love life was to keep feeding me booze. It had been working for a while, but little did they know that Ben was always on my mind. Being drunk didn't necessarily prevent it. It just slowed down my reaction times.

I couldn't stop thinking about Jessica's visit earlier. She was so sweet to me; it was almost unbelievable. That woman was a revelation. Ben wasn't wrong to feel the way he did about her. She was perfect.

Not to mention completely fucking gorgeous. She really was a knockout. And she was in her thirties, and a mother, so she had a level of maturity that girls my age most certainly did not have. She was nurturing and supportive, but you also got a vibe from her... Like, a silent blazing sexuality. She was wanton and enigmatic.

I bet she's a freak in the sheets. I don't even really need to imagine... I've watched her and Ben together twice. And both times I almost came in my pants.

I closed my eyes, and shook my head, grabbing another shot and slugging it back fast.

"She didn't say 'Alex', did she?" Kayla murmured, her eyes squinty from all the booze.

"She was getting there... making that desperate face," I grumbled, allowing the alcohol to spread its warmth through me, hopefully removing these crazy thoughts about my fuck-buddy's wife from my brain.

"I think you should... slow down," Alec hiccuped. "I don't feel like cleaning up your vomit tonight."

"Like you'd be cleaning it..." Kayla muttered.

"Do you think they went back home?" I asked, my fuzziness forcing the question out of my mouth before I even explained what I was talking about.

"No one got out yet," Alec murmured, pointing at the screen. "But I think they're gonna get early release..."

"No, not them," I huffed. "Ben and Jessica. I think they were checking out of the hotel today and driving home... But Jess came here after one. Hotel check-out is noon."

"Ryan, you need to stop obsessing," Kayla rubbed my back. "He'll call. Just give it some time."

"He doesn't even have my fucking number," I grunted, running my fingers through my hair in exasperation. "We have to DM each other on Instagram."

"Well, then he'll DM you," Kayla replied. "Just stop worrying. It'll work itself out."

I pouted again, slouching back in my seat. I tried watching the show, but I couldn't concentrate. My phone was burning a hole in my pocket.

What's the harm in one little message? Just to see how he's doing...

I glanced over at Kayla and Alec, who were cuddling up on the couch, getting all cozy. It was making me jealous. I was such a third-wheel. I hated that feeling. I hated being jealous of everyone...

My best friends, Ben and Jess... Everyone had these great relationships. Why couldn't I have made it work with Hailey? Or Dahlia...

Okay, this is getting ridiculous. Do not think about her.

"I gotta take a piss..." I grumbled, getting up and strolling casually toward the bathroom. Anticipation was coursing through me. Kayla didn't know I had my phone in my pocket...

I secured myself in my bathroom and locked the door, sitting down on the edge of the tub. I breathed hard and took my phone out, pulling up my Instagram DM's with Ben. I was about to type when I noticed something at the top of the screen. It was like a little video chat icon. I had never paid attention to it before.

It must be for video calling... Hm.

My drunken state easily convinced me that video calling Ben right now would be a great idea. *Just to say hi...*

With no thought at all, I clicked the icon, and sure enough, it started a video call.

I gulped, thrumming my fingers on my thigh as I held my phone up to my face, fixing my hair and my beard up a little on the screen while it rang. It rang a bunch of times, and my stomach was in my throat. *He's not going to answer... He's busy with his wife. Or maybe he doesn't even know what it is. Ben doesn't do social media much. Just forget it. This was a stupid idea.*

I was just about to end the call, choking on my self-deprecation when it connected, and Ben's face popped up right in front of me.

I almost fell backwards into the tub.

"Hey..." he rumbled, his bright blue eyes shining right at me, all sparkly and beautiful. His brow was furrowed a little, like he was confused as to why or how I was calling him through Instagram.

"Hi," I croaked, clearing my throat. I was completely hypnotized by how good he looked. And how much I had missed him. My stomach was doing all kinds of twisting, and I felt momentarily dizzy. "Sorry to call you like this..."

"It's okay," he spoke softly, his head cocking to the right. His hair looked damp, like he had just gotten out of the shower. And he wasn't wearing a shirt... So yea. *Fuck me.*

"I just wanted to make sure you were okay..." I mumbled, then stopped. I observed the background of his video and saw a bedroom. Not his. Definitely a hotel.

Oh my God, they're still at the hotel. They're still here.

"I'm fine," he answered, his face still mostly serious; sort of intimidating, and so very *Ben Lockwood.* "Actually, I'm great. I've had a... crazy day." He huffed out a soft little laugh and his smile almost broke my phone into pieces. *Jesus Christ... His smile is... debilitating.*

"Yea?" I asked, grinning back at him.

"Ryan, I know that Jess came to see you..." he said, his smile fading, though his face was still bright. He looked refreshed... illuminated even. *Giving the stars a run for their money.*

Jesus, you're so corny.

My eyes fell away for a second and I nodded. "Yea... she did. Look, I was going to tell you, but it's not my place. I shouldn't be getting involved in your marriage."

"Hm..." his jaw clenched visibly. "We'll come back to that. But it seems like everything is okay for now. It was a fucked up night... and morning... to say the least, but it all worked out. I'm glad she went to see you."

"You are?" I asked, raising my brows in surprise.

"Yea. Jess is..." he paused for a moment. "She just needed to figure out how she felt about it. About me and you."

"Oh..." I murmured, not really knowing what to say. I wasn't sure what he was talking about and I was still pretty drunk. My brain felt like a scrambled egg.

"How's your day been going?" Ben asked, changing the subject, though he seemed genuinely interested, giving me his full attention, which made my heart thump.

"Good... My roommates know about us," I told him, the words coming out before I had fully decided whether I should tell him.

"They what?" he barked, eyes widening in shock.

"Yea... I guess they could hear us last night," I replied. "Then Kayla saw you, so..."

"Jesus..." he grunted, running his hand through his hair. "Are they freaking out?"

"No," I shrugged. "They're actually super supportive and cool."

"Well, that's good, I guess," he breathed out of relief. "So you guys have just been hanging around?"

"Yea. Watching TV and stuff," I rumbled, pursing my lips. *I wish you were here...*

"Drinking from the look of it..." Ben smirked, his pretty, blue eyes shining right through me.

"What's that supposed to mean?" I slurred.

"Ryan, you're trashed," he chuckled, showing those sexy dimples that gave me a crazy confusing sensation in my belly. "I know what you look and sound like when you're drunk."

"So you do..." I rasped, trying and failing to hide my smile.

"Why are you getting drunk, baby?" he hummed, and my breathing shallowed. "Trying to forget me again?"

"No..." I grinned and bit my lip. "I gave up on that. It doesn't work."

"Well then, what's wrong?" he asked, a little more serious now, his forehead lined as he stared at me through the screen. "Is everything okay? Talk to me."

I huffed out hard and closed my eyes. This conversation was making me weak. He was just so... *everything.* Sweet, and charming, and bossy, and beyond sexy. Everything that was exclusive to Ben. Everything that made him so fucking perfect.

And the more I wanted him; the more I felt like he was mine, the more I realized that he wasn't.

This is why I need booze, Ben.

"It's just..." I sighed, shaking my head. "This is all so... fucked." *I miss you.*

Ben sighed back to me and nodded, his eyes filled with worry and guilt. I didn't want him to feel bad, like this was his fault. I was a grownup. I was responsible for my own actions, and my own heart. It wasn't his fault I was hopelessly infatuated with him.

"I don't know what to say..." he whispered. "I don't want you to hurt, Ryan. I just... I can't navigate around this shit. It's so... complicated."

I nodded slowly, agreeing fully with what he was saying. It certainly was complicated, to say the least.

"Can I see you?" I asked, instantly regretting how needy I sounded.

"You are seeing me," he smirked, that cocky fucking thing that made me want to smack him on the ass.

"Don't fuck with me," I grinned. "You know what I mean."

"I know..." he blinked slowly. "I don't think it's a good idea right now."

"You're still at the hotel..." I said, pointing out the fact that he was still in the city, and come tomorrow, he wouldn't be. If there was a chance of me seeing him again, it would be now.

He nodded slowly. "But you know... Jess is here. I can't leave her again."

"Where is she?" I asked, wondering how he was openly having this whole conversation if his wife was around.

His eyes moved away from the phone screen. "She's in the other room."

"Does she know you're talking to me?" I raised my brows.

"I think so..." he shrugged.

"And she doesn't care?" This was all very puzzling.

"I guess not..." he mumbled, looking just as confused as I was feeling.

"This makes very little sense, Ben," I told him.

"I know," he nodded, appearing a bit lost. "I don't understand what's going on at all. She knows I think about you... I think she knows... how I feel. It's sort of crazy. We spent all day... together..." He stopped and watched my face for a reaction to what he was saying.

My pulse started to increase, and I felt my chest tightening.

"You guys were..." I whispered, my voice trailing off.

"Fucking," he said, his voice deep and rough. Hearing him say that word made my cock jump. "All day... We fucked for hours."

A soft gasp flew out of my throat. "You did?" He nodded at me. This would explain the sated look on his luminous face. "Wow..." I breathed, because I didn't know what else to say. I was feeling so many things at the moment, and none of them made a lick of sense.

"Does that make you jealous?" Ben cocked his head to the side as he stared at me.

"No," I grunted, shaking mine slowly. I could feel my eyes radiating sexuality in his direction, even through the phone.

"Does it turn you on...?" he asked, his voice soft and inquisitive. "To think about Jess and me... *fucking.*"

I whimpered and blinked slow at my phone. "Yes."

"Good," he licked his lips.

"Ben..." I gulped, wanting so much more. I wanted to be there. I wanted to touch him. He was goddamned irresistible, and I think he knew that.

"Yes, Ryan..." he hummed.

"Um... I..." I was stuttering like an idiot. But I didn't know what to say. I wanted to know more...

"Ask me whatever you want," he spoke, so quiet and soft it was almost inaudible.

"How did it feel...?" I asked, my face warming under his intense blue stare. "Inside her... How does it feel?"

He groaned softly, and I could see the very beginning of his chest moving up and down.

"Do you want to know how it feels when I slide my hard cock deep inside my wife's tight, wet pussy?" he growled at me, the look on his face so dangerously sexy.

I couldn't help the slight moan that erupted from my throat. My dick was filling rapidly, straining against the material of my pants.

"I want to see..." I croaked, gripping the side of the tub with white knuckles as I held my phone in front of me. "I want to watch you fucking her."

"You mean like you did Thanksgiving night?" he smirked, his eyes dark. I swallowed hard and nodded. *Holy fuck, he knew I was there?! He knew...Jesus, of course he knew.* "You like watching me, don't you, Ryan?"

"I fucking love watching you," I rumbled, giving him the same deep, arousing tone.

"Mmm... I get so hard when I know you're watching..." he breathed, his eyes drooping shut for a moment. He looked so fucking sexy I couldn't stand not being near him. I loved that look on his face, when he was turned on and ready for whatever.

"Let me come over..." My voice was raspy and pleading. "I want to play with you and your wife."

Ben chuckled a growly, arousing laugh that sent shivers across my body, and straight down to my rock-hard dick. He glanced away from the phone again and raised his brow at something. Then his gaze came back to me.

"I'll work on it, baby..." he hummed. "Let me see what I can do. I can't guarantee tonight, but maybe soon..."

"But you're leaving tomorrow..." I whined out of frustration and Ben laughed softly.

"I'm not going to Mars, baby. I'm just going home," he grinned as his eyes sparkled with a devious desire. "It's only a few hours away."

I pouted, and he laughed again at my face, which made me smile. "Don't laugh at me..."

"Don't be so fucking cute," he murmured.

"I'm not cute, Ben. I'm a man, not a puppy," I squinted at him, and he laughed yet again. My chest swelled with pride at making him laugh like that. It was such a great sound, and he looked downright lethal all smiling and stuff.

"Mmm... sorry. I meant sexy, and hot..." he placated me, grinning big. "And well-endowed."

"Listening..." I smirked.

A sudden loud knock on the bathroom door startled me out of my flirty video call bubble.

"Ryan! Don't do it, man!" Alec shouted through the door. "Put down the phone!"

"Yea, Ry! You don't need to let him win!" Kayla shrieked. "Resist!"

I huffed and shook my head.

"What's that?" Ben raised his brow.

"It's my roommates," I sighed. "They want me to play hard-to-get."

Ben's lips morphed into a giant, straight-white-toothed, All-American drop-dead-gorgeous boy next door smile, which almost made me fall to my knees, and he wasn't even here.

"I thought you said they were supportive," he faux-pouted.

"They are, but they just don't want me to get hurt," I explained, ignoring the sounds of Alec and Kayla banging on the door, shouting things at me from the other side.

Ben's face dropped, and he looked taken aback, like I had slapped him in the face.

"Ryan... I would never hurt you," he spoke quietly, his tone very serious all of a sudden. "I don't want to hurt you..." He paused and breathed out hard. "I hope I haven't..."

"No, baby," I whispered, shaking my head. "You're not hurting me. I know this is a fucked up situation, but I'm fine. I can handle it."

"Are you sure?" he asked, blinking over wide eyes.

"Yea... yes," I nodded firmly. "Totally sure. Trust me, babe. I'm good. I just want to see you..."

He sighed out hard. "I know. I want to see you, too... I'm gonna work on it. Let me work on it, okay?"

"Okay," I hummed, knowing that we had to end the call. Alec and Kayla were really freaking out.

I heard Jess's voice in the background. It sounded like she was calling Ben. My heart leapt into my throat.

"Yea, babe! Coming!" Ben shouted at her. "I've gotta go, sexy. Talk soon?"

I pouted but nodded reluctantly.

"Don't be sad," he breathed, standing up as the camera angled down his exposed torso. "Will you think about me? I know I'll think about you..."

I was so busy drooling over all the hard clusters of muscles everywhere, I almost missed what he'd said. *Jesus, his body is insane. How the fuck does he look like that?*

"I'm definitely gonna think about you," I mumbled, and he laughed.

"Good," he smiled. But there was one more thing I wanted before I let him go...

"Show me your ass, please," I commanded, soft and pleading. But I sounded hungry, which was accurate.

Ben chuckled and aimed the phone at his butt, which was covered by dark grey sweatpants. He tugged them down just enough so that the top of his full, sexy ass was showing. It looked damn good. I just wanted to take a big ol' bite out of it.

"How's the hickey doing?" I rasped with a wicked grin.

"Watch it, kid," Ben growled through an even bigger smile. "Maybe I'll give you a hickey on your dick."

"That doesn't sound like a punishment to me, Benjamin," I chuckled, running my thumb over my bottom lip.

"Okay! I have to go!" he barked at me, laughing that soft, adorable laugh of his.

"Okay, goodbye, Ben," I sighed, not wanting to hang up at all.

"Bye, Ryan," he grinned, biting his lip before disconnecting the call.

I breathed out hard, shaking off all the emotions of that fucking amazingly tortuous video call, and opened my bathroom door. Alec and Kayla were standing there, arms crossed over their chests, feet tapping on the floor as they gave me scolding looks. I couldn't help but laugh.

"So how's Ben?" Kayla asked, her face lighting up with excitement. Alec elbowed her once again, and she pouted.

"He's good," I murmured, still riding the Ben-high.

"What did you guys talk about?" Alec asked, sounding like a parent who was about to ground me.

"We just talked," I sighed. "Guys, it's fine. I just wanted to talk to him for a minute. And he was happy to hear from me. I mean, I would've liked to go over there, because he's still in the city. But his wife is there, so... you know."

"Yea, we do know," Alec shook his head. "You're torturing yourself. He'll never leave his wife for you."

"I know that! Jesus, I don't want him to leave his wife..." I grumbled at them defensively. "That would be crazy. They're perfect together."

"So then what do you want, sweetie?" Kayla asked, being the more coddling of the two.

I sighed and shook my head, trying to think of the best way to describe what I wanted. It didn't make any sense, so saying it out loud would just make me sound like a lunatic.

"I don't... know..." I bit my lip, leaning up against the doorway and banging my head softly. "I want to be with him... And I want him to stay with his wife. I want them to be happy, and me... as well. I want to be happy... with them." I closed my eyes tight. "Jesus Christ, what the fuck am I talking about?"

"I don't know, bro," Alec shrugged, patting me hard on the shoulder. "That just doesn't sound like it makes much sense."

"Yea, no shit..." I grunted.

My phone started ringing in my hand. It didn't sound like a regular ringtone.

I lifted it before my face and saw another Instagram video call coming in from Ben. I squinted at my phone in confusion, wondering why he would call me right back. Alec and Kayla's faces were still, both of them apparently shocked.

I swiped to answer the call, expecting to see Ben's gorgeous face again, but was thrown off hard when Jessica came up on the screen. Her blonde hair was up in a messy bun on top of her head, her dark blue eyes shimmering like ocean water. And her face, like Ben's, was glowing–obviously from all the sex.

I swallowed over my dry throat.

"Hi, Ryan," Jessica smiled into the phone, her full lips curved as she blinked at me over the call.

"Hi, Jess," I murmured, glancing behind the phone at Alec and Kayla who were gaping at me, mouthing all kinds of things. I shushed them, turning away to get some privacy.

"Sorry to call you from Ben's phone..." she whispered, and it looked like she was walking too. "I don't have your number..."

"I could give it to you," I rumbled, then paused, realizing how stupid I sounded. "I mean, at some point. Just in case..." I breathed out slowly, and Jessica smiled, glancing at the ground.

"Listen, I don't have much time to talk..." she spoke quietly. "Ben doesn't know I'm calling you."

I froze. "He doesn't...? Why not?"

"No time to explain," she brushed off my hesitations. "Can you come over to the hotel?"

It felt like the world around me was moving in slow motion. I was in complete shock, gawking at my phone screen, at the beautiful blonde who was staring back at me, waiting for me to respond.

"You... want me to come over? To the hotel?" I huffed, my heart racing with excitement. I was acting like I wasn't sure if I should, but I already knew in my heart that I was going to. Whether Ben knew about it or not.

"Yea, could you?" she asked again, sounding much more casual than me.

"Ben doesn't know...?" I raised my brows.

"I'm sure he won't mind," she grinned, looking positively wicked.

I bit my lip to keep from grinning. I wasn't sure why, but my face wanted to mirror hers. It was weird. I couldn't believe I was even entertaining this, but I also couldn't fight the anticipation running through me.

I had no clue why she wanted me to come over, but I could only hope it was for something dirty. *A guy can dream, right?*

I exited the elevator on the eighteenth floor of the hotel, strolling down the hall. My palms were sweaty, and my heart was already racing. I was so nervous, I almost couldn't catch my breath. I was unsure of what I was doing there, but I knew that whatever happened, it would be an interesting night.

Seems like I've been having a lot of those since I met Mr. and Mrs. Lockwood...

I stepped up to the door of their hotel suite-room eighteen-eighteen, as Jessica had instructed on the phone only about twenty-minutes ago-and took a long, deep breath, holding it into my lungs. I was feeling much more sober now that I was freaking out. Still, I had taken an Uber over to the hotel because I was in no condition to drive. I could feel the warm and fuzzies floating through my bloodstream from all the booze of the day. It was working to keep me slightly calm, although inside I was panicking just a little.

I didn't know what I was doing, or what was going on in my crazy life. I was just living in the moment for now, which made everything that much more exciting.

I knocked on the door and waited, bouncing around in place, wringing my hands and smoothing out my t-shirt over and over.

The door opened slowly, and I saw Jessica standing there in a bathrobe, smiling a shy smile at me. I gulped and blinked a few hundred times, already feeling a myriad of emotions that there wasn't enough time in the day to identify.

"Hey... Come in," she whispered, quickly glancing behind me. She grabbed my arm and dragged me into the room, closing the door, but not without first slipping the *Do Not Disturb* sign on the handle.

Sweet Jesus...

"I'm so glad you came," she crooned by my side, tugging me along with her, over to the minibar which separated the living room and kitchen.

"Thank you for inviting me..." I replied, trying to sound casual.

The hotel suite was massive, and super nice. I had never been inside a hotel room that big before. It was almost the size of my apartment, from the look of it. As I glanced around, taking in my surroundings, I couldn't help but search for some sign of Ben. Jessica had told me on the phone that he didn't know I was coming over, but

I wasn't sure if she told him after we hung up.

"This place is... amazing," I breathed, as Jessica sat me down on a chair next to her. She made sure to sit close, her knees touching mine. She was barely dressed. The robe was pretty short, and I was willing to bet she was naked underneath. I tried to be subtle looking at her while she sat beside me; the robe resting high on her thighs, showing all of her smooth, toned legs, which were dangling off the chair because she was so short. Her feet were bare, and her pedicured toes were wiggling. It was kind of cute, and sexy. Thinking of such things was causing a burning in my loins. I tried to control it by focusing on what she was doing.

Jessica grabbed two glasses and poured us each some champagne from an open bottle. There were a few empty bottles on the counter already, and it was clear she and Ben had been getting their drink on today, which eased my mind a bit. I really didn't want to be dealing with sober people while I was still sort of sloshed myself.

She handed me a glass and took hers, holding it up to mine, still wearing that sweet little smile, with her cheeks slightly flushed. I had never seen her hair up and messy like that before. She looked... breathtaking.

We clinked our glasses and sipped slowly, eyeing each other over the rims. I was already feeling some significant heat in the air, and I wasn't sure if it was just hot in the room, or if I was burning from the inside out. Actually, the balcony door was opened and there was a breeze blowing the curtains around.

Jessica followed my gaze. "Ben's out on the balcony. He's smoking..."

"Smoking?" I raised my brow in question.

"Cigar," she grinned, taking another sip of her champagne.

"Oh, right..." I nodded, tracing the stem of my glass with my finger. "He still doesn't know I'm here...?" My gaze lifted to hers. She was already watching me.

She shook her head slowly. "He's gonna be surprised." Her lips curled, and I started chewing the inside of my cheek.

"You don't think he'll be mad?" I asked, skeptical of this whole situation.

"I doubt that," she murmured, cocking her head to the side. "Listen, Ryan, I know he wants to see you. But he was unsure of how I would react... I was sort of unsure myself." She paused and glanced down at our touching knees.

"If it's weird for me to be here, I can leave..." I mumbled, my stomach dropping a little in disappointment and insecurity.

"Don't be silly. I asked you to come over for a reason," she smiled at me, her blue eyes holding me in place. They were so deep and dark, not light like Ben's. It was hypnotizing. Her whole presence was. She was like a mysterious force, and I found myself desperately intrigued by her, though I wasn't sure why.

"What's the reason?" I asked, my voice coming out quiet and curious.

"I wanted to see you, too," she whispered, then reached over and took my hand in hers, pulling it forward to rest our joined hands on her thigh. Our fingers instinctively locked in that same way as earlier... The way they did with Ben.

Jessica hopped off her seat and stood up, scooting herself in between my legs. I swallowed hard, my brow furrowing in anxious confusion. I lifted my glass with the other hand and gulped back the rest of my champagne, hoping it would calm my nerves a little.

She watched my face for a moment before her eyes dropped to our joined hands, straightening our fingers, palms pressed together. It was baffling how my movements always seemed to mirror hers. When she moved, I moved. When she smiled, I smiled. When she touched... I touched. We were in-synch, which was crazy, because I really didn't know her well at all. Either we had some kind of connection, or I was like her pet. I couldn't tell... Or I didn't care.

We both watched our hands, admiring the feel of our fingers together, and how much smaller hers were than mine. Her hands were dainty and delicate, nails perfectly manicured a deep red, which looked great with her skin tone. And of course her wedding rings... She wore a big, giant sparkling rock on her finger-it screamed *Ben*-with a simple yet stunning platinum band. I had noticed Ben's wedding ring before, but I never really thought about it until now.

Until I was holding his wife's hand. Her sexy, soft little fingers... My mind started to drift, imagining what they would look like touching me... Maybe scratching my chest.

God... What is happening right now...?

Her eyes slid back up to mine, giving me a wistful look.

"You look good with a beard," she spoke softly, her lips curling into an innocent smile before she looked down again, biting her lip. "I meant to tell you that earlier."

"Thank you..." I hummed as my chest tightened and burned. I curled my neck to catch her gaze. "You look beautiful... Mrs. Lockwood." She grinned, I grinned. "Sorry if that's too... I don't know. Forward?"

She giggled out a breathy little sound. And then I did, too. *This is getting out of hand.*

"That's not forward, Ryan," she tugged my hand again, this time moving it down by her side. "But I like when you call me Jess. It makes me feel younger... Like less of a mom."

She let go of me, and I swore she wanted me to touch her. Like she was saying it with her eyes and her suggestive actions. So I did.

I rested my hand on her waist, and she didn't pull away. I breathed out slowly.

"You're the sexiest mom I've ever seen," I told her, my voice deep and very raspy. I kept fearing that I would cross some line, and she would slap me in the face. But she didn't. Instead, she smiled wider.

"You think?" Her tone was as sweet as candy. She looked and sounded like a woman ten years younger than her age. She could have been an actress or a model. Seriously, her and Ben were the hottest couple I'd ever had the pleasure of encountering.

At mention of Ben in my mind, I immediately tensed up, glancing at the doorway to the balcony. I couldn't see him, because the balcony was huge, and it was dark outside. But I could smell the faint cigar smoke. It reminded me of Thanksgiving night; the memory heating my flesh.

"Do you think Ben would be mad that I'm... here with you...? Like this?" I asked, glancing down at my hand resting on her waist. I could have taken it away, but I really didn't want to. The robe was so soft, and I could feel her body beneath it. My fingers moved ever-so slightly.

"I don't know..." she shrugged, and her eyes came alive with mischief. "Maybe we'll find out."

Oh boy... Is that part of her plan? She wants to use me to get back at Ben for cheating? That wouldn't be good. I don't want to be in the middle of their marital problems.

Although... I think I am their marital problem. Fuck. I am a home-wrecker. That's very disappointing.

"Ryan, relax, sweetie," Jessica crooned, reaching up to run her fingers along my jaw. "There's no way Ben would be anything but excited to see you."

"Are you sure?" I leaned my head into her touch. I didn't even realize I was doing it until I was, which blew my mind. This woman completely captivated me. "I would hate to... intrude on your alone time together..."

I sighed and shook my head. I didn't know what I was saying or doing. I couldn't tell if I was so mesmerized by Jessica because she was such a beautiful, sexy, vibrant woman, who smelled fucking delicious, or because she was Ben's wife. Was I only attracted to her because I knew she was Ben's, and I was infatuated with every aspect of his life?

"Honey, you're not intruding," she cooed to me, in that calm, slightly seductive voice. "I invited you here. I wanted to see you. Ben wants to see you. We both do..." Her nails grazed through the scruff on my face and I blinked slowly, savoring the feeling. "I enjoyed seeing you earlier. I didn't want you to worry about everything. And I thought I would need more time to think, but it turns out I didn't. It was much simpler than I thought it would be."

I could barely understand what she was talking about, but I was afraid to ask. I noticed that my hand was gripping her waist pretty hard, holding onto her for dear life. She giggled, and I smiled back at her, slightly abashed, releasing my grip as my hand slowly drifted...

Yea, no. This has nothing to do with Ben. I'm turned on as fuck by this woman... She's so goddamned gorgeous. And she keeps looking at me like that... It's driving me crazy.

Okay, so knowing she's Ben's makes it a little more exciting. Ben likes to be controlled in the bedroom, and what's more surrendering of control than letting someone else play with what's yours?

"I liked seeing you today, too," I whispered as my eyes locked on hers. I pulled her closer until her body was snug between my legs, my hand resting dangerously low on her hip. Her hand slid from my jaw down to my chest. "I'm glad we talked. And I'm glad you came back to Ben. He told me you guys had a... fun afternoon." Her eyes widened and sparkled up at me as she bit her lip. "He told you that?"

I nodded slowly, standing my ground, trying not to get tripped up in second-guessing everything. She grinned big and moved her hand down to my thigh, drawing circles on it through my pants. I could tell she was feeling curious, thinking; wondering what all of this meant. The chemistry between us, with Ben right outside, unaware of anything happening in here. It was like a high. I knew she was feeling it, because I definitely was.

"It was mind-blowing, Ryan," she gasped, her cheeks covered in a rosy natural blush that was so fucking cute and sexy. "He was unstoppable... like some kind of sex-crazed orgasm machine. You know how he gets when he's feeling dirty like that..." She beamed up at me, sliding her tongue over her bottom lip.

It should have been weird, talking to a guy's wife about sex and how turned on he gets after you've fucked him in the ass multiple times. I was really searching for some kind of awkwardness, because I felt like it should be.

But it just wasn't there. Jessica was hot. She was a blonde bombshell, standing with her tight little body pressed up against my crotch, her fingers trailing up and down my thigh, moving purposely and teasingly close to my dick, which was inflating more and more by the second. I was trying not to allow myself to become fully hard, but it was difficult. She looked like she wanted me to talk to her about her husband's sex drive, because I was the only other person in the world who knew about it like she did.

Mrs. Lockwood liked sharing.

I nodded slowly, running my hand down to where the material of her robe ended and her bare flesh began. She made a soft little purring noise, squeezing my thigh tight with her fingers.

"He's got stamina, I'll give him that," I rasped, and she giggled.

"That must be why you're glowing..." I blinked at her, giving her a seductive smile.

"Mmm... I was pretty worn out. And a little... sore..." she whispered, raising her brow just enough. I chuckled deviously and nodded again. *Yes, Ben's dick is very big. Mhm... This conversation is killing me so good.*

"I hope he took care of you," I gave her a little pout and she flushed more.

"We took a bath for a while," she answered, breathy and appealing. "That tub in there is massive. You should see it." She gave me another one of those faux-innocent, tempting looks.

"Maybe later," I rumbled. She was fingering the hem of my t-shirt, while I did the same with her robe.

I decided to push a little further, moving my other hand to the front of her robe, trailing my index finger along the opening. It wasn't tied very tight. In fact, it was hanging open a bit. Not too much. Just enough for me to see the beginning curves of her breasts.

I played with the front of it a little, while she watched me, fascinated, looking like she wanted me to tear it open suck on her big, beautiful tits. Which I wanted too, by the way. Like, *really* bad.

"But yea, the bath helped," she kept talking to me while I leaned in closer to her, my eyes on hers while my fingers teased her lack of sufficient clothing. "It was soothing enough, though I'm still a little swollen. So... *if* I were to do anything else tonight... it would have to be gentle. At first..."

She tugged her lip between her teeth and my heart stopped. I swallowed hard, wondering if I had just imagined that. *Did she really just say that...? Was that real? Is she propositioning me??*

Sure, we were flirting pretty hard, and touching, and talking about sex. All signs were pointing to this being a wild night, but I had no clue what kinds of things would happen. Ben was the one I was used to banging, not his wife. And now, here I was with her, not him, talking about fucking. It was crazy.

And my dick was suddenly so hard, I could feel it throbbing.

She wants me to fuck her. Jesus, I want to fuck her...

But wait, what would Ben say? I'm not sure he would mind... After all, he's said it before. He wants to watch me with her... Maybe that's what she has in mind. Could I really do that? How would it work?

Before I could say or do anything else, Ben came sauntering through the doorway from the balcony, wearing nothing but his dark grey sweatpants that sat deliciously low on his hips. My first instinct was to pull back and act like nothing had been happening. My heart was beating so fast I felt like it might explode right out of my chest.

Jessica didn't seem worried in the slightest. In fact, she stayed right where she was, slipping her fingers underneath the fabric of my t-shirt, grazing her nails through my happy trail. It made my already-hard cock twitch.

Ben paused when he saw me, his eyes widening and his jaw dropping slightly. He blinked a few times, staring at us, appearing thoroughly shocked.

I remained frozen in time, watching him watch us, likely trying to decide how to react to what he was seeing. I gulped, attempting to remain aloof, though I had no idea what I was doing. This had to be one of the most bizarre situations I had ever been involved in.

"Hi, baby," Jessica chirped at Ben, smiling sweetly with her hands still all over me. "I invited Ryan over. I hope you don't mind..."

Ben was still standing there in stunned silence, his eyes bouncing back and forth between me and his wife. Then I saw him register where my hands were, and where her hands were. It looked like his jaw clenched a little, but it was hard to tell with him all the way across the room. I wasn't sure if he was angry, or jealous, and if so, who it was directed at. And it didn't look like he knew either.

Finally, he snapped out of it and continued walking slowly, approaching us with a dangerous look on his face. He stepped over to the minibar, grabbing Jess's glass of champagne and slugging it back, before pouring himself some more.

He turned to face us, leaning up against the counter, sipping from the glass again, this time much slower.

"Of course I don't mind," he muttered, his blue eyes locked on mine. He was staring at me so hard, I felt like I could pass out. He raised his brow in that scary Ben way that ran a chill down my spine. "Hi, Ryan. I didn't think I would see you tonight..."

"Me neither," I croaked, trying to find my voice again. "Your wife is full of surprises..." I glanced down at Jess and she blinked over wide, enraptured eyes.

"So she is..." his gaze fell from mine, taking in the sight of Jess and I together. His eyes were blazing; a bright blue inferno. And I couldn't tell for sure, but it appeared as if he liked what he saw.

He gulped his drink again, killing the champagne, before going for something stronger.

"Don't let me interrupt," he grunted, picking up a tumbler and pouring himself a scotch from what looked to be another open bottle. "You want one?"

"Sure, thanks," I answered as calmly as I could manage.

"I was just telling Ryan how good he looks with a beard," Jess purred, grabbing me by the jaw again, a little harder this time, yanking my face down to hers.

I let out a soft gasp as I stared at her, my eyes darting down to her lips for a second. Long enough for me to admire how soft and pink and full they were. Her eyes did the same, lusting after my lips like they were a candy she wasn't allowed to have before dinner.

"Doesn't he look good with a beard, Ben?" she murmured, pupils still dancing between my eyes and lips.

"Mmm... He does," Ben answered from behind her, setting my glass of scotch down hard on the counter next to me, causing me to flinch. "So good..."

He moved over to us, dropping a possessive hand on my back, rubbing me gently while he kissed his wife on the cheek.

"I'll give you two some privacy," he whispered, his voice hoarse and growly, like some kind of animal; his tone a mixture of jealous frustration and curious arousal. "Let you get more... acquainted."

Then he turned and stalked off, glass in hand, toward the bedroom.

Holy fuck, that was intense.

I breathed out slowly, watching the doorway to the bedroom that Ben had just disappeared into.

"Was he being serious?" I asked Jess quietly, fearing that I would fail some test by not going after Ben.

"Yes," Jessica answered, tugging my face back to hers. "Ryan, do

227

you think Ben would let someone else near me if he didn't want it?"
I shook my head. She had a point.

"So then..." I cocked my head to the side as I leaned in even closer
this time, until our faces were only inches apart. "Where were we?"
Jess grinned wickedly, her eyes set on my mouth. "I think... we were
right about... here."

She pressed her soft lips on mine, so gently that I could barely tell
she'd done it. The warmth of her breath gave it away, until she took my
bottom lip between hers and sucked it, purring as she went.

I gasped softly, completely bewildered by the fact that I was kissing
Ben's wife-my ex's mom-with his permission. It felt so bad, so naughty.
It was such a high, one that I never wanted to come down from. I
wanted more... *So much more.*

I parted my lips, sliding my tongue in to meet Jess's, and she
actually whimpered. It was so hot. I could tell she was excited, the same
way Ben was excited the first time we hooked up. She hadn't kissed
anyone other than him in nineteen years, not that I knew of, which
seemed to be confirmed by how her lips were quivering, and how much
she was panting. It was just kissing, but she was enjoying it on another
level, because it was new, and *bad.*

We started kissing a little harder, and deeper, our tongues mingling
and our lips sucking. Jessica kissed different from Ben. She was much
softer and sweeter. She treated kissing like an entrée, when with Ben it
was usually just the appetizer.

She nibbled at my lower lip with her teeth, her hands running all
over the place. I palmed her ass hard, squeezing it until she mewled
between my lips. Her ass was wonderful; so plump and juicy. She
clearly did Yoga or Pilates, or whatever all those housewives do. It felt
amazing to cup it and massage it while pulling her closer to me. Between
Ben and his wife, I had really lucked out in the butt department.

Jessica was rubbing herself on me, grinding her body in between
my legs, the friction making me ache. It was fire, what was happening
between us. As much as she was clearly amped over our make-out
session, she still had that hesitance in her actions, reminiscent of my
first time with Ben. It turned me on to be a new, exciting thing for this
couple. That factor alone was my motivation for all of it.

"Are you okay?" I asked in between us mauling each other. I needed to make sure she wasn't having doubts, or just letting me do this because she thought it was what Ben wanted.

"You're so sweet," she giggled, biting my lip again. "I totally see why my husband likes you." Her hands ran down the length of my torso, feeling me up a little. "And you have a sick body."

I chuckled, squeezing her ass again. "Yea so do you. And so does your husband..."

"Mhm... We all look really fucking good, don't we?" she rasped, then we giggled together at how cocky we were being. But it was true, so whatever.

Jessica pulled her lips off mine for a second, both of us breathing heavy while she peeked up at me, eyes hooded with desire. Then she casually untied her robe, letting it hang open, biting her lip in one of the most seductive displays I had ever witnessed.

Sweet baby Jesus...

I could see so much. Not everything, but just enough for my dick to feel like it had its own pulse. Her big, round tits were on display, nipples just barely covered. My eyes locked on them for a moment, before traveling down over her toned stomach, landing below her waist.

Her pussy was bare, except for one tiny little landing strip of blonde hair, which was the cutest, sexiest thing I had ever seen. It looked immaculately groomed. I just wanted to run my thumb over it.

"Wow, Ryan..." Jess murmured, the sound of her voice pulling my gaze away from her tasty-looking cupcake.

"Hm...?" I grunted, unable to speak actual words at the moment.

"Look at you," she grinned, her hand covering the massive outline of my erection. I gasped, as did she while stroking me over my pants.

"Jess," I panted, reaching out slowly, moving my hand inside her now open robe and sliding my hand over her bare breast. "Fuck, that's nice." I cupped it, caressing gently, then gave it a little squeeze.

"Ryan..." she mewled, giving me a curious look. "Does Ben touch you like this?" Her hand gripped my cock as she jerked it slowly, through my jeans.

I groaned softly, watching her face close. "He loves it," I nodded and massaged her tit again, brushing my thumb over the hardened peak of her nipple.

She moaned and chomped on her lip, practically climbing on top of me. She held onto the back of my neck, her other hand fondling my throbbing hard-on while she clung to me and ordered my lips back to hers. Her movements had become desperate. She was so hungry for all of me; it was making me insane. Her lips tasted like champagne and cherries, and she smelled wonderful. I wasn't sure what the scent was exactly, something like jasmine and vanilla, but it smelled so damn good, my mouth was watering.

I held her on me by her ass, kissing her harder and deeper until I was dizzy. I moved my lips along her jaw, down to her neck, licking and sucking all over her creamy flesh. When I finally made it to her tits, I was starved for them. I took her pert nipple between my lips and I sucked it gently, flicking my tongue over it then nipping it with my teeth. *Oh my God... Oh. My. God. This is amazing. This is fucking wondrous.*

Jess moaned my name, tugging me by my hair while her other hand worked at the button on my jeans. I continued suckling at her nipples like a fiend as she unzipped my pants and shoved her hand inside, grabbing me by my shaft.

"Jess... Fuck, be careful..." I gulped, kissing her gorgeous big tits everywhere. "I don't wanna come too soon."

She giggled out an insanely erotic laugh. "Why...? Do you like this?" She whipped my dick out of my pants, although I was still seated, then proceeded to stroke me from the base all the way up in one, long, slow motion. I groaned softly, my eyes drooping shut.

"Your hands are... so... soft..." I breathed.

"Do you like this when Ben does it?" she asked, and my cock pulsed in her hand. "Does my husband play with your big dick like this?"

I nodded, panting and trembling. "Yes... I love how you both play with my cock."

We moaned together, my face buried in her tits while she jerked my dick off so fucking good. Then I slid my hand between her thighs, gliding my fingers through her slit. She was so slippery I could feel my own excitement seeping from the head of my cock.

"Ryan," Jess whimpered, holding onto my dick for dear life. "Is it bad if I want you to fuck me?"

I groaned out a ragged breath. I was so fucking excited to fuck this girl I was about to lose it.

"Yes... It's bad..." I grunted. "Very bad... So bad it's *fucking* amazing," I whispered to her, finally leaving her tits to come back to her sweet, hot mouth. "Would you let me...? Fuck you...?"

She kissed me hard, nodding while she whined out all these needy, sexy little noises.

"We have to show Ben..." she breathed over my lips. I felt like I was in a dream. Everything was fuzzy and warm. It was euphoric.

"Show Ben how we fuck?" I swirled my fingers around in her wetness.

"Mhm," she nodded then bit my swollen lips.

Excitement vibrated through me like I had stuck my fingers in an electrical socket. I had never done something so purely kinky, and dirty, and devious. Even fucking a guy was a new sexual exploration, but it wasn't as wicked as this. I was going to fuck both of my ex-girlfriend's parents, together. I was going to screw Ben's wife while he watched.

And it would be *fucking* phenomenal.

Jessica reluctantly peeled herself off me, standing up and breathing hard. Her face was so flushed and it made her look even more amazing. I couldn't wait to see what she looked like during sex...

I slipped my fingers into my mouth, all the while holding her eye contact, sucking her delicious flavor off them. She gasped and bit her lip, eye fucking the shit out of me, before grabbing my glass of scotch and taking a sip.

She handed it to me, and I sipped it slowly, reveling in the burn. I sipped again then set the glass down.

"You taste better," I rumbled, and she grinned, grabbing my hand and dragging me toward the bedroom. We were basically running, scampering into the room with haste.

The bed was huge. California King. Definitely big enough for three people.

In the bedroom, I instantly felt a strong, powerful presence. And when I turned to my left, I saw Ben, sitting in a chair, leaned back, sipping his glass of scotch. His eyes set on us, and they were wide, dark, and filled with a thrilled hunger. The look on his face was dangerous. It made the hairs on the back of my neck stand up.

Jessica sauntered over to the bed, faced Ben and let the robe fall from her shoulders, the material pooling at her feet. I witnessed him swallow hard, blinking slowly, while having some kind of telepathic conversation with his wife as he held his glass hard in his fingers. He looked so scary-and sexy-like he could eat both of us alive and was using every single bit of his strength to keep himself seated.

Jess turned to me then fell back onto the bed, holding herself up on her elbows so she could aim her lustful gaze in my direction. She motioned for me to come closer with her finger, and I went to her without hesitation, like I was her slave. She spread her legs for me, and I kneeled in between them, grabbing her face and kissing her soft. She hummed between my lips and I kept going, deeper, sucking her lips and making her melt.

I was immensely aware that I was being watched. I could feel Ben's burning eyes on me, and it made me nervous and energized at the same time. I was electrified. I wanted to give him a show, like he did for me both times at his house. He deserved to get off watching me fuck his wife.

I tugged my shirt over my head and tossed it, holding back my prideful smirk at Jess's obvious appreciation for my body. She clearly had a type. I pushed my pants and boxers down, kicking them off my legs, then came back to Jess, grinding my thick, aching erection along the apex of her thighs, her wetness coating me.

I was going out of my mind. It felt so good. I couldn't believe I was doing this.

Fuck... I can't wait to fuck this beautiful woman and her wet pussy, with her husband watching. Her husband who is also mine. Mmm... yes. I want to see him. I want to watch him watching me.

I kissed Jess a few more times, grabbing her tits and squeezing them, running my lips down her neck. She was moaning and panting soft breaths, yanking me down to her by my ass so she could rub herself on my dick. I planted soft kisses across her chest, licking and sucking all over her big tits. I was trying so hard to pay full attention to the performance I was putting on, but it was difficult. I wanted to look at Ben so bad.

I finally gave up the fight and glanced to my left. Ben was still sitting in the chair, his broad chest and shoulders leaned back, heaving up and down with what appeared to be rapid breaths. His brow was slightly furrowed, and he looked almost pained at having to sit there and watch all of this. His eyes met mine and for a moment I was afraid that he wanted me to stop.

But then his lips curled slightly into the faintest evil smirk and his blue eyes sparkled at me with excitement. He was into it. *Really* into it.

I sat up fast and pulled Jessica with me by her hips, flipping her over onto her stomach, and facing her toward Ben. Then I yanked her hips back, forcing her up onto all fours, her full, round butt right in front of me. I positioned myself behind her and ran my hand up her back, caressing her softly as I dragged my erection through the wetness between her thighs.

She tilted her face up at me, licking her lips and giving me a hungry look. She reached back and grabbed my dick, stroking it up and down in her soft hand.

"Are you going to fuck me now, Ryan?" she asked, her voice shaky with anticipation.

"Is that what you want?" I growled, running my fingers through her slickness, feeling her tremor as I circled her clit.

"Yes!" she gasped, pressing my dick into her entrance.

I glanced up at Ben, watching his reaction to all this. He nodded subtly, his hand creeping slowly toward his own erection, adjusting it in his pants.

I breathed out slowly, all too ready to oblige the two of them, taking my cock from Jess and pushing the head inside her.

We both moaned together, absorbing the sensation. It was so new... So unfamiliar, yet so fucking exhilarating. I pushed in a little more, my whole body tingling all over. She was so tight, and wet, and warm. It already felt incredible. I grabbed her hard on the ass, thrusting into her further, letting her take in the feeling. She was clearly loving it.

"Ryan! Holy *fuck*... your dick feels amazing..." she whimpered, and I groaned quietly. I heard another noise and looked up to see Ben's eyelids drooping as he dug his fingers into the arm of the chair. He looked so turned on. It was hot as fuck. He was making the same face that he made when I fucked him, and it burned my flesh like I was on fire.

I forced my thick cock further inside his wife's pussy, feeling every ridge of her, those plush walls stroking me inch by inch. I pulled back and pushed in again, developing a rhythm, keeping my eyes on Ben the whole time.

Jessica was making the sexiest noises ever. I was used to them, having watched her in bed with Ben a couple times. Her sounds were driving me to pick up the pace a little, pumping into her over and over. And Ben's face was just driving me insane. He looked like he was about to break, his head lolling back, Adam's apple bobbing in his throat when he swallowed, watching me take his wife for a ride on my cock.

I glanced down for a moment, biting my lip at the sight of my dick moving in and out of Jess's tight pussy. I gripped her ass hard in my hands, spreading her cheeks open so I could really see. It was fucking marvelous.

When my eyes came back up to Ben, he had his hand in his sweatpants, and he was stroking himself slowly, his eyes moving back and forth between me and his wife. I looked at Jess's face, her gaze stuck on Ben, too. My eyes fluttered shut for a moment while I grunted through stroking my cock in and out of her. I loved the fact that she and Ben were watching each other. I fucking *loved* that they were still so connected even with me in the picture.

"Ben..." Jess moaned, and he whimpered, his strong hand wrapped around his long, thick erection while he jerked himself, half of his huge dick sticking out of his pants. I licked my lips, lusting after his perfect manhood while I pumped into his wife, my balls smacking the underside of her butt.

"Jessica..." he growled, rough and gravelly, his eyes unblinking.

"Come here," she demanded, her voice uneven with my thrusts. He raised that cocky eyebrow at her, and my dick pulsed in her pussy.

"Come here, Ben," I added, giving him one of my own hungry looks.

He stood up slowly, stepping over to the edge of the bed and dropping his pants. He reached out and held his wife's jaw, stroking himself right by her face.

"Does it feel good, baby?" he asked, his voice soft and erotic.

"Yes..." she told him, while taking every inch of me.

"How does his dick feel inside you?" His eyes stayed on hers, his own big dick in his hand.

"Mmmm... so fucking good," she breathed as her walls clenched on me.

"Open wide, wife," he commanded, his eyes dark and shiny.

She parted her lips, and I watched, fascinated, as he pushed his dick into her mouth, and she started sucking.

"*Fuck*..." I groaned, keeping my thrusts in line with her mouth, moving up and down on Ben's giant cock.

"Good, baby..." Ben guided her, keeping his eyes with hers while she swallowed his cock, taking him deep in her throat while I continued drilling into her and pulling back; almost all the way out, then slamming back in. "Suck my dick while you get fucked. You're so hot, baby... I fucking love you."

"Jesus, Jess..." I grunted, watching her mouth. "Your pussy feels so good..."

She was still moaning, even with Ben's erection sliding in and out of her face. It was so hot, I couldn't even handle it. I could feel my orgasm looming, and I needed to focus.

"Ryan..." I heard Ben's voice calling me, and I looked up. He reached out and grabbed my face, pulling my lips to his.

I whimpered into his mouth as he kissed me, his lips capturing my sounds. He sucked my bottom lip over and over, shoving his tongue inside and flicking it on mine. I ran my fingers through his hair, tugging him even closer, kissing him back hard while I pounded into his wife, forcing her mouth onto his dick.

It was like pleasure overload. I could barely process how much was happening. My dick was buried inside a tight, warm, dripping wet pussy, stroking deep, and I was making out with the hottest guy in the world while he got head. The air in the room was heavy and filled with lust. It all just felt so incredible.

"You like it, baby?" Ben growled on my mouth, tracing my bottom lip with his tongue.

"Yes..." Pulling out and slamming in.

"Tell me, Ryan... Tell me how good my wife's pussy feels."

"Ben... it's so fucking good. *So* tight and wet..." Pound, pound, pound.

"God, I love watching you fuck..." he pressed his forehead against mine as he fucked his wife's mouth. "Make my wife come, Ryan... *Fuck*, make her pussy come on your cock."

I groaned loud, and I felt Jess's insides quivering. Her legs were stiff, and I could tell she was close. She was really going to town on Ben, gobbling his dick like it was her chosen profession. I slid my hand between her thighs and ran my fingers over her clit, brushing it gently until she cried out with her husband's cock sliding down her throat, her chest falling forward as she let go.

Ben pulled out of her mouth and held her up while she screamed, her walls constricting on my dick. She was suddenly even tighter, her pussy squeezing me like a fist as she came, hard, gushing all over me. I bit my lip and slowed my thrusts, letting her ride it out. She was mumbling out garbled cries, a mixture of swears and both of our names. It was the hottest thing I had ever experienced in my life.

As soon as she finished coming, her body collapsed onto the bed. I pulled out of her and laid her down on her back, kissing her lips softly. Her eyelids looked heavy. Actually she looked exhausted, and so damn gorgeous. I hadn't thought her face could flush any more than it was before but clearly, I was wrong.

"Oh my God, Ryan..." she whimpered, running her nails over my abs. "Jesus Christ..."

"You feel good, gorgeous?" I grinned, correcting my breathing.

"Mmmm..." she nodded slowly. "Now I want you to come."

I laughed softly and shook my head, watching her tits move up and down with her heavy breathing, her sweet pink nipples perked up in the air.

"Ben, tag in," Jess murmured, tapping her husband on the thigh.

I glanced up at him and he raised his brow at me. I pulled my lower lip between my teeth. *Oh, Ben...*

Ben crawled up on the bed, lying down on his stomach in front of me. I sat back on my knees and swallowed hard, watching carefully as he slid his tongue under my head, causing my dick to flinch. I was so hard I was throbbing. Seeing Ben's mouth on my dick was threatening to destroy me.

"Mmm..." he grunted, sucking my dick gently for a moment, then popped his mouth off. "I can taste your delicious pussy on his dick, babe."

"Do you like it?" Jessica drawled, rolling onto her side to watch with a curious excitement all over her face.

"Uh-huh..." Ben hummed, sucking me more, deeper, keeping his eyes on mine the whole time. I loved when he did that. The blow-job eye contact was excellent.

"Ben..." I gasped, my head lolling back in pleasure as I reached out to hold his face, reveling in the soft feeling of his tongue sliding underneath my shaft while he sucked my cock deep into his throat. "Your mouth feels... uh, so good, baby."

"Ben, I want your cock," Jess mewled, pleading with her husband.

Without question, he tugged his mouth off me, stroking my dick in his hand a few times while he positioned himself between his wife's thighs, easing his cock into her slowly. He moaned softly, kissing her lips nice and soft, building up a rhythm, thrusting into her deep, holding her thigh around his waist.

I jerked myself off watching Ben move. It looked just as good as I remembered.

"Baby, you're dripping wet," he panted, and she cried out loud. "Did you come nice and hard?"

"Yes!" she squealed.

"You wanna come again for your husband?" he growled, grabbing her tits.

"Yes, Ben... fuck, I love your dick..."

Ben's hooded eyes came back to mine. "Ryan. Dick, here. Now."

I obeyed his command, moving over to his face. He immediately lowered his lips on my cock and resumed sucking me, while fucking his wife slow and deep, his hips and perfect ass looking magnificent thrusting into her.

"God, Ben... Suck my fucking dick..." my voice cracked. It felt so good, I was seconds away from exploding.

Ben groaned with me in his mouth, pumping over and over into Jess's pussy while he blew me. I closed my eyes and shivered.

Fuck, I'm gonna come...

"Ben!" Jessica cried.

"Ben!" I cried.

He teased my balls with his fingers then squeezed gently, his head bobbing up and down my length until I let go and started coming. My dick erupted so hard I could barely breathe. It pulsed and throbbed between his lips, my hot, slick load shooting into his mouth while he hummed and swallowed it all.

He grabbed my hand fast and held it tight. He was coming, too. I knew he was coming inside his wife.

I pulled my dick out of his mouth and he kissed Jess's lips, eyes sealed shut while he roared, "Fuck! I'm coming... Oh God, I'm fucking coming in you, Jess... so... *hard...*"

"Yes, Ben! Come with me!" she squealed again, finding her own release, her nails digging into Ben's muscular back, leaving red marks in their wake.

I couldn't help but touch Ben everywhere, still marveling in my post-orgasm high. I fell back onto the bed behind him, running my hands up and down his hips, rubbing his ass, smiling a lazy smirk at the hickey that was still there from last night.

Ben and Jess were grunting and gasping, heaving as they came down from their orgasms. We were all just a big pile of sweaty limbs, mussed up hair and sex juices. It was mind-blowingly perfect. I couldn't have asked for a better, hotter, kinkier threesome. Ever.

"Oh... my... God..." Jessica squeaked, her fingers trailing down Ben's back, over mine. She grasped my hand, and we locked fingers.

"That was... fucking... perfect..." Ben sighed, running his hand through his hair, which was all over the place, making him look adorably sexy.

"So perfect," I added in a sated purr, scooting up to Ben and kissing his shoulder.

He turned to face me for a moment, taking my jaw in his hand and kissing me gently until I practically melted all over the place. Then he flopped over and grabbed his wife by the waist, tugging her closer to him, planting soft kisses all along her neck.

"I love you, baby..." he whispered. My eyes fluttered shut.

"I love you..." Jess hummed, squeezing my hand.

I love you.

CHAPTER 13

Ben

OPENED MY EYES FAST. Blinked a few times, allowing them to adjust to the lack of light.

It was very dark in the room. Almost too dark to see anything.

I lifted my head and looked around. I was in a bed, much bigger than my own.

Right... The hotel. What time is it?

I glanced to my right, looking over my wife's sleeping body toward the alarm clock on the nightstand. It was four in the morning.

I yawned and brushed my Jess's messy hair away from her face, gazing over her beauty, admiring how peaceful she looked. She was completely naked, not so much as a thin sheet draped over her waist. She looked luminous.

I kissed her forehead, then rolled back over to my left, where Ryan was sleeping with his back to me. He was also naked, and had nothing covering him, because I'd come to realize he was a million degrees when he slept, and he kept kicking the blankets away from him, apparently so as not to set the bed on fire.

I smirked to myself and shook my head, reaching out hesitantly to run my fingers down his back. It was so new and thrilling to have someone else in the bed. And with my wife on the other side of me... I felt like I was tripping on some far-out drug that's high lasted for hours and hours at a time.

I had no idea how to even begin to comprehend what happened tonight...

It was wild. Crazy. Insane. Something I never thought I would do in a million years. And I felt completely at ease doing it.

At no point during tonight's activities did I feel uncomfortable, or question what was going on. It just felt *right* the whole time. I knew it was because of the people. Jessica was my wife of nineteen years. I did everything with her, and wherever she was, I was comfortable and happy. And Ryan and I had a thing going on. We'd only known each other for two weeks, but we'd already explored our sexual feelings for one another a handful of times, and it was always amazing. So naturally bringing the two parties together was like the best fantasy being lived out.

I hadn't gotten a chance to talk to Jessica about whether she felt the same way, but I could already tell that she did. I asked her if she was okay, right before we all passed out in bed together, exhausted, sweaty, and sated. And she'd told me, with a smile, that she'd *never been better*. So I had to take her at her word for now, and trust that I knew her well enough to sniff out when she was secretly feeling off about something.

But Jess's level of comfort with the situation seemed like a direct result of Ryan's part in this as well. For whatever reason, unbeknownst to me, Jess and Ryan had a kind of bond. I wasn't exactly sure what it was, or where it had stemmed from, since they didn't really know each other all that well. But they seemed to really vibe on each other. Sometimes when I watched them interacting, I caught them mirroring each other's movements or facial expressions. And the weird thing was that it didn't seem intentional. It appeared to just happen, and it was strange, but also kind of wonderful to witness.

I already knew there was something different about Ryan. I had picked up on it when we first met, and it just continued to build after we started hooking up. He had a lot of really wonderful qualities, outside of the physical, that drew me to him. I had to imagine that Jess picked up on that stuff, too. Maybe she was feeling the same way that I was...

I was a jealous person by nature. When dudes hit on Jessica out at bars or parties, I always felt the rage bubble inside of me, like a Hulkish caveman. So the fact that I could watch my wife getting fucked by someone who wasn't me, and actually be turned the fuck on by it, meant that there was something else going on here. It was undeniable.

Ryan mumbled something in his sleep and started tossing again, flopping onto his other side and grabbing me by the waist. I smiled to myself and rolled over, deciding to let him spoon me for a minute until his scolding hot flesh got to be too much.

As soon as I pushed my back against his front, it became clear that he was dreaming, or something. He had a raging hard-on. I bit my lip to stifle my laughter, his giant erection poking me in the back as I stared at Jess's face, watching her sleep. She looked so cute and sexy. My wife was one-of-a-kind. The most amazing woman on earth.

Just remembering how fucking hot she looked when she was staring at me, bent over on all fours while Ryan got all up in her guts made me tremble, my semi-hard cock inflating. It was the most incredible thing I'd ever witnessed. It was like fucking in front of a mirror. That is, if you also wanted to suck your own dick and get fucked by your reflection.

My thoughts were getting me turned on again, as was the feeling of Ryan's super-sized cock flinching against my butt. I bit my lip as the arousal got the best of me, and began slowly writhing around a little in frustration.

I ground my butt against Ryan's dick, excitement lancing through me when it pushed in between my cheeks, making me warm and tingly all over. It was the middle of the night, pitch dark, and I was in bed with two hot-as-hell naked humans. If that wasn't a recipe for naughty behavior, then I didn't know what was.

I continued moving slowly, gliding my ass up and down Ryan's long, full cock, listening to him pant in his sleep. I wasn't sure if he had woken up, but I didn't really care either way. It just felt so damn good. I pushed my hips back harder, bending slightly at the waist so I could really get him in there. His smooth, thick head slid over my asshole and my dick started throbbing.

Oh fuck, this feels too good. Should I wake him up to dick me down? Should I wake them both up? Maybe I should just keep teasing and see what happens...

A few more minutes and I was becoming desperate. Ryan's dick was so hard, and it was basically right there, ready to push inside me. I wanted it so bad; I was burning up.

Just when I was about to grab my dick and start jerking off, I felt Ryan's hand massaging my ass. His lips found the back of my neck, kissing everywhere, across my shoulders and down my back. *Thank God, he's awake.*

Neither of us said a word. We didn't have to. The passion and lust were there, ready to be explored. He reached around me, caressing my front with curious fingers; my chest, my abs, my pelvis, purposely avoiding my erection, teasing me in a way that made me quake. He scooted in even closer, moving his lips to my ear, breathing softly while he took my earlobe between his lips and started sucking.

I wanted to moan out loud, but I was trying to keep quiet. I didn't necessarily want to wake my wife... It was much hotter this way. The forbidden aspect. If she woke up while Ryan and I were fooling around, who knew what she would do. And that was the most exciting thought of all.

Ryan's strong hand slithered back down to my ass, grabbing it hard in his palm. He slipped his fingers between the cheeks, and I instinctively tightened at his touch. He panted my name in my ear, giving away how fully turned on he was, as his finger probed me. I whimpered from the feeling of him fingering me, curling it to tease that spot that sent shivers across my entire body. He did it a few more times, then took his hand away for a second, coming back wet.

Fuck. Yes.

He started pushing his hips forward, swirling his head around on my hole. I relaxed a lot, more than usual because I wanted it so bad, and I was turned on like crazy. I closed my eyes and pushed my hips back to him, begging him, without words, to fill me quick before I burst into flames.

Ryan shoved his cock inside my ass slowly, his head slipping in first, breaking through my entrance. I gasped, as quietly as I could manage, gripping the sheets in my fist. He pushed in more, and more, penetrating me slow and steady, and I could tell it was driving him crazy. I was so fucking needy for him; I had to pop my butt out further, allowing him to thrust deeper. He grabbed my ass in his hands and held on tight while he pulled back and drove in, his thick monster cock ripping me apart.

"Ryan..." I whispered, unable to hold back anymore. "Fuck, that feels good..."

"Ben, you're so tight, baby," he growled, lifting my butt with his hands, fucking me deeper and deeper. "I love fucking your sweet ass."

"I love when you fuck my ass..." I rasped, trying too damn hard to keep quiet.

"You need me inside you, Ben?" he panted from behind me, kissing and nipping my neck, tugging my hair.

"Always," I moaned in a whisper. I went to reach for my cock, but Ryan swatted my hand away, taking it in his fist and stroking slowly up and down.

He met every thrust with a stroke. Just the best at reach-arounds.

We were going at it, hard, trying to be subtle, but it was pretty difficult when I had a huge cock in my ass. Ryan was pumping me from behind over and over, screwing me so good, I could barely breathe. My eyes sealed tight as I chomped down on my lip, taking the pounding I was being given and fucking loving it.

And then suddenly, I heard another voice.

"Oh my God..." Jess whimpered, and my eyes flew open. I caught a startled look on her face, but it didn't last long before she was launching herself at me.

She grabbed my face and kissed me hard, shoving her tongue in my mouth, gasping and moaning all kinds of erotic noises over my lips. She licked and sucked all over my jaw, and down my neck, biting me and scratching me with her nails.

I felt Ryan slowing a little, as if he didn't know what was going on, but then Jess's hand covered his on my cock and I moaned softly.

"Ryan, keep going..." she commanded in a whisper, and Ryan

didn't hesitate. He picked up the pace, thrusting into me hard from behind, moving his lips in to kiss my shoulders. It was the perfect combination of rough and sweet.

Jess and Ryan's linked hands jerked me off, and it felt so fucking wonderful I couldn't even comprehend what was happening. Then I felt Jess move her front up even closer and she wrapped her leg around my waist.

"Ben... put your cock in my pussy, please..." she whimpered, taking my dick and aiming it into her tight wet opening. "Fuck me while you're getting fucked, please. I need it."

My dick throbbed in her hand. Ryan was so deep in my ass, hitting my spot over and over, I knew I would come soon. And from the sound of him, so would he. The idea of coming inside my wife while Ryan came in me was too much for my erection to bear. It was about to burst just thinking about it.

I yanked Jess as close to me as I could get her, swooping her underneath me a little. Ryan got the hint and held my hips up enough to get a good angle. Then I slid my cock inside my wife, inch by inch, all three of us groaning out loud simultaneously.

"Ryan, can you... *fuck*... can you move... with me?" I panted, seeing stars in the room's darkness.

"Just follow my lead, baby," he rasped in my ear and I almost came just from that.

He continued to draw back then thrust inside me, and every time he did, I moved into my wife. It was like Ryan was controlling the whole thing which was fully mind altering. It was *so* good. I wouldn't be able to hold out for very long.

"Ben..." Jess squealed, feeling up my chest, legs spread open wide, while I pounded into her with Ryan's thrusts. "This is... *amazing*..."

"Mmm... baby... *yes*."

"How does it feel?" she purred, licking my lips. "Do you like it?"

"I love it..."

"Does Ryan's dick feel good inside you...?"

"Fuck, yes... Baby... I can't..." My brain was scrambled. I had no idea what I was saying, and everything was fading away from me.

"Are you gonna come from his huge dick?" she kept going,

moaning, pushing me while I pushed in her.

"Fuck! I'm gonna come... inside you..." I gasped, feeling my balls get super tight. "Ryan... baby, you're making me... come!"

"Come inside your wife, Ben," he growled in my ear, licking it, kissing my neck and jaw. "Come with my dick inside you..."

I gasped out loud and let the orgasm crash down on me like a tidal wave. I couldn't even recognize my own voice, grunting and panting and mumbling all kinds of things as my dick set off like a volcano and I poured all of myself inside my wife's tight, warm pussy.

She was squealing along with me, and as I was coming down, I felt Ryan finding his own release inside me, while Jess's walls were trembling on my cock with her own rocking orgasm.

They both made me come and then came together. It was the hottest, craziest, most ludicrous thing I'd ever been a part of.

After that, I blacked out for a while. I'm not sure if I fell asleep or was just in some kind of bizarre orgasm trance, but I felt like I was floating on a cloud made of cotton candy.

I vaguely recall Ryan and Jess falling onto the bed on either side of me, both of them kissing me in all kinds of places, whispering things. But I was barely conscious enough to do anything other than wrap my arms around them, pull them into my chest, and knock the fuck out.

When I reopened my eyes, it was light out. I stretched out my arms and legs in bed, feeling some serious muscle strain, all over my body. I turned my head left and right, slowly processing the fact that I was alone. It was then that I noticed the music coming from the other room. And the smell of food.

Yes, thank God for food. I'm starving.

I rolled out of bed, quickly stumbling to the bathroom so I could brush my teeth and wash up. I needed to wake up a little. I felt dazed from everything that had happened in the past forty-eight-hours. It was sort of like a booze and sex hangover, only much more refreshing. I felt... *alive.*

Once I finished in the bathroom, I got dressed in just my sweatpants and made my way through the suite, following the smell of bacon. I heard voices talking and laughing over the faint sound of the Rolling Stones' *Beast of Burden.* I sauntered toward the kitchen, unsure of what I would find.

I paused for a moment, taking in the scene before me.

Jess and Ryan were sitting at the living room table. They were both wearing robes, sipping cups of coffee, talking animatedly and laughing back and forth. There was a whole spread set up on the table, and it all looked delicious. But I was still too stunned to move.

I wasn't sure why, but for some reason I hadn't expected Ryan to still be there. And I definitely hadn't expected him to stay for breakfast. It was disorienting but also a surprising relief.

I forced myself to keep moving, wandering over to them to see what the hell was going on. My eyes found the food, like magnets, my mouth beginning to salivate as my stomach rumbled. All the activities from last night made me ravenous.

"Good morning, baby!" Jess chirped, gazing up at me with a smile covering her beautiful, fresh face. She looked rejuvenated; glowing, even. Clearly last night was good for her.

"Good morning," Ryan added, also smiling. He too looked incandescent. *Jeez, I wonder if I look that good...*

"Morning..." I murmured, plopping down on the love seat across from them, pouring myself some coffee.

"Are you hungry?" Jess asked, sounding very perky considering the lack of sleep.

"Famished," I grunted, sipping my coffee, then immediately grabbed a plate and scooped on some of everything. Pancakes, eggs, bacon, home fries, fruit. My plate was filled to the max, and I glanced up to see Ryan and Jess staring at me, both with the same knowing smirks on their faces. "What...?" I grumbled, raising my brows.

"Nothing," they both rasped at the same time, then peeked at each other and started giggling.

Okay, this is too weird.

"Recovering a little..." Ryan huffed, still wearing his cheeky little grin. "I get it."

"Yea, I already put away like three pancakes," Jess kept giggling.

"More like one and a half," Ryan teased at her, poking her in the side. "Then you made me eat the rest for you."

"No way! Shut up..." she squealed, smacking him playfully in the arm, before tucking a loose strand of hair behind her ear. Her cheeks were all sorts of rosy.

I squinted at them. "How long have you two been up?"

"Not long," Jess muttered, sipping her coffee.

I shrugged to myself, digging into my food. It was still warm, so it couldn't have been there for more than fifteen-minutes. I shoveled food into my mouth fast, basically inhaling everything because I was freaking starving. I hadn't been that hungry in a while.

"We have to check-out in two hours," Jess pouted. I glanced up at her in between massive bites. "I don't want to leave this big, beautiful hotel suite."

"Do you have to work tomorrow?" Ryan asked me, appearing thoroughly interested.

"I have a lunch meeting with some contractors," I mumbled. "We're bidding out a new job."

"They're building a new mall in Los Cruces," Jess added. "It would be a huge job."

"That sounds cool," Ryan nodded, looking back and forth between Jess and me.

I didn't know what to say, so I just nodded along, continuing on with my breakfast. It was sort of strange, sitting there with my wife and Ryan, after everything that happened the night before. I wasn't sure exactly what was going on, but Jess seemed fully content with Ryan being there, hanging around with us in the morning. I was a little thrown off by it. I had assumed she would want him to leave, though I didn't really know why.

I pushed the confusing thoughts out of my brain as I finished my food. Jess and Ryan were chatting back and forth about Ryan's classes, and what he was looking forward to this semester. Apparently, he was stressing out a little because he hadn't had the chance to work much lately, what with his friend's company being short on jobs. He seemed uneasy regarding his school loans, but he brushed it off when Jess tried asking about it.

Ryan's phone started ringing on the table, and he stared at it for a moment, swiping the screen, apparently to dismiss the call.

"It's just my roommate," he told us, flopping back against the couch. "He keeps calling to make sure I'm not dead."

"Shouldn't you answer and let him know you're not?" Jess grinned.

Ryan chuckled and shook his head, draping his arm on the back of the couch, his fingers playing with her hair.

"He'll be fine," he winked.

"Did they know you were coming over here?" I asked, narrowing my gaze at him. There was a tightening sensation in my stomach and it was making me uncomfortable.

"Mhm," he grunted his answer which annoyed me.

"His roommates were *concerned* about his relationship with me," I told Jess, popping a strawberry into my mouth.

"Yea, but I assured them that everything is fine, and I have it all under control," he said to her, glancing at me quick, giving me a look, before returning to my wife.

"Well, I can understand why they would feel that way," Jess squeaked, eyes bouncing back and forth between Ryan and me. "It is sort of an... odd situation."

"It is odd," Ryan nodded.

"Very *odd*..." I rumbled, watching him closely. He was so close to my wife... And I wasn't sure if I was actually jealous, or if I just felt like I *should* be.

After all, how could I justify being jealous of Ryan flirting with my wife when we had all fucked each other last night?

Or maybe I was jealous of Jess...

I shook my head and grabbed the rest of the bacon.

"Anyone want more bacon?" I asked, just to be polite. I definitely wasn't giving it up. "Too slow. It's all mine."

Ryan laughed out loud and Jess started giggling up a storm. I had to smile. I couldn't be jealous of these two. I liked them too damn much...

"Well, I'm gonna go take a shower," Jess sighed, standing up slowly, stretching her arms behind her back. "Or maybe another bath..." She reached out to brush Ryan's hair back with her fingers. "I'm going to miss the fuck out of that tub."

He grinned up at her, and she peeked at me, sliding her tongue over her bottom lip. I winked at her and she skipped off toward the bathroom.

Ryan gazed across the table at me, and I took a deep breath. He was giving me a look that I couldn't really interpret, and it was making me uneasy.

Before I could say anything, he got up and ambled over to the love seat, plopping down next to me. He scooted up to my side, wrapping his arm around my back and resting his head on my shoulder. I wasn't sure where the display of affection was coming from, but it felt really nice. I leaned back, placing my hand on his chest, fingering the opening of the robe.

"Are you okay with me being here?" he asked quietly, grasping my hand in his and locking our fingers.

"Of course..." I murmured, taking in the warmth that came from being able to just be near him; to hold on to him without worrying about someone finding out. It was so unfamiliar and overwhelming, it made me feel drunk.

"Because you looked a little upset about me getting close to Jess..." he rumbled, picking his head up to look at me. I gaped at him, unsure of what to say. Maybe I had been a little jealous at first, but only because it was so weird to see Jess acting like that with anyone who wasn't me. "If you ever feel uncomfortable with something, I want you to tell me. We have to be open about this stuff."

"It's just different..." I told him, running my fingers through the scruff along his jaw. "I'll get used to it."

"Is that... what you think will happen?" Ryan asked, his eyes wide and uncertain. "We're going to get used to it? The three of us...?"

"Jesus, Ryan, I don't know..." I shrugged, shaking my head slowly. "I have absolutely no idea what's going on. Last night was... mind-blowing. It was the craziest thing I've ever done."

He grinned at me. "It was pretty amazing, huh?"

"It feels so good being with you..." I whispered, leaning in to kiss him softly. He hummed on my mouth and I felt it below my waist. "And with Jess. I love watching you two together. I love the idea of both of us being with her... And both of you being with me. The combinations are endless." I grinned, and he chuckled on my lips.

"Do you think she's as amped over this as you are?" he asked, pulling back and raising his brow.

"I don't know, baby. You tell me," I smirked. "You guys seem to have an interesting bond..."

"We do," he breathed, gazing into my eyes. "It's weird. I feel very connected to her."

"Mmm... yea. I witnessed your *connection*," I grumbled, quirking my brow at him this time.

"You obviously liked it..." he teased me, sticking his tongue out. I licked it and he pretended to fight me off.

"Ben! Ryan!" Jess's voice bellowed from the bathroom. "Come help me get clean!"

Ryan and I paused our play fight and stared at each other with excitement sparkling in our eyes.

"I'll race you," he jumped off the couch and stumbled to his feet.

"You're goin down, kid!" I chased after him, grabbing him by the waist.

"Is that a promise?" he sneered, giving me a salacious grin before biting his lip as we shoved each other around, stammering toward the bathroom.

The second I stepped inside I froze, my jaw dropping through the floor. And it appeared that Ryan had the same reaction.

My wife was standing completely naked in front of the giant bathtub, staring at us with a wicked smirk on her beautiful face.

"Mmm... hi, there," she rasped at us, and we both just blinked. She turned and bent over in front of us, pouring some lavender body wash into the flowing water of the tub which was now about half full.

My dick was filling rapidly as I gawked at her gorgeous ass, all round and luscious, on display and waiting for me to grab it. I glanced at Ryan out the corner or my eye and he looked like he was drooling.

Jess faced us again, and now I was staring at her front parts; big, perky tits and her sweet little cupcake of a pussy. *Yum... My wife is a fuckin snack.*

I decided to make the first move, taking a slow step toward her. But she held up her hand, stopping me in my tracks, which made me pout. She giggled in response.

"There's something I want to do with you two," Jess purred, her bright eyes dancing between us.

"What did you have in mind...?" Ryan muttered, sounding like he was about to combust. I couldn't stop my eyes from dropping below his waist, noting his impeccably hard cock, poking through the material of the robe he was wearing.

"I will tell one of you to do something, and you have to do it," she started, explaining the rules to her made-up sexy game, which was really just *Jess Calls the Shots*, something we played often at home.

I raised my eyebrows at her. "So you just tell us what to do?"

"Yup," she squinted at me. "I'm feeling a little... curious. And I think we should play one more time before we go home, don't you agree?"

Her eyes stuck on mine, then they darted over to Ryan quick before coming back to me. *Ah, I see what she means. She wants us to enjoy our remaining time with Ryan by doing something fun and kinky before we have to leave him... Well, I'm down.*

I nodded at her slowly and she grinned, giving me a slightly wistful look. I definitely knew where she was coming from.

"Are you ready?" she asked, looking primarily at Ryan, who appeared sort of nervous. He swallowed visibly and nodded. "Okay!" she clapped. "Ben, I want to see how you and Ryan kiss."

I chuckled softly and shook my head. "You've already seen it..."

"Yea, but that was last night during all the sexcapades," she grinned widely.

"*Sexcapades?*" I laughed, crossing my arms over my chest. "Really?"

"Don't make fun of my cool word," she scolded me with a smirk. "I think it fits."

"I'd have to agree on that one," Ryan added.

"Okay, fine," I huffed, conceding to them. *I imagine I'll be doing a lot of that from now on.* "So you want me to kiss Ryan?"

"Yes, please," she nodded, looking like such a mischievous little kitten, I couldn't stand it.

I stepped up to Ryan quick and grasped his face, holding his jaw with my hand. He looked slightly taken aback, but his eyes set on mine then fell to my lips. I could tell he wanted it. And I did, too. I loved kissing him, after all. It felt fantastic.

I inched my face closer to his until I could feel his breath on my lips. My eyes fluttered shut, and I kissed him, so soft that he whimpered into my mouth. He grabbed me by the waist while we both parted our lips, tongues touching in the middle. I was already panting; it felt so nice. And knowing Jess was watching was just egging me on even more.

We kept on, kissing deeper, sucking at each other's lips with haste, my hands tugging him by his neck and hair, while he pulled my body closer to his, our erections grinding together through our clothes.

Finally, we parted, both of us breathless, eyes closed and lips brushing gently. I traced his lower lip with my tongue and he growled, barely audibly, but I could feel it, like a tremor running through me.

"Jesus... you two are so hot..." Jess murmured, and I opened my eyes to look at her.

She turned off the water and stepped slowly into the tub, her creamy flesh slipping beneath the bubbles as she sat down.

"Do we get to join you?" Ryan asked, now watching her, too.

"Not just yet," she rasped, licking her lips. "But soon. First, I want you to undress each other."

I took a breath, trying to steady my raging libido. This game was turning me on like crazy. I had no idea what Jess was playing at, but I knew it would be dirty, and sexy, and very fun.

Ryan went first, pushing my sweatpants down slowly, over my huge hard-on, which bobbed out, ready for action, then down my ass and thighs, letting them fall to my feet. I stepped out and kicked them away, untying his robe and pushing it off his shoulders, grinning at the fact that his eyes were stuck on my dick.

"Mmm..." Jess hummed from in the bath, leaning back against the tub, her eyelids drooping slightly in that way that let me know how aroused she was. Her right hand was already missing under the water, and I knew she would be touching herself soon.

"What next?" I asked, gazing at Ryan, flicking my hips forward to rub my cock against his.

"Touch each other..." Jess commanded, her voice soft and raspy with desire. "Slowly."

I moved in closer to Ryan, sealing the gap between our bodies so we could really grind on each other. He reached down and grabbed our dicks together in his hand, stroking so slow that my eyes closed, and I groaned softly. I placed my hands on his back, running my fingers along his muscles, tracing them with my fingers.

"Ryan, kiss Ben's neck," Jess panted. "He loves it..."

"Mmm..." Ryan groaned, moving his lips down my jaw and onto my neck, kissing and sucking all over.

I ran my hands around to his front, feeling up his chest and abs, grabbing his dick and rubbing it in tender motions. He breathed on my skin and I was burning up. His hands were on my chest, treasuring me while I jerked him slowly, making him tremble.

"Ryan..." Jess's voice moaned from the tub and he grunted a response, his tongue gliding over my throat. "On your knees, please."

"God damn, baby..." I breathed, not really sure which one of them I was talking to. Most likely both. It was such a trip, having two of them... It made my dick so hard it felt like it might break off.

Ryan happily dropped to his knees in front of me and licked his lips, gazing up at me with hunger in his eyes. I loved that look on him. It reminded me of the first time, in the basement...

"You know what to do," Jess gasped, and I peeked at her. She was leaning back in the tub, her wide eyes stuck on what we were doing. Her chest was moving up and down with rapid breaths, and she looked super into it.

Ryan wasted no time slipping his tongue under the head of my cock, tonguing it slowly before sucking me between his parted lips. I groaned, biting my lip and brushing my fingers through his hair while he went to town on my throbbing cock.

He was sucking for a while. Jessica was moaning out loud, rubbing her pussy in the bath. My eyes couldn't decide where they would rather be; on her or Ryan's mouth, sliding up and down my solid flesh. He was getting really good at blow jobs. I found myself wondering if I had gotten any better since the first time...

Finally, Jess stopped us, begging us to get into the huge bathtub with her, which we obviously did, without hesitation or argument. The water was warm, and it smelled like that body wash, which was calming. Still, my heart was pounding in my chest in anticipation of what would happen... I couldn't remember if I'd ever actually had sex in a bath before, but I didn't think I had. Especially not with two people at once...

Ryan and I sat side by side, across from Jessica, whose cheeks were flushed, her eyes dark with the obvious arousal she was feeling. She was looking at us like she wanted to devour us both. It was insanely hot.

She sat up slowly, scooting over to us, grabbing my face first, kissing me soft and sweet, purring on my lips, making my dick twinge in the water. Then she pulled Ryan's face over so we could all kiss at the same time. It was such an experience... When all three of our lips touched it sent an electric chill through me, from my groin up to my chest. *Mmm...*

Before I knew what was happening, Ryan and Jess were licking and sucking down my neck and chest, yanking at my hips to get my dick above the surface of the water so they could blow me together.

Their eyes met and their mouths came together right over the head of my cock. I groaned out loud, because *holy fuck...* There had never been a more intense blow job. Two mouths, on my cock. Two tongues, two sets of lips... It was like they were making out, with my super-hard dick in the middle. *Jesus Christ... This is incredible.* I barely noticed how hard I was gripping the sides of the tub until my hands started to ache.

"Baby?" Jess squeaked, her voice trembling.

"Yea?" Ryan and I both answered at the same time, and we all giggled.

"I want to watch you getting fucked by my husband..." Jess told Ryan, their eyes locked, faces only a couple inches apart. He nodded slowly, his eyes dropping to her lips. "While you... lick me..." she whispered, then slid her hand between her thighs under the water. "Here."

"Fuck, baby..." Ryan growled, brushing his lips over hers, while he took my cock in his hand, stroking it slowly. "I want to taste you again so bad."

"Again?" I grunted, and they both looked at me with sparkling eyes and faux-innocent smirks on their lips. Ryan crawled over me, kissing my lips slowly.

"I want you to fuck me again..." he hummed, and I took his plump bottom lip between my teeth, feeling his cock flinch against mine.

"Again?" Jess gasped, and we pulled apart to give her some dirty, wicked smirks of our own.

"Yea... Our boy can ride my dick like a cowboy," I rasped, giving Ryan a lascivious look before kissing him again, running my hand over his sweet ass beneath the bubbles. My finger slid between his cheeks and I felt him tense as he groaned softly.

"Hmm... So you both fuck each other?" Jess murmured, pushing herself back to the other side of the tub. "That is... very exciting."

"Everybody gets fucked in this threesome, sweetheart," I winked at her. Then I sat up, taking Ryan by the hips and forcing him to spin around to face my woman. "Now, lift your hips, wife. I think Ryan's still hungry..."

I slapped him on the ass, and he whimpered, taking Jess's ass in his hands and lifting her enough to get her thighs around his head. I got up on my knees in front of him, massaging his ass and watching in fascination as he lowered his mouth onto my wife's pussy and slowly began licking her.

My cock was already weeping. I took it in my fist and gave it some long strokes, while Ryan's tongue swirled around on my wife's clit, slipping inside her while he kissed and sucked. Jessica was panting hard, her breasts heaving up and down, nipples hard as little pebbles. She dug her fingers into Ryan's hair as he moved, lapping at her over and over.

My fingers glided between Ryan's ass again, my thumb circling his tightness a few times until I felt him relax. Then I pushed the head of my cock up to his hole, spreading him open so I could watch myself enter.

He was already making some very erotic noises, his face buried in my wife's delicious pussy. Jessica looked like she was close. I nudged my dick into Ryan's ass, the head slipping inside with the wetness from the bath. He groaned out loud, and I felt him shudder. I ran my hands over his hips, caressing his smooth flesh with my fingers while I pushed in further.

"Jesus Christ, Ben..." he moaned, his voice muffled by Jess's pussy. "You're so fucking big..."

"Mmmm... he is, isn't he?" Jess gasped, opening her eyes to watch what was happening in front of her. I bit my lip and thrust in more.

"Oh yea... fuck my ass good..." Ryan grunted, popping his butt in front of me. I chuckled, out of breath and already about to explode, forcing my dick further into his body, giving him inches until I was up to my balls in his backside.

"You like it deep, don't you?" I hummed at him, pulling back and driving in again.

"So deep..." he drawled.

I kept on fucking him, steady and slow, but deep, making him cry out my name into my wife's warm wetness. He was eating her so good, so dedicated, I could tell Jess was loving it. Her eyes were back and forth between mine and Ryan's, just like mine were back and forth between hers and my dick moving in and out of him.

The whole being with two people at once thing was still such a high... I didn't see how I could ever tire of it. There was so much to look at, so much to touch, to feel. It was like sensory overload. I felt like a kid in a toy store or something. *Probably not the most appropriate analogy, but let's face it. Appropriate went out the window a while ago...*

My hips were thrusting over and over and over into Ryan from behind while he ate my wife's pussy hard, licking and sucking in between groaning and grunting out his own pleasure. Jess came first, exploding into a trembling orgasm that I could feel, and I wasn't even really touching her.

Then she held onto Ryan, kissing his lips and jaw and neck, stroking his dick under the water until he gave in and started coming. I followed his lead, feeling him convulsing while I filled him with my climax, the three of us collapsing all over one another, struggling to catch our breath.

An hour later, we were all cleaned up, dressed and packed, ready to give the amazing hotel suite back. I was feeling slightly bummed, because we'd had such a great time there. We had made some seriously insane memories in that hotel room...

If these walls could talk... Let's just be glad they can't.

Jessica volunteered to hang back and get us checked out while I gave Ryan a ride back to his apartment. We agreed that it might look sort of strange for us both to drop him off. So they said their goodbyes, and I couldn't help but note the slightly glum looks on both of their faces as Ryan and I left Jess behind in the suite.

When we were securely inside the car, driving toward Ryan's apartment, I took a moment to breathe again. It had been such a whirlwind, the past two days. I could barely even process everything that had happened.

Ryan was squeezing my hand over the center console, as he had been since the second we got settled in the car. He was gazing out the window, seemingly deep in thought. I wanted to ask him what he was thinking, but I was willing to bet I already knew what it was.

Where do we go from here? I'm going to miss him again... Just like every other time we leave each other. Nothing has changed now that Jess is in the picture. If anything, it just makes it all the more complicated.

"So..." I finally broke the silence, tracing his thumb with mine.

"So..." he repeated, resting his head back against the seat.

"Do you have any plans for this week?" I asked, trying to make conversation and lift the mood a little. "Other than school, I mean..."

"No," he grunted, and said nothing else.

"No work, or anything coming up?" I pressed on.

"Uh-uh," he shook his head.

"I could maybe try to find you something if you need money," I offered. "I know some landscaping companies who might need part-time help."

"Yea but aren't they out by you?" he asked, turning his head slightly.

"Well, sort of..." I mumbled, racking my brain for any companies I knew that did jobs up this way.

"Forget it," he grumbled. "It's just... too far."

"It's not that far," I huffed, though I didn't really believe my argument. Five hours was far. I knew that was bumming him out.

"Yes, it is, Ben," he bit out. "You're going to be *so* far away from me. It's not like I can just drive for five hours... There and back is like a whole day in travel."

"Baby..." I whispered, shaking my head. He wasn't talking about work. He was talking about us not being able to see each other. I already knew it.

"*Baby* what?" he turned to face me fully in his seat. I concentrated harder on the road. "What do you want me to do, Ben? Just forget about this and move on?"

"No," my brow furrowed. "I don't want you to forget..."

"Then what am I supposed to do?" His tone making me feel sick. "I already missed you before... Last time I left you, I was miserable. And now it's even worse, because I'll be missing you *and* Jess." He breathed out hard, dropping his chin. "I don't know why I keep doing this to myself..."

"Ryan, I'm going to miss you too, ya know?" I responded, trying not to let my frustration out in my voice. "I'm going to miss you like crazy. I always do..."

"Yea, but you still have Jess. I have no one."

"You still *have* us... We just have to be apart for a little bit. It won't be too bad. I'll try to figure out a time when we can see each other again."

"Great. That makes me feel so much better..." he muttered sarcastically.

"Why are you acting like you're the only one who's affected by this?" I asked, peering at him out the corner of my eye. "It hurts me, too. You don't think I want to see you all the time? I..."

I forced myself to stop talking quick before I said something dangerous. I swallowed hard, trying to regroup my thoughts.

"I care a lot about you, Ryan," I squeezed his hand. "I hope you know that by now."

He was quiet for a moment. Then I heard him breathe in and out slowly.

"I do," he replied softly.

I nodded in acceptance of him accepting my words. "Maybe we can meet half-way next week or something. Have dinner, where no one knows us."

"What about Jess?" he asked with hesitation in his deep voice.

"She can come if she wants," I told him, my stomach twisting with many confusing emotions. I couldn't understand how I was feeling anymore.

I had thought when I was sneaking around with Ryan that adding Jess to the equation would bring everything out in the open. But now that it had happened, I was even more lost. As much as I loved fooling around with them together, I still wanted my alone time with Ryan. And I always loved my alone time with Jess, obviously. Maybe Jess wanted alone time with Ryan, too...

I had no clue how the hell we would figure all of this out. *In my effort to smooth things out, I really just fucked it up more. That's great. Good job, Lockwood.*

We arrived at Ryan's apartment, and I pulled into his driveway, alongside his BMW. I left the car running, unbuckling my seatbelt so I could touch him and kiss him everywhere. I was feeling the goodbye looming over me like a dark cloud, and it was making my chest ache.

Ryan unbuckled his seatbelt and immediately reached over the console to pull me closer to him. We kissed soft, but desperate, his hands gripping my waist as mine ran through his hair. There were no hesitations anymore when we did this. We were fully confessing of our feelings for one another when we kissed and touched... and said goodbye. It still hurt, only now all the pain was out in the open.

My surroundings came back to me and I opened my eyes, pulling back slightly as I glanced outside the vehicle. There wasn't anyone around, but I still wasn't sure if I wanted people to see us like this. What if someone around there knew Hailey? It wasn't unreasonable. It was the school area, after all.

"Sorry..." Ryan breathed, giving me an apologetic look as he realized what was suddenly tripping me up. I didn't want him to feel bad. It wasn't that I didn't want people to see us together... There was just still so much in the way.

"Don't apologize," I hummed, tugging his face back so I could kiss him again. "I'll miss you, baby."

"Me, too," he whispered, his voice rough with uncertainty.

"We'll talk soon, okay?" I asked, pushing his hair back with my fingers as I stared into his eyes. "You have my number now..."

He grinned a reluctant little thing that was fully adorable and nodded. "Yea. I do."

"Okay. Good," I winked at him, and he backed up further, breathing out hard. "Now get that sexy ass inside and try not to get drunk today."

"Can't make any promises," he smirked, opening the car door. "Some hot older guy turned me into an alcoholic."

I growled at him and he laughed, then leaned back inside to kiss me once more before he was out of the car, and on his way inside his apartment.

I breathed out a slow, shaky breath, glancing down at nothing. My smile had fully faded, and I didn't really know what to think. Everything was so fucked up, and I knew it was just going to get worse.

My life had gone from completely stress-free and dull, to drama-filled and bordering on excruciating. My mind couldn't possibly determine what to do next, so I zoned out and drove back to the hotel to pick up my wife. And then we went home.

"How long do you need to get started?" I asked, leaning up on the table, making some notes with a black sharpie.

"We should be good by next week," John, one of my subcontractors replied, hanging his tape measurer back on his tool belt.

"Good to hear. We need to get the jump on this. Their deadline is aggressive," I murmured, running my fingers along my jaw. "Who the hell starts a job right before Christmas?"

"I'm not sure, but these plans are on point, Lockwood. This will make us all a lot of dough."

I nodded at John, my eyes scanning the papers one more time before rolling them back up. This was my second meeting with the teams about our new project in Los Cruces. They had drawn up the contracts last week, and everyone was ready to go. I felt good about it. It would be a tough job, but my guys were the best in the state. I was sure everyone would be happy with the outcome.

John and I left the site, removing our hard hats and tossing them in the back of his truck. The sun was setting, and I needed to get home. Jess had already texted me that dinner would be ready in ten, and I was a good twenty-minute drive from home.

"Hey, you wouldn't happen to know of any landscaping companies up by ABQ that need help, would you?" I asked, tossing my stuff onto the passenger seat of my SUV.

"Um, not off-hand, but I could make some calls," John answered. "Why? What's going on up there?"

I looked up at him quickly. "Nothing really. It's just, um... one of Hailey's friends from school is looking for work." I tried not to seem as awkward as I was feeling.

"Oh. Yea, let me see what I can do," he nodded.

"It's no big deal," I shook my head casually, then extended my hand. John shook it hard. "I'll talk to you in a few days."

"You got it, boss," he rumbled, stalking over to his truck and hopping in, starting it up then honking at me as he drove away.

I got into my car and breathed out slowly as I left the lot. I kept the radio on as I drove home, but I wouldn't have been able to tell you what was playing. I was so deep in my thoughts; I was basically in a trance.

It had been over a week since Jess and I came home from Albuquerque. I was working a lot which left me little time to obsess over everything that had gone down. But still I was restless more often than not, and I hadn't gone to bed earlier than two in the morning in longer than I could remember.

On the outside, everything looked normal. Jess and I were back to our routine, living our regular lives. Working, having dinner at home, and gardening. Our friends came over on Friday night. The girls drank wine and gossiped upstairs while the guys played poker in the man-cave. It was all very standard behavior. It seemed as if nothing had changed at all, when in reality the opposite was true.

I had barely spoken to Ryan since we left him. We texted here and there, and I called him the other night when I couldn't sleep, just to see how he was doing. He seemed like he had fallen back into his own routine as well, going to school, studying, working out and spending time with his friends. I knew he was busy with his own life, and the last thing I wanted to do was disrupt his flow. But I still missed him. And while he assured me he was fine over and over again, I could tell by the distance in his messages, and in his voice on the phone, that he wasn't happy.

The guilt was palpable. Not only from lying to and betraying my daughter but also for leaving Ryan to fend for himself. I knew he didn't *need* me. He was a grown man, and an extremely independent one at that. But I felt like I had come crashing into his life, shaking everything up like a damn earthquake, and then just took off, leaving him with nothing but rubble. I had never felt like more of an asshole in my life.

Jessica refused to talk about him. I discovered our first day back home, after that crazy weekend, that she became edgy and tense when I mentioned Ryan. So I just stopped doing it.

Still, now and then I would catch her staring off into space with an odd look of longing or nostalgia in her eyes. I knew she was thinking about him, but I couldn't ask her about it. Mainly because I was afraid of what she would say.

I pulled into the driveway, turning off the ignition and just sitting in the quiet darkness of my SUV for a minute. I stared at my house, all the downstairs lights on inside. It looked so quiet and typical... so suburban. It was a nice house; nicer than all of our friends' houses. I had done a lot of work to it, and I was proud of that fact. But looking at it now, all I felt was suffocation.

There was a sneaking thought that came creeping into my brain, one that hadn't made an appearance in quite some time...

I should've had another kid. I should've gotten Jess pregnant again...

I loved being a father. I would have loved to have another child, before. But now it was too late. We were too old to start all of that again. I just wished we could've tried harder a few years back. Maybe it would have changed something...

I shook all these unnecessary thoughts from my head and got out of the car, making my way into the house. When I stepped inside, the entire downstairs smelled amazing. I had no idea what Jess made for dinner, but my mouth was already watering.

"Baby?" I grumbled, kicking off my work boots and walking

through the hall, toward the kitchen to find my wife.

I turned the corner of the dining room and saw Jess in the kitchen, leaning against the island with a glass of red wine in her hand.

"Hi, gorgeous," I crooned, stepping over quickly, grabbing her waist with my hand and pressing a soft kiss on her cheek. "Smells fantastic in here."

"Thanks. You're late," she scolded me with her eyes, though she was smiling.

"I know, I'm sorry," I squeezed her butt, making her squeal. "Meeting ran long. I texted you in my mind."

She giggled, then bit her lip to stop herself, still pretending to be mad.

"Your mind must have bad service because I didn't get it," she sneered, and I gave her a broad smile. "How'd everything go?"

"Great," I replied, picking a tomato out of the salad bowl while she smacked my hands away. "John's guys can probably start getting set up next week. I suppose they'll just prep for now and then it'll be full-speed ahead January second." I popped the tomato into my mouth. "How was your day?"

"Fine. I talked to Hailey. She's obsessing over some crazy paper she has to do before winter break," Jess told me, pouring dressing onto the salad. "And Rachel is already nagging me about the Christmas Eve party. She wants us to have it here."

"Really?" I huffed, giving her a look. "I thought they were doing it this year?"

"Yea, but I guess their house is a mess because of the baby," she pursed her lips then peeked up at me, wearing a purely guilty expression.

"What...?" I narrowed my gaze at her. Her eyes darted back down to the food. "What did you do, wife of mine?"

"I told her we'd do it..." she murmured quietly, knowing full well I would not be pleased.

"Jess..." I sighed, shaking my head.

"I know, I know. But it won't be that bad," she squeaked, trying to convince me. "Actually, it might be nice. Hailey will be home that week. We can decorate the house, wrap presents... It'll be fun!"

"Yea, I know we'll have fun with Hailey," I rolled my eyes. "I just don't see why we need to have a bunch of people over. I'd rather it be just us."

"Ben, don't be such a hermit," she said in an admonishing tone, bringing the salad bowl over to the table.

I raised my brow, following her into the dining room. I sat down in my chair and she opened a casserole dish, scooping out some delicious-looking creation onto the plate in front of me. It looked like baked ziti or something. I was already salivating.

"I think you just enjoy doting on people," I rumbled, glancing up to watch her as she set me up with my dinner. My mind started flashing back to the dinners she used to make for us when Hailey was little.

I would come home from work exhausted, and Jess always had a hot meal ready and waiting for me. She would plop Hailey into her highchair and cut her up little hot dogs or whatever, then serve me my food, making sure everything was just right. She was so caring and loving, and attentive. She was the best wife and mother on the face of the earth; I was sure of it.

Jess smiled a shy smirk at me, then sat down by my side, making herself a plate. Everyone else always came first.

Is it too late...? Maybe we could try again. Could we have another baby?

I gulped and clenched my jaw, my stomach twisting at the direction my thoughts were going. I just wanted to ask her. I wanted to know if I was wasting my time even thinking about it.

I took her small hand in mine and brought it to my lips, kissing her knuckles.

"Thanks for dinner, baby," I murmured, my eyes locking on hers. "You're the most amazing woman in the world."

She grinned at me with love in her eyes. "It's just a little pasta, Ben."

I chuckled softly and shook my head, letting her hand go so she could eat. "No, it's the best pasta. From the best wife."

She giggled to herself and we both dug in, eating her delicious meal in the comfortable, easy company of one another. I couldn't bring up the baby stuff now... We had such a good thing going. Did I really want to shake things up that much?

We already had some intense recent events under our belts to prove that we weren't the ordinary married couple I had once feared we were. What would a baby bring to the mix, other than more stress? Late-night feedings, crying, diaper rash... Preschool and playdates. More time and money when we finally had our lives to ourselves.

Jess and I gave up our freedom at seventeen, and we had just gotten it back. If we had another kid now, we wouldn't have alone time again until we were in our fifties.

Why the hell are you trying to talk yourself out of this? You already know it's not going to happen. It was a nice thought way back when, but it's too late now. Just enjoy your time with your wife and move on.

I pushed all my hectic thoughts out of my mind and ate my dinner. Jess and I talked about nonsense, our usual dinnertime conversation; movies and books, and what our friends had been up to. When we were done, I did the dishes while she watched TV in the living room.

We went upstairs shortly after to watch Conan in bed. It was just a regular evening, and my eyelids were starting to droop when I felt Jess's fingers teasing my happy trail. My dick woke up immediately.

I rolled over onto my side and started kissing her. Jess purred in between my lips while we made out, panting quietly, touching everywhere. My wife loved kissing. I considered myself somewhat of a master. Most of our sexy times started out with slow, sensual kisses and gradually heated up to us tonguing each other down, ready to devour one another.

Once I lost my pajama bottoms and Jess ditched her panties and my oversized t-shirt she slept in, it was go time. I could sense that she was about to reach for the nightstand, and unless she was going for the random buttplug we had in there for special occasions, it likely meant she wanted me to put on a condom. Which I totally did not want to do.

I was all ready to distract her when she switched it up on me.

"Baby..." she whispered while I was skimming her sweet flesh with my tongue. "You know what would be totally hot?"

"Mmm..." I grunted, grinding my rock-hard dick between her thighs. She was still reaching, but when her hand came back, she was holding something else.

"If we made a video..." she murmured, holding up her phone and giving me a wicked look.

My cock flinched. "A video...?"

"Yea..." she breathed, scratching her nails across my back. "It would be so dirty if we recorded ourselves fucking."

I pulled my face back and raised my brows at her. *God damn, my wife is perfect.*

"You want to make a sex tape?" I huffed.

"I don't think anyone says that anymore," she giggled, and I grinned slowly. "But yea. We should record it. You look so fucking hot when your dick is inside me..."

I growled and slid my tongue over my bottom lip. "You look fucking hot when I'm balls deep in your sweet pussy..." I kissed her softly, and she groaned.

"I want to..." she mewled on my mouth. "Do you?"

"I want to do everything with you..." I drawled, my head feeling fuzzy.

"Good," she grinned and turned her phone on. She started recording, holding the phone up while I licked and kissed her tits, sucking her nipples and making her purr.

I moved down her stomach to the apex of her thighs and licked her pussy, kissing her clit and tugging it between my lips.

"Oh God, Ben... that's so good," she moaned, and my eyes peeked up quickly, noting the phone in her hand, capturing what I was doing. She was right. It was totally hot.

I ate her out for a few minutes, but when I could tell she was close I stopped, causing her to pout at me. I took the phone from her and aimed it below her waist, taking my cock in my hand and pressing the head inside her.

"Spread your legs wide for me, baby," I commanded, and she did. I took her thigh in my hand and pushed inside her slowly, groaning at the tight, wet warmth of her engulfing my aching erection. "Jesus, Jessica. You're so tight..."

"Mmm... I think your dick is just massive," she giggle-moaned at me, which made me smile. I thrust in further and she gasped.

I watched the phone screen closely, fully angled in on my long, thick cock moving into my wife's pussy. It looked so good, I almost couldn't control myself. I drew my hips back and drove in all the way to the hilt, my balls soaking with her juices. And then I really started to move.

I picked up the pace, keeping a steady tempo; in and out, over and over, fucking her deep and hard while her camera recorded every movement. I held it up higher so I could get her big, round tits bouncing as I pounded into her, grunting as I went.

Jess lifted her legs and wrapped them around my waist, and I paused to rest the camera on the nightstand, getting a full view of our naked, sweaty bodies, grinding together in passion. I licked and kissed her everywhere; her mouth, her neck, her tits. All the while sliding my cock in and out of her sweet, tight walls.

"Ben... mmm fuck me, baby," she gasped, tugging my hair then grabbing my ass, forcing me as deep as I could go. "You're so fucking good at fucking..."

"I love how your pussy swallows my cock..." I groaned, feeling like a dam was about to burst.

"I'm gonna come, Ben," she whimpered, grabbing my face and pulling it down to hers. "Make me come with your giant dick."

"Come for me, baby..." I croaked, out of breath and hoarse, ready to fucking explode.

"I'm coming for you..." she hummed, then kissed my lips hard while her pussy tightened, squeezing me like a fist. "Oh, God, Ben! Yes!"

"Fuck yes..." I gasped, her pussy becoming extra slippery as she came all over me. She was squealing out all kinds of words, but it sounded echoey because my loins were being ripped apart by a killer orgasm.

I groaned out loud and let go, pouring myself deep inside her, my strokes slowing. My throat was dry and my voice raspy as I sang her praises, kissing her lips and jaw as my hips came to a gradual halt.

"Holy fuck..." she squeaked, her fingers roaming all over me. "You're the fucking best."

"You're the fucking best..." I mumbled, falling down gently on top of her as we caught our breath.

Eventually I rolled over, pulling out of her and remembering the camera. I grabbed her phone and stopped the video, tossing it down on the bed.

"That was..." I huffed then swallowed over my scratchy throat.

"Hot?" she finished my thought, and I grinned at her, wrapping my arms around her waist and tugging her closer to me.

"So hot," I hummed. "Just make sure that video stays on your phone, Mrs. Lockwood. The internet is a vast entity, and the last thing we need is friends, coworkers, or dare I say... *our daughter* seeing it."

"Really? I was planning on sending it out as a Christmas e-card," she teased, smirking at me.

I laughed and shook my head, kissing her a handful of times before we both passed out.

I had just finished a dinner meeting with a few of the business owners for my new development. The project was coming right along. John's team had started work on Monday, and we decided to go out to dinner to celebrate the successful end to our first week.

These guys were sort of loco. It was supposed to be a business dinner, but it seemed like all they wanted to do was drink. And once the three of us were one bottle of scotch deep, they wouldn't stop talking about going to a strip club.

"Guys, as fun as it sounds, I think I'll have to pass," I grumbled, taking a long sip from my glass of water. "I have a forty-five-minute drive home. I need to sober up."

"Come on, Lockwood. Don't be a baby," Frank, one of the partners who was funding half the project, goaded me. "The club off sixty in Corona is really something. You know they have private rooms in the back..."

"Why am I not surprised you know that?" I grunted, rolling my eyes and flagging the waitress for some coffee.

"He's right, man," Hector, one of the other partners, chimed in. "You can ride with me up there and sober up. I'll get you back to your car when you're done."

"Done with what, exactly?" I raised my brow at them, and they laughed. "You do remember I'm married, right?"

"Yea, so what?" Frank huffed. "I've been married twice."

"I can't imagine why it didn't work out..." I rolled my eyes again. They were just rolling back and forth at that point.

"Come on, Ben. You're working for us," Hector added. "One drink. If you want to bail, I'll pay for your cab back to your car."

I sighed and shook my head. My attempts to call it a night were futile. I'd known these guys for a few years, and every time we had similar dinners like this, they always ended the same way. I conceded, though I was the picture of unenthused. We paid our bill and left the restaurant, all hopping into Frank's Mercedes G-Wagon. He probably shouldn't have been driving, but he seemed more sober than I was. I knew it was irresponsible to let him drive, but he was a grownup. And clearly, he did this all the time.

I called Jess from the backseat to tell her what was up, and she wasn't surprised in the slightest.

"I sort of knew this would happen," she giggled over the line. "Just promise to be safe. And if you're too drunk to drive, there's nothing wrong with getting a hotel for the night. Only if you're alone, though!"

"Oh my God, I can't believe you'd even say that to me," I muttered, running my hand through my hair. "Trust me, I'm done drinking for the night. I'm just going to give it an hour then head home."

"I know, baby," she sighed. "I just want you to be okay. I mean, you can get a lap dance if you really want to..."

"The only lap I want to dance with is yours," I grinned, and she laughed in my ear.

"Benjamin Lockwood, sober up please. And be good!" she scolded me, though I could hear her smile. "I'm absolutely not driving out there to bail you out of jail."

"I'm hanging up now," I grunted.

"Love you, baby," she giggled again.

"Love you more." I hung up and sighed.

"How in the hell have you managed to stay married to the same broad you dated in high school?" Frank instantly started berating me. "You wasted your twenties on one girl! Jesus Christ, in my twenties I saw more pussy than my wife's gynecologist."

"I thought you were divorced..." I muttered, and Hector laughed.

"Yea, well. I know it doesn't make sense to you savages, but I love my wife. Always have, always will."

"I mean... she *is* insanely hot," Hector spoke quietly, and I shot him a look.

"You're telling me you've never cheated? Not even once?" Frank shouted at me from the front of the car.

Without my permission, images of Ryan and me together started flowing through my mind, twisting my stomach into a knot. I swallowed hard and took a deep breath.

"Nope," I hummed, gazing out my window.

I hadn't talked to Ryan in a while. Our last message was over the weekend, and while it was nice to know that he was okay, I was feeling like we were drifting apart. The thought made my chest ache with the desire to see him and touch him.

I still missed him like crazy, but there was nothing I could do about it. We were both living separate lives. It made little sense to dwell on what had happened when there was no way for us to see each other...

Although... I am almost halfway to where he lives. I wonder if he...

I shook my head. No. Bad idea.

Tonight was already getting a little too wild. I needed to focus on sobering up so I could get home to Jess.

My curiosity and thoughts of Ryan mixed like a strong cocktail, and I glanced down at my phone in my hand. *Maybe I could call him...Just to talk.*

I was probably just drunk, and it was making me miss him. Even though I always missed him. But being drunk really accentuated my feelings. I decided to be creepy and check his Instagram. Just because.

I pulled it up on my phone and then froze.

Ryan had just posted a new picture a few minutes ago. It was of him and some friends at the casino in Santa Rosa. That was only an hour away.

My mouth was suddenly dry, and I began breathing heavily, a whole slew of different emotions running through me. But I had no time to obsess over them, because we had arrived at our destination.

Frank pulled up in the parking lot of the strip club, *Crownz*, and turned off the engine. We all hopped out of the vehicle, and I tucked my phone into my pocket, trying not to think about the fact that Ryan was only an hour drive away from where I was at this very moment as we walked inside.

The bouncer recognized Frank, but more specifically his friend, Ulysses S. Grant, and led us over to a private table. I barely had time to sit down before girls in skimpy bras and black thongs were bringing over a bottle and three glasses. Frank was already hitting on them.

"Jeez, calm down. We just got here," I chuckled, bouncing my knee beneath the table.

"You don't have to play hard-to-get, Lockwood. We're paying them," Frank chortled and what do you know... My eyes rolled again.

I decided that sobering up now would never work and poured myself a drink, sipping it slowly as I looked around. There was a long stage that wove around basically the entire place, with five poles, each equipped with a topless girl, swinging around to the music of Motley Crue.

Three girls spotted us and sashayed over with dollar signs in their eyes. The two blondes went to Frank and Hector, and for some reason the brunette came up to me.

"Hi there," the short girl in very high heels crooned, running her fingers along my neck. "How about a dance?"

"No thanks," I rumbled. "I'm the designated driver."

She glanced at the drink in my hand and gave me a look like she was slightly put-off.

"Come on, baby..." she purred, moving in closer to my ear. "We could go somewhere more private... and talk."

"Talk about what?" I asked, just trying to fuck with her a little. I didn't do the whole stripper deal. It was never my thing. The only time I had ever even been near one was my bachelor party in Vegas, where I had basically been strapped to a chair and forced to let her give herself rug burn from my jeans.

"Whatever you want," she licked her lips. "You're hotter than any of the guys who come in here. I think we could have some fun."

Oh God, she wants me to pay her for sex? This is crazy. Why did I let these morons drag me here?

"I'll tell you what," I huffed, pulling a twenty out of my pocket. "I'll pay you to go dance over there." I nodded toward the other end of the bar, then stuffed the bill between her fake tits.

"Asshole," she scoffed, and stomped away with my twenty dollars. Hector laughed out loud, and Frank shook his head.

The minutes were passing by and I was bored. I had already turned down more dances than I could count on two hands, while Frank and Hector were blowing through girls like they were trying on clothes. Eventually, they both elected to take a couple of them up on their offer for a private show, and retreated to the back, leaving me alone with my scotch.

I decided to just go outside and call a cab. But when I got there, and I had my phone out, my fingers were dialing Ryan's number, and before I knew it, I was calling him.

The phone rang a few times while I paced, chewing on my lower lip. I couldn't believe how crazy this all was...

I was out at a strip club, filled with hot girls who wanted to fuck me—some of them had even offered it for free—and yet I was out in the parking lot calling my daughter's ex-boyfriend. It didn't make any sense at all, but I couldn't help what my heart was screaming at me to do.

"Hello?" Ryan's voice finally came over the line, and my pulse was instantly racing.

"Hey... hi," I stuttered, feeling immensely stupid for some reason.

"Hi. What's up?" he shouted over all the background noise. He was clearly still out.

"Nothing much... I just... I'm at a strip club," I said, and then kicked myself. *Why is that what you would say right now?!*

"Oh yea?" he asked, sounding amused.

"Yea... Um, I was just bored, and I wanted to say hi," I blurted out, then huffed. "I mean, I didn't just call you because I was *bored*. I called you because... I wanted to hear your voice."

My hands were shaking a little, which was highly ridiculous.

Ryan was quiet for a moment, though I could still hear all the casino noises in the background, including his friends yelling about something.

"Really?" he whispered, almost inaudibly. The softness of his voice made my stomach clench. "Ugh, hang on. I'm going somewhere less noisy so I can hear you."

It sounded like he was walking, and the background music faded away.

"So you're out, too?" I asked, choosing not to reveal that I knew where he was.

"Yea. Some buddies and I came to the casino in Santa Rosa for a guys' night out," he answered, his voice just as deep and masculine as I remembered. I hadn't talked to him on the phone in forever and hearing him now was making me weak. "What the hell are you doing at a strip club?" he chuckled.

"I had a business dinner, and they dragged me here," I mumbled.

"So why aren't you in there getting your swerve on?" he asked, and I couldn't tell if he was fucking with me.

"Yea right..." I scoffed. "I don't need any of that shit. I have the ultimate stripper waiting for me back at home."

Ryan laughed softly. "Yea... True story. How is Jess doing?"

"She's great..." I murmured and then paused. I didn't want to talk about my wife. There was only one thing I wanted, and it was killing me inside not to have it.

The line was quiet again, and I could physically feel the distance between us. Not even the hour drive, but the emotional distance. I didn't want it like this. I wanted to close the gap and be with him again. I missed him so much; it was excruciating.

"Ben..." he whispered, and I closed my eyes.

"Ryan..." I gulped.

"I hate this," he hummed, breaking my heart in two.

"Me, too," I whimpered. "Baby, what are we doing?"

He let out a pained noise that crushed me even more.

"I know it's for the best..." he started then stopped. "But it doesn't feel like it."

Fuck this.

"Ryan... Hang on for a second please," I commanded. "Don't hang up."

I pulled my phone away from my face and Googled hotels in the area, pulling up one between my location and the casino.

"Ben? Are you there?" I could hear Ryan yelling at me. "What the hell are you doing?"

"I'm here, baby," I answered, out of breath from the mere idea that I would see him soon. That was, if he said yes. "Will you meet me at the Hyatt on sixty? I'll text you the address."

"What...?" he asked, sounding confused. "How... Where are you, Ben?"

"I'm like an hour away from you, at some strip club in Corona," I answered, my entire body coursing with adrenaline. "I'm going to get a cab to the Hyatt right now. I'll wait for you in the hotel bar."

Ryan was silent and I could almost see his stunned face which made me smile.

"Hurry up and decide, baby. I need to call a cab," I grinned.

"Uh... yea. Okay. Yea, I'll meet you," he stuttered, sounding excited, which had my heart jumping. "The Hyatt. Sure. Text me the address. I'm coming now."

"Okay, awesome," I breathed, and bit my lip.

"Yea... awesome." I could hear the smile in his voice. *Baby...*

"Ryan?" I spoke softly, brimming with nervous anticipation.

"Yea?"

"Don't keep me waiting."

CHAPTER 14

Ryan

I WAS IN A DAZE. My heart was leaping against my chest as I drove down the highway, trying to stick to the speed limit, since I had been drinking a little. Not much. I wasn't drunk or anything, but I still needed to be cautious. I couldn't let anything stop me from getting to that hotel.

I was so excited to see Ben; I was actually shaking. I still couldn't believe he'd called... I was in shock.

We hadn't been talking much since he and Jess left a few weeks ago. Honestly, it was depressing me more than I'd ever thought it would. It was worse than the worst break-up I'd ever experienced.

I admit, I felt a bit foolish for dropping everything and running to him the second he called. I knew that I should have been playing hard-to-get, at least a little. But I couldn't help myself. I missed him more and more each day, and before my phone rang with his name on the screen, I had been considering some things I'd never expected myself to consider.

But none of that mattered right now. I was going to see Ben, in just a few more miles...

I was freaking giddy.

Understandably my friends had been confused as hell when I told them I was leaving. As a group we'd agreed that we would stay out all night, drinking, gambling and having a wild night. Then we were going to find a waffle house to sober up enough to drive home. The night had been fun thus far. But of course, the potential to see my man tossed all of that right out the window.

I made up some lame excuse about Alec and Kayla needing my help with something, and bounced quick, before they could ask too many questions. I knew it looked sketchy, but I didn't really care about that. I didn't care about anything other than getting to that freaking hotel. *Damn, I seem thirsty... Whatever. Sorry not sorry.*

I drove for another fifteen minutes or so before I saw the Hyatt. I pulled into visitor parking and darted through the lot, making my way toward the restaurant entrance. They had some steakhouse there, attached to the hotel, and I assumed that was the bar Ben was referring to. I wasn't sure how late they were opened. It was already almost one. But when I stepped inside, I heard live music and a bunch of chatter.

I tried my hardest to walk casually when really I wanted to be running. I spotted the bar and instantly my eyes set on Ben.

I stopped for a moment to take him in. He looked *so* devastatingly good. It was completely unfair.

He was sitting alone at the bar, staring at his glass of what I assumed was scotch, wearing dark jeans and a navy blue button down which fit every intricate contour of his large, muscular frame. His dirty blonde hair was slightly longer and mussed up, as if he had been running his fingers through it, which was exactly what I wanted to do... It looked so soft and silky. The stubble that lined his perfect jaw was longer, too. Not quite a beard, but just enough to make him look rugged and sexy. And it was Ben, so his knee was bouncing up and down, most likely out of fidgety nerves, because he was always moving. The sight made me smile.

Just as I was about to walk again, I saw a woman approach him. She was tall and slender, with long black hair. She moved up close to him and said something, biting her lip and twirling her hair around her finger. She was obviously hitting on him, which was adorable. I couldn't blame her in the slightest. He was by far the hottest guy in the whole damn place.

Ben smiled politely at her and shook his head, responding to whatever she was saying, likely letting her down easy. She pouted a little but nodded, then slinked back over to a booth where she sat down with some other women, all of whom were sipping martinis. I chuckled to myself and shook my head. *Irresistible Ben Lockwood... He has no idea the power he has over people.*

I stepped slowly over to the bar, and Ben looked up, immediately locking me in place with those bright blue eyes. I felt a tremor run through me, catching my breath in my throat.

The shimmering blue hypnotized me as he got up, stalking toward me in long strides. I saw him swallow hard as he sealed the gap between us. And then he smiled.

It was such an incapacitating smile; it knocked the wind out of me. And before I could say or do anything else, he grabbed me hard, wrapping his strong arms around me and hugging onto me for dear life.

I melted against his strapping body and squeezed his waist, pulling him as close as possible while he held my back, running his fingers along my shoulder blades. I inhaled deep, taking in that mouthwatering smell of him, like clean laundry and musky soap and Ben freaking Lockwood. The best smell in the entire world. His face burrowed in my neck and he trailed his lips tenderly along my skin.

"Hey, baby..." he crooned, that deep, sexy voice vibrating through me. "Miss me?"

"Shut the fuck up," I whimpered, and he laughed softly, his breath tickling my flesh and making my cock jump against his waist.

We finally pulled apart, though he kept his hands on my biceps, burning into my soul with those blue irises.

"I'm so glad you're here," he murmured, cocking his head to the side. "I almost can't believe it."

"I know, me neither," I shook my head subtly. "I'm still kinda shocked. I definitely didn't think I would be seeing you..."

"I know," he grinned, biting his lip. His cheeks were almost flushing, and it made my heart thump. *He's so happy to see me... What is this? How can this be happening? Am I in a dream?!*

"Come on. Let's get you a drink," he commanded, taking my chin briefly in his fingers, before turning back to the bar, forcing me to follow him like damn puppy.

We both sat down at the bar and Ben ordered me a scotch while I checked out the surroundings for a moment. It was a nice place. Dim lights, candles, all blacks, deep reds and oak furniture everywhere. The band was playing some Bob Dylan song and didn't sound half bad.

Ben turned to face me, his knees touching mine as he leaned up on the bar, inching closer to me. The bartender set a drink down in front of me and I took a fast sip in an attempt to calm my nerves.

"So... casino?" he rumbled, showing off a tragically sexy dimple.

"So... strip club?" I retorted, and he laughed.

"Yea. Those business dinners always somehow go rogue," he grinned, sipping his drink. "But I'm glad I went with them." He said nothing more but kept his eyes on mine. He didn't need to elaborate. I knew what he meant.

"Me, too," I hummed, licking my lip.

"How have you been, kid?" he asked, his eyes slipping down for a moment before he raised his brow. "You look good."

"Ben Lockwood... are you coming onto me?" I rasped, and he laughed again.

"Mm... Not just yet. But hopefully soon," he smirked that cocky grin that made me want to pounce on him.

We talked for a while, finishing our drinks and ordering more. He asked me about school and my friends, then I asked him about work. He was delighted to tell me all about this new project he was working on, and he was very animated describing all the details. It felt so good to just sit and talk to him. To merely be in his presence was like a high of its own.

By our third round, we were both feeling nice. We were sitting very close so we could hear each other over the music. And yes, we were just talking, but even that was winding me up. He kept watching my lips and licking his. I could tell he wanted to kiss me, and I wanted it so bad I was almost desperate.

Still, I couldn't get over how at ease I felt with him. It was comforting on a whole other level. I always knew I missed him when we were apart, but I guess I never really knew the full extent of it until we were back together; and I never wanted to be away from him again.

"So... How's Jess been?" I finally asked about her, surprised that we hadn't mentioned her up until that point.

"She's wonderful," he replied, tracing his glass with his index finger. "You know Jess. She's always perfect, no matter what else is going on in the world."

"That's true," I nodded, feeling an odd emptiness. "Does she know you're with me?"

He shook his head slowly. "I told her I was too drunk to drive home, so I was staying in a hotel tonight." He paused, some serious emotion flashing briefly over his face. "I'll tell her tomorrow."

I gulped the rest of my drink, trying to cover up the strange sensation of guilt that was trying to fight its way through my bliss. I wasn't sure what I had to feel guilty about. Jess knew about Ben and me. She didn't care. We had all been together at that point. But still it was irking me that this negative feeling was attempting to rain on my parade.

So I stuffed it down and inched closer to Ben.

"So... you have a room here?" I raised my brow at him.

"Mhm," he nudged my knee with his. "Right upstairs..."

"That's... interesting," I murmured, my fingers twitching with the desire to touch him everywhere.

"Very interesting..." he hummed, then took his plump, tasty-looking bottom lip between his teeth. He moved in closer until we were barely apart. His hand reached out slowly, maybe even slightly hesitant, as his fingers slinked up my arm. "Maybe we could... go upstairs for another drink...?"

"That sounds fun," I whispered, and his eyes sparkled. I couldn't stop watching his mouth, imagining all the delicious things I wanted to do to it. It was burning me up.

We were so damn close to each other, I could feel the warmth radiating off of him. And he was touching me so softly, there was noticeable movement below my waist. I swallowed hard, making a snap decision to place my hand on his hip. I actually heard him whimper from my touch and it had me ready to combust.

"You make me dizzy..." he breathed, leaning in like he was going to kiss me, though his eyes were still watching me closely.

"Maybe we should... go somewhere private," I stuttered through my nerves, briefly glancing around us. There were still a few people nearby. I wasn't sure if it was the best idea for us to be doing this in public.

"Who cares about these people?" he huffed, moving his hand down to my thigh and sliding his fingers along my jeans. "No one knows us here."

"I know..." I gulped, breathless. "But... I just..."

"What's wrong, baby?" he rumbled. "Does this make you nervous?"

"*You* make me nervous," I replied, my voice unsteady. "Always have."

He chuckled out a deep little laugh. "You know what you make me..."

I barely even noticed that I was gripping his shirt in my fist. I released it and nodded at him.

"I do," I hummed, moving my hand up to the top button of his shirt, running my finger along his exposed clavicle; the top of his broad, defined chest. "You do the same to me."

Ben growled, going back to caressing my arm with his long fingers. The look in his eyes was one of pure hunger, and it appeared to be taking every ounce of his strength not to rip both of our clothes off right there.

Some chatter happening nearby caused us both to look up. The ladies from before were now drunk, up and dancing-more like stumbling-around with a few guys. It snapped Ben out of his trance a bit, and we realized simultaneously that while we didn't actually know anyone around here, it probably wouldn't be wise to start making out in the middle of a bar.

Ben cleared his throat and leaned back, signaling to the bartender for the check. He paid quickly, and we both got up together.

"You wanna come see my room?" he rasped, giving me a salacious grin.

"I would love to see your room," I breathed and bit my lip.

The two of us left quickly, exiting the restaurant and walking casually through the hotel lobby. We shuffled into the elevator, and as soon as the doors closed, Ben pushed me up against the wall and kissed me, hard yet somehow so soft that I was already coming undone. He pinned me to the wall with his hips, grinding on me slowly while he held my jaw, parting my lips with his tongue.

"Baby... I fucking missed you so bad..." he purred as I dug my fingers into his hair, kissing him harder and deeper.

"God, I missed you," I panted in between hot, slippery kisses of pent-up lust and desire.

The elevator dinged at our floor and we forced ourselves apart, stammering out into the hallway. Ben dragged me by my arm to his room, opening the door quickly and shoving me inside. He slipped the *Do Not Disturb* card on the door and I grinned, remembering when Jess did the same thing a few weeks back.

As soon as we were securely inside the hotel room, we became like wild animals, attacking each other in pure desperation. We didn't even turn the lights on. It was so dark, but the moon was shining in from the glass door of the balcony, making everything that much more sensual.

Ben was kissing me so hard, my lips were swollen, and my dick was throbbing. We both undressed one another fast, ripping at our clothes, frantically trying to make the other naked. I ended up naked first, and Ben's pants and boxers were around his ass, his button-down hanging off his shoulders as he dropped to his knees and started blowing me.

I couldn't help the groan that flew from my mouth as he sucked my dick slow and deep. His lips stroked me long, up and down, his head bobbing in front of my waist. I held his face, watching him in fascination as he gave me the best head of my entire life.

"Ben... Baby, you suck me so fucking good," I mumbled, slipping my fingers under his chin. His eyes met mine, and even in the room's darkness, I could see the brightest blue ever, shining up at me, almost glowing.

He moaned with my cock in his mouth; the vibrations rippling through my whole body. I could tell he was horny as fuck by the way he was going to town on me. He was loving every second of it, and obviously so was I. I could already feel my balls tightening.

I yanked my cock out of his mouth and stood him up, ridding him of his shirt and pants for good. Then I grabbed him by the waist, kissing him softly, flicking my hips to rub our erections together.

We kissed our way to the bed, and I pushed him onto his back, licking, nipping and sucking down his neck and throat, then onto his chest. I took his nipple between my lips, toying with it, toying with him, making him shudder. Then I moved down the rest of his torso, gliding my tongue between all the rippling muscles until I reached his big beautiful dick, in all its glory.

"Tease my cock, Ryan," he breathed, his tone pleading. "With your sweet lips and your warm tongue."

"Fuck, Ben..." I moaned quietly, taking him in my fist and stroking, from his balls all the way up to the crown and back. His eyelids drooped and his head fell back. "You have the best dick ever."

I swirled my tongue around the tip, tasting the saltiness of his arousal, causing my own dick to pulse between my legs. I licked him in long, tender strokes, up and down every inch of his manhood, really savoring how smooth and hard and warm his solid flesh was in my mouth. I sucked him gently at first, playing with him, feeling him tremble before me. And then I gave him everything I had.

I sucked Ben's big dick slow and hard, drawing out all of his sexy sounds, letting him slide down my throat until I couldn't fit one more inch. I was fucking him with my mouth, and I could see him losing his edge, gripping the comforter in his fists. His glorious muscular body was splayed out and ready for me to devour him.

"Ryan... baby... holy fuck," he gasped, panting, pushing himself down my throat until my eyes began to water. "You are so fucking good at sucking my dick. No one's ever done it like you..."

I groaned at his words, picking up the pace a little. I was like a machine. The world around me was blurring as I chased his orgasm, desperate to taste his hot, slick come. Ben was falling apart in front of me. He was about to let go, any second.

"Uh... oh God... baby..." he grunted, writhing around, ready to burst. "I'm gonna come. You're gonna... make... me... come!"

He cried out softly, my name flying from his sweet lips while he erupted into a staggering climax, shooting all in my mouth and down my throat as I struggled to swallow all of him. It was so much, but I wanted it. I needed it. I *loved* it.

I was so thirsty, I couldn't get enough. When he was done, I sucked the head of his dick and he gave me a little more. *He is so fucking hot, oh my God.*

I crawled over him while he was fighting to catch his breath and pulled his face up to mine.

"Kiss me," I demanded, biting and sucking his curved lips. "Taste how delicious you are, baby."

"Holy... fuck..." he whimpered, grabbing my ass and pulling me closer. "Ryan... you're so amazing. How are you even real?"

"Ben..." I gulped, a strange, heavy tightness in my chest. I felt like I was about to say something that I shouldn't. So instead I rolled him over on his side and positioned myself between his long legs. "I'm going to fuck you so good, baby."

"Fuck me, Ryan..." he begged, reaching for my dick. "I've been waiting for you."

I growled and licked my hand, massaging some lubrication on my dick before pressing it up to his opening. I couldn't stop staring at him, just admiring how fucking good he looked. His hair was really a mess now, but it made him look young and gorgeous, like a model or something. His cheeks were blushing, his lips moist and swollen. His eyes were barely staying opened, and he looked like he could pass out.

I held him open and forced my cock into his ass, both of us groaning together. He was so tight; I felt like I was in a dream. I pushed into him further, feeding my dick inside him, slowly, until he relaxed enough to let me move.

"How's that feel?" I mumbled, and he gasped out something I could barely understand, his hands holding my waist tight. "You like how I fuck you, huh, Ben?"

"I love it," he moaned, and my dick pulsed inside him. "Fuck me harder."

I obliged him, fucking him deep and hard, pounding myself into his tight ass over and over. The sounds of us fucking were ringing through the room, and we definitely weren't being quiet, but I didn't give a fuck. I was exactly where I needed to be. I was with my man, making love to him.

He's my man. All mine. His ass, his dick, his sweet lips and blue eyes and golden skin. He's. Fucking. Mine.

"You're mine, aren't you, Ben?" I drawled, getting lost in my rhythm, barely even aware of the words I was saying.

"Uh, yes..." he grunted, his whole body moving up and down on the bed with my forceful thrusts.

"Tell me," I commanded, caressing his balls, making him twitch.

"Tell... you..." he mumbled incoherently, his eyes rolling back in his skull out of euphoria.

"Tell me you're mine." I pounded into him, drawing back then diving in. His tight ass was stroking me so good, I was losing any semblance of control.

"I'm yours," he gasped, digging his fingers into my flesh. "I'm yours, Ryan. Baby... oh God..."

"Fuck, Ben, I'm gonna come in you," I panted, gripping his ass hard.

"Come inside me," he growled. "Please..."

I had no idea why, but hearing him say that, in that way, set me off like fireworks. My orgasm rocked through me, bursting out of my cock with all its might, emptying inside Ben's ass so deep. My dick was aching, my balls contracting as I came, so hard I could barely breathe.

And then somehow Ben started coming again, his dick twinging out even more come on his abs, which I hadn't ever thought was possible. He was panting and whimpering out my name and all kinds of noises as I collapsed on top of him and he caught me.

We held each other in our arms, breathing and recovering from the most intense sex ever.

It was everything I ever thought sex could be. And it was all because of Ben. He was just so goddamned perfect.

I love him.

I had hearts floating behind my eyes as I pressed my head up to his chest, feeling his heartbeat against my cheek as I drifted off to sleep.

"You're gonna have to stop that..."

"Why?"

"You know I'm ticklish there."

I grinned. "Where... here?"

Ben giggled then cleared his throat trying to give me a more manly face, though he just looked adorable. "Yes, there. Now stop before I punch you."

"You wouldn't," I gasped, trailing my finger along his naked hip.

"Wanna bet?" He raised his brow.

"Fine, fine. What about... if I did it... with my lips..." I murmured, drifting down to his pelvis, brushing my lips through those sexy V-shapes in his muscles.

"Mmmm... baby," he whined, closing his eyes and biting his lip. "You can't do that. I'm exhausted. I don't think I could even get hard again if I tried."

"Hmm... I think we should test that theory out," I grinned wickedly as I continued to play with him.

"Ryan, it's six a.m." he huffed, running his fingers through my hair. "We've been fucking for hours. Listen to my voice! It's like gone." He chuckled, and I had to laugh.

He had a point. He sounded worn out. *And so damn sexy, I can't even stand it.*

I glanced over at the partially drawn curtain, barely covering the glass door to the balcony. The sun was rising.

I stretched out my sore limbs then wrapped my arms around Ben's waist, pulling him closer so we could cuddle some more. We'd already been doing this for a while. I honestly wouldn't have even known how much time had passed if he didn't say something.

Last night was the best night of my entire existence.

It seemed like every night I had with Ben was better than the last. I wasn't even sure how it was possible for us to regenerate quickly enough to have sex as much as we had. I mean, I had stamina, but shit... Ben really just brought out my inner sex-fiend.

I held him close, trailing my lips along his throat and onto his chest, nuzzling the soft, light little patch of hair beneath his sternum. He smelled so freaking good it made my mouth water.

He slipped his leg in between mine and played with my hair, his big giant arms holding me; protecting me from the outside world. It was dangerous how good I felt when I was with him. It was like nothing or no one could ever penetrate this bubble.

Still, in the back of my mind I knew there was a timer on this state of ecstasy I was in. Ben would have to go home soon. And I would have to go back to school and finish out my classes before winter break. And then who knew what would happen...

"Are you hungry?" I murmured, distracting myself from my painful thoughts.

"Ryan, I will get lock-jaw if I suck your dick again..." Ben huffed. "You're too big. I need a break."

I laughed softly, shaking my head as my fingers trailed along his lower back.

"No, Ben, I meant hungry for *food*," I chuckled, pulling my face back to look at him. He was biting the inside of his cheek, clearly trying hard not to laugh. It made him look so adorable and sexy I couldn't deal.

"Oh," he rasped, gliding his fingers along my jaw. "Then yea... I am very hungry for food. I'm starving, actually. I think I might die."

"Well, we can't have that," I grinned, kissing him softly on his pouted, albeit slightly swollen lips. "Should we order some room service?"

"I don't think they do that here," he smiled, tilting his head as we stared at each other. "It's not like the suite in ABQ. This place isn't fancy enough for breakfast in bed." I chuckled and blinked slowly, still touching him everywhere. I just couldn't stop. I was fully addicted to having my hands on him. "Plus, I gotta get going soon. I don't want Jess to worry. I still have to get back to my car."

"I'll drive you to your car," I told him, my tone letting him know this should be obvious.

"Are you sure?" he asked, his forehead lined in question. "It's like forty-five minutes in the opposite direction from where you need to go..."

"I don't mind," I whispered. *I would do anything for you, Ben. Don't you know that by now?*

"Really?" he gave me some appreciative look that made my stomach twist. I nodded quick. "Thanks, baby."

Anything to spend more time with you...

I smiled at him to keep myself from blurting out all these crazy thoughts swirling around in my over-stimulated mind.

"Why don't we shower and get dressed, then we'll hit up waffle house on the way to your car..." I suggested, brushing his silky hair away from where it wanted to flop over his forehead.

"Oh my God, don't even *say* waffle house right now," he rumbled, his eyes lighting up. "My stomach is growling. I'm surprised you can't hear it."

I laughed and kissed him again. "Well then, let's get going. I need to keep my man fed."

Ben hummed against my lips, but I opened my eyes quickly to see if he was freaking out over the fact that I just called him *my man*. He looked a little serious, but not completely spooked, which I took to be a good sign. I needed to be careful. I couldn't risk scaring him away by saying something crazy. Even though it was all I was feeling at the moment.

We finally peeled off each other and got up, both of us moving glacially slow because of all the muscle strain. I felt the same way I usually did after I went really hard at the gym. *Aside from the sore butt thing...*

We got into the shower and washed up, trying hard not to get distracted, though it was difficult. Just being near Ben made my cock hard, and clearly he felt the same way. He let me wash him for a little bit until he accused me of being *frisky* and pushed me away. I had to laugh, though. He was just so cute and sexy. He was such a controlling, intimidating *man*. It made me swell with pride at the fact that I could get him to drop his guard, even just enough to let me wash his hair.

We got out of the shower and got dressed, gathering up all of our things and getting ready to leave.

"I really hope they wash these sheets," Ben grunted, shaking his head.

"I'm sure they will," I chuckled. "We're definitely not the first people to have a crazy fuckfest in here."

"Ew! Ryan... that's gross," Ben scolded me, and I laughed again. "I don't want to think about other people's jizz in the bed."

"So it's different if it's our jizz?" I raised my brow, unable to stop giggling at his face.

"Stop saying *jizz*," he smirked, walking to the door. I followed behind him.

"You said it first," I muttered, and he turned to face me, giving me a warning look.

"Don't push me, kid," he growled, a wicked grin tugging at his lips. I stepped up to him and ran my hands over his chest.

"When are you going to stop calling me that?" I hummed, feeling up his muscles beneath the soft material of his shirt.

"When you stop acting like a punk," he whispered, grabbing my ass and squeezing while he pulled my body against his. His eyes dropped to my lips, fluttering closed before he kissed me so soft I couldn't help the involuntary groan that slipped from between my lips.

"Ben," I breathed, sucking his bottom lip tenderly before tracing the top with my tongue.

"Ryan," he panted, holding my waist hard.

"What are you doing to me?" My lips melded with his and we kissed it out, slow and deep; passionate.

"The same thing you've been doing to me since that first night in the basement," he moaned quietly over my lips, making me tremble.

We finally pulled apart, and he rested his forehead on mine while we caught our breath.

"I think about that night all the time," I whispered.

"Me too," he spoke softly. "I was so... afraid of you. Of how good you made me feel."

"I was afraid of how badly I wanted it..." I told him, and he whimpered, kissing me once more, quick.

Then he huffed out a breath and reluctantly let me go, but not without first caressing my jaw with his long fingers.

"Let's go, baby," he gave me a small smile, and we left the hotel room. *Jesus... That was intense.*

We walked through the hallway to the elevator, waiting patiently for it. Well, *I* was being patient. Ben couldn't stand still, as usual, and was all tapping his foot and touching everything. He literally never stopped moving. He was like a big kid, and it made me smile.

"We're totally doing the walk of shame right now," he murmured as the elevator arrived at our floor.

"I have some t-shirts in my car. You can borrow one if you want to change," I told him, and he smiled at me as the doors opened.

The elevator had people in it already, and as we stepped inside, I realized that they looked sort of familiar.

It was the woman from last night, with the long dark hair. The one who had hit on Ben...

She was with one of the guys she and her friends had been dancing with before Ben and I left to get our freak on. And she was clearly walk-of-shaming it herself.

Ben and I stood side-by-side, opposite the woman and her one-night-stand. Ben was smirking, crossing his arms over his chest, looking hot as all fuck. And I was just trying not to laugh, leaning up against him a little.

"The someone you were waiting for?" the woman asked Ben, raising her brow and showing off a small, knowing grin.

He nodded slowly in response, his face illuminated with the most charming, straight white-toothed smile I had ever seen on any human before. He peeked over at me and winked.

"You're a lucky guy," the woman swooned, batting her eyelashes at the two of us. Her one-night-stand just looked tired and hungover.

"I know, right?" I grinned, and the elevator doors opened, the four of us filing out into the lobby.

I followed Ben, who was chuckling to himself and shaking his head, over to the desk to check out.

"What did you say to her last night?" I asked him, and he turned to face me, leaning against the counter.

"Nothing really," he shrugged. "She asked if I was alone, and if she could buy me a drink. And I told her I was waiting for someone."

"Hmm... So I'm *someone* now?" I teased, crossing my arms over my chest.

"Baby, you're more than just a someone," he whispered, his voice deep and raspy. "You're *my* someone."

My stomach flipped, and I bit my lip, breaking our intense stare, glancing at my shoes. My face felt so warm, and I just knew it was likely turning red.

"How are you so fucking sweet?" I grumbled, peering back up at him.

"I can be nice when I want to be," he smirked. I took a deep breath, trying to steady my out-of-control pulse as Ben checked out of the hotel with the lady at the desk.

It took all of two minutes, and the next thing I knew, he was grabbing me by the hand, tugging me outside. I saw him scanning the lot for my car, so I pulled the keys out of my pocket with my free hand and unlocked the doors with the remote. We walked through the parking lot toward my car, holding fucking hands. Like we were a couple or something.

My mind is being blown right now.

I opened the rear door first and grabbed two clean t-shirts out of my gym bag.

"Here," I called to Ben, and he looked up, grinning at me. "White, or grey?"

"Grey, please," he answered, and I tossed the shirt at him. He unbuttoned his dress shirt and shrugged it off his broad shoulders, while I subtly ogled his delicious shirtlessness. Then I pouted to myself when he slipped the t-shirt over his head. "You don't mind if I borrow this?"

"Of course not," I scoffed, tugging my old t-shirt over my head and replacing it with the fresh white tee. "I like that we can share clothes. We're the same size."

"Yes, we are..." Ben hummed, and I glanced up to see him checking me out. I laughed softly.

"Will you drive?" I asked, flinging the keys to my BMW at him.

He raised his brows at me in surprise. "Yea?" I nodded.

"Please."

"You got it, baby," he grinned as he opened the driver side door. "Anything for *my man.*"

I rolled my eyes at him, but on the inside I was jumping up and down. I couldn't tell if he was fucking with me, because he had that damn cocky *Ben* look on his beautiful face. But still it was making me feel tingly all over. *Does he really want to be my man???*

We got into the car and buckled up before immediately holding hands again, like we always did in the car for some reason. Our fingers laced together, and I relaxed against the passenger seat, watching Ben out the corner of my eye as he left the hotel parking lot and drove us toward food.

I actually hadn't been in the passenger seat of my BMW since it was my dad's, before he passed away. He never let anyone but me drive his car, and he always knew I loved it. That was why he left it to me when he died. And probably because he knew I was in school and couldn't afford to buy a car of my own. The fact that I was letting Ben drive was a bigger deal to me than I would ever let him know.

The drive to the waffle house was only about twenty-minutes, heading in the direction of the restaurant where Ben's car was parked, according to him. I wasn't too familiar with this area, so as soon as I dropped him off, I would definitely be GPS-ing it home. The mere thought of having to say goodbye to Ben again was making me sad already, but I couldn't let the impending sorrow ruin my time with him.

Ben was in rare form. He was actively smiling at nothing, bouncing around in his seat, singing along to the songs on the radio. If I were misinterpreting the situation, I could easily convince myself that his stellar mood had something to do with us, or me. But I didn't want to get my hopes up, so I ignored those thoughts. He was probably just excited to eat.

Ben parked at the waffle house and was power-walking to get inside fast, though still clutching my hand in his, yanking me with him as we plopped down in an available booth. The waitress came over to drop off the menus and Ben ordered coffee before she was even done saying hello.

"What are you getting?" I asked, skimming the menu. I glanced up at Ben, who was not looking at his.

"Waffles, hash browns, eggs over medium, bacon, sausage and toast," he replied in one breath then smiled, apparently pleased with himself.

"Damn, babe," I chuckled. "Save some food for the rest of us." He shook his head slowly, and I laughed. "You have quite the appetite."

"Mhm," he grunted as the waitress brought over his coffee. She asked for our order and he repeated the same thing he had just said to me, only faster this time, which even had the surly waffle house waitress laughing.

"And for you, darlin?" she turned to me.

"Just waffles, bacon and OJ, please," I smiled, and she stomped off with our order.

"Psh. Amateur," Ben scoffed at me. "I thought you worked out like crazy. Wouldn't you need to eat way more than that to stay your size?"

"First of all, I don't work out *like crazy*," I grumbled at him and he rolled his eyes.

"Baby, you told me you were in the gym every day last week," he raised his brow, calling me out.

"Okay, fine," I conceded. "But that was only because I was trying to distract myself."

Ben's face went still as he gaped at me. "Distract yourself from what...?"

I shook my head and looked down at the table, fiddling with the silverware.

"Nothing. Forget it," I mumbled.

"Ryan," his soft voice slithered inside me, and I swallowed hard. He reached across the table and took my hand. My eyes darted back up to his. "I hate the thought of you being sad..."

"It's not your fault," I whispered, my tone laced with uncertainty.

"Baby, I miss you so much when we're apart," he hummed. "You know it's not easy on me either, right?" *You're gonna have to stop saying things like this to me, Ben...*

"I know," I replied, glancing around us to see if anyone was looking. I was more than a little nervous to be holding his hand out in the open like that, though my insides were twisting up over the fact that he really seemed to love calling me *baby.*

Ben caught onto my reservations and shook his head. "Who cares about these people, Ryan? We don't know them. We're never going to see them again."

"I know, but... I just..." I stuttered, feeling the warmth spread down my neck.

Ben abruptly stood up and circled the table, sitting down right next to me, on my side. He reached out and ran his fingers along my jaw, sending shivers all across my body.

"Kiss me, Ryan," he commanded, though his tone was soft and nurturing.

I gaped at him like he was insane. "What? Why?"

"Because. I want you to know that it's okay," he told me, sounding confident and heart-stoppingly sexy. "We can't do this everywhere... I know it's a problem. There's still so much standing in the way. But here, in this goddamned waffle house, we're miles and miles away from anyone who knows us or our situation. So I want you to kiss me... Out in the open. While we still can..."

I gulped and took a deep breath, peering to my left, then to my right.

It certainly didn't appear that anyone was paying attention to us. And even if they were, why should we care? Ben was right. We didn't know anyone there. We weren't near school, or Ben's house, or anyone who might tell Hailey. For all these people knew, we were just some random gay couple.

This was what I had wanted; what I had been trying to convince myself I didn't want, even though my heart was constantly telling me otherwise. I wanted Ben. I wanted to be *his*. Jessica was his woman. And I was his man.

He leaned in closer to me, forcing my eyes back to his. They were as blue as the sky. *He wants me to kiss him...* He *wants* me.

"I'm here, baby," he whispered, running his hand down my neck. "Isn't this what you want?" His face moved in closer and my eyes fluttered shut.

"Yes..." I breathed on his lips. *I want you, Ben. So bad...*

"Prove it," he demanded, gently. "Show me..."

I hummed and kissed his sweet lips, soft and slow, causing him to groan out this little sigh of contentment. I held his jaw with my hand, tugging his lips with mine, blocking out every hesitation and insecurity trying to steal my bliss. And suddenly it was just us, alone on our own private island. Just me and my man.

"You're destroying me, Benjamin Lockwood..." I whimpered on

his mouth and he smiled, kissing me back, breathing gentle, calming breaths while we sucked at each other's lips in just the perfect way. In our own little bubble, until...

A throat cleared, loud. "Alright, here we are!" the grumpy waitress barked, startling both of us out of our reverie. She set down our plates on the table, then scoffed, shaking her head as she walked away.

Ben and I stared at each other, then burst out laughing. He sighed and ran his hand through his hair, before scooting away to go back to his side of the booth. Except that I grabbed his arm to stop him.

"Stay," I murmured, pleading with my eyes. He smiled a wide, fully debilitating smile and scooted back in, pushing me over to make room. I grinned to myself, acknowledging how different my heart thumped when he was near me.

Ben brought his eight million plates closer, and we ate sitting side-by-side, sharing bites here and there, talking and laughing and teasing each other. It was by far one of the best trips to a waffle house I'd ever had.

Once we were sufficiently stuffed, it was time to go. I paid while Ben was in the bathroom which made him whine and scold me for minutes on end. But it was totally worth it. He was so cute when he was annoyed and being forced to give up control.

I let him drive again, back to his car. And while we were on the road, he called Jess with his phone on speaker. I was nervous to hear her voice, but even more nervous for her to find out Ben and I spent the night together alone. I wasn't sure if she would be mad. And I really had no desire to hurt or upset her in any way.

"Baby?" Jess answered the phone after two rings, her sweet, melodious voice floating through the speaker like a siren song.

"Hey, babe!" Ben shouted at her, and I flinched. "Just wanted to call and let you know I'm almost on my way home. We're heading back to my car now."

"Okay. You're still with the guys?" she asked, and I saw Ben's eyes dart to me briefly.

"No, actually... I'm with Ryan," he spoke firmly, and I cringed inside. *Please don't be mad. Please don't be mad.*

"Ryan?!" she squeaked. "How??"

"Well, it turns out he was at that casino in Santa Rosa with some friends, which was only like a half-hour drive to the strip club I was at. I didn't want to stay there, but I was pretty drunk, so I went to a hotel nearby and he... met me."

"He met you at the hotel?" Jess asked, and I couldn't exactly gauge her tone. She didn't sound mad. Just surprised.

"Yea... We stayed there last night." I could see Ben's hands gripping the steering wheel tight. He was obviously nervous, too. "He was in no condition to drive all the way home either."

"Oh... Jeez. That's crazy..." she murmured. I swallowed hard over my suddenly dry throat. "Did you guys have fun...?"

From the way she asked the question, I could instantly tell she wasn't mad. She was curious... Maybe a little turned on. I recognized it in her voice.

"Yea," Ben grunted. "Lots of fun."

"I bet," she whispered, and my dick flinched in my pants. *Jessica likes it. She gets turned on thinking about Ben and me together.* "You're in his car now?"

"Mhm," Ben barely replied, then nudged me.

"Hi, Jessica!" I crooned. "I miss you, love love."

"Oh my God, I miss you too!" she squealed, and Ben shot me a look, narrowing his gaze. I smirked at him. "How are you doing out there all by yourself?" I could hear the pout in her voice.

"I'm alright... Sorta bored," I huffed. "I miss you guys. I was so excited when Ben called last night."

"I'm sure," she purred. "Well, I'm glad you guys got to spend some time together. Hopefully, I can see you very soon."

"I know, I know," I sighed. "I need to see you..."

"Are you going to see your mom for Christmas?" she asked, being her usual caring, attentive self.

"I think so," I replied, not at all wanting to get into this conversation. "I have a couple finals due this week and then I'm on break. I can't wait."

"Oh wow, you get done before Hailey then."

"Yup. Almost time..."

"Alright well please drive home safe. I don't want to be worrying about both of you," she said firmly, and I smiled. When I peeked over at Ben, he was smiling, too.

"Will do, honey," I rasped, and she giggled.

"Bye, babe. And Ben I'll see you soon?" she chirped.

"Yes, baby," he answered. "Should be home in about an hour."

"Okay. Love you," Jess murmured sweetly to her husband, and I bit my lip.

"Love you, too," he rumbled then hung up the call. I breathed out hard for some reason.

Ben and I were quiet for a minute. I was still reveling in the high from hearing Jess's voice, having her comfort me with her sweetness, like she always did. And the fact that she was completely accepting of Ben and I having alone time. It was pretty wonderful.

"I'm so..." Ben started, then paused. "Happy."

I turned in my seat to face him. "Are you?"

"Yea," he sighed, then shook his head. "I love the fact that Jess is okay with us still seeing each other. Honestly, I wasn't sure what she'd say..."

I nodded slowly. "She seems fine with it."

"Yea. It's great," he huffed. "I get to have my time with her... and you. It's all I want."

"Good, baby," I murmured, squeezing his hand. "I'm happy you're happy."

Ben nodded and went silent again. He clearly had many thoughts bouncing around in his pretty head.

"Did you... want alone time with Jess?" he asked, hesitantly, his eyes darting to me for just a second.

I wasn't sure what to say. I enjoyed having alone time with Jess, but mostly just because she was such a loving person. I liked having her as a friend.

And yes, I also liked fucking her, and eating her pussy, but I'd never thought about doing it without Ben there.

"I just don't want it to be unfair, you know?" he continued, tapping his thumb on the steering wheel. "Like, I don't want it to be like you're both doing whatever *I* want."

"I don't think it's like that, baby," I told him. "It's just a very... new, unfamiliar thing for all of us. It would take some getting used to for us to figure out a rhythm."

"I wish we had more time..." Ben pouted. "I wish the three of us could be together more."

"Me, too," I whispered. My head was spinning.

We drove the next few minutes in silence before we pulled into the restaurant parking lot. Ben let out a relieved sigh when he spotted his vehicle unharmed. I walked him over to his SUV, and he turned to face me, sighing out a sweet, soft noise.

He rested his arms on my shoulders, and I placed my hands on his abs as we stared at each other. *I hate this part...*

"Can we talk more often this time?" I asked him, not wanting to sound like a desperate, clingy loser, but then not really able to help it.

"Of course, baby," he answered, calm and assuring. "Last time... I don't know, I just wasn't sure what we were doing. But that was wrong of me. I always miss you so much. And if I miss you, I should just call you. No more fucking games."

I raised my brows. *Wow...*

"Okay... good," I nodded, reaching up to hold his face. "No more games."

We both leaned in, meeting in the middle and kissing slowly. It was so warm and sweet, it almost made my teeth ache. We kissed for a few minutes, touching each other everywhere, panting and humming, grinding our hardened dicks together.

"I can't wait to see you again," he whispered.

"I'll be counting the minutes," I breathed on his lips and he grinned.

"Sappy fuck," he teased, and I hit him in the stomach.

We finally pulled apart and forced ourselves to say goodbye. I got in my car and watched as Ben drove away, waving at me as he left the parking lot.

I sat there for twenty-minutes in silence before I finally started my engine and headed home.

Fuck yes.

I sighed out a breath of relief as I packed up the rest of my books and slung my backpack over my shoulder.

That was it. I was done with my last class before winter break.

I had just gotten back a paper from my Torts class. Fucking ninety-five. I was psyched.

I left the classroom, nodding at a few people here and there as I exited the building, making a b-line for the parking lot. I was more than thrilled to be finished with school for the next couple weeks, and I just wanted to get the hell off campus for a while. I had been busting my hump since the beginning of this semester, and I was definitely due for a break.

I sauntered over to my car but paused when I heard a familiar giggle. I turned over my shoulder and saw Hailey, standing with a few friends, talking and laughing. I recognized all of them, except for one. A tall guy who was smiling down at her while she held onto his arm.

I swallowed hard. It didn't look like they were together or anything. For all I knew they were just friends. But for some reason my pulse was increasing, and my chest felt tight.

I hadn't seen Hailey since we broke up. But I would be lying if I said I hadn't thought about her a few times... And stalked her social media just a little.

You have to move on, man. You're not together anymore. Hailey's allowed to see other guys...

Before I could even process what I was doing, I was walking over to them. I approached slowly and Hailey spotted me, giving me a sweet, if not slightly sympathetic smile.

"Excuse me a sec," she murmured to her friends and stepped over to me, tilting her head to the side.

"Hey," I hummed, forcing a weak smile. After-break-up encounters were always awkward, whether you wanted them to be or not.

"Hi, Ryan," Hailey said my name in that same sweet tone she always had. "How's it going?"

"Good," I nodded. "Just finished classes. I passed that crazy torts nonsense..."

"Wow, good job," she squealed then shook her head. "I'm so

dreading that one."

"Yea, it wasn't easy," I huffed. "How have you been doing?"

"Great, actually," she smiled and for some reason it made my stomach turn. Not that I wanted her to be devastated by our break-up or anything... But we were together for almost five months. It stung to see her moving on so effortlessly. "I still have papers due and an exam in two days."

"They really work you up to the end, huh?" I chuckled awkwardly, shoving my hands in my pockets.

"Yea..." she sighed. I glanced at her friends behind her and the guy she had been talking to made brief eye contact. *Fucker.*

"It's good to see you, Hales," I mumbled, my lips quirking up.

"Yea, you too, Ryan," she blinked those gorgeous blue eyes up at me before looking down at her shoes. "Well, I'd better head to class..."

"Yea, sure. Don't let me keep you," I muttered, leaning down to kiss her cheek. It felt so different now. I almost couldn't believe that she was my girlfriend a month ago... "Be good. And hey, don't be a stranger, huh?"

"Mhm," she hummed, smiling at me before biting her lip. "See ya around... *Heartthrob Harper.*"

"Watch it," I squinted at her and she laughed, scampering off to rejoin her friends. I went back to my car, watching them out the corner of my eye. I saw one of her girlfriends take her by the arm and whisper something in her ear, most likely about me, while the tall guy continued to grill me with his eyes, clearly trying to be subtle.

But I wasn't worried about it. Hailey and I were over. There was no going back to that, which did still feel kind of shitty, but there was nothing I could do about it now.

And as it would seem, I was in something of a new relationship.

I hopped into my car and started her up, driving back to my apartment. I was exhausted from staying up late the last few nights to finish my paper, and all I wanted to do was relax for the rest of the day. Plus, I needed to call my mom and figure out what the hell was going on for Christmas. I still didn't know if she wanted me to come home for the holidays... She had yet to call me, which unfortunately was not out of the ordinary for my mother.

My phone started ringing through the Bluetooth system in my car and I checked the screen, my face immediately breaking into a massive smile.

"Hi there," I answered the call, my fingers twitching on the steering wheel.

"Hey, sexy ass," Ben's deep voice rung through the speakers, giving me chills. I could picture the cocky smirk on his face and it already had me panting.

"What's up?" I asked, nestling myself into my seat.

"Not much. Just got home from a quick meeting at the site," he told me, sounding cool, calm and confident. That typical *Ben* tone I was so used to at that point.

"That's cool," I bit my lip to stifle my giddiness. *Jesus, a two-second conversation and you're swooning... Take it easy.*

"Well? Don't leave me hanging in suspense!" Ben growled at me over the phone. "How'd it go?"

I grinned and stayed quiet for a moment, knowing it was driving him crazy, while reveling in satisfaction.

"Ninety-fucking-five," I finally answered him, beaming with pride.

"Hey! There you go, kid. That's what I'm talking about," he rumbled with an obvious smile in his voice. "I'm so proud of you."

I chuckled, my cheeks heating like a furnace. "Thanks. I busted my ass on that paper. My professor was impressed."

"Yea, so am I. I had no fucking clue what you were talking about when you read me that one paragraph," he laughed, which was just about the cutest thing ever. I couldn't even believe how happy I was at the moment. I felt high.

"Yup. All done now. No more school for three weeks," I sighed.

"You deserve the break," he went on, and I heard Jess's voice in the background. Ben mumbled something to her that I couldn't hear. "Do you want to tell her, or can I?"

I laughed softly and shook my head. "You can." I heard Ben telling Jessica about my grades and she started cheering. I honestly felt like my face was going to break in half.

The three of us had been talking a lot more since the last time I saw Ben. And while I still missed them both every day, and desperately wanted to see them, it certainly made me feel a lot better that we could at least do this strange long-distance thing we were doing.

We texted all the time and talked on the phone at least once a day. Usually Ben was the one to call me, but Jess always ended up hijacking the phone from him at some point during the conversation. The other night I talked to her for two hours. It was crazy.

I honestly had no idea what we were doing anymore. All I knew was that I loved talking to them. They definitely brightened up my day.

"Celebrating tonight then?" Jess asked, sounding so excited for me that my heart wanted to burst out of my chest. It was pretty incredible having people who gave that much of a shit about the things I accomplished. My friends were all sort of self-involved, not that I would blame them. And my own mother barely ever called me about anything, let alone to ask how school was going.

"Honestly, I'm just excited to go home and relax," I breathed. "I don't want to look at another law book for the next three weeks."

"You earned it, sweetie," she purred, her voice making me warm and fuzzy.

"What are you guys doing tonight?" I asked, pulling onto my street. "Anything good?"

"Not really," Ben answered. They must have had me on speaker. "I'm cooking a delicious roasted chicken for dinner, with potatoes and... all kinds of crap."

I laughed out loud and heard Jess giggling with me.

"Come on! Why is it so hard to believe that I could be cooking dinner?" Ben griped.

"Sorry, baby," I chuckled. "But Jess told me about the last time you tried making her dinner..."

"He almost burnt the house down," Jess laughed.

"It wasn't that bad..." he grumbled defensively.

"Sure, babe," Jess added, and I could hear him playing with her. It set a longing in my chest. *I wish I was there with them...*

I parked in my driveway and sighed. "Well, I have to go, crazies. I just got home."

"Okay, baby... Can you call me later?" Ben huffed.

"Of course," I answered, my stomach twisting into a knot.

"Talk to you soon, muffin!" Jess chirped. "And congratulations! You rock, you sexy almost lawyer!"

I laughed softly. "Bye, guys."

"Bye!" they both shouted at the same time, and I hung up before I could miss them anymore. I was already in agony.

I got out of the car with my bag and headed toward my apartment. My phone started ringing, and I grinned, pulling it out of my pocket, expecting to see Ben's number again.

But this time, it was a different number. One that I was beginning to recognize...

I froze and stared at my phone screen for a moment, watching the incoming call. I bit my lip as my stomach turned. I eventually swiped to decline the call and tucked my phone away again.

I can't deal with that. Not now.

I made my way inside, and was immediately hit with blaring Christmas music, echoing off the walls. Kayla was dancing around, decorating the whole place with all kinds of tinsel and cut-out snowflakes. It looked like Santa's Workshop exploded inside our apartment.

"Jeez..." I murmured to myself, tossing my stuff on the floor and stammering over to the kitchen for a beer. Alec was already in there doing the same.

"Hey, man," he grabbed me a cold one, twisting off the cap before handing it over. "How'd it go today?"

"Aced it," I grinned, clinking my bottle on his and taking a long sip.

"That's awesome, bro! I'm so glad," he patted me hard on the back. "You really went hard on that paper."

"Tell me about it," I replied, looking around at all the decorations. "Kayla's sort of going overboard this year, don't you think?"

"About that..." Alec started, giving me a slightly guilty look. My smile faded. "Her parents are actually coming up for Christmas this year..."

"Oh yea?" I asked, sudden unease sliding through me.

"Yea... And she wants them to stay here," he continued, eyeing me carefully. "Is that cool? You're going to Denver anyway, right?"

I took another sip from my beer, even longer this time. The truth was, I wasn't sure if I was going to see my mom. The fact that she hadn't even called me about it yet, and Christmas Eve was in a few days, didn't exactly bode well for my *holiday plans.*

"Um yea. Yea, it's cool," I grunted, faking a smile for my best friend. "Don't worry. I'll be out of your hair."

"You know it's not like that, man," Alec frowned. "It's your apartment, too. You're obviously welcome to stay. I just figured you'd rather chew broken glass than spend Christmas with us and Kayla's parents. They're kind of... different."

"I heard that!" Kayla shouted from the living room, and Alec and I gaped at each other.

"How the hell does she do that?" I gasped and Alec shrugged.

I decided to retreat to my room for a bit. I needed a break. And I sort of needed to figure out what the hell was going on with my mom.

I dialed her number and paced my bedroom as the phone rang, over and over. I was chewing on my bottom lip, wondering if she was actually going to ignore my call, when finally...

"Hi, baby!" my mom's pitchy, fluttering voice came through the phone. "I'm so happy to hear from you!" I breathed out slowly.

"Hi, Mom," I greeted her soft, immediately feeling like I was eight-years-old again. It was an uncanny thing that happened whenever I spoke to my mother. Good thing I didn't speak to her that often...

"How have you been?" she asked, sounding chipper, if not slightly distracted, as per usual. "How are you doing in school?"

"Good. Great, actually," I told her. "I'm done with classes for winter break..."

"That's great, sweetie! Are you spending Christmas with Hailey?" she asked, and my stomach twisted.

"Uh, no... Actually, Hailey and I broke up," I replied, quietly. I felt guilty for some reason. Although, she would know more about what was going on with me if she bothered to call every once in a while.

"Oh no. Ryan... What happened?" she asked, oozing sympathy, but as soon as I opened my mouth to respond, "She was a sweet girl. Are you sure you can't make it work?"

"No, Mom. We can't," I grumbled. "It's been a month. It's over."

"Really? A month?" she squeaked. "Didn't you meet her parents at Thanksgiving?"

"Yea..." I gulped, barely realizing that I was walking fast around the entire circumference of my bedroom. "It's okay though... It was mutual."

"You didn't get on well with her family?" she kept pushing, and now it sounded like she was talking to someone else in the background. I wondered why she was asking me all these questions if I didn't even have her full attention.

"I did. That wasn't the issue..." I huffed and rubbed my eyes. "Look, Mom, I'm not with Hailey anymore. So... did you want me to come home for Christmas?"

The line went quiet. I checked the screen to make sure the call was still connected. "Mom?"

"Yea, I'm here, baby," she finally spoke again. "You can come for Christmas if you want."

My brow furrowed. *If you want...? Jeez, thanks, Mom. Love you too.*

"Well, if you don't want to see your only son, then I guess I won't bother..." A wave of rejection swept through me, burning my insides like acid.

"No, it's not that, Ryan," she gasped defensively. "Of course, I want to see you." I breathed in deep and nodded, trying to convince myself that this was true. "It's just... the flights are so damn expensive around the holidays. I didn't want you to worry..."

I cringed. My mom still had no money. She'd never really had money, even when I was a kid. After she and my dad split, he would send child support and whatnot, but my dad wasn't exactly rich either. We weren't poor, but we definitely didn't have money to throw around.

And I still didn't, what with work being so damn slow right now. I was burning through my savings faster than I would let myself think about. So if I were to fly home for Christmas, clearly I would be expected to pay for it.

But before I could comment on that any further, she kept going.

"And also, I'm spending Christmas at Fred's house," she murmured, sounding completely normal. Like she wasn't fully fucking with me right now.

"Who the hell is *Fred?*" I hissed, the confusion evident in my voice. I already felt a headache coming on.

"Oh, I didn't mention Fred...?" she asked, her voice coming out genuinely surprised. She always sounded like that. My mom was a total airhead. She was a sixties, hippy flower child who still smoked just as much pot now as she probably had back then. I couldn't tell if it was the constant weed smoking that made her so scatter-brained, or if she was just like that. My mom was a huge space cadet. Always had been.

"Mom, when would you have mentioned *Fred?*" I grumbled at her over the phone, raking my hand aggressively through my hair. "You haven't bothered to call me in months."

"I'm so sorry, Ryan," she whined, huffing out a soft breath. "I've been busy. You're such an independent boy... You've been like that since you were little. Sometimes I just... feel like, you've got this."

You've got this?! Really, Mom?? Maybe I wouldn't have needed to be such an independent kid if you actually paid any attention to me...

"Fred is a man I've been seeing..." she kept going with the information, and I was feeling a wave of nausea come over me. "We've been dating for a few months. He's great. He's in a band!"

Oh Jesus fucking Christ...

I plopped down on my bed and rubbed my temples with my fingers. "You've been dating this guy for months and you're just now telling me about it?"

"Well, I wanted to make sure it was serious before I introduced you," she muttered, sounding guilty; like a child being scolded by a parent. The irony was irritating the shit out of me.

"Okay, introducing us I understand... But you could have at least mentioned it," I mumbled and shook my head to myself. "So... you're going to *Fred's* for Christmas? I guess it's sort of serious then..."

"A little," she replied, her vagueness and refusal to provide me with a straight answer irking me to no end. "He has two kids. Brandon and Layla. They're eight and twelve. It was important to him that I spend the holiday with the three of them..."

All of my childhood insecurities were coming on, full-force. My mom was actually blowing me off-her own son-to spend Christmas with her new *boyfriend* of only a few months and *his* fucking kids. This was utter bullshit.

"Alright, Mom. I get it," I sighed. "Don't worry about me. I'll be fine."

"Hey! How about I come see you after New Year's?" she chirped, using the same tone she used to give me when I was a kid and she was trying to make up for missing my peewee football games. And then my high school football games. And my debate club finals. And my fucking graduation. "I've been meaning to come out there again and stay with you for another weekend! I had so much fun with you and Hailey over the summer..."

I forced a queasy smile and closed my eyes tight. "Sure, Mom. Sounds like a plan."

She started yelling at someone. "Brandon! Pick up your skates, please! Someone's going to trip and die! Daddy will be home soon." *She's fucking taking care of this guy's kids already? Jesus, that was fast... Well, maybe not. This is my mother we're talking about.* "Ryan, baby, I have to let you go. But I promise I'll call you very soon."

"Okay, Mom," I hummed, confusing tears attempting to sneak out from behind my eyes. "Love you..."

"I love you so much, sweetie," she murmured. "I'm so proud of you. You're the best kid a mother could ever ask for."

Because I never expect anything.

"Bye, Mom," I grunted, my voice hoarse from the impending emotional breakdown. I hung up the phone fast and tossed it on my bed, flopping onto my back.

I covered my face with my hands, squeezing my eyes shut even tighter as I struggled to catch my breath. My chest was heaving a little, and the tears were coming, whether or not I wanted to let them.

I had never considered my childhood to be bad. Not compared to how awful some other people had it.

I was never abused. I never went hungry, or cold. I always had a roof over my head and food in my belly. My parents loved me. I knew they did.

But it was the neglect that I hadn't even realized was a thing until I grew up and saw how some of my friends' parents treated them. They showed up to all their activities, games, and school events. They picked them up and dropped them off whenever they needed it. They didn't leave them home alone until they were well into their teens.

I got none of that. My dad left my mother when I was only six, and of course neither of them would ever tell me why, other than that they *couldn't be married to each other anymore.* I don't remember much of anything before my dad left. I had a few memories here and there of him playing with me.

My memories of my dad were always good. But that was all they were. Memories.

After he left, I didn't see him again until I was twelve, when he came to visit. It was a pretty mediocre father-son weekend. I was twelve and used to spending all my time alone, or with my friends. I had no interest in getting to know the father who'd abandoned me six years earlier.

The visits after that were infrequent. The first time I ever went to Santa Fe to see him was when I was fifteen. He bought me a ticket, and I flew down by myself. It was then that I knew I'd like to live down there someday. I liked the weather and the people. I just didn't necessarily like my dad.

Of course when he got sick, I had to be with him. It was an emotional roller coaster of a time for me. I barely knew my father, and that made me feel insanely guilty because he was dying. And after he was gone, I would never get another chance to know him.

Those nine months, with my father in and out of chemo, were honestly the best times we'd ever had. We actually spent time together; as much as we could, anyway. I got to know his new wife, Bernadette. She was sweet, but she had kids of her own, too. She didn't have time to be catering to a seventeen-year-old with abandonment issues.

I promised my dad on his deathbed that I would do whatever made me happy. And so far, that was what I thought I'd been doing. It had been a dream of mine to be a lawyer when I was in high school, and my dad seemed really proud of that. I wanted to make him proud. I just wanted him to love me... Both of them.

I groaned out a pained sigh and sniffled through my tears, wiping my eyes and trying to steady my out-of-control breathing. My mom was right. I was independent. I didn't need anyone or anything. It was me against the world.

My mind flashed back to the phone call from earlier... The one I had ignored. My throat constricted, as I considered what was on the other end of that call... The message that was likely sitting, unanswered in my voicemail box.

What is the right thing to do here...? What would really make me happy?

I sat up and blinked over my scratchy eyes. Maybe I could just stay home for Christmas. It wouldn't be that bad, dealing with Alec and Kayla, and her weird parents... After all, how weird could they be if they actually loved her enough to come visit for the holidays?

But the thought of being that awkward friend who hung around the house while my best friend spent time with his girlfriend's family made me sick to my stomach. I couldn't do that. I would never let myself be that desperate.

I barely even wanted to see my mom, anyway. I just felt like I *should* see her, because it was the holidays. But if she didn't care, then why should I?

There were only two people I actively *wanted* to spend time with... And they wanted to spend time with me, too.

They cared about me, and what I was doing. They cared enough to listen to me talk about my schoolwork, and my interests. They cared enough to call me the second they knew I was done with classes to find out how I did.

That was love. It was what I wanted... *What I need.*

Before I could even process what I was doing, I began pacing around my room again, this time packing clothes into an overnight bag. I had a plan, and I needed to believe that this would be the right thing for me. I was feeling so lonely, so rejected. I needed to be with people who wanted me. I was fortunate enough to have found not one, but two of them. They would give me what I needed.

I need some love.

CHAPTER 15

Ben

WAS LYING ON MY BACK ON MY COUCH IN THE BASEMENT, nursing my fourth beer, watching some Netflix show about serial killers.

I glanced at the clock on my desk. It was almost two in the morning. I huffed and set my beer down on the table, picking up my phone.

Still nothing from Ryan.

I had texted him a couple hours ago, because I was missing him, and I expected him to reply back like he always did. But he didn't. So now I was worried.

Sure, he was allowed to have his own life. I didn't expect him to drop everything to reply to his long-distance secret married whatever-the-hell I was to him. But I had gotten sort of used to him always responding to my texts right away. I just hoped he was okay...

I pulled up his Instagram account like a fucking stalker and checked to see if he had posted anything. *Nope. Figures.*

He wasn't on there much anyway. But still, sometimes he posted when he was out with his friends.

Maybe he's seeing someone... Maybe he's having sex.

I closed my eyes and shook my head. I didn't know why this was the first place my mind went as soon as he didn't answer a text. It wasn't my business. He was his own person... A hot single guy. He was certainly allowed to date, although the very thought of him seeing someone other than me or Jess made me feel extremely murderous.

What about Hailey? He dated her... Your daughter.

I groaned and rolled over onto my stomach, tossing my phone on the floor. I was such an asshole. I couldn't believe I was actually entertaining the idea of a relationship with my daughter's ex-boyfriend. And now I had dragged Jess into it, too. *What a piece of shit you are.*

My phone started ringing, and I jumped, sitting up fast and grabbing it. My heart lodged in my throat, which was such a bizarre reaction to a phone call. And when my eyes landed on the screen, it began thumping even harder in my jugular.

"Hello?" I answered fast, out of breath from nothing.

"Ben..." Ryan's voice rumbled into my ear, and for some reason I was nervous. He sounded strange.

"Baby... Are you okay?" I asked quietly, my whole body completely still. *Please God, let him be alright.* "You didn't answer my text..."

"I'm sorry about that... I was driving," he murmured, and my forehead creased.

"Driving...? Where?" I asked, gripping my phone hard in my hand.

"What are you doing right now?" he ignored my question, asking his own.

I squinted in confusion. "Nothing much... Hanging out in the basement, watching TV."

"You miss me?" His voice was so deep and sexy, my breathing instantly shallowed.

"You know I do," I leaned back on the couch. "I wish you were here..."

"Mmmm... I was hoping you'd say that." I heard a grin in his voice, and it made my dick twitch against my thigh. I smiled and bit my lip.

"Did you call just to fuck with me?" I growled, and he chuckled quietly.

"A little," he rasped. The desire to touch him was overwhelming. I wanted to see him and kiss him... Feel his warmth and his smooth skin. It was amazing how much I actually missed him now that I wasn't hiding from it anymore.

"Baby, do me a favor," Ryan commanded in a soft tone.

"Anything," my pulse raced inside me.

"Come upstairs and let me in," he pleaded, and I almost dropped my phone. *What the fuck?!?*

I stood up fast. "What... How...?" my voice flew from my throat in a gasp. Ryan chuckled.

"Don't keep me waiting out here, Ben. It's cold," he murmured and my whole body started buzzing with excitement. *Is he really here? Oh my God... What?!*

I darted up the stairs, phone still in hand, plastered to the side of my face as I raced through the house to the front door. I got there and whipped it open, anticipation coursing through my veins.

"Hi," Ryan smiled at me, also still holding his own phone up to his ear. I huffed out softly, my hand slipping down by my waist.

"You're here," I mumbled, eyes widened in shock. I couldn't believe what I was seeing. I was just missing him so bad and *poof!* He appeared out of thin air.

"Uh-huh," he nodded, grinning at me, his dark eyes locked on mine.

"Oh my God, you crazy fucking asshole," I whimpered and launched myself at him.

I kissed him hard and fast while he was still giggling, those little noises slipping between my parted lips. I held his face in my hands, my fingers savoring the feeling of the scruff that lined his perfect jawline while I kissed his soft lips over and over. I slid my tongue into his mouth, and he groaned, placing his hands on my chest to feel me up through my t-shirt.

"Baby, I missed your lips," he panted, sucking on my bottom lip so sweet, I was already on fire. "Your tongue... your fucking taste."

"Ryan..." his name flew out of my mouth into his as he pushed me against the doorway, causing me to grunt. We were full on making out, hard, and it took a few moments for me to realize we were out in the open.

Yes, it was the middle of the night, and no one in our neighborhood would be looking out their windows right now. But still it wasn't smart.

"Come on," I forced my lips away from his, breathing heavily as I dragged him inside and closed the door, locking it behind him.

"Is Jess up?" he asked, still holding onto my body, his curious fingers touching me everywhere.

"She's sleeping," I tugged him by the waist, running my hands up his torso, across his strong, broad shoulders. I shoved him up against the wall in the foyer and ground my hips into his.

My erection was already rock hard, and I wanted him to feel it. Judging by the gasp that escaped him as my crotch brushed his, he could. And he clearly liked it.

"Should we wake her up?" he asked, raising his brow, eyes dropping to my lips. I kissed him gently, gliding my tongue in to meet his.

"Not yet," I hummed, yanking him with my hands grasping the nape of his neck. "I want you all to myself right now."

I took a fist of his shirt and pulled him with me, toward the basement. Our eyes were set on each other, and I could see a fire burning inside him. His desire for me was visible, and it was such a damn turn-on.

I took a moment to look him over. He looked fucking gorgeous. From his tousled dark hair, perfectly trimmed up beard lining his jaw, defined arms and chest, showing themselves through the fabric of his long-sleeved Henley; narrow waist, fitted jeans sitting low on his hips, and those long legs. He was just so fucking hot. I could barely control my breathing when I looked at him. When he was looking at me...

We snuck downstairs quietly, and I caught him glancing around the basement, with a wistful look on his pretty face.

"I haven't been down here since... that night," he murmured, his eyes coming back to mine as he tilted his head, nostalgia gleaming in those dark green irises.

"Mmm..." I hummed, stepping over to the couch to take a seat. Memories of that night were flashing through my mind now, like a dirty slideshow. "You were so ballsy, coming down here like that."

He sat down right next to me and I turned to face him.

"I couldn't help myself," he raised his brow. "You're just so goddamned irresistible."

I smirked. "Hmm... Coming onto an older married man is a bold move, kid. What if I said no?"

"That was a risk I was willing to take," he breathed, scooting in closer until we were only inches apart. My dick was already hard, fighting against the material of my sweatpants.

"When did you know...?" I asked quietly, my eyes bouncing back and forth between his eyes and those plump curved lips.

He slid his hand onto my leg. "Know what?"

"That you were going to make a move," I went on, eager for information. "When did you decide you wanted to try me?"

He breathed out a soft noise, his fingers trailing up and down my thigh.

"On Thanksgiving night..." he said, his face fully serious. "The first time I saw you with Jess... I watched you fucking her, and I was... in *awe*." I bit my lip to stifle noises wanting to escape. "I couldn't see much of her. Only you... All those muscles in your back and arms, your smooth, golden skin. Your sweet ass."

I chuckled deviously, and he grinned, moving in slowly to brush his lips over mine. I started to tremble, my cock flinching between my legs.

"Do you even know how fucking good your ass looks?" he kept talking, his deep voice all hoarse and growly with his arousal. "I couldn't stop staring at it. Before you, I had never looked at any guy. I never would have... But then I saw your full, round delicious ass, with your hips thrusting into your wife... And all I could think about was touching you. *Fucking* you."

I groaned and licked my lips. "You wanted to fuck me, baby?"

"Oh God, yes," he nodded slowly. "It was all I could think about. But I didn't come down here the next night expecting anything. I just wanted to be near you." I swallowed hard. "And then I saw how nervous you were... When I got close, I could tell you were curious... About how it would feel. And what we could do together..."

He lifted his hand and took mine, placing it on his abs, the way he had that first night. I rubbed up on him gently, watching his face while I touched him, slow and sensual. Then he leaned in, pressing soft kisses along my jaw and down my throat.

My skin was so hot it was almost stifling. I laid back on the couch slowly and he moved on top of me, sliding my t-shirt up my frame and tossing it on the floor. His warm, wet mouth moved down my chest, kissing my pecs, sucking my nipples, soft and ravening. He nibbled one a little, and I gasped, my dick painfully stiff beneath him while he dry-fucked me.

"Ryan, holy fuck..." I grunted, ripping at his shirt to get it off him. He pulled it off his long arms and threw it, then pressed his heated soft skin on mine.

"Ben..." my name slipped from his mouth like a prayer. *Good God, what have I gotten myself into...*

We kissed deep and slow, fucking through our clothes for a while before we eventually lost our pants. His dick was so full and thick as he rubbed it on mine, flicking his hips in long, fluid motions, making me dizzy. My heart was rocking in my chest, and it felt so familiar.

Every time I had been with Ryan since that first night was just like this. It was us, together. We were insatiable for each other, and I fucking loved it.

Eventually Ryan slid my boxers off slowly, and moved his head between my parted thighs, taking my aching cock in his mouth and sucking my dick so good I couldn't breathe. Just like that first night. Watching his head vigorously bob, his lips sliding up and down, had me going crazy. I was ready to burst in a matter of minutes.

I stopped him before he could make me come and he looked desperate, sparking inside me a voracious desire. I flipped him beneath me and took off his boxers, making my own slow descent down his big, hard body, kissing and licking everywhere I could reach.

I took him in my mouth and sucked slow, swallowing his long cock until he was trembling before me. I left his big dick nice and wet then sat astride his hips, sliding his length between my ass.

"Ben..." he purred my name, running his hands up my hips, holding on tight. "Fuck me. I need you so bad, baby."

My cock pulsed, and I gripped his pecs with my hands, steadying my body on top of his. I reached behind me and relaxed, keeping my eyes on his as I guided him inside me. His eyes fluttered, and he groaned out loud as I pushed myself down on his dick.

"Fuck, Ryan... You're all I need," I told him, arousal seeping from the head of my cock as he filled me.

I rode him slow at first, working my ass on his inches as we grunted and gasped together, falling apart in pure ecstasy. It was so perfect and needy and carnal, that before I knew it, I was fully fucking him; riding his cock with my ass, watching his face before leaning down to kiss him, moaning into his mouth while his dick dove so far inside me, it felt like every atom in my body was on fire.

Harder and harder, I kept going, kept moving, taking all of him as we held each other. He curled his fist around my cock and stroked as he started to come in me, and I exploded into orgasm with him.

I had never felt more complete than I did with Ryan. Our sex was unlike anything I had ever experienced before. A balance of perfect imperfection. Forbidden fate.

We kissed for so long I lost track of time. Because time was standing still, for us.

I woke up the next morning in my own bed. With my wife. And my boyfriend.

I hugged Jessica against my body, lining the nape of her neck with kisses because she just smelled so damn good.

Ryan and I had made our way upstairs a little while after our *alone time*. It was five in the morning when we got into bed, and we were exhausted. The second we hit the mattress we were both out cold. And Jess had been deep in her usual slumber the entire time all of this was going down.

So basically my wife would be waking up to a big surprise.

I wasn't exactly sure what time it was now, but there was sun streaming in through the windows, meaning it was probably at least eight. Ryan was clearly still asleep, judging by the adorable little breathing noises coming from behind me.

Jess started tossing, pressing her butt against my crotch. I smiled on her sweet flesh, my lips trailing down to her shoulders while my hands rubbed up on her hips.

"Good morning, Mr. Lockwood," she purred, and I chuckled.

"Good morning, Mrs. Lockwood," I growled. "I have a surprise for you."

"It's not a surprise, Ben," she murmured, and I raised my brow. "It's huge and jamming into my back."

I laughed softly and hummed, kissing her skin a few more times. "No, not that. Look behind me."

Jess rolled over fast and lifted her head. She gasped out loud, her mouth hanging open and her eyes wide with shock. I had to laugh again.

"Where did you get him?!" she squealed, crawling over me, almost kneeing me in the stomach, to get to Ryan.

"He showed up last night," I grinned, watching her climb on top of Ryan and straddle his waist.

He groaned softly, his brow furrowing, eyes still closed. Jess and I snickered. The poor thing was so tired and now we were fucking with him. *Well, if he didn't want to play with us, he wouldn't have come over.*

Jess leaned down and hugged Ryan's body, pressing an adorable kiss on his chin, while I just watched, running my fingers along her lower back.

Ryan finally opened his eyes for a moment, then smiled this big, heartthrob thing, closing them again.

"Good morning," he murmured, grabbing Jess hard on the ass, making her squeal.

"Morning!" she chirped, pulling back to look down at him. He opened his eyes again. "I can't believe you're here."

"Me neither," he hummed, licking his lips slowly, the sight of which made my cock move.

"I'm going to make you guys breakfast," Jess said, the excitement obvious in her tone, and the radiant look on her face. "Come down when you're ready." She kissed Ryan's lips quick then rolled off the bed and stammered into the bathroom, closing the door behind her.

Ryan leaned up on his elbows and glanced at me. "She's the best."

"Mhm," I grunted, wrapping my arms around his waist and pulling him closer to me.

"You're the best, too," he grinned down at me as I nuzzled his neck and throat, running my lips all over his heated flesh.

"I am?" I trailed down his chest, stomach, pelvis... Ryan gasped.

"Fuck, Ben..." his eyes fluttered shut, and he flopped back down onto the pillow while I continued to work on my blowjob skills. *Practice makes perfect.*

Jess emerged from the bathroom a few minutes later, passing by us fast, smirking to herself. I had sort of expected her to join us... I knew she wanted to. Maybe she knew we'd be hungry after more sex and figured the breakfast was necessary.

I made Ryan come with my mouth, and then we took a quick shower, during which he returned the favor. After that we made our way downstairs, bouncing around all happy like we were walking on a goddamned rainbow.

We sat down at the table and Jess immediately brought over plates of blueberry pancakes and bacon, and lots of coffee. I gave my wife the most appreciative eyes ever, because she was fucking amazing, and she returned my telepathic compliment, tugging her bottom lip between her teeth. I knew she was turned on like crazy, especially because Ryan was there, and I found myself wondering if I should let the two of them have some alone time. They had never really fooled around alone before...

"Jessica... this is so delicious," Ryan's voice rumbled through my thoughts, as he gave my wife a sweet look. "Thank you so much, babe."

"You're so welcome, sexy," she grinned at him. "I'm really glad you're here. What made you decide to come?"

Ryan paused for a moment and something strange flashed over his face. He looked serious, as if he was contemplating something difficult. But he brushed it off then locked eyes with Jess and smiled.

"I couldn't stand being away from you two any longer," he spoke quietly, peeking at me quickly and winking.

"Such a sweet thing you are," I growled, and Jessica giggled.

She joined us for breakfast, the three of us chatting casually, mostly about Ryan's classes and how proud of him we were for his awesome grades. I couldn't get over how impressed I was that he was Pre-Law. It was something I knew almost nothing about, other than what I heard from Hailey, though Ryan was obviously further along.

He seemed very dedicated to his school work, though I couldn't help but notice how he never mentioned that it actually made him happy. I think he was proud of himself for focusing and buckling down with his studies, but I could tell he saw it as more of a *job* than an actual *passion*.

I remembered what he had told me over Thanksgiving weekend, about how he didn't have many hobbies, other than that he enjoyed working outside and had an interest in rebuilding old cars. I found myself wondering if maybe something like that would make him happy...

I want him to be happy. I want to make him happy.

Maybe I could find him an old car to restore. That would be fun.

I shook my head at where my thoughts were going. It definitely wouldn't look great... Me buying a car for the younger dude I was banging. Wouldn't that make me a sugar daddy?

I cringed internally. *That's sort of creepy. I'm not old enough to be a daddy... Am I?*

I zoned back in on the conversation just in time to hear Jess telling Ryan about the Christmas Eve party.

"Usually Bill and Rachel do it at their house, but what with the baby and everything they asked if we could have it here," Jess explained, sounding much more excited about the idea of this party than I was. "So now I have tons of decorating to do."

"I'll help you decorate," Ryan offered, sipping his coffee. "I mean, if you need help. I don't want to intrude..."

"No, oh my God, that would be amazing!" Jess replied gratefully. "Thank you so much! I know Ben was dreading hanging up all the lights by himself."

"Yea, because they're a pain in the ass," I grumbled, and caught Ryan smirking.

"Wow. If you were green, I would swear I was sitting next to The Grinch right now," he teased, and Jess laughed.

"Oh, just you wait," she interjected with a grin. "He goes full-Scrooge until Christmas morning, and then he finally lightens up when he gets to watch Hailey opening her gifts."

At mention of Hailey, the smiles fell from all of our faces simultaneously. It was as if we were so swept up in whatever this was we were doing that we had completely forgotten how fucking fucked up it was.

I took a deep breath and glanced down at my empty plate. I swallowed hard, though I couldn't swallow down the guilt that was trying to rise like bile. This was all my fault. I was the one who hooked up with Hailey's boyfriend while she was here in the house. And then I got Jess mixed up in all of this, too. I didn't feel like The Grinch. I felt like the damn devil.

Jess got up and cleared our plates, bringing everything to the kitchen, most likely to escape the tension and remorse that was now hanging over all our heads like a dark cloud. Ryan and I remained silent, both lost in our thoughts.

I loved the fact that Ryan was there with us, and it was a problem because I didn't want him to leave. But he had to.

Hailey would finish her classes in a couple days, and then she would come home for Christmas. And Ryan most certainly *could not* be there when she did.

I exhaled a swift breath, stuffing it all down, to be dealt with at another time.

"Come on, kid," I grunted, rising from my seat with purpose. "Let's go hang up some lights."

I parked my SUV in the parking lot and the three of us hopped out, making our way over to the trees. The place was all decorated to the fullest, complete with fake snow, ornaments, plastic reindeer everywhere; the works. It was a regular winter wonderland, there in the Southwest.

It wasn't always easy to find a Christmas tree, being that pines didn't exactly grow naturally there in most areas. Typically, it took some time, effort, and money to locate a proper Christmas tree. But I had managed to track down some good places over the years, since Jess and Hailey would not settle for anything plastic in our house. We had to have an authentic tree. They demanded it.

This year we had driven out further than usual, mainly because we had Ryan with us, and we didn't want to risk running into anyone we knew. It was a bit like a date or something, and we needed to be very careful. At first I was hesitant, being out in the open like that. But seeing Jess and Ryan's faces light up at the sight of all the beautiful evergreens told me I'd made the right call. I just wanted to make them both happy, and so far it seemed to be working.

"Oh my God, do you smell that?" Jess squealed, taking Ryan by the hand and tugging him over to the rows and rows of big green trees. "It smells like Christmas!"

"I love the smell of real pine trees," he replied, running his fingers over the needles on the branches. "It reminds me of back home."

"Denver?" I asked, taking a big whiff of the smell while giving him the side-eye. I never heard Ryan talk about where he grew up. It was sort of a mystery.

"Yea," he nodded. "Colorado has lots of trees like this. And snow, obviously."

"I've never been, but I'd love to see it someday," Jess added, the three of us studying the wide selection. "Snowy winters are so cool. Ben and I took Hailey to Boston in the winter once when she was like thirteen. We had such a great time. Ice skating in the commons. It was great."

"I've always wanted to see New England..." Ryan murmured quietly, his voice filled with a soft hesitation I couldn't quite figure out. "My aunt lives out there..."

"Are you going back home for Christmas?" I asked him, watching Jess scamper around out the corner of my eye.

"Um... yea," he replied, his tone slightly clipped. But before I could ask any more questions, he quickly changed the subject. "Let's get a tall one. Like this."

He nodded at a ten-foot tall balsam fir, which had a slightly bluish hue to it. It was big and bushy; probably grown indoors somewhere. But still it looked nice. I could already imagine it decorated with lights and all the little ornaments Jess and Hailey had accumulated over the years.

Jess came skipping back over, holding two Styrofoam cups, one in each hand.

"Hot chocolate for my darling men?" she smiled, handing the cups out to us.

I grinned and took one, looking to Ryan who did the same, sipping his slowly.

"Mmm. Thank you, baby," he rasped and leaned in to kiss her on the cheek.

"You wanna share this one?" I asked her, taking a sip of the warm, chocolatey beverage.

"No, thanks," she hummed. "I think I'll just taste it like this..." She grabbed my jacket in her fists and yanked me down to her lips, kissing me softly. I groaned and slid my tongue between her lips, giving her a taste of the sugar while she purred into my mouth.

When we pulled apart, I was breathless. Jess wrapped her arms around Ryan's waist and held onto him tight, checking out the giant tree in front of us.

"You like this one?" he asked, holding her close, nuzzling his nose and mouth in her hair as he kissed her head. It was very sweet to witness. Almost as sweet as the hot chocolate.

Watching them together gave me an interesting sensation. It made my stomach twist and my chest tighten up. If I didn't know any better, I would say it was jealousy and arousal mixed together, like some strange treat that's ingredients didn't quite make sense, but oddly still tasted good. Like bacon ice cream.

"I do, actually," Jess answered, reaching out her left hand and tucking it into the back pocket of my jeans. "It's really nice."

The three of us stood together, staring at the tree while what little sun was left when we got there disappeared, and it became night. It was suddenly much darker, and they switched on all the lights. The entire place was lit up with Christmas lights of all colors, shapes and sizes. Some were still, some twinkling and flashing. It looked really cool. Big, tall bushy green trees, lights and fake snow fully surrounded us. Our own Christmas hideaway.

"This is so romantic," Jess squeaked, peeking up at me. I smiled down at her. She was so beautiful, her perfect face illuminated by the lights.

Then I looked at Ryan. When he glanced at me, his dark eyes sparkling, I felt buzzed. Being there with the two of them, out in the open... It was thrilling. I looked around to see if anyone was watching us, prying eyes trying to figure out our situation; the two guys and the girl who were all huddled together to escape the slight chill in the air. It didn't really appear that anyone cared, but maybe it was just because I didn't.

I was having too much fun to give a fuck what anyone else thought. The only two people I cared about in that moment were Jess and Ryan. My woman, and my man.

This is so fucking bizarre. It feels great... marvelous, even. But how long can we go on like this? Can we really ever be together, the three of us? Probably not, because of the Hailey aspect... But even putting that aside, which we never could. Would they want that? How would it work?

I knew in my heart that it probably wouldn't. But I didn't want to let my doubts and insecurities ruin our lovely evening together. So once again, I stuffed it all down, and nestled my side up against Jess's.

"Let's get it."

I wandered off to find someone who worked there, so I could pay for the giant tree and have him strap it on top of my vehicle. The thing was expensive, to say the least, but it was worth it. Just seeing how excited and joyous Jess and Ryan were made me want to buy five more just like it.

Fifteen-minutes later the tree had been tied up to the roof rack on my SUV, and we were ready to head home. I hopped into the driver's seat, starting up the engine and blasting the heat to warm my frigid hands. After about a minute, I realized I was still alone in the car, and turned over my shoulder to look out the windows and see what the holdup was with my passengers.

My stomach flipped when I saw Jess and Ryan making out by the rear window. *There's that odd feeling again...*

I watched them closely, registering the burning sensation in my loins. I felt jealous, though my dick was also stiffening in my pants, which was just so confusing. I had never known I could feel these two things at the same time until the night in the hotel suite, watching them together. It was such a rush. My stomach always bottomed out at first, like I was free-falling off a cliff. It was exhilarating, and scary.

Finally, Jess opened the passenger side door, giggling, her cheeks flushed and her lips moist. It was a great look on her, I must say.

Ryan hopped into the back and our eyes met in the rearview mirror. I gazed at him and he bit his lip. My dick was unbearably hard.

"Ready?" I asked, my voice deep and hoarse. They both said nothing and nodded at the same time. I breathed out slowly and drove away.

Jess turned Christmas music on the radio, and spent the entire drive back home singing along to every song that played, forcing Ryan and I to join in. I wasn't much of a Christmas carol guy, but I begrudgingly sang along to appease them. Ryan spent most of the ride laughing at the two of us, and it was very cute.

His phone rang once while we were driving, and although he didn't accept the call, his face got awfully serious as he watched the screen. I really wanted to ask him who was calling and if he was okay, but I didn't want to pry. He would come to me if he needed to talk about anything. At least, I hoped he would.

When we got home, Ryan and I brought the tree inside and got it set up in the living room. The thing was gigantic. Luckily, we had high ceilings otherwise we would've had to maim the top of it.

"Are we going to decorate it?" Ryan asked, nestling up against me on the couch while Jess watered the tree with a great deal of focus and dedication.

"We can put the lights on tomorrow after the branches set a little," she answered, looking so tiny standing next to the massive thing. "But we have to wait for Hailey to decorate it on Christmas Eve. It's a tradition."

I felt Ryan still next to me and I peeked down at his face, trying to be subtle. I caught a brief look of disappointment, but he covered it up with a smile that quickly turned into a yawn.

"Are you tired?" I asked, trailing my fingers along his jaw. He gave me an impassive shrug, and I wasn't sure what it meant.

We hadn't even asked him when he was going home, nor had he mentioned it. We had just assumed he would stay, even though I didn't understand why. There had yet to have been any conversations about when he was leaving. It just felt good having him there. I supposed none of us wanted to ruin the wonderful day we were having by talking about anything serious.

"Bed time?" Jess asked, standing before us with a wicked gleam in her dark blue eyes. The corner of her mouth quirked up into a sexy smirk and my pulse instinctively sped up.

Without any further discussion, Ryan stood up and took my hand, pulling me to stand. Jess sauntered toward the stairs, purposely sashaying her hips in front of us as we followed her lead, ascending the steps toward the bedroom.

All the lights were off upstairs. That exotic moonlight coming in from our bedroom windows was the only thing illuminating the room, which I loved. It was very seductive.

I chose to get things rolling first and tugged my shirt over my head, stepping out of my pants until I was in only my boxer-briefs. I sat down on the edge of the bed, looking up at the two of them, waiting to see what they would do next.

Ryan followed my lead and removed his shirt and pants, then sat down next to me, making sure our arms and legs were touching. We both stared at Jess, and she began undressing, much slower than we had, giving us a little striptease.

She slithered out of her pants, then lifted her shirt over her head, tossing it at me, which make me chuckle. Then she removed her bra, flinging it at Ryan. My dick was already growing harder by the second just from looking at her big tits, her little pink nipples pert from the slight chill and the excitement.

She slid her panties down her legs so tantalizingly slow. Ryan reached over and placed his hand on my thigh, caressing gently as we watched my wife's sensual display, his curious fingers inching dangerously close to my erection.

Jessica stood before us, completely naked and unashamed–why wouldn't she be? Her body was incredible. Her eyes were twinkling as she bit her lip and stepped closer, slowly, until she was standing right in front of us, looking down with lust in her eyes and a sweet blush on her cheeks.

"Touch me," she whispered, her tone pleading as her pupils danced back and forth between Ryan and me.

We both reached out, my hand gliding up the back of her thigh to cup her ass, squeezing with my fingers, while Ryan fondled her tits. She closed her eyes and quietly moaned, both of us pulling her closer, our hands exploring every inch of her naked flesh.

Jess climbed onto Ryan's lap, straddling his hips and holding onto the nape of his neck. She kissed his lips, softly at first, but then they began to heat up, and they were making out as she ground herself on him. I watched closely, swallowing hard, staring at their mouths as their tongues pressed together, the blood rapidly filling my cock.

Ryan moved his lips down her neck and onto her tits, kissing and sucking all over them while Jess panted. I could see her trembling and it was burning me with desire. She reached out and grasped my jaw in her hand, tugging my face to her chest. I leaned in, kissing her left tit while Ryan worked on the right. I pushed her down harder on him by her ass, sucking her nipple between my lips.

"Oh, my fucking God..." she gasped, and I groaned, swirling my tongue around her peaked flesh, nipping at it with my teeth. I felt Ryan's hand slide between my legs, and he started palming my dick over my boxers.

"Fuck..." I moaned quietly with my wife's nipple between my lips.

Ryan paused the titty love for a moment and kissed me, both of us breathing heavy as our tongues touched, lips moving together in those hungry kisses that made me weak.

"Ben..." he whimpered my name and my cock throbbed in his hand. "I love your lips."

I hummed, sliding my finger between Jess's ass cheeks. She was so wet, basically dripping. It made me wild with hunger, for both of them.

"I want you to fuck me..." Jess mewled, and Ryan and I pulled apart, breathing heavy. "Both of you."

"Jess... I need to feel you inside," Ryan groaned, and she nodded quickly.

He grabbed her by the hips and laid down on his back, scooting further up on the bed, positioning her on top of him. I got up on my knees and watched as they kissed each other hard, Jess's wet pussy gliding up and down on Ryan's hardened length through his boxers.

I pulled them off for him, and then took mine off, stroking my cock in my fist, the veins in my dick pulsing. Ryan massaged Jess's tits in his hands while she took his cock in hers, pressing the head up to her entrance. He moaned softly, and I bit my lip, fully aware of how amazing it felt to slide the head of my own dick into that tight, wet warmth.

My wife pushed her soaking wet walls down on Ryan's erection, allowing him to fill her up, inch by inch. My eyes stuck on her behind, watching him move inside her slowly. It was fascinating.

"Holy fuck..." I hummed, gazing at the sight before me; my wife riding another man's cock, right in front of my face.

Jess moved up and down on him, swiveling her hips, looking so graceful as she took his dick, her hands gripping his hard chest, steadying herself on top of him.

"I missed this, baby," Ryan whispered, and my stomach clenched, a fire burning me from the inside out, all the way up my chest. I glanced at his face, their eyes locked on each other's. "You feel so good... Fuck me, Jess... Fuck my cock."

"Your dick feels amazing," she purred, whipping her head back slowly, her tits bouncing while she rode him. A chill washed over me. "Ben...?"

"Hmm?" I croaked.

"Will you... please..." she gasped, her voice trailing off into a moan.

"Will I what, baby?" I asked, getting lost in their rhythm, hypnotized by what I was watching.

"I want you to..." she whimpered, her voice quiet and hesitant, yet dripping with lust and mischievous hunger. "Please... fuck me..."

I raised my brow at her back. "You want me to...?"

"Fuck me... please," her voice cracked. "Fuck me with Ryan. I need you, Ben."

My dick began to ache. I had to take my hand off it because I was afraid I might come already. *She wants us both... at the same time?? Jesus Christ, that's fucking hot. Oh, my God. I'm going to combust.*

"Are you... sure?" I had to ask. The most we'd ever done was use the butt plug while I was fucking her. But that thing was almost nonexistent compared to the size of my dick. It wasn't cockiness, it was just a fact. And Ryan's dick was basically the same size as mine. This would fill her up like nothing she had ever experienced. But I was sure it would feel good...

Probably fucking euphoric.

"Yes, baby," she pleaded. "Ben... I need you in me. Now... please."

I heard Ryan groan softly and even that had me coming undone. If I did this, I could feel him, too. I fucking wanted it so bad; I felt like I might pass out.

I moved up to Jess's ass, cupping it with my hands and lifting her up and down on Ryan's dick, causing him to moan out some of the hottest noises I had ever heard. I slid my fingers between her thighs, touching Ryan's shockingly hard dick as it moved in and out of her slippery wet pussy. I gasped, as did Ryan. It was fucking incredible. *This is too much for my dick to handle.*

I slid my cock between her cheeks, using her natural lubrication to get it nice and wet. Ryan spread his legs wider, and I positioned myself between them, running my fingers over his balls. I felt him tremor at my touch.

"Fuck... Ben..." he groaned, and I held onto his thigh, taking my cock in my hand and pressing the head up to my wife's other entrance.

"Tell me if it's too much, baby, okay?" I said to her in a calming voice. She panted and leaned back against me. "Relax all your muscles, gorgeous."

I could feel her relax a bit and I pushed gently, trying to be as easy as possible. We hadn't had anal sex in probably almost a year, and even before that, it definitely didn't happen often. At that point, I had probably fucked Ryan in the ass more times than I had my wife in the past few years.

I forced my head a little more, her body struggling against my size, especially because of how full of another huge cock she already was. Her movements on Ryan's dick had slowed, but she was still grinding on him, which was allowing me to work myself inside. But she still needed to relax more.

I moved my face up to her neck and kissed all over the nape, across her shoulders; gentle and sweet, humming out some soft noises for her. "Baby, you're so beautiful..." I whispered on her skin, brushing my lips everywhere I could reach. "I love you so fucking much..."

She relaxed more, and I ran my left hand up her side, massaging and caressing her breasts from behind. She let out a quiet moan, and I could tell she was ready. So I gave her a push, the head of my cock breaking through her ass.

"Ah! Ben!" she gasped, her voice shaky, and so erotic.

"Is that okay, baby?" I asked, moving in a little further. She nodded fast, and I fed her another inch. It was so tight I could barely breathe. "Jesus, Jess... My dick is in your sweet ass... Does it feel good?"

"Yes..." she moaned. I was suddenly aware that not only could I feel Ryan's cock inside her but also my balls were rubbing against his, and it felt fucking divine. "Oh God, Ben... fuck me more."

I held her waist and thrust in further, allowing her to fuck Ryan's cock while I filled her ass with mine. A few more thrusts and I was all the way inside her, every single inch of my erection being swallowed up by the tightest thing I had ever put my dick inside in my entire life.

We found a rhythm together, and Ryan took over on his end, holding her ass in his hands and pushing inside her over and over, while I fucked her behind slow and deep. Jess leaned down to kiss Ryan's lips raw, moaning into his mouth while I held her hips and drilled into her.

My fingers began to explore a little, and I grabbed her tits, palming and squeezing them, before I moved onto Ryan, holding his hip then touching his chest, tracing his muscles with greedy hands.

"Ben... oh God, baby... *Fuck*, I can feel your dick on mine," Ryan grunted, pumping into my wife's pussy hard.

"Mmm... yea it feels fucking amazing," I drawled, sucking and nipping my wife's neck and shoulders. "How do you like it, wife?"

"Oh... my... God..." she cried, her voice hoarse as her whole body trembled.

"You like getting fucked by two guys at once?" I growled, spreading her ass open so I could watch my dick moving in and out.

"Yes! Holy fuck..." She sounded like she was right on the edge.

"You're so full of us, baby..." Ryan and my hips were in sync, both of us pushing in and pulling out at the same tempo.

The feeling of Ryan's dick rubbing on mine through the wall of my wife's pussy was too much for me to bear. I was definitely going to come soon.

"Are we hitting your spot, Jess?" Ryan hummed, his voice also coming out strained. *Oh, please... Let us all come together. That would be so fucking good.*

"Yes... yes... oh my God, yes!" she wailed, her muscles tightening up. "You both fuck so good... Holy fuck I'm gonna come..."

"Come for us, baby," Ryan begged, his legs stiffening beneath me. I could feel my orgasm coming. I was almost there...

"Fuck you're ripping me apart with your big cocks... I'm coming! I'm coming so... fucking... hard..." Jessica gasped out loud and started convulsing, her whole body shaking with her staggering climax.

"Fuck, Jess, I'm gonna come..." Ryan panted, and I could tell he was letting go, which pushed me right over the edge.

"I'm coming," I grunted, then groaned out loud, releasing deep in my wife's ass.

"Me, too," Ryan whimpered, and I could've sworn I felt his dick pulsing as he came inside her. "We're coming in you, baby..."

"Fuck yes!" Jess squealed, still shaking as Ryan and I trembled, all three of us holding each other, letting the wave of sensation wash over us at the same time. I had experienced nothing like it before.

We were in some kind of parallel dimension where everything felt amazing all the time. A sexual Utopia. My entire body was quaking, and I could feel theirs, too. In that moment, it was just us.

The three of us... We were all one.

The next morning, I had a breakfast meeting with the developers, so I woke up before anyone else. My body was sore, and the hot shower felt incredible on my aching muscles. It was like I had run a marathon the past two nights in a row.

All the sex was certainly taking a lot out of me, but I loved it. I treasured every single subtle strain. I had never felt so invigorated. So alive.

I got dressed quietly, so as not to wake the sleeping beauties. As I was getting ready to leave, I caught them wriggling around in the bed. I stepped over and kissed Jess on the forehead, then brushed Ryan's hair back with my fingers, watching them for a moment.

Ryan slipped his arm around Jess's waist and pulled her against him. She nuzzled her face on his chest, resting her head over his heart. A longing set in, and I suddenly wanted to blow off my meeting and just crawl back in bed with them. It looked so warm and cozy. And they looked so comfortable.

Okay. I need to leave now, or I won't be leaving at all.

"Bye, baby..." I said to both of them. "Be back soon."

"Love you, Ben," Jessica murmured through her sleepy voice.

"Bye, babe," Ryan rasped.

I breathed out slowly and left the room, heading downstairs to be on my way. I left my heart back in that bed, and just my body was out the door, in my car, then driving away.

I was distracted during the entire twenty-minute drive to the meeting. I found myself constantly wondering what Jess and Ryan were doing. Would they wake up and make breakfast together? Would they want to do their own separate morning things? Would they brush their teeth side-by-side? Would they take separate showers, or would they shower together? Would they stay in bed and have sex?

My palms grew sweaty and my heart raced. Maybe that was exactly what they were doing... They could have very well been fucking at that moment. Would there have been anything wrong with that?

Not really... Ryan and I fucked alone all the time. And obviously Jess and I did. It wasn't unreasonable that Jess and Ryan would use the time alone to their advantage.

For some reason, the idea of Ryan in my bed with Jess, between her legs, stroking his big cock in and out of her pussy brought on the strangest version of nausea I had ever felt in my entire life. I felt like I was going to throw up, but I had an erection at the same time. It was so confusing; I became dizzy, fearing that I might have to pull over.

But I pushed past it, focusing on the facts. Ryan had already fucked my wife, twice. I had witnessed him fucking her. It wasn't a big deal. I had wanted it. Hell, I *loved* it. It turned me on like crazy.

Still, my body seemed to have a slightly different reaction when I thought about them doing it without me present. It felt like I was being betrayed. Like they were trying to hide something from me.

It was ridiculous. It wasn't like that at all.

Was it?

No. When Ryan and I were together alone, without Jess, we weren't hiding it from her.

Were we?

No. At least I didn't think so.

Okay, so we were hiding it the first few times. And then when I met Ryan at the Hyatt that night, I didn't tell Jess until the next day...

Shit, even when he showed up at the house, I stowed him away in the basement for our own secret private time before we went upstairs to Jess. Was that hiding it? Were we being sneaky?

Maybe that was part of the excitement... And if it was, then I had absolutely no right to tell Jess she couldn't do the same thing with Ryan. It needed to be equal.

Holy fuck, this is confusing.

My head was spinning. This was by far the most complicated, fucked up relationship status I had ever come across.

My breathing was out-of-control by the time I parked at the developer's office and turned off the engine. I sat in the car for a few minutes with my eyes closed, just taking in deep breaths, holding onto them for a couple seconds, then releasing them slowly. I reminded myself of that yoga crap Jess was always making me do with her. It actually worked a lot to calm me down.

I couldn't control what was going on at home. And I couldn't worry about it right now. I had business to attend to, and that was where my focus needed to be.

I eventually got out of the car, feeling much calmer and ready to work. I met the developers, and we got a lot done. I ate a bagel, too, which helped. I hadn't even noticed how hungry I was. That probably had something to do with my panicked uneasiness. I always felt off when I skipped breakfast.

The meeting lasted a few hours, and by lunchtime I was finally on my way home. I managed to keep myself focused on work the whole time I was there, but sure enough, as soon as I was in the car and driving back home, I was becoming antsy again. I caught myself speeding down the highway a few times. Luckily, I didn't get pulled over.

When I parked in my driveway, the anxiousness and unease were bubbling over. I was all ready to jump out of the car and storm into the house, as if I expected to catch my wife in the act. It was completely ludicrous. My mind was running away with me.

I sat in the car for a moment, breathing hard as I stared at the house. Everything looked normal. I didn't see Ryan's car, but that was because we'd parked it inside the garage, so as not to arouse suspicions if someone we knew drove by.

In my heightened state of paranoia, I decided to sneak into the house quietly, to see if I would catch the two of them fucking. Not that there was anything wrong with it if they were... But for some reason, I just wanted to catch them. Like that would somehow change the way I felt about it...

I got out of the car and tiptoed over to the door like a fucking idiot. I opened it slowly, stepping inside and gently closing it behind me. I stood in the foyer, holding in my erratic breath while I listened for any noises. My blood was rushing in my ears, and it was making it hard to pick up on anything else. But I didn't hear screaming or moaning coming from upstairs. That was a good sign. Or just... *a* sign. Whatever.

I crept through the hall, past the living room, glancing around the corner. No one there.

Then I heard a giggle from the kitchen, and I paused, my whole body going still. Voices. It was obviously Ryan and Jess, but they were just talking. I heard the sink turn on, then off, and I breathed out a rough sigh.

They were just in the kitchen, talking and laughing, probably making lunch. Nothing was happening, and I felt like the biggest fool on the face of the Earth, because why would I care even if something *was* happening? This was the nature of our weird little three-way relationship. I couldn't get mad about it...

Well, I *could*. But I shouldn't. That would be selfish and hypocritical. I couldn't expect Jess to be fine with me and Ryan fucking behind her back if I couldn't be okay with her doing it. I desperately needed to figure this out, otherwise we would have to end it with Ryan, and I definitely didn't want that.

I shook my head, mentally scolding myself as I stalked toward the kitchen. When I turned the corner, my heart lodged unexpectedly in my throat.

Ryan had Jess pressed up against the counter and they were kissing. It wasn't a big deal. I had seen them do this before. But instead of continuing to walk into the room like I wanted to, I slid back around the corner, out of sight.

My heart hammered inside me as I wondered what the fuck I was doing. I was being so sketchy for no reason. It was stupid. I felt stupid.

I peeked around the corner again to see what they were doing. Ryan's hands slid up Jess's waist, and he grabbed her tits, squeezing them softly while she grated her body against his. My mouth was as dry as a bone.

Jess's hand covered Ryan's hard-on, stroking him over his boxers. He whispered something to her that I couldn't hear, and she giggled softly. They looked like they were having fun... They looked good together.

I should just leave them alone... After all, that's what Jess did yesterday morning when I was sucking Ryan's dick in bed. She gave us privacy. Maybe that's what I should do...

But my body had other plans. It wouldn't let me leave.

My wife pushed Ryan's boxers down below his ass and dropped to her knees. I gulped past the wave of nausea that washed over me as I watched her take his dick in her mouth and start sucking.

Ryan held her head, his fingers combing through her blonde hair while she moved her lips up and down on his solid flesh. I was having this crazy out-of-body experience; as if I was watching myself give Ryan head.

I had done it countless times already. I was so familiar with his dick, I could almost feel it in my mouth. I could hear Ryan whispering to her the way he did to me... *Baby, that feels fucking amazing. You suck me so good. You like this dick in your mouth, don't you? Suck the come out of my dick, Ben...*

Except that time he said Jess's name, not mine. And then he started coming, having an orgasm between her lips, blowing his hot, slick load down her throat while she swallowed all of him. Like she did to me.

Like I did to him. Like he did to me.

I was so confused I felt like I could retch. My dick was as hard as a fucking rock, but my stomach was turning violently. I slipped into the downstairs bathroom as quietly as I could manage, closing the door behind me as I struggled to catch my breath. I had absolutely no idea what was going on inside me, but I physically felt my body vibrating.

This is it. The drama. This is what you wanted. You wanted to feel alive, remember? Leave that boring, ordinary married-guy lifestyle behind and try something different... Well, here you are. Happy now?

I huffed a few more times, doing the yoga-breath thing again, when I heard Jess's voice outside the bathroom door.

"Ben? Is that you?" she called to me, sounding nervous. *Nervous like she just got caught?*

"Yea! In here!" I grunted, running my hand through my hair. "Sorry... I'll be right out."

"Okay. Shit, you scared us," Jess giggled. "We thought someone broke in and was going to murder us with a hatchet."

"I didn't think anything about a hatchet," Ryan added, and I laughed. *Okay, that was cute.*

I opened the bathroom door slowly, and they were both standing there, staring at me. They were smiling.

"Hi," I mumbled, fidgeting in place.

"Hey," they both said at the same time.

"You just missed the party..." Ryan smirked, and Jess smacked him in the stomach. I raised my brow at them.

"How was your meeting?" Jess asked, her cheeks slightly flushed, and her eyes set on mine in that way she always looked at me when she was asking me about my day. She'd been doing it since we were eighteen and got our first place together. It made me feel warm and relaxed. And loved.

"It was great," I smiled, finally leaving the bathroom, walking with them back into the kitchen.

"We were just making lunch, and we got side-tracked," Jess bit her lip. "But it'll be done in a couple minutes."

I huffed and nodded, welcoming the relief. They weren't hiding anything. They wanted me to know what they were doing. Because we were together, all three of us.

Ryan wrapped his arms around my waist and gave me a sweet, soft kiss.

"I'm glad you're home," he murmured over my lips. "We missed you."

"I missed you, too," the words flew out of me before I even knew I was saying them.

It had been three days since Ryan showed up and basically moved into our house.

Don't get me wrong; I *loved* having him there. I missed him terribly when we were apart, and I was always happier wherever we were together.

But unfortunately, in this case, we were together in Jess's and my home. The home which also belonged to our daughter, Hailey. Ryan's ex-girlfriend. Who was coming back tomorrow.

We still hadn't talked about it. The three of us had just been lounging around the house, watching movies, cooking meals, laughing and playing and fucking nonstop. Yesterday we spent hours after lunch decorating the whole house for the Christmas Eve party. It was fun and the three of us had a blast. So... No time for the serious, apparently.

It was honestly starting to drive me a little crazy. I hated leaving things up in the air. I wasn't that kind of person. Jess was more the *take it easy, life is a highway*, optimistic going-with-the-flow sort of person. But not me. I hadn't been a *free-spirit* since I was seventeen and I held my daughter in my arms for the first time. Now I needed a plan. I needed order and control.

But nope. Not with these two. Ryan and Jess were two peas in a pod. They agreed on everything, supported everything the other said, laughed at all the same jokes and waxed the same pseudo-spiritual hippy peace-and-love philosophies.

I knew where Jess got it from. Her grandparents were like that. Her parents, not so much. Actually, it irked them to no end. They were like me. They needed information and answers; solutions.

I figured out that Ryan got this same easy-going personality trait from his mother. Finding out details from Ryan's life was like piecing together a very complicated puzzle. He never gave anything away. Even when I asked him questions about his parents, their divorce, or his life back in Denver, he would answer with such vagueness, it drove me mental.

Unfortunately for him, I was no ordinary interested party. I paid attention to everything, and I was learning Ryan well enough to know how to read between the lines and decode his hieroglyphic-esque answers to questions about his past.

I picked up on the fact that he had a complicated relationship with his mother, and that when his father was alive, there wasn't much more guidance and support coming from that side either. Ryan was insanely independent for someone his age, and I gathered that he'd been that way for quite some time. I recognized it, because I grew up the same way. I didn't have the same issues with feeling starved for attention from my parents, while they were alive, anyway. But both of my parents passed away before I turned fifteen. After that, my younger brother and I were raised mostly by my aunt, who had her hands full with her own life. Jacob and I were on our own.

I wanted Ryan to feel like he could talk to me about things; his life, his worries, his doubts, his insecurities. I wanted him to confide in me so I could help him. But he was so closed off. Not in a selfish way. More so in an almost underwhelmingly magnanimous sense. It was as if he didn't want to burden people with his issues. I could tell he was used to taking on the world by himself, which was a slightly depressing thought.

The mysterious phone calls were just one example I had come across since he came to stay with us. His phone rang frequently throughout the day, and he never answered it. But he didn't just decline the calls either. Instead, he stared at his phone screen, watching it ring until it was done.

I'd seen him do this a few times already. Each time I asked him who it was, he'd say something along the lines of *no one important*, then try to distract me with kisses, or change the subject. It forced me to let it go, because I didn't want to push him, but I was starting to worry a little. I just hoped he was okay.

While all of this other bizarreness was going on, I also had my daughter to think about. She was coming home tomorrow for the holiday, and her ex-boyfriend was here, staying in our house, engaging in lots of very bad stuff with me and her mother. I supposed I would have to talk to Ryan. Jess was no help, anyway.

I had asked her earlier if she knew when Ryan was leaving, and she brushed me off. She didn't seem concerned with it, which was baffling. Hailey was her baby girl. I found it hard to believe that she thought everything would just *work itself out.*

Ryan and I were alone in the house. Jessica had gone out to finish up some last-minute shopping with Rachel for the party. She was due back soon, and I was waiting for her to send me a warning text so I could take Ryan to go hide out in the shed for a bit, in case Rachel wanted to come inside, which was a likely possibility. Jess had no good excuses to keep her friend from coming in. She couldn't very well tell her we were secretly harboring our daughter's ex-boyfriend for sex and cuddling.

I breathed out slowly and went to the dining room to pour myself a scotch. I sipped it slowly, praying for some solace that maybe alcohol could give me. This whole situation was so fucked up.

I had no regrets. Ryan was such a part of my life at that point; for Jess, too. If I could go back in time, I don't think I would have changed anything, which was much more troubling than it should have been. I couldn't understand why I was so quick to potentially sacrifice my relationship with my daughter for this man. It clearly wasn't just about sex. I was afraid to admit it out loud, but I knew it was much more than that.

I finished my glass quick and poured another, my staggering thoughts coming to a screeching halt when my phone vibrated in my pocket. I pulled it out quick, noting the text from Jess. Fifteen-minute warning.

I sauntered through the house, over to the stairs.

"Ryan!" I called to him, feeling suddenly more jittery than usual.

"Come on, we have to go."

"Coming!" his voice bellowed from upstairs somewhere. I wasn't sure what he was doing, but we needed to move quick. I absolutely could not risk Rachel, or anyone for that matter, finding out Ryan was there.

Luckily, he seemed to have picked up on the sense of urgency, and hopped down the stairs fast, freshly shaven and showered. I faltered for a moment looking at him. He was just so damn beautiful. It was overpowering. The attraction I felt to him was so strong, like a calling on some deep level I couldn't even understand.

He gave me a nervous smile, stepping around me, but not without trailing his fingers along my lower back.

"Let's go," he huffed, and I nodded, the both of us making our way out back, toward the man-cave. It would be our hideout for however long it took Jess to get rid of her friend.

We got settled in the shed, door locked and blinds securely closed. I put some Netflix movie on and we cuddled up on the couch. We sat there in silence, pretending to watch for at least ten minutes before we realized that we really weren't paying attention. Well, I wasn't. I was still lost in my thoughts. And Ryan seemed to be in his head, too. I could tell by the way he was methodically stroking the nape of my neck with his fingers.

"Baby?" I finally spoke, softly, the nagging questions becoming too much to ignore.

"Yea," he grunted, still with the hair fingering.

"I was thinking... You know I just got the first deposit for this new job. So, I have plenty of money to float around..." my voice trailed off, and I tried to figure out how to continue without offending him.

"Are you just bragging?" he curled his neck and peeked up at me, smirking. "Or is there a reason you're bringing this up?"

"No, I'm just saying... I know you haven't really been working much," I stuttered, trying hard not to waver under his deep stare. "So, I wanted to let you know I can lend you some money, if you need it."

Ryan stared at me for a moment, his brow furrowing in confusion. I swallowed hard.

"I'm not going to take your money, Ben," he eventually whispered, looking less angry than I thought he would, but definitely more hurt.

"Not *take*," I corrected him, reaching out to hold his jaw with my fingers. "Borrow. You can pay me back whenever you're ready."

"Ben," he sighed, briefly closing his eyes.

"Ryan, don't be difficult," I muttered. "It's just money. I have more than enough to lend you some. Just until you start working again. What do you think? Like five grand?"

"Ben..." he grunted my name again, visibly clenching his jaw.

"Ten?" I kept on, raising my brows, waiting for him to answer me. I was fully prepared to just keep saying numbers until he stopped resisting and accepted my offer.

"Jesus. How much money do you *have*?" he gaped at me like I was insane.

"Enough," I shrugged. "Here." I wriggled my phone out of my pocket and pulled up my mobile banking app. "Just give me your account number and I'll transfer five to start. I might have to call my accountant for more... I'm not sure if there's a cap on mobile transfers–"

"Ben!" Ryan barked at me and I stopped talking, gazing at him. He was so cute when he was annoyed. "I'm not taking money from you! God, what do you think I am? Some kind of hooker or something?"

I wanted to laugh, but I held back because I knew he was being serious, and clearly wasn't in the mood for teasing.

"No, baby. I'm sorry... I didn't mean it like that," I hummed, brushing his hair back with my fingers. "I'm just trying to help. I don't want you to worry about anything."

"I'm fine, Ben. I don't need help. I can handle my shit on my own," he grumbled. "Thanks for the offer, but I'll find work."

"Ryan, trust me, I know you can handle yourself," I told him, my tone firm. "You're almost shockingly independent. I mean, putting yourself through Law School is... incredible." I slid my hand down to his chest, feeling up the muscles beneath his shirt. "I just want you to know I'm here for you. I don't want you to stress. Like, maybe I can find you some work... Something close to school."

Ryan's eyes were wide as he stared at me, his forehead lined with some emotion I couldn't decipher.

"Actually, I was thinking... I know a guy with a garage just outside of Albuquerque," I kept talking, trying to pacify him with my words and ideas. "I remember how you said you wanted to restore an old car... And I think he has one you might like. Maybe I could buy it and you could–"

He stopped me mid-sentence by grabbing my face and pulling my lips to his. He kissed me hard, and I gasped in his mouth, his soft lips sealing over mine. His tongue pushed gently between them to stroke my tongue, slow and sensual, melting me. I hummed and pulled him closer, kissing him back, deep and eager for more. It felt so good, all my thoughts were immediately silenced. And all there was left was us. Kissing and touching, breathing and trembling in devotion.

"Baby..." I whimpered, leaning back, bringing him with me. He settled between my legs, grinding on me and kissing me so good my lips were raw, and my cock was aching. This control he had over me was intense; the need consuming.

"What have you done to me, Ben Lockwood?" he whispered over my lower lip, greedy hands running everywhere. "You're ruining me..."

"You've done the same to me, Ryan," I breathed, gripping his ass and pulling him down to rub his crotch on mine. My brain was fuzzy and the world around us was a blur. It probably wasn't smart for us to be doing this with Rachel inside the house, just a couple yards away. But I couldn't help it. I just wanted him so bad, all the damn time.

"I don't know what I'm feeling anymore..." he drawled, lifting my shirt a bit then unbuttoning my pants, tugging them down enough that my dick was peeking out. He ran his thumb under the crown, and I flinched from the sensation. "I want you all the time, baby. I can't stand the idea of being away from you..."

I groaned softly and unzipped his jeans, pulling his cock out so we could rub them together a little. My skin was so hot it was about to set our clothes on fire.

"Me neither, babe..." I murmured, holding him as close to me as possible. He trailed his lips across my jaw and down my neck as I savored the feeling of his newly shaved face, kissing and sucking.

My eyes were closed and my lips quivering while he teased my flesh, making me yearn for him to take me over in every way possible.

I was so ready.

"Ben..." he breathed my name like he was falling. His tone twisted my stomach, and my chest started to burn.

I shook my head a little... Something was happening. There were emotions in his movements, in his voice... I tried to ignore it, grabbing his face in my hands, holding him in place and kissing him deep.

He's just turned on, that's it. Everything's fine.

He broke free from my lips. "Ben, I think..."

Don't do it, kid.

He teased his way across my jaw. "I think I'm..." his voice trailed off, and he whimpered.

I swallowed hard.

Please... Don't. Don't say it...

He gasped, lips shivering by my ear. "I'm falling in love with you..."

My heart sank in my chest and I squeezed my eyes shut. I was heaving with uneven breaths as a chill washed over me. I gulped over and over again, my mouth filling with saliva. *Oh God, please...* Fear was clutching my windpipe, making it hard to breathe.

My body reacted to my nerves, and I pulled away.

"No..." I grunted, moving my hands off of him as my eyes opened slowly. "You can't."

He sat back, gaping down at me. "I *can't*?"

I shook my head repeatedly. "No... no no no." I wriggled out from under him, forcing him back. I needed space. This was too much.

"Are you fucking kidding me right now?" he huffed, his face appearing confused and wounded.

"Ryan... you can't say that. You can't *feel* that. Not now... Not... yet." I closed my eyes, rubbing them with my fingers. "This can't happen."

"Why the fuck not?" he asked. I said nothing, trying hard to steady my breathing. I felt a panic attack coming on.

What the fuck am I doing?? I can't do this... I need to get out.

"Ben... I just..." he started, then paused, grabbing my hands and yanking them away from my face. "I thought you would want to know..."

"No." I shook my head some more. "You can't tell me that. This isn't supposed to be happening. You're my daughter's ex-boyfriend.

We shouldn't be doing this..."

"You can't be serious," he gasped. "So after everything, that's all I am? I'm still just Hailey's ex-boyfriend...?"

I stared at him with wide eyes. I didn't know what to say. I didn't want to hurt him. It pained me inside... But I couldn't let him tell me that. I couldn't let him fall for me...

Too late. I cringed at my thoughts.

"I thought we had something..." he whimpered, his tone wrought with devastation. "You, me and Jess. I thought this was real..."

I scoffed and backed up more, yanking my pants up fast.

"Real?! You want to talk about *real?* Why don't you tell me who's been calling you five times a day... Tell me who you've been ignoring. Tell me about your life... about why you're not going home for Christmas." His face fell, and he looked crushed. Confused, guilty and lost. I hated myself for making him look like that. But I couldn't stop... "This isn't real, kid. This is make believe. We're all just hiding from our real lives."

I stumbled to my feet and started pacing in front of the couch, yanking my hair at the roots.

"So you never actually cared about me...?" his shaky voice rippled inside me, straight through my chest. "I was just an interesting way to pass the time? A new fuck to shake up your boring life..."

His words stung, like salt in a wound. I didn't know if I actually believed what my head was telling me... Or if I just felt like I should.

"No... Maybe... I don't know..." I rasped, shaking my head. "I don't know what's going on. All I know is that you can't..." I quickly stopped myself from saying the words. As if speaking them out loud, breathing them into the air would make them real.

"Don't fucking tell me what I can and can't feel, asshole," he hissed, standing while zipping up his jeans. "News flash, Ben! You can't control everything around you! You don't own my feelings."

"Why are you doing this?" I narrowed my gaze at him, trying like hell to stop from shaking.

"Because I fucking feel it, Ben! Because *I* allow myself to feel it! Unlike you, you fucking hypocrite! Jesus Christ, did it ever occur to you that this would happen? No. Let me guess, you never let yourself think about it."

"Because I can't!" I roared at him, stepping up to his face, anger and frustration burning from my eyes into his. "I *have* to be in control, Ryan! I don't have a fucking choice! For my wife, and my daughter... I have to protect them. This can't happen..."

"Yea, well, guess what? It already did," he seethed, grinding his jaw as he glared at me. "Your wife loves me. I know she does."

"How would you know that?" My voice was so low, it was almost inaudible.

Ryan cocked his head to the side, moving in even closer to me, until I could feel his breath on my lips.

"I just know," he growled, his eyes dark with rage. His tone was almost condescending, like he knew something about my wife I didn't, and he was happy to hold it against me.

"You barely fucking know her, kid," I squinted at him, standing my ground, not ready to back down, ever. "She's been mine since you were in diapers. You're a shiny new toy. Very exciting... Not love."

I saw him falter, visible pain flashing in his eyes, before he quickly covered it up with more anger.

"You know she sent me that video of you guys, right?" he held my gaze hard, fury burning behind his deep green irises. "She was thinking about me even then... She wanted me with you two."

My heart was hammering in my chest, my mind running a mile a minute. I didn't want to believe him, but I knew he wouldn't lie. *Jess sent him the video of us fucking...? Why would she do that?*

"She made that video for me," he kept going, pushing me with his words. "She missed me. You said it yourself... We have a connection."

"It doesn't matter..." I grunted, swallowing hard. *She didn't make the video because she thought it would be hot. She made it so she could send it to Ryan.*

I couldn't help wondering why she wouldn't have just told me that's what she was doing. Why be so secretive about it?

I pulled my phone out of my pocket and texted Jess, telling her to get rid of Rachel. We needed to talk. This all needed to be hashed out, right the fuck now. No more avoiding subjects and waiting for things to sort themselves out. I was going to sort it out myself. Now.

"It does matter, Ben," Ryan huffed. "She wanted it... She wanted me. She thought it was what you wanted, too..."

"Don't fucking talk about my wife like you know more about what she wants than I do," I hissed, my fists clenching at my sides. "You have no idea what it's like to be with someone for nineteen fucking years. I've spent more than half my life with that woman. We have a goddamned child together. You don't understand that kind of connection."

"Okay. There we go. I knew it," he nodded, his brow creasing with obvious hurt. "You never gave a fuck about me. I was nothing more to you than a strange new fuck."

"That's not true..." I closed my eyes.

"Yes, it is," he muttered. "Everything you said to me was bullshit. You didn't want it to be the three of us. You're a selfish piece of shit."

"Fuck you, kid," I grumbled. "You don't know what you're talking about."

"No, fuck you, Ben," he barked. "Fuck fucking you! You're just scared. You're afraid to admit you're feeling something more than just an obsession with my cock in your ass. You're all too ready to push me away because you don't want to face the truth. You love me, too."

"Stop fucking saying that shit!" I snarled, shoving him away from me with my hands on his chest. I stomped past him toward the door, but he grabbed me by the arm. I yanked it out of his grip and turned back, getting up in his face. "Try me, kid. I fucking dare you."

He squared his shoulders, standing his ground, his face inches from mine. "I'm not fucking scared of you, Ben."

"You should be," I growled, clenching my jaw. The anger was coursing through my veins, clouding my mind.

"Go ahead then," he rumbled low. "Hit me." My chest was heaving. I thought I was seriously going to hit him for a second.

I heard a noise behind us. The door handle was jiggling.

"Ben? Ryan?" Jess's voice came from outside as she knocked on the door over and over. "Open the door! She's gone."

I took a deep breath and forced myself to step back, spinning to open the door for my wife. Jess stepped inside, her eyes bouncing between Ryan and me. Her face turned serious.

"What's going on?" she asked, raising her brows, her voice quiet and dripping with unease.

"Did you send that video of us to him?" I asked her, my burning gaze now aimed directly at my wife.

She stood, frozen and silent for a moment. She glanced at Ryan quick before her eyes came back to mine.

"Yea..." she murmured. "So? What's the big deal?"

My jaw clenched again, and I crossed my arms over my chest. "Nothing, I just thought that was for us. I don't understand why you wouldn't tell me you wanted to make a video for him..."

"It's getting too serious for Ben," Ryan mumbled. "He just wants me on call. To come over and fuck whenever he's in the mood. Maybe I should take the money... If I'm nothing more than a fun lay when you're bored."

"What?" Jess gasped in stunned distress. "What is he talking about, Ben? What money?"

"Forget about that..." I grunted, shooting a look in Ryan's direction. "I was just trying to help. I care about you, Ryan. Don't act like a bitch."

"Yea, sure. You care just enough so you don't have to feel like you're taking advantage of me," he hissed. "Not enough to love me, though. God forbid you let me get fucking close enough..."

"You fucking can't, Ryan! Don't you fucking get that?" I barked at him, my whole body shaking in anger. "My daughter is coming home tomorrow! You can't be here. We can't do this... Any of it!"

"Ben, where is all this coming from?" Jess squeaked at me and I blinked slowly, trying to calm myself down. It wasn't working.

"Did you fuck her...?" I asked Ryan, ignoring my wife. My voice was low and hoarse with rage. His brow lifted. "Yesterday. After I left... Did you fuck my wife?" I turned to face Jess again. "Did you?"

The look on Jess's face answered my question before either of them said anything. It felt like the ground had been ripped out from underneath me.

"Of course I fucked her," Ryan's voice crept inside me, taunting me with images of them, in my bed, together. Without me. Behind my back. Fucking... and hiding it from me.

"Get the fuck out," I whispered, feeling violently ill. The bile was rising.

"Ben, how hypocritical could you be?!" Jess yelled at me. "So it's okay for you to fuck him... To fucking *cheat* on me with him. And just because I told you I was okay with it, now you think you can dictate when and where and how we can be together?! That's so fucked up! This isn't yours! You don't get to call the shots when there are two other people involved!"

"It's not about that..." I squeezed my eyes shut. "This is too much. It's all just... too fucking much!"

"Well, guess what? You got us into this," Jess whimpered, like she was about to burst into tears. I glanced at her and her lip was quivering. "None of us know how to navigate this shit, but we're supposed to try *together.*"

I stared at her for a moment, watching my wife; the woman I loved. She looked so lost. And she was right. It was all my fault.

I couldn't take back what I had done... What I'd started. But I could still try to save us from any more pain. I could still save Hailey. If I stopped this now, I could protect her from the truth.

"I can't," I breathed, shaking my head slowly, then turned to face Ryan. "I'm sorry... But you have to go."

"That's what I thought..." he muttered, immediately stomping past me, toward the door. I could've sworn it looked like he had tears in his eyes. I wasn't sure if they were from anger, or sadness. Probably both.

He pressed a chaste kiss on the top of Jess's head. "I'm sorry..." he whispered to her, the sound of his unsteady voice smashing through my chest like a sledgehammer to a sheet of glass.

He left the shed and didn't look back.

I stood in stunned silence, unable to comprehend what the fuck had just went down. I was numb.

Did that really happen? Did I end it? Am I really going to let him leave??

"Ben!" Jess squeaked, tears rolling down her cheeks. "Do something! Stop him!"

I shook my head slowly, pressure threatening to burst from behind my eye sockets.

"It's too late, Jess..." I croaked. "He has to go. We can't do this...

Not to Hailey."

Jess rushed over to me and wrapped her arms around my waist, collapsing against my body, shaking as she cried hard. I rocked her slowly, gripping her tight as I struggled to hold it together. I couldn't let myself feel it. I needed to block it all out. All the pain, frustration, sadness and guilt. I had to force it down and never let it free. It was the only way I could survive this.

"What did we do?" Jess wept, her tears soaking into my shirt.

"I don't know..." I whimpered, swallowing hard. "I'm sorry, baby. I fucked us up so bad. It's all my fault." My eyes stayed on the door, willing him to come back, though I knew it was too late.

It was over.

CHAPTER 16

Ryan

I JOLTED OUT OF AN UNEASY SLEEP, glancing around me in panic, my heart thumping in my chest.

I closed my eyes tight and took a deep breath, flopping back against the seat. I was sweating, but cold at the same time. My back was stiff, and my mouth was dry. My eyes were burning, and my temples throbbed.

The sun was up, but I had no idea what time it was. I plucked my phone out of the cupholder. It was dead. *Great.*

I stretched out my arms and legs, as much as I could in the driver's seat of my BMW. The sounds of clinking bottles and cans on the floor rang through my ears, causing me to cringe. Condensation covered my windows, and I could barely see anything in the parking lot.

I opened the door and slowly stepped out, the cool morning air stinging my exposed skin. I reached inside the car and grabbed my sweatshirt, pulling it on and zipping it up fast. I blinked over my hangover-grogginess, checking my surroundings for somewhere I might use a bathroom and get some water.

There was a McDonald's across the parking lot where I'd slept in my car last night, after killing a pint of tequila and a six-pack. I had been trying to drown my sorrows, and I guess it worked at the time. But now that I was awake again, I remembered everything. All the pain came flooding back to me and I felt sick.

Before I could process what was happening, I bent over and hurled all over the place, throwing up the excessive booze from last night.

I steadied myself on the side of my car, feeling spent, emotionally and physically. I couldn't bring myself to move. I just wanted to lie down in this random parking lot and die.

After I fled the Lockwood residence, I drove around in circles for a while. I didn't want to drive all the way home, because Alec and Kayla were still entertaining her parents. Plus, they thought I was in Denver, and I didn't feel like explaining to them why I was back so soon, and a complete emotional train wreck.

There was really nowhere else I could go. So eventually I hit up a liquor store, parked in a random parking lot and drank my pain away, until I passed the fuck out.

Once I was all puked out, I grabbed my bag and walked over to McDonald's. I ordered an egg McMuffin because I needed something to soak up the remaining alcohol, a water and a large coffee. While I waited for my order, I used the bathroom, brushing my teeth, washing my face, and changing my clothes. I was more than relieved to have all my stuff with me. I definitely felt slightly better in clean clothes and fixed up a little. I think I left a t-shirt and some pajama pants at the house. Oh well. They were gone now.

My stomach turned again, and I darted to the toilet, leaning over. But it was a fake out. This nausea was less about the booze and more about the fact that I was alone again... This time for good.

I still couldn't even wrap my head around the fact that we were done. It had just come out of nowhere. One minute I was blissfully happy with my two favorite people in the world, and the next thing I knew, Ben was telling me he never cared about me, and he never would.

Okay, not in so many words. But I could tell he was just trying to spare my feelings. The look on his face said it all.

I told him I loved him, and he told me to leave.

It was all my fault, really. I always knew it wouldn't end well. But I kept going back anyway, like the masochist I so clearly was.

Ben didn't love me, and he was probably right about Jess not loving me either. She was too sweet to ever say it to me, but he was her husband. He knew her better than anyone. I was just the fling, and the fling always fades.

I just thought I had a little more time. I guess that was stupid of me...

I thought if I could just be with them enough, and show them how good it could be, then maybe I could make them love me. That was even stupider. You can't force someone to love you. I had learned that with Dahlia. I should've been prepared. But instead I dove headfirst into the shallow end and left my heart open for the thrashing. And that was exactly what had happened.

I dragged my tired, depressed ass up to the McDonald's counter, grabbed my food and sat at a table. I forced myself to eat half the McMuffin, even though the mere act of chewing was so strenuous I could barely manage it. Every bite just tasted like nothing. The world around me was grey.

I chugged my water in three big gulps, then sat and sipped my coffee, staring off into space. The clock on the wall said it was just after six in the morning. People were coming and going around me, going about their lives, completely unaware of just how pointless it all was. Nothing mattered. We were all just waiting around to die.

Jesus, get ahold of yourself. It's a break-up. Just find someone new to fuck and you'll be fine.

I remembered my phone, pulling my charger out of my bag and plugging it into the wall, waiting for it to get enough juice to power on. I drank half my coffee while my phone charged and bought two more bottles of water. I finally turned my phone back on, holding my breath, secretly praying for a message from Ben.

My phone started buzzing with a couple texts and my heart lodged in my throat as I checked them.

They were from Jess.

Jess: Hey...
Jess: Sweetie I'm so sorry. We never meant for this to happen.
Jess: Ben's just... he's having a hard time w this. He feels guilty because of Hailey
Jess: I know that's not an excuse but I just wanted you to know
Jess: Just let me know you're ok... please?
Jess: You're so important to us. You have to know that

I groaned and dropped my head in my hands. My brain was throbbing, and my chest hollow.

I had no idea when the messages came in, because my phone had been off, so they all just showed up now. I so badly wanted to respond to her, but I couldn't. I couldn't torture myself like that. I needed to give it up.

It was over.

A couple girls around my age came in, giggling their way over to the counter, ordering breakfast. It jolted my memory to where I was. I was still in Ben and Jess's town. And Hailey was coming down from school today.

Sure, Jess had said she wasn't coming until later, but still. I couldn't risk anyone they knew seeing me. I had to get out of there.

But where could I go? Was I really going to spend Christmas Eve in my car?

That was the most depressing thought ever.

I gathered up my stuff and headed back to my car. But once I was inside, I realized that I still hadn't decided where to go, so I ended up sitting there, staring at nothing for like an hour.

I needed to just bite the bullet and go home. Whatever I said to Alec and Kayla was the least of my problems at that point.

I just couldn't stand the idea of going home to my apartment and sitting around, alone, on Christmas Eve. Although, I wasn't sure what I would have done if things hadn't ended with Ben and Jess. I still would've had to leave their house regardless, because Hailey was coming home. I think some delusional part of me was praying that they'd try to keep me around. Or at least not rip my heart out and toss it down the garbage disposal.

I wished I knew someone in the area I could hang out with. Someone nearby who would tolerate my pensive grouchiness, and my desire to get shit-faced. Someone who didn't give the tiniest fuck what was going on in my life and wouldn't harass me for information; who would just hang out with me casually to pass the time.

Hm. Wait a minute. I do know a someone like that... And he might just be around.

I grabbed my phone and looked up the contact, wondering if I could actually call him. It wasn't even eight in the morning. It was a very odd time to be calling people I barely knew...

But he was a banker, so he was probably used to getting up early. What was the harm in trying? I pressed call and anxiously chewed my lower lip while the phone rang in my ear.

"Well, shit. Definitely didn't expect to hear from you..." Tate's voice crooned at me, and I could already hear that wicked smirk in his voice.

"Hey..." I rasped, feeling suddenly shy. I was so drunk the last time I saw Tate. You know... after we fucked in the bathroom at a sleazy bar outside Santa Fe. "Sorry to call you so early..."

"Early for me is four in the morning," he hummed. *I knew it.* "How's it going, Harper? Merry Christmas Eve."

"Yea... Merry Christmas Eve," I sighed, trying not to sound so despondent. "What are you up to?"

"Not much... Just hanging around at home. There's a thing later," he told me, his tone casual. "What about you?"

"Nothing really..." I murmured. "Actually, nothing at all."

"Well, that sucks," he rasped, and for some reason it made me laugh. He was just so blasé and unaffected by everything. I kind of liked it.

"I'm in town..." I blurted out, sliding my index finger along the car window, drawing a frowning face in the condensation. "Um... in Tularosa. I was wondering if you were around...?"

Tate made a little noise, which I couldn't interpret. "Did you come with Hailey?"

"No... Hailey and I broke up a month ago," I spoke softly, praying he wouldn't demand details about why I was there without Hailey.

Fortunately for me, Tate wasn't really the type to give a fuck what was going on in other people's lives when it didn't affect him.

"Oh... Sorry?" I could hear the grin in his voice, and it made me chuckle.

"Whatever, fuck you," I huffed. "So do you want to hang out or not?"

"Mmm... definitely," he rumbled. My pulse picked up. "I'll text you my address. Come over whenever you want."

I nodded slowly, even though he couldn't see me. "Okay."

"See ya soon, Harper," he said, then hung up fast. I was left sitting in the driver's seat of my car, staring at my phone in my hand with my head spinning.

I wasn't sure if it was a good idea to see Tate... After all, I didn't really know him. Plus, Ben had strictly forbidden me from seeing him again.

I scoffed to myself. *Well, then. I guess that's a perfect reason to see Tate.*

My phone vibrated in my hand. It was the text with Tate's address. He only lived about fifteen-minutes from where I was. This whole thing should have been making me much more nervous but if it was, I was too out of it to notice.

I didn't want to think about Ben, or Jessica, anymore. I just wanted to forget they existed. Tate was a good-looking guy, with nice eyes and lips, a hot body and a big dick. He was entertaining enough, but more than anything, he was *here.*

I just didn't want to be alone on Christmas Eve. Not this time. Not after yesterday...

I turned my engine on and fixed my seat so it was upright again. I switched on the GPS, which would guide me to Tate's. But before I could leave the parking lot, there was one more call I needed to make...

It was time. I couldn't put it off anymore.

I finally had my answer.

I followed Tate inside his apartment, and he closed the door behind us. His place was nice; wide open with big windows, high ceilings and lots of natural light. It was spotless and organized, but according to him this was because he was barely ever there.

He had told me the last time we hung out, in Santa Fe, that he traveled a lot for work, and spent at least half the year living out of hotels. At first, I thought it sounded sort of depressing, but then he explained to me that the hotels were usually always nicer than his apartment. Plus, he never had to worry about cooking or cleaning up after himself. He seemed to enjoy it, so who was I to judge? I had only stayed in nice hotels like twice in my entire life.

I forced my brain to stop where it was going, before I could obsess. *We're not thinking about them, remember? We're not even going to say their names in our mind.*

Tate and I had just gotten back from brunch. As soon as I arrived at his place almost three hours ago, he told me he was starving and insisted we go for food and bloody Mary's. Apparently, rich people called that *brunch.*

He took me to some bougie, overly expensive place, where he ate, and I just drank. I assured him that a bloody Mary was basically a meal, what with the celery, tomato juice and horseradish. This place even put bacon and shrimp cocktail in it, not that I had eaten much of that part. I was only interested in drinking at that point.

But Tate was more than fine with it. He didn't pester me, study my every move, or try to control me like someone else I knew. He just sat back and watched me, smirking and occasionally biting his lip. He was very enigmatic, while also leaving all his cards on the table. He was straight-forward with who he was, and I liked that about him. There was no hiding, or confusing behavior from Tate. He was just... Tate.

Still, being that we were in Hailey's hometown, and I knew she would be around, most likely now, I was feeling slightly jumpy. I kept fearing that she would walk through the door to the restaurant while we were there, and Tate proceeded to bust my balls over the entire course of our little meal.

When we were done, and I was feeling nice and fuzzy from the booze, we came back to his place to hang out. I didn't really know what we were going to do... He mentioned that he had plans later but hadn't yet told me what they were. The idea of sleeping in my car again tonight-on Christmas Eve-was putting a damper on my attempt to prove how fine I was.

Tate kicked his shoes off and wandered around his apartment, saying nothing. It was almost as if I wasn't there, and I couldn't tell if I liked it because he was comfortable with my presence, or if I just felt invisible.

I walked over to a bookshelf that had some framed pictures on it and decided to snoop a little. Tate had a great book collection. All the classics; *The Great Gatsby, As I Lay Dying, Lord of the Flies, Of Mice and Men.* I felt like I was back in ninth grade English class all over again.

I checked out the pictures and saw an older man and a woman, holding each other and smiling, most likely parents or something. Then a picture of a slightly younger Tate and a girl who was probably ten or eleven. My eyes fell on the third frame and my heart plummeted into my gut.

It was of an even younger Tate and some other boys of roughly the same age, some slightly younger, some older. They were outside at what looked like a cookout and some boys-Tate included-were wearing football jerseys. I recognized Bill, from Thanksgiving, and Ben's brother Jacob. And then sure enough, there was Ben himself. Wearing his high school football jersey, and a wide, all-American boy next door smile, his dirty blonde hair slightly longer and matted on one side, likely from a helmet.

I stared hard at the boy in the picture, amazed by how much he still looked like that now, even in his mid-thirties. He couldn't have been more than fourteen in this picture. But it was definitely Ben, just with rounder cheeks and younger eyes; and minus the displeased scowl.

My chest tightened and burned, the pain I was feeling inside so strong and aggressive, I had to look away. I almost couldn't stand up anymore. I felt weak, like my knees wanted to buckle.

I heard Tate shuffling around behind me and I forced myself to push past the agony ripping through my insides from my broken heart, then turned to go find him.

"You got any booze?" I asked, watching as he fiddled with some weird little device in his hand.

"Wow," he chuckled, his eyes bouncing up to mine. "Trying to party, are we?" I shrugged, because I didn't have any other words to say. He lifted the device in his hand and I realized what it was. "Wanna smoke?"

"Um... sure," I mumbled, a giant wave of *fuck-it* washing over me. I really just wanted not to feel anything anymore. The pain in my chest was too much. I couldn't take it for one more second.

Tate opened the sliding door to his terrace–yes, he had his own terrace, complete with chairs, a table, plants, the works–and stepped outside as I followed behind him. We sat down in chairs, side by side, and he took a long drag from his pen, holding it in for a while before he breathed out a thick cloud of pungent smoke.

He handed it over to me and I did the same, taking a much smaller hit, letting the drugs settle inside me and ease my mind.

We repeated this a few more times, passing the thing back and forth until Tate started messing with it again. I already felt much calmer. I was aware of my surroundings, but seemingly oblivious to everything going on outside of Tate's apartment.

I leaned back in my chair and stared over the railing of the terrace, checking out the view of the other buildings nearby and a small park. Most of the visible windows were decorated with Christmas lights and tinsel. There was green, red, silver, and gold everywhere, which reminded me it was Christmas Eve. I honestly hadn't been thinking about it much.

I wondered how Alec and Kayla were holding up, with her parents in the apartment. I missed them already, and I'd only been gone for a few days. *I'll miss them...*

I wondered what my mom was doing. Probably catering to her new boyfriend's kids; maybe baking cookies or wrapping presents. I couldn't help but notice that the jealousy, insecurity and rejection I had been feeling toward my mom and her new life in my childhood home had fizzled. It was the drugs for sure. I felt like I was sitting inside a cloud, floating around in the sky, the cool air burning my cheeks. I was so high... above everyone and everything down on the ground.

"So, since you and Hailey broke up, I take it you're not going to the Christmas party at Ben's tonight..." Tate's voice broke through my bubble, and I turned my face slowly toward his. His eyes were slightly squinted, and he looked like he could potentially pass out.

I shook my head, raising my brow at him. He looked really sexy for some reason. He had more stubble than the last time I saw him. It made him look rugged and masculine.

"Well, I have to go," he huffed, pulling a pack of cigarettes out of his pocket, removing one, and sticking it between his lips. "It's sort of a tradition. Like the Thanksgiving thing. Jacob and his wife are like family. I'm the twins' godfather, which is fucking scary." He chuckled and flicked his lighter. His eyes darted up to mine. "You want one?"

"I'm good," I politely declined. I wasn't a cigarette smoker. Plus, my mouth was really dry. *I could go for that drink...*

He grunted out a little noise, flicking the lighter again, this time lighting his cigarette and puffing on it.

"I only smoke cigarettes when I'm high," he grumbled. "I don't know why. It's like relaxing or something–"

"So you're going over there tonight?" I interrupted him, my mind wanting answers to so many questions, there wasn't enough time for my slow mouth to ask them all.

"Uh-huh," he nodded, tapping the ash off the end of the cigarette on an ashtray in the middle of the table. Then he took another long drag. I was staring at him, waiting for him to tell me more, but it became clear he wasn't going to. So I asked...

"What time?" Good thing I was high, otherwise I would've sounded much more desperate.

"Eight," he replied, then put the cigarette out. "Let's get drunk." He didn't wait for me to respond before he was getting up and wandering inside his apartment. Of course I followed him.

He walked over to a bar by the kitchen and grabbed a half-empty bottle of scotch. He held it up and raised his brows at me, silently asking if that was what I wanted. I nodded for yes.

It was interesting that we didn't really need to speak. We barely knew each other, and yet we had a kind of kinship. It must have been from making each other come. I guess orgasms bring people together.

Tate poured us each a glass, and we clinked, sipping slowly. He watched me carefully for a moment, his eyes dark. I had absolutely no idea what he was thinking, and I wasn't sure that I really cared.

"You can stay here if you want," he rumbled, cocking his head. "While I go to the party."

I gaped at him. "Are you sure?" He shrugged and nodded subtly. "You barely know me... What if I was some psycho?"

He giggled and bit his lip. "If you were going to murder me, I think you would have done it by now." I laughed softly, shaking my head and sipping my drink, a little faster this time. "You can rob the place if you really want to. Like I said, I'm never here. I don't need half this stuff."

I grinned wide, which made him smile; a devious, white-toothed smile. He winked at me.

"Thanks," I mumbled, swallowing hard, breaking our eye contact.

"Are you doing okay?" he asked, quietly. "You seem a little fucked over this break-up. Or maybe something else..."

My eyes shot back up to his, and I froze. I so badly wanted to tell him about Ben and Jess. I needed to talk to someone. It was killing me to keep it bottled up inside.

"I'll be fine," I muttered, not allowing myself to say anymore.

Such was my curse. I was doomed to forever walk the earth dealing with every single problem in my life on my own. No one to share the burden. No one to confide in, or console me with words and actions of comfort. If it didn't happen with Hailey... If it didn't happen with Ben and Jess, it wouldn't happen ever. I'd just have to learn to accept it.

Tate huffed a soft noise and pouted at me. Then he walked over and grasped my jaw gently in his fingers. His face inched in close to mine and I felt him exhale slowly as his eyes dropped to my lips. I reached out to hold on to his waist, pulling him flush against me as his lips found mine.

He kissed me soft, sensual, parting his lips and letting me meet his tongue with mine. I sucked on his bottom lip, remembering how much I enjoyed doing so. It was a pouted curve, brushing over mine, just enough suction to make me tingle. It felt so different than it did with Ben... And obviously different from Jess.

I growled and kissed him harder, deeper, determined to push away all the thoughts and memories of the last few days. I ignored the hollowness in my chest from kissing someone who wasn't them.

They didn't want me. Tate did. He was here. They weren't.

"Let me help you," he purred, running his hands down my chest, caressing me, until he reached the waist of my jeans. He unbuttoned and unzipped them, pushing them down my thighs.

I tugged his face as close to mine as possible without swallowing him up, kissing him with fervor until he broke it, leaving me breathless and wanting more. He trailed his lips over my throat, humming as he went, dropping to his knees and wasting no time taking my dick in his mouth.

I groaned softly, continuing to sip my scotch while I watched him, servicing my cock. He was so good at sucking dick. He was drawing soft moans out of me, bobbing in front of my hips, sliding me in and out of his warm, wet mouth. His eyes locked on mine as he took me all the way down his throat, basically choking on my cock while palming my balls.

I leaned back, my eyes closing as I gripped the side of the bar. He was sucking the life out of me and I was so high and drunk I barely even knew where I was. Then for some reason Ben's face appeared behind my eyes. The slightly devastated look he gave me when I told him I fucked Tate. The vulnerability in his eyes... The very same I'd seen in the shed, right before I left.

I swallowed hard and pushed the images away, holding Tate's jaw and thrusting, fucking his face hard, making him grunt. He sucked up and down every inch of me until I let go and started coming; the orgasm pulsing out of my cock into his sweet mouth. He was moaning while I came down his throat, and he swallowed every last drop, looking like he was about to get off himself.

He pulled his mouth off me and stood up, kissing me hard, forcing his tongue between my lips so I could taste myself. I groaned and grabbed his cock through his pants, jerking him slowly.

"You're so fucking good..." he drawled, breathlessly. "Fuck me..."

My heart rocked in my chest, guilt trying to shove its way out of the back of my mind. My first instinct was to stop, because I didn't want to hurt Ben. But that was a stupid reaction.

Ben hurt me. He didn't care... He didn't love me.

"Get a condom," I demanded, breathing ragged. He nodded and

peeled himself off me, running his fingers through his hair.

"Come to the bedroom with me," he said, his tone pleading and dripping with lust. Then he turned and stumbled down the hall.

I breathed out hard and killed the rest of my scotch, ignoring the burn. I poured another glass, my hand shaking a little. I wasn't sure why I was so uneasy, but the fact was that every time I was with Tate, I ended up thinking about Ben. I just couldn't help it. It was miserable.

I drank most of my second glass then sauntered into Tate's bedroom, feeling the buzz. He was sitting on the edge of his bed, staring up at me. His face was slightly flushed as he watched me, blinking slowly.

I approached him, tugging my shirt over my head. Then I pulled his off and pushed him backward with a hand on his chest. He fell on his back and scooted further up on the bed as I crawled on top of him, kissing across his chest while I unbuttoned his pants, yanking them off with his boxers.

I ran my hands up his hips, touching him slow while I licked all over his erection, sucking the head, running my tongue underneath.

"Fuck... Ryan..." he gasped, burrowing his fingers in my hair. He reached behind him and grabbed a condom and a small bottle of lube, tossing them next to me on the bed.

I stroked my rapidly hardening cock a few times, tore the condom wrapper open with my teeth and rolled it on. I squeezed some lubrication on my dick, coating myself over the condom, then slid my wet fingers between his cheeks. He moaned and his eyelids fluttered.

I pushed his legs open wider, wedging myself between his thighs, taking my cock in my hand and probing his ass with the head. He was watching my every move carefully, his defined chest moving up and down with his heavy breathing.

I forced myself inside him and he took me willingly, both of us grunting together as I filled him slowly. He wrapped his legs around me and I moved over him, kissing his lips hard as I pulled back and drove in deeper.

"Jesus..." I growled on his mouth, pumping into him over and over. "You feel so good."

"Fuck my ass, Ryan..." his voice cracked, uneven with my rapid thrusts. "Fuck me harder with that big dick."

I went on, giving him everything I had, getting lost in the rhythm. His hands gripped my ass, pulling me deeper while I continued to thrust, balls deep inside him. We were both grunting and groaning, the sounds of us fucking echoing off the walls. I curled my fist around his cock and jerked while pounding into him, taking him for a ride until he cried out loud.

"I'm fucking coming..." he gasped, his dick shooting out his orgasm all over his abs. "Fuck yes..."

"Mmmm..." I hummed, pushing myself further until I gave up and erupted into another climax, pouring it deep in his ass inside the condom.

I was seeing spots behind my eyes as I collapsed on top of him, pulling out while we caught our breath. He trailed his lips all over my neck, his fingers combing through my hair. I kept my eyes closed, for fear that if I opened them, I would have a major freak out.

I couldn't believe that yesterday I woke up in bed with Ben and Jess, cuddling, kissing and touching; fully content and happy. Blissful, even.

And now I was heartbroken, engaging in rebound sex to hide from the fact that I was hurting, down to my core. There was nothing wrong with Tate. He was actually a wonderful guy, and I liked him a lot. He was smart, and charming, good-looking and fun. He gave great head.

But he wasn't Ben.

We laid in bed for a while, kissing and touching, teasing each other and laughing. I was trying so hard to distract myself from the pain, which was right beneath the surface. I knew Tate could tell I wasn't fully with him. But honestly, I didn't think he cared all that much. He wasn't looking for serious, anyway. He was casual and unassuming, which I appreciated to no end.

We got up and meandered around his apartment naked, pouring more drinks, getting faced. I think I was definitely more drunk than he was, but I didn't really care. I was trying to forget, after all.

We got into the shower together and fooled around some more. My head was hazy, and I felt so out of it. I needed to keep closing my eyes and forcing myself not to think about Ben, and the times we had showered together. They were such agonizing memories. His adorable face, his big, huge delicious body; his bossiness, his controlling nature and how he'd started to drop his guard for me.

I could almost feel my broken heart in my chest, fighting to keep beating, even though I was missing a huge part of myself. And just knowing that I was in the same town as him... And that Tate was going over there in a couple hours. It was driving me crazy.

A little while later, we were freshly showered, and I was lying on Tate's bed with my glass of scotch, sipping slowly while I watched him dress for the party. He was in his boxers, picking out jeans and shirts from his closet, holding them up in front of himself, asking my opinion. I felt very comfortable with him, which was good and bad. I kept feeling like I wanted to talk to him about Ben. Plus, I was pretty drunk at that point, and my filter was almost nonexistent.

"Grey or blue," Tate asked, holding up two button-downs and raising his brow.

"Blue," I grunted, sipping my drink, my eyelids heavy as the alcohol swam through my bloodstream. "It brings out your eyes."

He grinned and tossed the shirt next to me on the bed, stepping into his jeans.

"Have you talked to her at all?" he asked, zipping up.

"Who?" I blinked slowly, my vision blurring.

"Hailey," he spoke quietly, slipping his long arms into his shirt.

"I saw her a few times at school," I slurred. "We're fine. The whole thing was... amittable. Amiable...?" I blinked a few times. "Amicable." I giggled, and Tate laughed out loud.

"Jesus, you're sloshed," he chuckled, giving me an evil grin. "It's pretty adorable."

"Fuck off," I muttered with a smirk and he laughed again.

"If it's so *amicable*, then why are you getting fucked up?" he asked, raising his brow at me again as he buttoned up his shirt. He did that a lot, but it didn't make me feel the same as when Ben did...

I gaped at him, my mouth hanging open a little.

"Look, I won't ask why you're here. In town..." he huffed. "It's none of my business. I just think whatever you're going through must be pretty rough, and if you want to tell me about it, you can."

I blinked at him a few times more times, watching him morph into two Tates. I swallowed hard. Could I tell him about Ben? He already sort of knew I had a thing for him... He had called me out on it the last time we were together...

But still, I couldn't risk him telling someone and Hailey finding out. It would ruin everything. And no matter how much Ben had hurt me, I never wanted him and Jess to lose the respect and love of their only child.

I watched Tate as he finished getting dressed, spritzing himself with some cologne that smelled nice. He looked great. I was a little jealous that he was going to this party and I wasn't. I wanted to see Ben and Jess... and Hailey. I knew I was just fucked up, and nothing was making much sense right now. But I really wanted them all to see me with Tate. I wanted to make them jealous. They needed to see what they were missing out on.

I'm a catch. They don't deserve me. It's their loss.

Tate is hot. He looks fucking good. Imagine how satisfying it would be... The look on Ben's face, seeing me with Tate. He would be so fucking jealous.

I almost giggled at the thought.

"It's just fucking Ben, you know?" I started rambling, not even aware of what I was saying. "He thinks he's so in control of everything all the time... You can't just do that. You can't just boss people around and string them along... You can't control everything, you know? You have to let your guard down sometimes. But no, not Ben. He has to be *in charge*... It sucks."

Tate gave me a look, one much more serious than I had ever seen on him before, and I feared that maybe I'd said something bad. I could barely remember what I had just said. The weed and the booze, the sex... and the heartache. It was a lethal combination.

"You know, Ben and Jake's parents died when they were teenagers..." Tate told me, standing in front of his mirror, fussing with his hair. "It was really rough on them."

I flinched. Hailey had told me about her father's parents passing away when he was younger. Apparently, they were killed in a car accident. Hailey didn't like to talk about it, and apparently neither did

Ben. I specifically remembered her warning me not to mention anything about his parents before I went home with her for Thanksgiving. I had taken that very seriously. Even after Ben and I became a thing, I made it a point never to ask him about it.

I had always just figured he would talk to me about his parents when he was ready. And yet he was mad at me for not talking about my past. How could he tell me I was being secretive when he did the exact same thing? *Hypocrite.*

"Anyway, I think that took a toll on him. That and having Hailey so young," Tate went on. "That's probably where the need for control comes from."

"Yea, I get that..." I huffed, closing my eyes and shaking my head. "But sometimes you have to let people in."

"You're right," he nodded.

"It's like, we've all got stuff going on. And yes, losing your parents is definitely a great tragedy. I mean, I lost my dad. So... it was fucked up. I get it," I mumbled, sloshing my drink around, spilling some on the bed. "But that doesn't give you the right to just shit on people. To take their hearts and just rip them out and stomp on them like fucking garbage."

"What did he do to you?" Tate gave me the side-eye, grinning at me a little. "Did you and Hailey break up because you're so clearly into him?"

"What? No," I scoffed, killing my drink fast. "I told you, Hailey and I mutually decided we didn't want to be tied down..."

"Because you'd rather be tied down by her daddy..." he smirked, wiggling his eyebrows at me.

"Please stop," I muttered, and he laughed out loud.

"Ryan, I don't give a fuck, you know that," he sighed out his chuckles. "I told you, I've thought about him like that before... More than once." He grinned, and I rolled my eyes. "I'm just saying, he's a hard dude to get a read on. I've known him since we were kids, and I still barely ever know what his deal is."

He nodded at me to follow him, which I did, and we went back into the kitchen to get more drinks.

"Have you ever dated girls?" I asked, feeling curious as I sipped my eight-millionth drink of the day.

"Not usually," he grunted, leaning against the bar. "I have before. But I really like dick." He winked at me.

"So you're like, a chronic bachelor?" I smirked.

He shrugged, very noncommittally. "I don't have time for relationships."

"The only single guy at all the holiday parties..." I giggled, sipping again, sucking on my lower lip.

"I like to be different," he laughed. "Shakes things up."

"Yea, well have fun with that..." I grumbled, pursing my lips as my eyes set on the glass in my hand. "I'll just stay here and wait for you to get back. Merry Christmas to me."

"You want to come with me?" he asked, and my eyes jumped up to his.

"What...?" I gasped, gawking at him like he just suggested I murder someone.

"Yea. Fuck it," he grinned, bringing his glass to his lips. "Crash the party a little. It'll be fun."

I was stunned speechless. I didn't know how to respond. *Is he being serious? Or is he fucking with me....?*

Could I really do that? Go to Ben's... With Hailey there. What would he think? Would he freak out?

I shook my head. I couldn't do that. It was stupid and irresponsible. I couldn't go to Ben and Jess's house, with all their family and friends, as Hailey's ex-boyfriend. It would be suicide.

But then... The thought of arriving at the party with Tate and seeing the look on Ben's face was immensely satisfying.

He had destroyed me. I told him I loved him, and he told me I couldn't. He basically dismissed my feelings, as if they were nothing. Part of me wanted to see him squirm a little...

But Jess and Hailey were innocent in all this. I didn't want to hurt them.

Though I wouldn't exactly be hurting them...

Tate was their guest. He never got to bring a plus one, since he was the bachelor of the group. Who was I to decline his invitation?

Plus, I didn't really care if I made myself seem crazy. Soon it wouldn't matter anyway...

It would be one last chance to see Jess and Hailey. And Ben...

"Don't you think they'd be mad?" I asked Tate, hesitance making my voice quake a little.

"Why would they?" he answered, shrugging. "You said you and Hailey split on good terms. She should be fine with it. Unless..." His voice trailed off, and he smirked at me again.

"Unless what?" I raised my brow.

"You're ashamed to be seen with me," he squinted. "Are you afraid for them to know we've been hanging out? Not even so much Hailey... but Ben. You don't want him to know about us, do you?"

I paused, staring back at him. It was like he was tempting me, calling me out a little. He seemed fully onboard with the idea of bringing me to this party. A party I was not invited to; not even slightly. And if he didn't care, then why should I? I had nothing to hide.

I wasn't ashamed. Actually, I was sort of excited.

"I don't give a fuck," I shrugged, trying to seem casual, although my insides were suddenly shaking with nerves. I tossed back my drink. "Let's crash this party."

Tate's face erupted into a wide, purely evil grin.

"Well, alright then," he finished off his drink quick. "Let's fucking go."

The ride over to Ben's was a blur. I didn't realize Tate had driven us there until we were parked on the street in front of the house and I was stumbling out of his car.

It was truly unsafe. Very, *very* irresponsible. He had been drinking for hours.

But I was in no shape to argue with anyone. I was in the middle of my own meltdown.

The outside of the house was lit up with the lights Ben and I had put up. There were decorations in all the windows, illuminated from the inside. It looked great. Cars filled the driveway and lined the street. There was clearly a party going on in there.

My heart was really going crazy. Not to mention that I could barely see straight or form a complete sentence. This was a terrible idea... But I was going along with it because I knew that after tonight, none of it would matter.

One last hoorah.

"Alright, come on, hot stuff," Tate grabbed me by the arm and dragged me up the walkway. "It's showtime."

"I'm gonna tell Ben about me and you," I slurred as we walked up the front steps, and Tate rang the doorbell.

"Is that right?" he chuckled, standing me up straight and pulling on the lapels of my jacket.

"Yea. He's gonna be *mad*..." I snickered, swaying back and forth.

There was loud noise coming from behind the door; Christmas music playing and people talking and laughing. It sounded like there were many people in there, and I was feeling nervous again. I needed to focus on not throwing up.

I need another drink...

The door flung open and my heart stopped. Jessica was standing there, all smiles and golden hair, curled and flowing down her shoulders. She was wearing a red dress and a Santa hat.

She smiled at Tate, but when her eyes slid to me, it immediately fell off her face. Her eyes widened, and she looked horrified. Her mouth hung agape as she stood there, muted.

"Merry Christmas," Tate crooned, leaning in to kiss her cheek. "I brought a friend. I hope that's okay."

"Uh..." a gasp flew from inside her throat, and she just gaped at me, blinking a few times. "Shit."

I swallowed hard, feeling suddenly like I'd made a terrible mistake. I shouldn't have gone there. *What the hell am I doing?!*

But instead of turning around and running back to the car, like I probably should have, I straightened my shoulders and cocked my head to the side.

"Hi, Jess," I murmured, forcing a small grin. "Merry Christmas."

"Um... Merry Christmas, Ryan," she squeaked, sounding breathless and looking oh-so overwhelmed. "What a surprise..."

We all stood there staring at each other for what felt like an eternity.

I so badly wanted to hug Jessica. It was actively killing me not to. I could smell her from where I was standing, and it made my mouth water. Her beautiful rosy cheeks, full lips, looking all glossy and delicious; wide, blue eyes gazing up at me.

God, I fucking missed her so much. Her presence was so calming. I just wanted to wrap her up in my arms and forget everything that had happened. I needed that comfort, and I just couldn't have it. It made my chest ache.

"I'm sorry... where are my manners?" Jess huffed an awkward giggle, stepping out of the way. "Come on in. Can I take your coats?"

"It's okay, I've got it," Tate replied, striding inside first as I followed his lead, trying like hell to walk normally.

He removed his coat, and I did mine, handing it to him to hang up. My eyes darted back down to Jessica, like magnets, and I quickly slid my fingers along her back, giving her a look. I wasn't sure if she picked up on everything the look was saying... It was a lot.

I'm sorry... I know this sucks... I miss you so much... It's so good to see you... You look beautiful... Please don't hate me...

Her eyes connected with mine and her brows pushed together. I opened my mouth to say something, but the words wouldn't come. She looked like she was having the same problem.

"Hey, Tate!" a voice bellowed from the living room. "Good to see you, man!"

"Hey, brother," I recognized Ben's brother's voice, glancing up to see him hugging Tate and patting him on the back. When I returned to Jess, she was scurrying away with her head down, toward the kitchen.

"Ryan?" another male voice said my name, and I meandered slowly into the room, bracing myself for whatever disastrous reaction I was about to receive.

It turned out just to be Greg, Jess's brother-in-law. He was standing with Bill and Jacob, and now Tate, all of whom were staring at me, looking thoroughly shocked by my presence. Well, except Tate. He was smirking like the damn devil he was.

"Did he come with you?" Jacob asked Tate, raising his brow at his friend.

"Okay, this is weird..." Greg mumbled.

"I thought Ben said you and Hailey broke up," Bill muttered, apparently trying to piece it all together. *Good luck with that, pal.*

"Yea, I brought him," Tate jumped in, looking pleased with himself.

Jacob was giving Tate some kind of look, his eyes burning right into him. Tate seemed unaffected by it.

One of the twins came scampering into the room, repeatedly tugging on Jacob's shirt.

"Daddy, Uncle Ben needs your help," she mumbled, then peeked up at me. "Hi, Ryan!"

She waved at me, and I smiled, waving back before she giggled and darted off, back down the hall. I gulped over my dry throat.

Jacob's eyes flicked between me and Tate once more, and he huffed a breath, shaking his head as he left the room, heading toward the kitchen.

"This is gonna be a shitshow," Greg chuckled, sipping his beer.

"I guess we can always count on your crazy ass to bring the drama, huh Trouble?" Bill sneered at Tate, patting him hard on the back.

Something crashed in the kitchen and I actually jumped. My heart was pounding so hard against my chest, I could feel it rocking my whole body. Tate must have sensed my unease and stepped over, taking me by the arm again.

"Come on," he hummed. "Let's go get a drink." I looked up into his eyes as he watched me closely for a reaction. I nodded slowly.

I could feel Greg and Bill's eyes on us as we walked down the hall to the dining room. My face and neck were so warm, I felt like I was on fire.

There were a few people I didn't recognize in the dining room already, talking and eating appetizers. Tate ignored them and went straight to the bottles of liquor, grabbing scotch and pouring us each a glass. I was already so drunk I could barely walk on my own... I definitely didn't need more booze. But then again, I was in Ben's house. And he was in the next room. With Jess. And probably Hailey.

So I drank.

"You okay?" Tate asked, running his fingers along my arm. I nodded fast, though I was anything but *okay* at the moment.

I could hear Hailey's voice in the kitchen. Her cousin must have told her I was there, because she suddenly swung around the corner, her eyes wide and her face still. I felt like I had been drop-kicked in the chest.

"Ryan..." she gasped, walking over slowly, looking like her head was about to explode. "What are you doing here?"

"I'm uh..." I mumbled and my voicebox gave out.

"I invited him," Tate answered, and said nothing else. The room was spinning.

"You..." Hailey's forehead creased as she stared back at us. "How...?"

"Hales, I just..." I finally started talking again, stepping over to her, slow and careful. I was afraid she might slap me. I stopped right in front of her, aiming my blurred vision down at her gorgeous face. I breathed out a sigh and shook my head. "Merry Christmas."

She blinked up at me then tucked her hair behind her ear. She was wearing sparkly bow earrings and a sweater with candy canes all over it. She looked so cute.

"Merry Christmas," she replied quietly. "I didn't expect to see you... Is everything okay?" Her eyes darted over to Tate for a second before coming back to mine.

"Everything is great," I murmured, wobbling a little. "Just hanging out, you know... The usual." I shrugged.

"I thought you would go see your mom for Christmas," she said with clear confusion in her voice and all over her face.

"She doesn't fucking care if I go see her or not," I scoffed. "She's got some new boyfriend... A new little family to focus on. I'm barely a passing thought..."

"Don't say that," she sighed, reaching up to caress my shoulder. It felt nice, which made me want to burst into tears for some reason.

"It's true," I grunted, cocking my head. "Not that I care, anyway. I'd rather be here with my friends." My tone was sarcastic, but I jutted my thumb in Tate's direction.

"How are you guys *friends*?" she asked in a whisper, most likely not wanting to offend Tate. Little did she know, Tate didn't give a fuck about anything.

"You want the details?" I raised my brow at her, and I heard Tate cough into his drink. I peered at him over my shoulder and he was laughing to himself.

Hailey's face froze, and she huffed out a noise, shaking her head slowly. But before either of us could say anything else, I heard a commotion. Ben stomped into the room fast, with his brother clearly trying to stop him. His aggressive movements came to a halt when he saw me, his eyes landing right on mine. I almost shit myself.

Ben's eyes were scorching. His nostrils flared as he shot laser beams out of his bright blue irises, directly in my direction. Then he glanced behind me at Tate, and he looked like he could burst out of his clothes any minute like the Incredible Hulk.

Regardless of how bad I had wanted to put him in his place before, I definitely wasn't doing that now. I was just standing there, scared out of my mind, trying not to pass out.

Finally, Ben blinked, though it wasn't much of a change to his face. He looked so angry, but also confused and slightly distraught. I just wanted him to accept me, but it was clear he didn't want me there. The realization crushed me.

Well, guess what, Ben? You don't get to control everything. Tate invited me. I'm here with him. So you'll just have to deal with it.

"What's he doing here?" he asked Hailey, and Tate; basically anyone in the room who wasn't me. "What are you doing here?" That time was for me.

"Dad, it's okay," Hailey spoke first. "He can be here. We're still friends, right Ry?" She gave me an expectant look, and I nodded slowly.

"Yea, of course," I rasped. "We're friends." My eyes flicked up to Ben as I silently warned him to back off.

I could tell it was taking every ounce of strength in him not to say anything. He was still glaring right at me, and I worried Hailey would pick up on the tension between us.

Without saying another word, he turned and stormed back into the kitchen, Jacob following behind him, leaving Hailey, Tate and me standing there in awkward silence.

"He seemed happy to see you," Tate muttered, and I shot him another look.

"I told him our break-up was mutual, but I guess he didn't believe me," Hailey sighed.

"Guess not..." I breathed. This whole situation was so fucked. I had no idea what I was doing, but my heart was racing, and my palms were growing increasingly sweaty. I sipped my drink again, trying not to spill it all over myself.

"Can I get you something to eat?" Hailey asked politely, appearing concerned, likely because of how obviously drunk I was.

"No thanks," I grunted. "It's okay, Hales. You don't have to dote on me. Get back to your party. It'll be like I'm not even here."

"I doubt that..." she spoke softly, then turned and left the room. I heard hushed whispers across the table and glanced up to see the other people in the room's eyes dart away from me quick.

"I need to get some air," I croaked, grabbing Tate's arm. "You got any more of those cigarettes?"

"Yea, sure," he nodded, and took me by the hand, leading me into the kitchen. I really didn't want to go in there, but it was the only way to get to the deck from inside.

As soon as we stepped into the kitchen, the conversation came to a screeching halt, like one of those record scratches. I could feel every single eye on me, and it was making me so nauseous I was almost certain I would hurl.

Jess was chugging her glass of red wine. Her sister Marie, their friend Rachel, and Jacob's wife, Laura, were all staring at me, hard. I didn't see Hailey, Ben or Jacob anywhere, but I didn't have much time to look around for them because Tate was dragging me to the door.

"Hello, ladies," Tate crooned, giving them all a broad smile. He looked and sounded so charming, but I knew from experience that he was actually being a dick.

"Hi, Tate!" they each shrilled, smiling enthusiastically at him. "Merry Christmas, sweetie."

"Merry Christmas," he replied, sliding open the door to the deck. "You all look lovely."

"Thanks," they answered together again, their cheeks flushing up a storm. Jess was still completely silent, though I could see the redness all over her cheeks, spreading down her neck and chest. "Hi, Ryan..."

They said my name, and I jolted.

"Hi..." I whispered, my voice coming out rough.

"Good to see you," Rachel, grinned, biting her lip slowly as Tate yanked me through the doorway and closed the door behind us, effectively shutting off the giggles and girl talk, which I could see happening through the glass. The three of them had surrounded Jess, like a pack of hyaenas. They were still looking at me through the door, in between the obvious gossiping, which made me jittery.

I took a deep breath, inhaling the chilly air, the world whirling around me. I tried to relax as much as I could. Until I felt Tate squeeze my hand.

"Hey..." his voice rasped from beside me. I assumed he was talking to me, and I rested my hand on his waist. But then I assessed my surroundings, which took longer than normal in my drunken state, and realized he was talking to someone else.

My eyes landed on Ben and a chill washed over me. Goosebumps sheeted my skin as he stared at me from across the deck, holding a cigar that may as well have been a gun. Because he looked like he wanted to murder me. Or rather Tate...

His eyes fell briefly down to Tate and my joined hands, and my hand resting on Tate's waist, which I instinctively pulled back. He raised his brow, but said nothing. Just continued to stare at us, taking a puff of his cigar, blowing out the smoke leisurely into the air. The smell of cigar smoke was so familiar to me now. I associated it with Ben, physically. It made every muscle in my body constrict.

Tate pulled a pack of cigarettes out of his pocket, removing two and sticking them between his lips, lighting both at once. Then he handed one of them to me and I took it, bringing it to my mouth and taking a small drag, struggling not to reveal how much my hand was shaking. I tried to tug my other hand out of Tate's grip, but he squeezed it harder.

"Since when do you smoke?" Ben asked, startling me. His voice was quiet and harsh, like a jaguar deciding if it was going to eat you.

"Since now," I forced my voice from inside me throat, locking my eyes on his as I took another drag, willing myself not to cough. "Only when I'm drunk."

"I thought you said you never get drunk..." he cocked his head to the side, eyes squinting. "Seems like bullshit, kid."

"Seems like none of your goddamned business," I grunted, blowing more smoke out, right at him. I actually felt his muscles tighten, and I wasn't even touching him.

Tate, on the other hand, I was touching. And I could feel him flinch next to me. Even he was getting a nervous now, which was worrying.

I heard some noises coming from the yard, and glanced behind Ben to see Jacob, his twin girls and Hailey, setting up what looked like fireworks in the grass.

"Tate, give us a minute," Ben rumbled, his eyes never once leaving mine. *Oh, great... Now he wants Tate to leave so he can yell at me and make me feel like shit some more. This is so fucked. Fuck this and fuck you, Ben.*

"Please," I growled at Ben, taunting him with my smart-ass remark in my drunken stupor, which was really not a good idea. He narrowed his gaze at me, looking like he wanted to strangle me with his bare hands.

"Yea... sure," Tate replied, conceding to Ben's asshole-ish command, but not without first running his hand visibly along my lower back.

He gave Ben a look and then descended the stairs, joining Jacob and the girls in the yard. I just stood there, casually smoking my cigarette, watching Ben and waiting for the inevitable scolding I was about to receive. I almost rolled my eyes before he even started.

"Really?" he finally spoke, his broad, firm chest and shoulders moving up and down with visibly forceful breaths.

"Really what, Ben?" I asked, my eyes struggling to stay open. I was so fucked up, I could barely even fathom what was happening.

"Really, you're here with him...?" he muttered, placing his cigar in the ashtray next to him. "Really, you're fucking shitfaced? Really... you just... show up with Hailey here?" He barked at me through a hushed voice so no one would hear him. "What the fuck, Ryan?!"

"Yes, I'm here with Tate," I whispered, my eyes hardened in frustration. "He actually likes spending time with me..."

"Don't be a brat," he grunted. "I like spending time with you, you know that."

My stomach flipped, but I forced myself not to acknowledge it. "Yea well, he doesn't hurt me..." I mumbled petulantly, flicking my cigarette on the ground, stomping it out. "You do. Hence the fact that I'm *shitfaced.*"

Ben looked momentarily wounded. "I wasn't trying to-"

"It doesn't matter," I cut him off, crossing my arms over my chest. "Tate invited me, so I came. Actually, I came more than once..." I raised a cocky eyebrow at Ben and saw him swallow hard.

The look on his face should have been satisfying. The obvious devastation; confusion, anger and sadness. It was what I had wanted when I first thought about going to the party.

But now that it was happening, I just felt sick to my stomach. I didn't want this. I didn't want any of it...

I just wanted to go back in time, back to Thanksgiving so I could stop myself from ever going near Ben. I would have been much better off.

I loved him. I still did. But I couldn't ever have him, and it was ripping my heart in half.

Ben's look of distress then shifted to one much more irate, and he clenched his jaw.

"Did you have to think about me again to get off with him?" he grumbled, leaning up against the edge of the deck.

"Fuck you, Ben," I scoffed. "If this is how you treat people you care about, then I feel bad for Jess."

His eyes were blazing at me, like the bright blue center of a flame. "Watch what you fucking say to me, kid. I won't hesitate to lay you the fuck out."

"Go ahead," I pushed, stepping forward. "Make my day. Make my whole fucking life. You want to ruin Christmas for your wife and daughter by fucking me up in front of all your friends and family? Be my guest. I don't feel shit anymore... I'm fucking numb to the world."

"Jesus Christ, Ryan..." he breathed, closing his eyes and shaking his head. "I didn't mean to do this to you. I never meant for any of this to happen..."

"Yea, you've already made it crystal clear that I misinterpreted everything between us," I huffed, running my hand through my hair.

"It's fine. Just forget it. Pretend none of it ever happened."

"I don't want to..." he breathed.

"Then what the fuck do you want, Ben?" I slurred, grabbing onto the table to steady myself. "Honestly... Is it just the sex? Because if so, I'm sure Tate would–"

"Shut the fuck up," he hissed, trying to keep his volume in check.

"I mean, usually he likes to bottom, but I'm sure for you he'd make an exception..." I went on, rambling through my fuzzy mind, snickering to myself.

"Don't fucking say that!" he growled, stepping up to my face fast. "Shut. Your. Fucking. Mouth."

"Or what, Ben?" I rasped, not backing down. "Or. Fucking. What?"

There was a war waging inside him, and it was visible. He was being torn between a blinding hatred, a gut-wrenching hurt, and an unwavering lust. I could actually see it in his eyes, especially when they dropped to my lips for a millisecond. It looked like he wanted to kiss me, then punch me, then kiss me again, then maybe throw me off the deck. It was a very overwhelming thing to see on someone's face while they looked at you.

I watched closely as his blue eyes bore through me, catching the sight of him swallowing hard, his throat bobbing slowly and his brow creasing for a moment in uncertainty.

Suddenly there was a loud pop right behind us that made us both jump. We turned to see Jacob, the twins, Hailey and Tate cheering as they lit off some small fireworks in the yard. They shot bright colorful explosions into the sky just above our heads, one after another. Ben and I just watched, our eyes glued to the sparkles.

The rest of the party piled out onto the deck to observe the fun. Ben and I made eye contact again, and he looked like he wanted to say something, but couldn't in front of all these people. That was the issue with us, and it always would be. It had to be a secret. No one could know... And I just couldn't do it anymore.

I couldn't hide anymore.

Tate jaunted back up the stairs, while Jacob and the girls were still lighting off red and green fireworks. He breathed out a soft sigh and took me by the arm.

"You want to go get another drink?" he asked, his pretty face serving as a nice distraction from the agony I was feeling inside.

"Sure," I gave him a small grin, and we headed back to the house. I paused for a moment and glanced back at Ben. "Merry Christmas, Mr. Lockwood."

Ben's face remained etched in all kinds of emotions, but I forced myself to ignore it and leave him behind, going back into the house with Tate. Pretending was the only way I would survive the rest of this evening. It was all I could do not to completely break down.

I had to hold it together. I had to keep my cool, even though the more I drank, the less fucks I began to give. I didn't care about this fucking party. I didn't care about making myself look like a dick. I really didn't care much about anything, because I was over it. I was done being the secret fling; the afterthought. For once I wanted to be the star of the show, or at the very least, a costar.

I had thought I could be that with Ben and Jess. I thought the three of us could be together... But it turned out I was just an experiment for them to see how kinky they could be. They had used me. It was one of the worst feelings I had ever experienced.

Tate and I stayed inside drinking while everyone else watched the fireworks. Eventually they all came back inside, huddling around the kitchen and dining room, which was where the food and booze were.

It hadn't been long since we'd gotten there, and I still wasn't feeling any more comfortable. I could tell everyone was watching me and talking about me behind my back. Every time I made eye contact with someone I didn't know, they looked away.

Jess was avoiding me, as was Hailey. And Ben was nowhere to be found. I was just wandering around the house, sloshing my drink in my glass, getting drunker and drunker with every sip. It was working to prevent me from feeling the excruciating pain deep inside my gut, though the overall awkwardness of being there was still palpable.

Eventually I stumbled into the living room, which was empty, making it the perfect place for me to be. I stood in front of the Christmas tree, staring at it, remembering the night we'd gone to pick it out. It was such a wonderful evening; the three of us together, holding each other's hands and enjoying one another's company; unfazed by the opinions of the outside world. We were just *us*. Me, Ben, and Jess. It had felt so *right* that thinking about it now made me want to retch.

That's my tree. This should be my life... With them. I deserve to be happy, too.

"We just decorated it today," I heard a soft, familiar voice from behind me and I closed my eyes tight, forcing back the tears.

Jessica came up and stood next to me, and I could already feel her warmth and tranquility.

"It looks great," I murmured, taking another big gulp of my drink.

Jess reached out and grabbed the glass from my hand, setting it on the table behind her.

"Ryan stop," she commanded, softly. She was demanding in such a different way than Ben. When she told me to do something, it wasn't like she was ordering me around. I actually *wanted* to do it.

"Look at me," she insisted, and I reluctantly slid my eyes down to hers, my brows knitting together. "You don't have to do this," she whispered. "This isn't you."

"How would you know?" I muttered, instantly feeling stupid for saying that. Of course she knew me. She probably knew me even better than Ben did.

"I just do," she replied, her dark blue eyes locked on mine. "You're so much better than this. You're strong and brave... You can handle anything."

"I can't..." I shook my head, breathing unsteady. "I can't handle this."

"You can," she ran her fingers softly along my back. It was so calming, like a direct contrast to what I was feeling inside. "Ryan, I'm so sorry... I never wanted this to happen."

"I know, I know..." I dropped my chin. "It's not *you*."

"You love my husband..." she breathed, and I whimpered, biting my trembling lower lip. "You love me..."

I closed my eyes and nodded slowly. She reached up to grasp the nape of my neck and pulled me down to her in the softest, most comforting hug I'd ever felt. I was coming undone. I was literally about to burst into tears.

"I love you too, Ryan," Jess whispered in my ear and my whole body started to tremble.

I gripped her waist and pulled her in close; so close it was like I was trying to make her a part of me.

"I love you," I murmured, and she nodded with her face stuffed in the crook of my neck.

"I know, baby..." she gasped.

"I love him, too..." I croaked.

"I know..."

"Why doesn't he love me back?" The tears were coming. I had to stop them. We had to stop this. Someone could see...

Fuck it. I don't care. I don't care who sees. I'm in pain. I need this...

"He–" Jess started and then we heard noises coming down the hall. We pulled apart fast right as a group of people stammered into the room, talking all loud.

"Oh hey," Tate hummed, sauntering over to me and wrapping his arm around my waist. "There you are."

I exhaled hard, still trying to recover from whatever had just happened with me and Jess. I so badly wanted to hear what she was about to say about Ben... I wanted to touch her more and kiss her. *God, I'm so fucking drunk. What the hell am I doing here...?*

Tate slipped his fingers under the material of my shirt, feeling up my side a little. Bill and Greg and their wives were staring at us in confusion and fascination. Jacob was rolling his eyes and Ben looked like he was about to erupt and start spewing hatred all over the entire room.

And then there was Hailey. I could tell she had never been more flustered in her entire life.

I couldn't tell if Tate was actually starting to like me, or if he was being all over me for my benefit, to make people jealous and stir up drama. It was definitely what I had said I wanted to do when I agreed to crash this party. But now all I wanted was to be alone with Jess and Ben, so we could talk.

I felt like such a desperate loser. Why was I so quick to sacrifice my pride for these two? It was like I couldn't stop myself. I was always chasing after them...

For once I wanted to be chased.

"Just let me know when you want to get out of here..." Tate whispered in my ear and I felt a chill run through me.

"Hey! Why don't we open some presents!" Jess squealed, obviously trying to distract everyone from whatever little show Tate and I were putting on.

They all gathered around in the living room, as presents were handed out. I wasn't really paying much attention, since I wasn't invited to this party, so none of these gifts would be for me.

Jess gave the twins and Greg and Marie's daughter, Maxine, stuff to open to keep them occupied for a while. Then she moved on to the rest of them, playing Santa's helper, the whole group *ooh-ing* and *ah-ing* over their gifts.

Everyone was thoroughly distracted by the festivities, and I felt so left out, it was physically killing me inside. If I wanted to feel like I didn't exist, I would have just gone home for Christmas.

"Excuse me..." I muttered, getting up from where Tate was sitting with his side pressed against mine. He glanced up at me for a moment, nodding and giving me some look that seemed like it said *Okay, I'll be right here.*

Are we like a couple now?? What the hell is happening??

I stomped out of the room, feeling everyone's gazes burning into my back as I slinked through the hall and up the stairs. I opened the door to Hailey's bedroom and snuck inside, closing it behind me, breathing out hard.

I walked over to her bed and sat down, dropping my face into my hands. I sat there for a little while, in silence, trying like hell to calm down. The room was spinning around me, and I really felt like I might be sick.

Suddenly there was a knock on the door, and I groaned to myself. The door opened, and I looked up to see Jess approaching me slowly in her gorgeous, form-fitting red dress, showing off her curves in all the right places. I watched her step over to me with her hands behind her back for some reason.

"Hey, sweetie," she rasped. "You doing okay?"

"Not even slightly," I grumbled, my shoulders slouching over, the weight of all this bullshit crushing me.

"I'm sorry to bother you when you want to be alone..." she frowned, her eyes wide and sparkly as she gazed down at me. "I just wanted to give you this."

She pulled her hands out from behind her back and she was holding a small box, wrapped in red wrapping paper with a green bow on top. She held it out to me, and I gaped at her in confusion.

"What's that?" I asked, my voice a soft, hesitant noise barely creeping out of my mouth.

"It's for you," Jess replied, blinking at me, her face still mostly serious. "Open it."

My mouth hung open in pure shock. I honestly wasn't sure that any of this was really happening until I took the box from her and examined it closely.

There was a tag on it with a reindeer that said *To: Ryan, From: Santa*

I struggled to breathe as my eyes slid up and down between Jess and the gift in my hands. I finally forced myself to react and started tearing open the paper slowly, revealing a nice matte black box. I took the top off and sifted through some green tissue paper until I felt something hard. I rested the box on my lap as I removed what was inside, my eyes widening in disbelief.

It was a super fancy, leather-bound journal, like the ones that all my law professors always carried around. Except that the cover was very different.

It had what looked like a flower inside it; a dried rose with three petals falling down. The whole thing had been preserved behind some clear protective plastic, which was making up the cover of the journal. And it said my name on it in a beautiful bold script: *Ryan Harper.*

I was still barely breathing as I ran my fingers over the smooth surface, admiring how intricate the details were inside. It was an actual rose; deep red, with leaves and thorns slightly browned, but still very elegant. And the three petals falling... It was breathtaking. It had actually taken my breath away.

I looked up at Jess, my forehead lined in question. *Where did she get this?*

"Ben and I made it for you..." she whispered, answering my unspoken question as she took a seat next to me on the bed. "It's a rose from the garden. I learned how to properly preserve them a couple years ago, and now I kind of love doing it." She reached over and ran her fingers over my gift. "The three petals are... for us. The binding is real leather. That was Ben's idea. He said a big-time lawyer would need a proper journal. For like, clients and cases and whatnot."

"Jessica..." I huffed, shaking my head slowly as I opened the journal and flipped through the smooth, cream-colored paper. "I don't know what to say..."

"You don't have to say anything," she murmured, her eyes staying on mine. "Merry Christmas."

"This is the most incredible, thoughtful gift anyone's ever gotten me..." I muttered, my heart rapping against my chest.

"We knew you would appreciate something like this," Jess gave me a small, hesitant grin. "More than just buying something expensive."

"You're completely right," I said. "But now I feel like a shit. I didn't get you anything..."

Jess giggled a breathy noise, and I almost smiled. *Almost.* It was hard... I was still hurting so bad.

"You don't have to get us anything," she told me, taking my hand in hers. "You already gave us the best gift..." My lip started quivering. "Your heart."

I closed my eyes fast and shook my head. "But... it's over. Ben said we couldn't..."

"Ben is just confused," she whispered, turning her body to face mine. "He loves you, Ryan. I know he does. He might be scared, but I know my husband. He's scared for a reason."

She reached out and ran her fingers gently along my jaw, tugging my face closer to hers.

"We can't..." I grunted, my whole body quaking in fear and anticipation.

"I know..." she breathed over my lips. "I just miss you so much..."

"God, I miss you," I rasped, holding onto her waist. "I miss both of you."

"Ryan..." she mewled, brushing her lips gently over mine. I was shivering. "Don't give up on him..."

I whimpered quietly, confusion and regret filling me like sand in an hourglass.

But it's too late. I already did...

My brain was racing over everything that had happened in the past twenty-four hours. I began to fear that I had made a horrible mistake...

Someone knocked on the door and Jess and I jumped, separating fast again. This kept happening. We were being very irresponsible.

The door opened slowly, and it was Hailey. My heart was hammering on my ribcage, and everything started spinning again.

"Hey..." Hailey hummed, tilting her head to the side. "Can I talk to you for a minute?"

"Me?" I asked, pointing to myself. Jess was already standing up and walking to the door.

"Yea... If that's okay," she raised her brow at me, then glanced at Jessica.

"Let me get back downstairs..." Jess breathed and slinked out of the room, closing the door behind her.

Hailey came to sit down next to me on the bed, and I felt like I was in the Twilight Zone or something. It was insane, what I was doing. I seriously needed to reconsider how I made life decisions.

"Ryan," Hailey turned to me, staring deep into my eyes. I swallowed hard. "Are you okay? Seriously... Is everything all right with you?"

"Um yea... I'm fine," I grumbled, trying to sound casual. "What do you mean?" I put my gift back in its box and moved it away on the bed.

"You just... seem like you're going through something," she said, speaking calmly. "Is this because of the break-up?"

When she said *break-up*, Ben and Jess were the first people who popped into my head. But then I quickly realized that she was talking about us. And I felt ridiculous, because *she* was the one I had dated for five months. Not her parents.

"Is what because of the break-up?" I asked, shifting in my seat.

"Tate..." she raised her brows. "What's going on with you two?"

I breathed out slowly. "Well... he invited me here..."

"Yea, but... why?" she asked.

"We're sort of... seeing each other," I answered, and she looked thoroughly confused.

"Since when?" Her forehead creased.

"Just... recently," I hummed, not really wanting to say much more. But clearly she wasn't letting me get away with being vague.

"Ryan, that's crazy..." she huffed. "You're not gay."

I squinted at her. "Well, I had sex with him, so..."

She gasped, and for some reason she looked offended. I had no idea why... Her face appeared put-off that I wouldn't have told her something like this. Or she wouldn't have been able to tell...

"So you're into guys now?" she cocked her head to the side in that way she always did when she was annoyed that someone had proven her wrong. It was kind of funny.

"I guess I am," I grunted, giving her the same pointed look.

"You're not gay," she muttered, narrowing her gaze at me. *Oh yea, she totally wants to be right. Typical stubborn Hailey. She's just like Ben...*

"How would you know?" I scoffed, knowing she would fully hate that response.

"Because, I know," she mumbled, smirking like she was ready to bring out the big guns. "You've fucked me Ryan... A lot." My mouth was getting dry. "You fucked my tits..."

My dick flinched in my pants. "So...?"

"You used to eat my pussy almost every day," she whispered, inching closer to me. "Sometimes twice a day..." I gulped, my breathing becoming shallow. "Sometimes three times a day..."

"Yea, well... I changed my mind," I croaked, my loins starting to burn. "I like dick now."

"You do?" she ran her fingers down my neck, onto my chest.

"Uh-huh," I nodded quickly, struggling not to give away how much she was affecting me. I was trying to prove a point, but I wasn't exactly sure what it was.

"So... you're gay?" she asked, pushing me back slowly as she climbed on top of me, straddling my waist.

"I'm so gay," I breathed, gazing up at her as she ground on me slowly.

"Prove it," she purred.

"How?" I gasped, my fingers itching with the desire to grab her by the hips. *She's winning. Dammit.*

"Let me kiss you... and don't get hard," she grinned, pressing the apex of her thighs down hard on my crotch. I could feel the warmth on my dick, which was *already* getting hard.

I was so going to lose this argument.

"Hailey, we're broken up..." I hummed, my eyes stuck on her mouth as she licked her lips slowly.

"Ryan, we're not going to fuck," she moved her lips over mine. "You're gay, remember?"

I breathed out softly, and before I could object to this any further, she kissed my lips, fast yet gentle, causing me to groan in her mouth. She took my hands and pushed them down on the bed as she sucked my lips, sliding her warm tongue between them.

"Fuck, Hales..." I wriggled beneath her, the blood rapidly filling my cock. She would be able to feel it any second now...

"Does that feel good, baby?" she whispered, mashing her tits on my chest. *God fucking dammit.*

"Okay... fine," I pushed my hips up to hers for some quick friction relief. "You win. I'm not gay."

"Yea, I know," she pulled back, smirking at me. Then she wiggled on top of my erection for a second, giggling out her victory.

"Whatever," I grumbled, pouting up at her. *Sore loser, right here.*

She sighed and rolled off of me, lying down by my side. "Why are you pretending to be gay?"

"I'm not *really* pretending," I huffed, turning onto my side to face her. "I had sex with Tate."

"Do you think you're bi?" she asked, seemingly interested. "Or just experimenting..."

"I don't have a clue, Hailey," I shook my head. "I barely even know who I am anymore."

"What changed?" she asked, brushing my hair back with her fingers. "You seemed like you were fine until we came home from Thanksgiving."

I swallowed hard over the words threatening to erupt from my throat. I was still so drunk. I needed to be careful not to say anything about me and her parents, but it was difficult. I was so comfortable with Hailey. She was still one of my best friends, despite everything that had happened.

I propped myself up on my elbow. "You really wanna know?"

"Yea, of course," she replied, gazing at me with those big, beautiful eyes.

"It was your dad," I spoke softly, trying to keep my tone in check.

"My dad?" she asked, brows pushing together.

I nodded. "Meeting him sort of... changed me. It was almost like I wanted to help him, or something. He reminded me of myself... Happy and grounded. But maybe a little... I don't know, stuck?" I paused and shook my head. "I don't want to sound like I'm talking shit about your parents, because they're just so damn perfect together... But for some reason they made me realize that I had no idea what I was doing with my life."

Hailey stared at me, giving me her full attention, apparently captivated by what I was telling her. Because for the first time since we met, I was actually opening up.

"Hales, I don't even know if I want to be a lawyer anymore..." I grunted, closing my eyes and flopping back on the bed. She wrapped her arm around my waist and rested her head on my chest. "I never knew how closed off I was until you ended it."

The room was quiet for a few minutes. We were just lying there, listening to each other breathe.

"Do you want to get back together?" she asked, sounding nervous.

With your parents, maybe... I shook my head slowly. "No... I'm sorry, babe, but–"

"No, Ryan, I don't want to either," she cut me off, and I breathed out a hard sigh.

"Oh okay... good," I chuckled, and she laughed, smacking me in the chest.

"I just want you to be happy, Ryan," she said, her tone of voice making me feel much better about everything. She was truly supportive and amazing. "And I think you need to do whatever will make that happen. Whatever you do, don't keep following a path because you're afraid to stop and turn around. Don't get yourself trapped, like my parents did."

My heart was aching for Ben and Jess, and I wasn't sure why.

"Not that I think they did anything wrong," she kept going. "Like you said, they're perfect together. I just think they have some regrets. I know my dad wanted another baby..."

My stomach clenched. I remembered my first night there, in the basement with Ben, when I asked him if he had ever thought about having another kid. He got so weird and anxious about it. He had mentioned to me before that being a father was his favorite thing in the entire world. I wasn't sure why he and Jess hadn't tried again, or at least talked about it. But I certainly understood the feeling of getting stuck on a path.

Hailey was right. Now was the time for me to figure out exactly what I wanted. And I couldn't let a relationship define that.

Ben had taught me so much about myself that I never would have known if it weren't for him. And Jessica brought out some of the best parts of me that were special. Between the two of them, they had pushed me in exactly the right direction.

Now it was up to me to find my path.

I was scared; terrified, even. But also determined. I knew what I needed to do. I couldn't let my fear of being alone stop me from finding myself.

I heard yelling, and Hailey and I sat up. We glanced at each other nervously, before a loud bang made us both jump.

In an instant, we were on our feet, running to the stairs.

CHAPTER 17

Ben

I WAS SITTING ON THE COUCH IN THE LIVING ROOM, watching all my friends and family gather up their unwrapped gifts. Everyone was talking and laughing and having a great time.

But not me.

I was the picture of pure misery. I think they were all chalking my bad mood up to the fact that I was usually the Grinch of the group. Little did they know it had nothing to do with Christmas, and everything to do with the asshole in the blue button down and Prada loafers.

I was watching Tate carefully, trying not to be obvious. But his presence was really bothering me at the moment. The way he was just sitting there, on his phone, not paying attention to anyone or anything around him. The one person he'd been hanging on all night had disappeared upstairs. Apparently the rest of us just weren't entertaining enough for him...

Fucking prick.

I desperately wanted to go upstairs to see what Jess and Ryan were doing. I knew she was giving him our Christmas gift, because I saw her pluck it from underneath the tree after he stormed off upstairs to be alone, and then she followed him. It was taking all of my strength not to go up there. I couldn't...

Ryan being there was fucking with me on so many levels. Not only had I been so wrought with guilt and depression after he left yesterday that I was on the verge of tears, but now knowing he'd run right over to Tate *fucking* Eckhart's... I felt like I had been stabbed in the gut and they were twisting the knife.

I absolutely *hated* the idea of Ryan and Tate together. It made every fiber of my insides burn with a white-hot jealous rage. And they actually had the nerve to show up together, flaunting their ridiculous relationship in front of everyone, including my daughter.

Ryan was just so drunk. It was worrying me. I hated seeing him in pain, and I knew it was all my fault. I just wanted to curl up in bed and sleep until after New Year's.

I hope he likes the gift... Maybe that will take away some of his anger and hatred towards me.

And I hope he finds the secret page...

Something caught my eye, and I glanced up to see Hailey going upstairs. My pulse quickened as I prayed that Jess and Ryan weren't doing something like fooling around up there... If Hailey walked in on that, it would all be over.

Even more over than it already is, I mean.

"So uh, Trouble, is this your new thing? Going for Hailey's sloppy-seconds?" Greg sneered in Tate's direction.

My pulse turned up another few notches, for many reasons. I hated thinking about Tate and Ryan together, that we knew. Also, mentioning Hailey in the same breath made me feel like I could punch someone. And lastly, Greg referring to Ryan as *sloppy-seconds* made me want to specifically punch him. Because... no one talked about my man like that.

"You jealous, Greg?" Tate murmured, his face still stuck on his iPhone. He raised his gaze briefly, mimicking a kiss in Greg's direction.

"Lockwood, you gonna weigh in on this?" Bill jumped in, and I stopped glaring at Tate for long enough to glance over at them. I shrugged, trying hard to pretend I didn't give a fuck what they were talking about.

"Yea, I mean come on," Greg added. "The dude's boning your daughter's ex. Didn't they just break up?"

"They've been broken up for a while," I grumbled, tapping my foot against the floor.

"Please don't talk about *boning*," Jacob sighed. "My kids are in the next room."

"You don't count. You always stick up for him," Bill huffed at Jacob.

"Maybe the three of them bone together," Greg laughed, and Bill joined in, both of them snickering like a couple of fucking children.

"He wishes," Tate smirked, and my blood was really starting to boil.

"Way to steal Hailey's boyfriend, Tate," Bill shook his head. "The poor kid's probably so confused."

"He didn't seem very confused to me..." he rasped, that damn fucking grin covering his stupid face.

Something in me snapped.

"Don't you ever get sick of toying with people?" I grunted, aiming my burning gaze at Tate.

He finally put his phone down, eyes meeting mine as he raised his brow.

"Look who's jealous now..." he murmured, his voice low and taunting. I squeezed my fist. "The kid can make his own decisions, Ben. No one's toying with anyone. In fact, he called me."

My chest was heaving, as I briefly registered the sight of Jess darting through the hallway, looking flustered. My eyes came back to Tate, and all I could see were images of him and Ryan together. It was making me sick to my stomach.

Ryan and Tate kissing, touching... Ryan's mouth on stuff... His dick in... places.

My jaw ticked as I swallowed down the jealousy-bile, blinking those thoughts away.

"He's going through something, and you took advantage of that," I sat up on the edge of my seat. "You need to leave him alone. You had your fun. Now it's enough."

Tate cocked his head to the side, squinting at me. "What *is* he going through, Ben? Hm?"

He was calling me out. I wasn't sure how much he actually knew, but I didn't care at that point. I was too angry.

"Stay away from him," I growled.

"Who the fuck do you think you are?" He huffed out a condescending laugh and my muscles stiffened. "Ryan was right. You *do* think you can control everyone, don't you? Well guess what, Lockwood... You don't own him."

His voice was terribly quiet when he said that last part, but I still knew the rest of the guys were watching us from across the room, trying not to be obviously nosy.

I stood up slowly and walked over to where Tate was sitting. He immediately got up, too.

"I don't have to own him to know that you're not good enough for him," I whispered, inches away from his face.

"Back off, Ben," he warned, his eyes dark. My whole body was vibrating with wrath.

"Not a chance," I shook my head slowly. "I'll fight for him if I have to."

He leaned in closer. "You don't. He's over you."

I swallowed hard, trying desperately not to let his words get to me. Tate was skilled in the art of fucking with people. I'd known him since we were kids, but he was always Jake's friend, not mine. Honestly, he pissed me off to no end, all the fucking time. I hated how arrogant he was, and how much he used people to get what he wanted.

Ryan was way too sweet and kind and caring for someone like Tate. Tate would chew him up and spit him out, and I would rather die than let someone do that to him.

I loved him, after all.

And I knew he still loved me. Not Tate. *Me.* I didn't give a fuck what this little prick said.

"I think you need to leave," I grunted at Tate's smug face, tightening my arm to keep it from swinging.

"Gladly," he huffed. "I'll just get *my* man, and we'll be on our way."

"Hell fucking no you won't," I hissed, my eye twitching from the fury that was about to explode out of me. "He stays. You go."

Tate laughed again, and I was grinding my teeth so hard my jaw was sore.

"Why don't we let him decide what he wants to do?" he sighed. "He's a fucking grown-up. He doesn't need you ordering him around."

"What would you know about what he *needs?*" I rumbled, trying like hell to keep my voice even.

"Well, he did call me when he was *going through something...* so..."

"He would never choose you over me," I spoke so soft, right by his face, ensuring that no one could hear what I was saying. Though I barely even cared anymore.

"He already did. More than once," Tate rasped, and winked.

That's fucking it. I saw red.

I lunged forward and grabbed Tate by his shirt, lifting him and slamming him up against the wall.

He coughed as his back connected, rattling the framed pictures hanging on the wall.

"Jesus..." he grunted, stepping forward again. "You want more, Ben?! You wanna know what we did?"

"Fuck you," I snarled, shoving his chest hard with my hands until he stumbled back again.

"Funny you say that, because... well..." he sneered, and I swung my fist at his face, connecting with his jaw.

"Shut up, or I'll shut you up, you fucking prick!" I roared at him, punching his face again, that time getting his mouth. And again, in the eye.

I had fully blacked out at that point. Everything around me was a blur.

The next thing I knew, a bloody-faced Tate and I were shouting at each other, throwing punches and grabbing at each other's shirts.

I faintly registered Jess screaming at me. Actually, everyone was screaming. There was so much commotion happening around me, I could barely even see Tate anymore.

I felt strong arms wrap around my waist from behind, pulling me backward, holding my arms. I recognized the feeling, and that scent instantly...

Ryan...

Jacob was holding Tate back, and Hailey was hollering at both of us. I heard a ringing in my ears that wouldn't stop, adrenaline coursing through my veins.

"Ben, stop! Jesus Christ, enough!" Ryan shouted as I tried to fight against him. He was the only one in the general vicinity strong enough to hold me down right now. Because I really wanted to kill that fucker. I wanted to permanently shut him the fuck up.

I just wanted to make sure he never touched my man again...

He's not yours anymore.

I finally gave up the fight and yanked myself out of Ryan's grip. I was breathing so hard, my chest heaving as I paced back and forth like a caged animal.

Tate's face was bleeding a little. He was swiping at a cut on his lip, and I could already see underneath his right eye starting to bruise. *Good. You fucking piece of garbage.*

I expected Ryan to be over checking on him, but to my surprise he was still with me. He moved in front of me and forced me to look at him.

"What the fuck are you doing?" he grunted, quietly, so as not to arouse suspicions. Though I was sure that had pretty much gone out the window.

I had just made myself look completely insane. But I couldn't help it. I *was* insane.

This love was making me crazy.

Jess grabbed me by the arm and yanked me away from the crowd of our friends and family, who were all standing around looking shocked and petrified. She pushed me into the dining room and sat me down in a chair.

"Benjamin Michael Lockwood. What the *fuck* is wrong with you?!" she huffed, looking over my face briefly to check for any cuts or scrapes.

"Please... he couldn't get one hit on me if I tied my arms behind me back," I grumbled, running my hand along my jaw. There was one sore spot where he might have barely connected, but I wouldn't ever admit it out loud.

"I don't fucking care, Ben! What are you doing? Have you lost your fucking mind?" Jess squealed, keeping her voice down. "It's Christmas

Eve, for fuck's sake!"

"I know, baby. I'm sorry," I closed my eyes tight, raking my hands over my face. "He was saying shit about Ryan, and I just... couldn't fucking take it."

"Okay, well you need to lock it up," she hissed. "We can't do this. End of fucking story."

I nodded over and over. "I know. I get it."

Hailey stomped into the room, her cheeks flushed and her eyes wide.

"Dad! What the hell did you do?!" she gasped. "Why would you punch Tate?"

"Because he's a fucking asshole," I growled. "Someone needed to shut him up. It's been a long time coming."

"Ugh..." Jess pinched the bridge of her nose. "I think this party is about done..."

She left the room to go check on everyone else, and I glanced awkwardly up at my daughter.

"I'm sorry you had to see that, baby," I muttered. "I hope I didn't scare you..."

"I mean, you were a little scary, Daddy," she huffed, leaning up against the chair I was sitting in, running her small hand along my jaw. "But also pretty freaking badass."

She giggled softly, as I scoffed and rolled my eyes.

"You were defending Ryan," she spoke quietly, and I froze. My heart was racing again, now for a different reason. I peeked up at her. "I think that's sweet, Dad. Ryan's going through a hard time right now... And I don't think Tate has the best intentions. Just the fact that you would defend him is pretty awesome."

I felt so guilty I couldn't move or speak. Hailey had no idea of *my* intentions in defending Ryan. I wasn't defending him as a friend, or his ex's dad.

I was in love with him, and I couldn't bear the idea of anyone else being with him and then bragging about it to my face.

I dropped my head into my hands and cringed as Hailey rubbed my back.

I sensed him before I even knew he was there. I pulled my hands away from my face and Ryan was standing in front of me, looking worried and sweet and so fucking adorable it made my soul ache.

For some reason Hailey got up and left the room, patting Ryan on the shoulder on her way out. I squinted in confusion.

"Are you alright?" he asked, staring down at me with his forehead lined.

"I'll be fine," I grunted, biting the inside of my cheek. "How's your *boyfriend?*"

"Don't..." he rumbled and shot me a look. "Tate's okay. He'll live. But I'm not talking to him right now... I'm talking to you. Why did you hit him, Ben?"

"Because..." I mumbled and glanced at the floor, raising my brow. "I didn't like the way he was talking about you." I swallowed, feeling stubborn and immature, and foolish.

"Ben..." he hummed, shaking his head slowly.

"You knew this would happen," I said, standing up, so we were face-to-face. "You knew what coming here with him, all hanging on each other, would do to me."

He was quiet for a moment as he gaped at me, chewing on his lower lip.

"Yea... so? Maybe I did..." he answered in a frustrated tone. "Maybe I wanted you to feel as out-of-control as I did when you told me I couldn't..." He stopped himself, his eyes darting to the doorway.

"I'm... sorry," I whispered, and it was physically killing me inside not to touch him. I actually felt it. Like I was being torn apart, one piece at a time.

"I know you are," he nodded, visibly shutting down. "I have to go..."

"Don't leave with him," I pleaded, my voice so soft it was almost nonexistent. "*Please*, baby..."

"Don't call me that," he whimpered and breathed out hard. "I have to leave with him. My car is at his place."

"Just... stay," I begged again, not even caring how desperate I sounded. "I'll give you a ride to get your car tomorrow, or–"

"Ben, stop!" he barked, and I flinched. "That makes no sense. Hailey is here. You said it yourself... This can't happen. It has to be over."

I was shaking like a leaf. Suddenly my whole body was freezing.

"Don't do this," I reached out to touch his hand, and to my surprise, he let me. "I told you I was sorry. You know I meant it..."

"It doesn't matter, though," he sighed, taking his hand back. "You were right. It never would have worked."

I felt so fucking helpless. I couldn't stand the thought of letting him leave with that fucking prick. They were both drunk... It was dangerous for him to get in the car with Tate. Plus, there was no way Ryan could drive anywhere once he got his car. He lived five hours away... Clearly his plan was to stay at Tate's... And they would sleep together... *Again.*

"Jacob will drive you both back to Tate's," I grumbled, glancing at the ground quick because if I looked at him for one more second, I would kiss him and not give a single fuck who walked in the room. *Bad, bad, very bad.*

I expected Ryan to argue with me about my demands; calling me *controlling* or *bossy.* But he said nothing. My eyes slid up his tall frame, landing once again on his beautiful face. *Baby...*

He nodded and gave me a small smile which confused the shit out of me and constricted my throat.

"Thanks for the gift, Ben," he hummed. "And for... everything."

He left the room before I could say or do anything else, and I just stood there with a disparaging look on my face as my knuckles throbbed.

I was lying awake in bed, staring at the ceiling.

I turned my head slowly to check the clock on the nightstand. *Four a.m. Great.*

I huffed out an annoyed breath, tossing and turning, trying to get comfortable, though it was no use. I had too much on my mind...

After the fight, everyone left our house. No one was particularly *disturbed* by watching me mash my fist into Tate's face, but it certainly put a damper on the rest of the evening.

But at that point I didn't give the tiniest fuck. It was after midnight on Christmas Eve. It was time for everyone to bounce.

So they all left, Greg and Bill glorifying me for whooping Tate's ass. Apparently, they hadn't heard what we were actually fighting about, which was a relief. They just thought it was hilarious to watch me toss him around a little.

As kids, we all used to scrap. We were a group of boys who were always together... Of course there would be fighting; all that developing testosterone. I came home bloody and bruised more times than I could count. If we fought with each other, we always made up after a couple days. Tate and I would probably be fine. We just needed to cool down.

That was what I had assured Jacob of, anyway. Little did he know that whether I could ever be in the same room as Tate again would depend on whether he smartened the fuck up and left Ryan alone.

Tate wasn't a relationship guy. There was no way he and Ryan would be anything other than a casual fling to make me jealous.

Then again, Ryan is fucking perfect. Tate would be an idiot not to want him around all the time. I do...

I grunted and flopped onto my stomach, smashing my face into the pillow. My thoughts were irritating me. I was so restless, I couldn't stand it.

And I couldn't even go down to the basement because it reminded me of Ryan, and I didn't want to spend the rest of the night wallowing in my own misery like I had the night before. Even though that was exactly what I was doing.

Remembering the look on Ryan's face as he left the house made me weak. I had convinced my brother to drive him and Tate to Tate's house, since they were wrecked, and I would sooner jump into oncoming traffic than put the guy I loved into a deadly situation like that. I wouldn't be able to live with myself if something happened to him...

When he was leaving, he didn't look anywhere near as devastated as he had the day before, when we... *broke up*, for lack of a term that made more goddamned sense. He actually looked slightly refreshed; determined, even. I wasn't sure what had changed, but he looked happy. Serious, but content.

I was dying to know what had happened upstairs with him and Jess and Hailey, before the fight broke out. Jess told me she had gone up there to give Ryan his gift and make sure he was okay. She said that he was so happy about the gift, he almost broke down. This thought made me swell with pride and retch with pain at the same time.

Nothing had changed. We still couldn't be together, and we all knew that. But seeing Ryan leave the shed that day, then seeing him completely fucked up with Tate, brought the feelings I was trying to stuff down into perspective.

I *did* love him. And I wanted him to love me.

There was nothing I could do to change our situation, and it made me feel more powerless than I had in years. The only other times I remembered feeling like that was when my parents died, and when I found out Jess was pregnant at seventeen.

The latter turned out to be the greatest thing that ever happened to me. I couldn't help but wonder if maybe falling in love with Ryan would turn out to be a good thing, too.

But I had rejected him. I turned him down and made him feel like loving me was wrong. I mean, it *was*, because of Hailey. But I shouldn't have dismissed him like that. I knew about some of Ryan's insecurities, and I think me negating his feelings hit some kind of nerve. It was a really fucked up thing to do, and I was sick over it.

Evidently, Jess and Ryan's conversation was cut short when Hailey came upstairs to talk to him, too. It surprised me that Hailey volunteered information about her conversation with Ryan. She seemed all too excited to tell me and Jess what they talked about, as if we were all friends, rather than her parents who theoretically had no business worrying what was going on with Ryan.

Hailey told me she wanted to ask Ryan about the thing with Tate. She had been confused about the nature and origin of their relationship and meant to confront Ryan about it. And according to her, he had never seemed more confused and lost since she'd known him.

Knowing that Ryan was hurting so bad broke my heart in two. I couldn't stand the thought of him feeling alone and unwanted, because it just wasn't true. I wanted him. I wanted him so damn bad... And I knew Jess did, too.

The talk with Hailey must have given Ryan some hope. That would account for the look of purpose and confidence on his face when he said goodbye at the door. It was four hours ago, and I was still thinking about it. I could only hope that he would figure some things out, and maybe we could see each other again soon.

"Jesus, Ben... Can you stop moving please?" Jess grumbled, flopping over on her side in frustration, her sleepy voice sounding less sleepy and more annoyed. "You're wiggling around too much. It's driving me crazy."

"I'm sorry..." I sighed, rolling onto my side to face her.

"I hate that you can't sleep at night... And I hate falling asleep without you, but you're making me realize why you spend so much time in that damn basement at night," she huffed, fidgeting with the covers.

"I can't go down there..." I whined, my voice deep and slightly vulnerable.

"Why not?" she asked softly. I swallowed hard, closing my eyes and breathing out slowly. "Oh, baby..." she murmured with a clear sympathy in her tone and reached out to brush my hair back with her fingers. Apparently, I didn't need to say anything. She already knew the answer.

"I ruined everything, Jess," I hummed, subtly shaking my head. "I pushed him away because I was scared..."

"Baby, you made a mistake. It happens," she whispered, trying to console me with her words and easy tone. "We're only human. We're allowed to fuck shit up sometimes."

"Yea, but not when it hurts the people we care about..." I rumbled, gazing at her with wide eyes. "What if..." I paused and gulped. "What if he can never forgive me?"

"Then he wouldn't be Ryan," she said.

We were quiet for a few minutes, just staring at each other, blue eyes melding in the darkness of our bedroom on Christmas morning. I reached out and grabbed her, pulling her small body into mine, holding onto her with all my strength. I breathed in her marvelous, calming scent, letting it fill me and give me solace.

"I... love him," I whispered into her hair, freeing the words, letting them fill the surrounding air.

"I know you do," she breathed, running her fingers along my back. "I love him, too."

I whimpered and squeezed my eyes shut tight, willing away the tears that were trying to force their way out.

"What if we can't get him back...?" I asked, my voice shaking. "What if we can't find a way?"

Jess breathed out an unsteady sigh and shook her head against my chest.

"I don't know, baby..." she replied, unease lining her quiet voice. "But we'll always have each other."

I nodded and gripped her harder, letting her warmth lull me to sleep.

"Merry Christmas, Jessica," I drawled, my eyelids finally drooping shut.

"Merry Christmas, my love."

Christmas day came and went like it always did: fast.

I woke early after getting only a few hours of sleep and decided that an abundance of coffee would be my gift to myself for the day. Jess made a wonderful, lavish breakfast, and despite how internally depressed I was, I ate with my family, forcing myself to put on a smile and build up the illusion that I was happy. And not going through a heart-wrenching *break-up*.

Jess's parents drove in from Arizona, and her grandparents from only about ten-minutes down the road, and we all sat around, talking, eating and opening presents with Hailey. Greg and Marie stopped over for a bit with Maxine to drop off more presents, then left to go do their own things. Then Jacob came over with Laura and the twins, though they could only stay for a couple hours because they had to spend half the day with Laura's parents, too.

The house was full of lively conversation and holiday cheer, and while not much of it was coming from me, I was enjoying watching Hailey and Jess open all of their gifts, and I loved seeing how happy they were when I begrudgingly opened mine. Jess got me a new Swiss watch, and Hailey got me some cute pajama pants that had kissy-face emojis all over them.

Having Hailey at home made everything good again. I could actually push all the drama of the past month out of my brain and spend time with my amazing, beautiful wife and daughter. It was the best part of the holidays, for sure.

Unfortunately, there was one thing nagging at me, and as the day went on it was becoming more and more of a distraction.

Tate's car was still parked outside on the street where he'd left it last night because he was too drunk to drive home. I knew that Ryan had stayed at his place last night. There was nowhere else for him to go. So the obvious thought would be that Ryan was, at some point, going to drive Tate over here to get his car.

All day I was anxiously watching that damn Maserati on the street, waiting to see if Ryan's green BMW would pull up. Eventually I got sick of waiting and asked my brother if he knew when Tate was coming to get his car.

"He said he'll be by in a few," Jacob told me after texting Tate. "He's going to see his parents, so I'm guessing he needs his car."

My stomach turned violently. *He wouldn't bring Ryan to meet his parents, would he? That would be fully ridiculous. They're not a couple. Tate doesn't do that whole... thing.*

Right...?

I was dying to ask Jacob if Tate had said anything about Ryan, but I didn't want him getting suspicious about why I was interested. Luckily for me, my daughter stepped in.

"Did Tate say if Ryan is still with him?" Hailey asked her uncle, her face covered in the same kind of disapproving irritability I was feeling, which made me uncomfortable.

"No, I didn't ask," Jacob grumbled.

"I still can't believe you let Ryan leave with him last night," Hailey aimed her scolding eyes and tone at me. "You should have let him stay here."

Jess gave me a quick, nervous look as she continued cleaning things up, keeping herself busy so as not to be distracted by the unease we were clearly both feeling.

"It's not my business to get involved in their... whatever it is," I huffed quietly, trying to act unaffected by the Ryan topic, though I felt like no one was buying it.

"Yea, okay," she scoffed sarcastically and rolled her eyes. "That's why you punched Tate in the face multiple times last night... Because you don't want to get *involved.*"

Jess coughed, and I froze, my mouth hanging open in shock. I wasn't sure what Hailey meant by this, but it seemed like she was calling me out, which had my heart suddenly pounding against my chest.

"Benjamin, really?" Jess's mother, Rebecca, gasped. "Punching? You're too old to still be acting like a teenager."

"Dad was right to hit Tate last night," Hailey interjected, crossing her arms over her chest as she sat back in her chair. "If he didn't, I would have done it myself."

I grinned subtly and bit my lip, attempting to stifle my smile when I caught Rebecca's disapproving grimace.

"She's right," I ran my fingers along my jaw. "Violence isn't the answer."

"Yea, well, I don't like Tate messing with Ryan's head," Hailey went on. "He's too sweet and kind for that nonsense. Tate is obviously just using him to entertain himself."

Yea, see?! I'm not the only one who picked up on that!

I cringed inside at the fact that I was agreeing with my nineteen-year-old daughter about the guy that we both happened to know romantically. *God help me...*

"I wouldn't worry about it," Jacob added, seeking to ease our minds. "Tate doesn't do serious. I'd be willing to bet he won't be seeing Ryan again after today."

I breathed out slowly, praying for my sake that this was true.

"Yea and that's the messed up part!" Hailey huffed. "Ryan deserves better than that. He deserves to be with someone who will treat him right."

"Didn't you break up with him?" Jacob smirked.

"Yea, but that doesn't mean I don't care about him," she grumbled defensively. "I broke up with him because I knew it wouldn't work and I didn't want to string him along. But he's still a great friend of mine, and I want him to be happy. Tate won't be there for him, you said it yourself."

"Hailey, sweetheart, why did you decide to date a gay fellow?" Jess's father, Robert, asked, and I nearly spit out the sip of coffee I had in my mouth. "There are plenty of hetero men out there for you to settle down with, but instead you choose the one who prefers the company of other men." He shook his head and Jess gaped at me with her eyes bugging out of her skull.

"He's not *gay*, Grandpa," Hailey scoffed, rolling her eyes again. "He's too real for those labels. He's a very unique person."

Jess's parents shared a look like they had no idea what in the world their granddaughter was talking about. But I couldn't help but smile at my daughter. She was so smart and mature, and open-minded. Of course, she didn't know how much this topic affected me as a person, and she never would, but still. It was nice to hear her understanding things on a deeper level.

"When I was your age, everyone experimented with the same sex," Jess's grandmother, Millie, chimed in from across the room, and we all glanced at her. "We believed in free love. None of this *gay straight bisexual* nonsense. We just loved who we loved. It was beautiful."

Hailey met my eyes, and we smirked. For a crazy old coot, the woman was pretty *woke*.

"Yes, Mother. And that's why to this day you're not sure if Daddy is my real father, or if I'm actually the product of one of your crazy week-long orgies," Rebecca gave her own mother a look of frustration, pouting to herself.

"It wasn't an *orgy*, dear," Millie's husband stepped in to defend his wife from their daughter's accusations. "We spent a lot of time with your mom's friend, Glenn, who was really quite the exhibitionist..."

Oh, dear Lord...

Hailey burst out laughing and Jess stomped back into the room.

"Okay, Grammy, Grampy, maybe that's enough of this conversation, please?" Jess whined, shooting me a look and mouthing *help*. I shrugged and gave her a sympathetic smile. There was nothing I could do to stop them. This was a normal occurrence any time the family got together and wine was involved.

After that hiccup, the awkward conversation was shifted to more appropriate topics, and I started zoning out. I couldn't help but think about what Jess's crazy old grandparents were saying. They had clearly dabbled in their fair share of *experiments* in their day. And they were open about it.

Then again, that was the sixties. A time when apparently everyone got it on with each other and never stopped to consider labeling it. I sort of wished the same could be done now. People today loved their labels. They claimed to be so accepting of everyone and their own individual preferences, but they secretly loved to put people in a box. It was like filling out a questionnaire. Sexual orientation: *Straight, gay, bisexual, etc.* All of those new, fancy words they were always making up to describe themselves and one another.

But what if you didn't want to *associate* or *identify* as one of those words? What if you just wanted to love who you loved? From one adult human to another?

I had fallen in love with a woman. And then I fell in love with a man. But I didn't *identify* as anything other than *me*. Benjamin Michael Lockwood. Wasn't that enough?

My brain hurt from all this overthinking.

The doorbell rang, and Jess was already rushing to answer it. I heard voices and immediately knew it was Bill and Rachel, with the baby. I was up fast, greeting them and taking their coats.

Everyone settled in the living room, and I took the baby, William Jr., off their hands so that the new parents could eat and relax for a few. I sat in the big chair, holding William in my arms, wrapped in his soft, cuddly blue blanket with white bunnies all over it. I rocked him gently, making funny faces at him, taking the occasional whiff of his little head. It smelled like heaven.

I stared at the small being in my arms, watching his tiny eyes blink up at me. He was adorable, as were most babies; a soft, small patch of dark hair on top of his head, which fit in the palm of my hand. I couldn't resist pretending to bite his itty bitty toes and fingers while he wiggled and cooed.

I glanced up when I felt someone watching me and noticed that Hailey and Jess were gawking. Hailey giggled and joined me, poking the tip of her finger to William's button-nose, making him squeal.

"You're a natural," she whispered to me, nudging my shoulder.

"I learned early," I hummed, peeking at her out the corner of my eye and raising my brow. "Don't get any ideas, please."

"Um, I'm all set!" Hailey griped, and I laughed softly, tugging William's sock back onto his tiny foot.

"Good," I sighed, marveling at the comfort I felt holding a baby in my arms. It just felt so right. A longing set in my chest, which made me feel like such a chick.

Get your ovaries in check, Lockwood. It's just a damn baby.

"Maybe you should start planting some ideas..." Hailey sang, and I glanced up at her. She nodded toward Jess who was still watching me, this time snapping pictures with her iPhone.

"Mind your business, brat," I grumbled. "You love being an only child."

"Yea, but I love you being happy more," she whispered, and my stomach twisted. "Mom, you want to make a baby with Dad, right?" Hailey taunted her mother, then started hysterically giggling at the panicked looks on both of our faces.

"She's a nuisance," I muttered, trying hard to stow my eager smile.

"Honestly..." Jess scoffed. "Is it too late to drop her off at the Fire Station?"

Hailey gasped in outrage and Jess and I laughed, sharing a lingering look that made my whole body tremble.

Eventually I had to give the baby back to his parents. Much to my disappointment, I couldn't keep him. I was wandering around the house, reluctantly helping Jess tidy up when I saw a car pull up in front of the driveway.

My heart instantly lodged in my throat as I darted to the door, opening it fast. I wasn't sure exactly what my plan was if Ryan was there. I knew I wouldn't be able to corner him and force him to talk to me, but I just needed to see him. It was driving me insane, all this waiting around.

But when I looked outside, I saw Tate getting out of the back of a black Toyota Camry, not Ryan's BMW. He had taken an Uber.

My forehead lined as the car drove away, and I stomped down the front steps, heading right toward Tate. I wanted answers, and he was going to give them to me.

When he saw me approaching, he rolled his eyes, but I couldn't help but notice that he looked worried. Under his eye was more bruised today, and the cut on his lip was swollen.

I stepped over to the driver's side of his car where he was standing with the door open. He obviously had no desire to stay and talk to me.

"What do you want, Lockwood?" he sighed. He looked tired and hungover. "Haven't you done enough?"

"That looks... pretty bad," I grumbled with my forehead lined in the slightest bit of remorse.

"Yea, thanks," he scoffed. "I'll be stuck doing phone meetings until this shit heals."

"Look, I'm uh... I'm sorry..." I grunted running my hands through my hair. That apology took a lot out of me.

He gaped at me for a moment, seemingly shocked that I was actually apologizing, and not trying to hit him again.

"It's fine," he shrugged. "I shouldn't go fucking around with someone else's man..."

I squinted at him. "Ryan's not my..." My voice trailed off when he gave me a knowing look. "Okay, fine. I have feelings for him. If you tell anyone, a black eye will be the least of your problems."

Tate chuckled and shook his head. "Your secret's safe with me, man. But if you ask me, the two of you have some serious shit to work out."

I wanted to know what he was talking about, but at the same time I had no desire to converse about my relationship with the fuck-face who had been sleeping with my boyfriend last night. Just thinking about it now was burning a ball of rage in my gut.

"I thought he would drive you over..." I mumbled, not doing a great job of hiding my disappointment.

"He left this morning," Tate told me. "Went back home, I guess."

I nodded and breathed out hard. I couldn't tell if I was upset that Ryan was gone, or relieved that he was far away from Tate.

"Thanks for understanding," I turned to leave. Tate slipped into the driver's seat of his car, but before he could close the door, I grabbed it. "If you ever go near him again, I'll end you."

Tate laughed softly and nodded. "Sure thing, Lockwood. But just remember... if you're ever bored and looking to fool around a little, you know where to find me." He winked, and I rolled my eyes, slamming his door shut for him.

I turned and stalked back up the walkway, flipping him off as I went. He honked a few times as he drove away.

When I got back inside, I immediately tugged my phone out of my pocket and pulled up a text to Ryan. I typed out a message, feeling a new level of desperation as I hit send.

Me: Hey, baby... Merry Christmas. I miss you so bad...

I stared at the screen for a little while, but after ten minutes he still hadn't even read the message. I mentally scolded myself as I tucked my phone away and went to find my family for a needed distraction.

Hours later everyone had left except Jess's parents who were staying the night. They had already retreated to the guestroom while Jess, Hailey and me cuddled up on the couch watching *A Christmas Story*.

I hadn't yet heard anything from Ryan. In fact, he still hadn't looked at my message, and it was making me edgy. I wanted to text him again, but I didn't want to seem like a loser, bothering him when he clearly wanted nothing to do with me.

Jess's head was resting on my shoulder, and I could feel her falling asleep, which was cute. Hailey was on the other side of her mother with her feet up on the arm of the couch, her face buried in her phone.

Suddenly, she gasped out loud, and I felt Jess startle out of her dozing.

"Oh, boy... That's weird," Hailey mumbled.

"What?" I asked, trying not to sound as worried as I felt.

"Ryan deleted his Instagram account," she replied, hesitantly.

I swallowed hard. "What does that mean...?"

"I don't know, maybe nothing," she said. Curiosity lanced through me.

"Have you talked to him today?" I asked quietly. I felt Jess's body stiffen against mine.

"He texted me earlier to let me know he got home okay," Hailey answered. The rejection stung. *So it's just me he's ignoring...*

I was glad to know he was okay, but I didn't understand why he couldn't at the very least look at my message. I didn't want to hurt him anymore... I just wanted...

Oh, who are we kidding? You have no fucking clue what you want.

I sighed and got up slowly, causing Jess to pout up at me with sleepy eyes. I grinned.

"Want me to carry you up to bed, my queen?" I asked, raising my brow at her. She yawned while nodding.

"Going to bed. Goodnight, Hailey bug," I crooned, lifting Jess up by her butt as she wrapped her legs around my waist.

"Okay, not that I want to think about it, but you guys go make a baby!" Hailey shouted at us as I climbed the stairs. I grumbled to myself, though my smile was overpowering.

In our bedroom, I laid Jess down in bed, and she immediately curled herself under the covers. I pulled my shirt over my head and changed into my new pajama bottoms Hailey had given me, climbing into bed next to my wife, who was already snoring. *No baby-making tonight.*

I plugged my phone in to charge on the nightstand, and I couldn't resist. I typed out one last message to Ryan. *Then I'll leave him alone.*

Me: Just let me know you're alright. I care about you Ryan, you know I do... Goodnight.

I rustled underneath the covers, spooning with Jess, waiting to hear the sound of my phone, when I knew damn well it wasn't going to happen.

I laid awake in the dark for hours.

It was New Year's Eve. Hailey was back at her apartment. I had begged her to stay home for all of winter break, and I managed to keep her for five days after Christmas. But she left yesterday because apparently there was some big New Year's party her friend was hosting, and she couldn't miss it.

It's the social event of the year, Daddy! She had told me as she packed up her stuff. I was brooding over it, but there was nothing to be done. She was a grown-up in college. She wanted to be with her friends. I understood it. But it didn't mean I was happy about it.

Since Hailey was gone, I had nothing left to distract me from how depressed I was. Sure, I had Jess, but she was acting sort of gloomy herself. It was like neither of us could fathom how the happiness we felt last week could just disappear in the blink of an eye.

And I still knew it was all my fault, which made the guilt harder to swallow than anything else.

I hadn't heard from Ryan at all since he left on Christmas Eve. I had been texting and calling him nonstop, but I hadn't received one response. I was obsessing over it.

My messages were going unanswered *and* unread. And all my calls went straight to voicemail. I was beginning to think he'd blocked my number...

He wouldn't do that... Would he?

There was only one way to find out. I went looking for my wife, who was upstairs in our walk-in closet, picking out a dress for tonight. There was some party happening at a bar, and all our friends were going. I would have sooner just stayed in and wallowed in my misery, but Jessica wouldn't have it. She insisted that we go out to this gathering and show face like a normal couple who wasn't in a funk over the loss of their secret boyfriend.

"Babe?" I called to Jess, stepping inside the closet.

"Which one is better?" she asked, holding up two dresses in front of her body. "The green or the silver?"

The silver was definitely shorter and would show off more of her legs if she wore heels. But the dark green one was low in the front and the back. And the color... It reminded me of Ryan's eyes.

"Green," I croaked, then cleared my throat. "Jess... Can you call him, please?"

She stopped what she was doing and closed her eyes in what looked like sympathy and exasperation.

"Ben... If he doesn't want to talk to us, we can't force him," she sighed.

"He's ignoring me, not you..." I pointed out. "Maybe he'll answer for you... I just want to know if he's okay. I think he blocked me."

"Baby, I know this is hard on you," she mumbled, giving me considerate eyes. "It's hard on me, too. Of course I want to talk to him, but I just feel like we put him through enough..."

"You mean *I* put him through enough..." I mumbled, leaning my head back against the wall.

She swivelled her head in my direction. "I didn't say that."

"You don't have to. I know you're thinking it," I closed my eyes tight. "I made him leave us... I told him it wasn't real."

"Ben, you have to stop beating yourself up," Jess spoke firmly. "Blaming yourself over and over again won't bring him back."

"Okay, fine," I huffed. "Please, just call him once and see if it goes through. Please, Jess? I'm begging you. I need to know..."

She stared at me for a moment, chewing on her lower lip before finally picking up her phone off the dresser. My stomach clenched in anticipation as I watched her pull up Ryan's contact information and place the call.

She brought the phone to her ear, and I was literally shaking. I could hear the phone ringing already, which meant that he had almost certainly blocked me. I hadn't gotten a single ring in the twenty times I'd called his phone this week.

Jess's face dropped, and she looked slightly despondent as Ryan's voicemail picked up. I could hear his voice on his message, and it made my heart hurt.

"Hey, this is Ryan Harper. I'm unavailable right now, but leave me a message and I'll call you back. Or maybe text me, because who the hell talks on the phone anymore?? Thank you, and have a wonderful day!"

The sound of that little smirk in his voice at the end drove me crazy. I had been listening to that message a lot over the past week...

And I had left my fair share of voicemails, too. Not that he was probably even listening to them... Or getting them.

Jess ended the call and tossed her phone on the floor. She pouted as she stomped over to me and hugged me tight. I squeezed her and buried my nose and mouth in her hair.

She was hurting, too. I knew she was. How could she not be?

This was all so fucked. I couldn't even breathe, and I was barely hanging on to my sanity. I needed to know why Ryan was ignoring us. I needed to talk to him and straighten this out.

I needed to see him.

I released Jess and I must have had some look in my eye, because she gaped up at me and shook her head.

"No. Ben..." her eyes widened. "No... Whatever you're thinking of doing right now, don't. I'm begging you."

"Baby... I'm sorry..." I whispered, backing out of the closet. "But I just have to do this. I have to."

"Ben! Wait..." she gasped and then she was chasing me.

I darted out of the bedroom and down the stairs, grabbing my car keys off the table by the door.

"I'll be right back," I grunted and whipped open the front door.

"Ben! What do you mean you'll be right back?!" she yelped, hopping off the steps. "Where are you going??"

"I'm gonna go see him real quick. I have to," I rumbled as I stepped through the door, turning back to catch the worry on her face.

"Ben, it's five hours away!" her voice creaked. "Don't do this..."

"I have to, baby," I gave her an assuring look. The best I could manage. "I promise, I'll be back in time for the countdown to midnight."

"But Ben..." she gasped, her eyes round and pleading with me. We stared at each other for a moment before she finally nodded and bit her lip. "You promise you'll be back?"

"I promise," I hummed, drawing an X over my heart. "I haven't missed kissing you at midnight in nineteen years, and I don't plan on starting tonight."

Jess reluctantly nodded again, her forehead creased with obvious concern.

"I love you..." she whimpered. "Please be safe."

"I will."

"And Ben?" I turned over my shoulder one last time. "Tell him... I love him."

I nodded and kept walking, Jess closing the front door behind me as I hopped in my car fast and drove.

I arrived at Ryan's apartment and immediately knew something was wrong.

His car wasn't in the driveway. I was kicking myself, because it was New Year's Eve, and maybe he was out, and what kind of moron drives for five hours to see someone without even confirming that they're actually home?

I shook my head and got out of the car. I wouldn't have been able to confirm his presence at home, anyway. He was ignoring my calls. Or he had blocked me. Or both.

Whatever, it didn't matter. He had no Instagram, no other social media, and I didn't have any way of contacting his friends, which I wouldn't have done anyway, because that would make me seem crazy. Which I definitely was. But I didn't need kids in Hailey's circle finding out I was stalking her ex.

I walked up the driveway toward Ryan's front door, my mind flashing back to the first time I went there. The night I left the hotel to sneak over and fool around with him. It felt like so long ago, when in reality it had only been a few weeks. So much had happened since then, it was almost unfathomable.

I took a deep breath and held onto it as I rang the doorbell. I stood there, shifting my weight back and forth as I prayed that he was home, and maybe just his car was missing for some reason.

The door opened, and I recognized the small, dark-haired girl standing on the other side as Ryan's roommate's girlfriend. *What was her name again....? Kayla. That's right. The one with the nice butt.*

"Oh, fuck..." she muttered, gaping up at me, her eyes wide and popping out of her head.

"Hi, Kayla," I spoke, forcing myself to sound normal. "I'm so sorry to just show up like this. I was just wondering if Ryan was home...?" She stared at me, completely silent, her jaw hanging open in obvious speechlessness. "I need to see him..." I pleaded with my eyes.

"Kayla! Who's at the door?" I heard a deep male voice bellow from inside, and I assumed it was probably Ryan's roommate and best friend, Alec.

"Um... no one..." she stuttered her response then whispered to me, "He's not here. You have to go."

"What... Why?" I huffed, shaking my head. "Look, I know he probably doesn't want to see me, and you guys are protecting him, and I get that. But I just need to talk to him. He won't answer my calls..."

"No, seriously, Ben. You have to go," Kayla warned again, looking and sounding terrified, which was confusing the shit out of me. "Hurry...!"

"Kayla, who–" a big guy with black hair and tons of tattoos stepped into the doorway, by Kayla's side, his question instantly fading away when he saw me. "Are you fucking kidding me?"

He glared at me, his eyes hardening.

"You must be Alec..." I observed calmly, standing firm, trying not to get burned by the flames he was shooting at me through his eyes. "I'm–"

"Yea, I know who you are," he grunted, stepping through the doorway, closer to me. I instinctively took a step back. "What the fuck do you think you're doing here?" His tone was downright chilling. I would know, because it gave me chills.

"Um... I just came to see Ryan," I rumbled, narrowing my gaze at him, wondering why he looked like he wanted to murder me. "He hasn't been answering my calls or texts and I just need to talk to him."

"No fucking shit, asshole!" Alec barked at me, moving closer again. "He's ignoring you because you broke his goddamn heart!"

He was really coming at me now and I had no choice but to keep backing up. I wasn't about to fight Ryan's best friend, but he was looking at me like a rattlesnake, coiled and ready to strike.

"I told him I was sorry..." I mumbled like an idiot, not knowing what else to say. "He knows I didn't mean to hurt him..."

"Oh, you didn't mean to?!" he growled. "Well, that's a fucking relief! As long as you didn't *mean* to..."

"Alec, please stop," Kayla's small voice squeaked from the doorway.

"You fuck with my best friend, basically rip his heart out and stomp on it in front of him, then you have the nerve to fucking show up here?! I should pound you into the ground!" His chest was heaving, and he was lurching forward, following me as I backed away.

Adrenaline coursed through my body, making me quake. The kid was pretty big. Not as big as me or Ryan, but he was close enough, and I really wasn't in the mood to fight. He had a reason to be pissed off at me... Obviously Ryan had told him what happened. I just needed to fend him off long enough to find out where Ryan was.

"Come on, man. I know he's your best friend, but what happened is between me and him," I held my hands up in concession. "Can you just tell me where I can find him so we can talk, please? We need to talk..."

Alec stopped in his tracks and gave me a look I couldn't understand, shaking his head slowly.

"You just don't get it, do you?" He eyed me hard, like I was the biggest piece of shit on the planet. "It's over, Ben. You fucked with him for the last time."

My jaw clenched, and I felt unwanted tears threatening to burst from my eye sockets.

"You don't know what I've been going through since he left," I whispered. "I'm in goddamned agony every day without him. I fucking love him, okay?! I fucked up. I need to know where he is, so I can tell him I made the biggest mistake of my life!"

"You're never going to see him again!" he roared at me, lunging forward, shoving me hard in the chest. I stumbled back, but regained my footing, stepping forward.

"Alec, stop it right now!" Kayla screamed at him.

"He's the reason Ryan left, Kayla! This asshole, right here!" he shouted and got up in my face. "You took my best friend, you fucking selfish piece of shit. I should fucking kill you for hurting him!"

He looked like he could hit me at any moment, but his words stunned me too much to care. My pulse was ringing in my ears and I wasn't breathing at all.

"What do you mean he *left*?" I asked, my voice so low and hoarse I wasn't even sure I had said anything.

"He's gone, man," Alec shook his head, finally taking a step back. "He applied to some transfer program and got accepted. They took him early..."

Everything started spinning around me, and I felt like the ground disappeared beneath my feet. My knees actually gave out, and I fell backward. Luckily my car was right behind me and I reached out to hold on to it.

"When...?" the word slipped out quietly.

"Four days ago," Alec sighed.

I felt so sick; I was sure I would throw up. My vision became dark and blurred. I blinked a few times, so completely stunned. I just couldn't believe what I was hearing.

He left...? Ryan's... gone?

"No..." my voice crept out of my throat and my head started rocking back and forth. "No no no... *No*... He wouldn't. He couldn't..."

"Yea, that's what I thought, too," Alec's voice grunted from somewhere in front of me, but I couldn't see anything. My eyes were opened, but everything was black.

"No... fuck. *Why*...?" I whimpered and covered my face with my hands, resting my whole body weight against my SUV. I squeezed my eyes shut and ran my fingers through my hair hard. *No... He can't be gone. It's not true. He wouldn't leave me without a goddamn explanation, would he?!*

Jesus Christ, I fucking love him! I'm in love with him... He can't leave.

"Where did he go?" I asked, murmuring into my hands.

"I don't... know," Alec grumbled, and I could tell he was lying. He knew where Ryan was, but he wasn't going to tell me.

Suddenly I felt a small hand rubbing my back in calming circles.

"Come inside, Ben," it was Kayla's voice. "It's cold out here." She grabbed me by the arm and forced me to stand upright. "Come on. In we go..."

She walked me up the driveway, inside their apartment and got me settled on the couch. Alec still looked angry with me, but mostly just depressed. Not that I gave a shit.

I was sitting inside Ryan's apartment, only it wasn't his apartment anymore. He had moved out. He left and moved away without even saying anything.

I was so heartbroken, I could barely function.

The whole apartment was silent for a while. The only thing I could hear was my rapid panting. I was chewing on my lower lip so hard it was about to bleed.

"Why would he transfer?" I finally asked, feeling so dizzy and lightheaded. "He loves New Mexico."

"He was really hurt, Ben," Kayla whispered. "I think he just wanted a fresh start."

"I made a fucking mistake," I dropped my head into my hands again. "I was scared. I told him I was sorry... Jesus Christ, if he would have just answered the goddamned phone, I would've told him..." I stopped myself and swallowed hard. "He should've at least said goodbye. I deserved to hear it from him..."

"His heart was broken," Alec pointed out again, and I opened my eyes to glare at him.

"My heart is broken too, okay?" I barked. "You don't understand the position I'm in. This is the most fucked up shit I've ever experienced in my life. I wasn't trying to hurt anyone, but I had my daughter to think about! I know I did this to myself. I fell for him... and I just needed a fucking *minute* to think..." I exhaled and rubbed my eyes. "But now it's too late."

Silence, again. No one was saying anything, and I realized they weren't going to.

They weren't going to comfort me. In their eyes, I was the bad guy. I guess in my eyes I was, too.

You fucked up so bad. You drove him away.

"Can you... please... just tell me where he went?" I opened my eyes to plead with them. I knew I looked desperate and hopeless and pathetic. I could see it on their faces.

Kayla's mouth dropped open, but she said nothing. She just shook her head over and over, then glanced at Alec. So I did, too.

"*Please...*" I begged again, my brow furrowing so hard I had a splitting headache.

Alec leaned forward, his eyes locked on mine. "I wouldn't tell you where he went if you paid me a million fucking dollars." I swallowed hard as the bile rose in my throat. "It's over, Ben. Move on and let him do the same."

My chest heaved up and down with heavy breaths. It was taking everything I had not to break down. I couldn't do it in front of these random kids, though I barely cared what I looked like to anyone anymore.

That was what falling for Ryan had done to me. I was in so deep, overflowing with regret, that I couldn't even recognize myself.

I needed to go. It was another five-hour drive back home, and it was already six in the evening. I needed to get to Jessica before midnight. Despite how badly I had fucked up with Ryan, I still had a wife who loved me; who would never give up on me, no matter how selfish and stupid I was from time to time.

I need my wife.

I huffed out a hard, unsteady breath and stood up slowly. My whole body was weak and heavy with sadness.

"Well... thanks, I guess..." I muttered, and sniffled. I walked away from them, heading toward the door.

"Ben, wait!" I heard Kayla's voice squeak, and I turned quickly.

She jumped out of her seat and stammered over to me.

"Kayla, don't you fucking dare..." Alec growled at her from across the room. She rolled her eyes then gaped up at me with concern covering her face.

"What if I can get a message to him..." she whispered, blinking rapidly. "What would you want me to say?"

"Kayla!" Alec shouted, and she flinched, but ignored him, her eyes still stuck on mine.

"Tell him I love him," I shook my head slowly. "And I'm sorry... And that I will *never* give up on him."

She swallowed visibly and nodded.

I breathed out a rough sigh and turned back to the door, leaving fast.

I got in my car and drove off, watching the road blankly. I was in a trance, barely even cognizant of what I was doing. I was just driving, toward home, my mind racing over everything that had happened in the last week.

The radio stayed off. It was silent. And I just drove.

A beeping sound from my car finally snapped me out of it, and I realized my gas light was on. I pulled over at a gas station off the highway and filled my tank. I ran inside to use the restroom, and once I was in there, I began to feel strange.

My pulse was racing, and a cold sweat broke out across my body.

I stood in front of the sink and splashed some water on my face. I peered at myself in the mirror and a wave of anger swept me up. I couldn't breathe, the devastation clawing at my throat.

I covered my face with my hands and growled out loud in frustration and fury. I rubbed my eyes so hard it hurt. I had never wanted to hurt myself so bad in my entire life.

I needed the physical pain, to block out the emotions. I needed to hurt myself for hurting him...

I roared a guttural sound from inside my throat punched the paper towel dispenser. It was made of plastic, so it immediately cracked down the middle. I punched it again, and it made a satisfying crunch-noise.

I drew hard breaths into my lungs as I grunted, punching the stupid thing over and over, smashing it to bits with my aching fist until my knuckles were bloodied and raw. I ripped the remaining piece of it off the wall and hurled it against the opposite wall, stomping over and kicking it until there was nothing left.

I gasped for air, crouching down on the ground and holding my head as the tears finally broke free, and I couldn't even attempt to stop them. My whole body was trembling as I cried softly to myself, feeling the crack in my heart, like the plastic I had just demolished. My knuckles were throbbing, which distracted me from the pain in my chest, but only for a moment.

I just couldn't believe he left.

He was *really* gone.

"I'm so sorry, baby..." I whimpered, my forehead resting on my knees as I curled into a ball on the bathroom floor. "You were right... I was afraid to feel it."

Minutes went by, and eventually I forced myself to stand up and leave the gas station bathroom, meandering slowly back to my car.

I drove away from my meltdown, far away from ABQ. It was over. It was time to go home.

As I grew closer to my town, the town where I had grown up; where I had been living my entire life, I realized that everything had come full circle. My relationship with Ryan was exciting, and new, and different. It was so unlike anything I had ever done before...

And that was what I had wanted.

But it had apparently run its course, and now it was back to normal. Back to the regular, ordinary, boring life of Ben Lockwood.

I just hoped that wherever Ryan was, he was safe and happy. No matter how sad I was, I was still grateful to Ryan for bringing excitement to my world. He pushed his way into my life and shook things up, just like I had wanted.

But there was no way for it to be anything more than that. I just had to accept it.

All I could do was pray that he would live a long, happy, healthy life doing what he loved. That he would meet a nice girl, or guy; fall in love. Get married, have babies. I wanted all of that for him.

Sure, I thought for a minute I wanted it *with* him... And yes, I entertained the idea of us having a *real* relationship, out in the open. Finding a way for Jess, Ryan and me to make it work.

But I couldn't hold him back like that. He was still so young; fifteen-years younger than us. He had his whole life ahead of him. He deserved to have a wedding and make babies with someone. To do all the things that Jess and I had already done together.

It wasn't fair to expect him to just fall into our already-made lives. He needed to make his own.

Now I understand why he left... It's better this way.

I checked the clock as I was pulling off the highway to see it was eleven-thirty. Only a half-hour until midnight, and I was about fifteen-minutes away.

I breathed deeply and stepped on the gas, driving fast toward the bar where my wife was with our friends. She had already been texting and calling me nonstop, blowing up my phone. I knew she probably thought I would miss the countdown, but I had absolutely no intention of doing that.

I had fucked up enough for one lifetime. I wouldn't disappoint anyone else.

I sped through the streets, racing against time, watching the clock in between navigating the route that led to the bar where the party was happening. But then I slowed down, mentally scolding myself as I thought about how my parents had died.

And how scared I had been to learn how to drive after that.

It was just an accident. No one's fault, really. Nobody had been drunk, or anything crazy. I guess my parents just weren't paying attention. One second they were alive, and the next second, they were gone.

I shook my head to myself. It wasn't worth me killing myself over. I would get to my wife, eventually. And I was sure she'd rather have me late and alive, than speeding to an early grave.

I felt a chill run down my spine.

Life was way too short... Too short to spend it on regrets and wondering *what if.*

An accident could take any of us away from this world any minute. And as much as I couldn't bear the thought of that happening, even worse was the idea that I would die before I could do everything I wanted. Before I could give my wife everything she wanted, too.

I made it to the party with ten-minutes to midnight. I parked and hurried inside, looking around frantically for my wife. I finally spotted her, standing with her sister and our friends, by the bar which had the big screen on the ball in Times Square.

I ran over to her and the look on her face when she realized I made it–I kept my promise–was enough to patch up my bruised and battered heart.

I grabbed Jessica in my arms, hugging onto her tight while our friends cheered for my arrival. I actually smiled, because it felt good to be back.

Jess glanced up at me, her smile fading as she raised her brows, silently asking what happened. I swallowed hard and shook my head.

She pouted, and I hugged her again, positioning myself behind her, holding her waist as we watched the TV. I let my lips linger in her hair, kissing her head over and over while she gripped my arms.

We had been through so much together, and clearly this was just the beginning. I could feel it in my heart. My life was far from over. We would have a million more adventures, and as long as I had this woman by my side, holding me and loving me, and supporting me... I would always be alright.

The crowd in New York cheered, and so did all of us. The ball began to descend, ready to lead us into a new year.

People were hollering, blowing horns and whistles as we counted down...

"Ten, nine..."

Jess took my hand and squeezed.

"Eight, seven..."

I nuzzled my face in her neck, watching the screen.

"Six, five..."

The ball moved lower, and I made a wish.

"Four, three..."

Keep him happy... No matter what.

Jess and I breathed out together, "Two..."

One.

CHAPTER 18

Ryan

Six months later...

"I CAN'T FUCKING BELIEVE I'M STILL ALIVE."

"I know, me neither..."

"Jesus Christ, I think that was the hardest thing I've ever done in my entire life," I rumbled, shaking my head as I walked across the commons, my eyes dry and burning.

"Are we fucking sadists or something?" my friend Henry asked, running his free hand through his unruly hair. We both looked like we'd been up for days on end, which was accurate. I couldn't remember a night in the past month when I'd gotten over three hours of sleep.

"Yes. Without a doubt," I scoffed, shaking my head.

We had just finished our final exams for the semester. Four finals, complete with two papers and a dissertation. I had no recollection of what a normal life was like. It was all about fucking Law School.

Thank God for Henry. He was my best friend in Boston, and he also happened to be in almost all the same classes as me, which was helpful. That way I had a pal to talk me off the ledge at two in the morning when I was studying so hard I felt like I was going blind.

I stepped over to the train station and turned to high-five him.

"I would say enjoy your summer break, but none of us will be relaxing until the grades are posted," he laughed.

"Very true," I nodded. "Text me when you wake up from sleeping until July. We can grab a beer."

He chuckled and nodded back. "Will do. Stay golden, Harper."

"Back at ya, boss," I grinned and waved him off as he walked away, heading in the direction of his apartment.

Henry lived in a two-bedroom loft in Downtown Boston with four roommates, all of whom were also students at Suffolk Law. We used to have study groups over there when I first transferred, but it started getting way too cramped, so Henry and I had taken to camping out in the Law Library. It was closer than going to my place.

I hobbled down the stairs feeling exhausted in every sense of the word, but also greatly accomplished. I had finished yet another year of law school. As long as I passed my finals, which I was confident I would, I could land this pretty sweet internship as a paralegal at a big firm there in town. Then I was only one year away from the bar. It was exciting.

Or so I kept telling myself.

I hopped onto the green line and nestled into an available seat, making the twenty-minute journey to my aunt's place in Allston. It was actually a really nice apartment, and she was a saint for letting me live there for free. What with school taking up every second of my life, I didn't exactly have time for a job, and had next to no money.

But my aunt Jill was great. After my dad died, she extended an open invitation for me to come stay with her, any time I found my mother to be too much, or if I couldn't make living in Santa Fe work. I never had to take her up on her offer, because I got accepted to UNM and found a place out there. But I had always kept her generous offer in the back of my mind. In case I needed an escape...

As it turned out, I did.

I unzipped my backpack and pulled out my journal, the one I'd gotten for Christmas six months ago. I ran my fingers over the preserved rose beneath the film, then opened it up to a free page. I bit the cap off my pen, holding it between my teeth as I began scribbling out words.

Saved from a savior's saving grace,
Far enough to change my pace.
Running from what would make me free,
Inside myself I no longer see.

I hummed and closed my eyes, chewing on the pen cap.

I started writing the day I moved from New Mexico to Boston. On the plane. I was having such a hard time, and I needed an outlet. If I didn't find a way to channel my feelings, I knew I would end up doing something I regretted.

So I wrote. Mostly poetry, some songs. A couple short stories. It was odd that I found time to do it, being that I was always writing papers for school. The train rides definitely helped. I loved having the additional free time.

Driving into the city was a nightmare. Plus, parking was an expense that I could not afford. I was lucky enough that my aunt had a driveway where I could keep the BMW. She had paid to ship it out right after I moved in exchange for letting her drive it when she needed a car which wasn't all that often. Those New England winters were no joke. I couldn't understand how anyone drove in four feet of snow.

I flipped through my journal to a page I had written in January, on a particularly frigid winter day...

The air is sharp, and it stings my face.
Everything is white.
How can this be right?
I wish I could share it with you...

My chest began to ache a little. My constant desire to torture myself won the battle between brain and heart, and I flipped to the back of the journal, to the second to last page. I stared at the handwriting for a moment, feeling myself tremble as I ran my fingers over it slowly, and read it again...

> *Dear Ryan,*
>
> *I hope you love this journal. I don't know why, but I just felt like you would. It seems like something you could use, and I wanted you to have something special and unique, because that's what you are.*
>
> *I don't want to write about everything that happened because I want you to fill these pages with good things. Like school stuff, or info on your big, fancy clients you'll definitely have some day. Or even just whatever makes you happy. You're going places, kid. I have no doubt in my mind that whatever you decide to do with your life, you'll be successful and great at. You're so dedicated it blows me away.*
>
> *I'll say one thing, and then I promise I won't make this about me...*
>
> *I love you. I do, and I'll never stop being sorry for not telling you when I had the chance. I can only hope that you still feel the same, because I know I'll never stop loving you. You changed my entire life, and I'm eternally grateful.*
>
> *There's so much more I want to say to you, but I'll wait to say it in person. Hopefully, you can find it in your big giant heart to give me the chance.*
>
> *Thank you for being brave and fearless when I couldn't. Never stop being who you are, because you're perfect.*
>
> *Merry Christmas, baby.*
>
> *Love always,*
>
> *Ben*

I took a deep breath and squeezed my eyes shut, fighting against the tears. I slapped the journal shut and tucked it back inside my bag, leaning my head against the window as I watched the train speeding underground. I sniffled and rubbed my eyes, wondering why I kept doing this to myself.

I had first discovered the letter from Ben about a week after I moved to Boston. It had really shaken things up at the time...

I had been doing a great job of not thinking about him or Jess. It was like I had built a wall in my mind, and I refused to let any of those longing thoughts, memories or urges penetrate it. I was moving on, and it was a very good thing.

Until I found that damn letter. And everything came floating back to the surface.

I was still proud of myself for not calling them. I had wanted to so bad... It was gnawing at me inside. I had to go out and hook up with a stranger to keep myself from doing it, and even that was a temporary solution.

But I pulled through. I had blocked Ben from my contacts on Christmas Day and still hadn't undone it. It wasn't even so much that I thought he would try to reach me, but more so for myself. In my mind, if I deleted my Instagram account and blocked Ben, then it would be harder for me to obsess over wanting to talk to him.

Of course, I hadn't blocked Jess or Hailey. I knew neither of them would try to reach out, because they respected my boundaries. Although Jess called once, a few days after I left...

I had considered calling her back, but I knew it would just make things worse. They couldn't know where I was or what I was doing. That would defeat the purpose of a fresh start.

I had spoken to Hailey a couple times in the last six months. I made it a point not to tell her where I was, just in case she ended up telling her father. Ben was the one person I couldn't have finding out where I was living. Because I knew he would come looking for me... And I just couldn't have that.

I still loved him and Jess. I knew those feelings would never go away. They were too strong, and powerful; too real.

But at the end of the day, regardless of whether Ben loved me or not, it changed nothing. We still couldn't be together, and it was just too painful to keep putting myself through the ringer. Being mind-numbingly happy and agonizingly sad at the same time had seriously fucked with my emotional sanity. I still felt it, even now. And it had been six months.

Hailey was understandably confused about why I wouldn't tell her where I was, but she accepted it. She was just supportive of me finding myself and following my path. She was a great soul. I had honestly never known anyone like her... Though it was clear where she got it from.

The only people who knew where I was were Alec and Kayla, and my mom. None of my other friends from New Mexico really cared that much, which I supposed was a positive and negative of cutting out social media. You find out who your true friends are, but it sort of hurts when you do.

Being a twenty-two-year-old college student was hard to pull off without an Instagram account. Lately I had been contemplating making a new one. After all, there was no way Ben and Jess were still thinking about me. It had been *six months*. That's half a year. I was sure they had moved on.

I mean, yes, Ben had said he would never give up on me... Apparently, he showed up at Alec and Kayla's on New Year's Eve looking for me. And he told Kayla that he loved me.

That too had made me go a little crazy when I found out. But Alec and Kayla were good friends, and they'd made it a point not to tell me until two months later when I was properly settled into my new life. At that point I had already found Ben's letter, so I knew he loved me... Or at least that he'd said so on paper.

But to find out he had actually said it, out loud, to my friend was overwhelming. I had to go out and hook up with another stranger to ignore all those stifling feelings, too.

That had been the extent of my love-life since I came to Boston. I went on a couple dates with a girl I met at Starbucks a few months back. And then I went on a couple dates with a guy I had met at a party on Valentine's Day. It was interesting, and fun, but I still never got those butterflies with anyone around here. That captivating, soul-crushing jolt to your nervous system that came from raw attraction and chemistry. I hadn't felt it since Ben and Jess, and I spent more time than I'd like to admit praying that I would find it again someday.

I couldn't stand the idea of having lost my only chance at true happiness.

But I was still young. There would be more chances at love, I was sure of it.

I got off the train at my stop and walked the four-minutes to my aunt's house, taking in the beautiful weather. The sun was out, and it was in the sixties with a nice breeze. The weather there was so different from New Mexico. Having four distinct seasons was very exciting. I had already gotten winter and spring, now we were almost at summer. I couldn't wait to see what fall was all about...

I climbed the stairs to the apartment and used my key to open the door. I stepped inside and was hit with a smell that instantly made my mouth water.

"Hey, auntie," I murmured, to my aunt's back. She was standing in front of the stove. "What the hell are you making? It smells delicious."

My stomach was already rumbling. *I guess I haven't eaten in days either.*

"Hey, sweetie!" Jill sang, glancing at me over her shoulder. "Blueberries are in season, so I'm makin' a pie. I got a crate of 'em at the farmer's market. Figured we'd celebrate the end of the semester!"

I smiled to myself. My aunt was truly amazing. She was a fully selfless person, unlike my actual parents. I was so lucky to have her.

"That sounds amazing," I crooned, stomping down the hall. "Do you mind if we wait a bit though? I'm so drained, I could use a shower and a nap."

"Of course, pumpkin," she replied, in that Boston accent that made me smile and cringe at the same time. It was one of those things you both loved and hated simultaneously. "The pie won't be done for a few hours, anyway. Go get rested up. I'll be here until about six, then I'm goin' to play Keno at Dolly's."

"Sure thing. Thanks," I smiled, sauntering into my bedroom and closing the door.

I tossed my backpack on the floor and immediately crashed onto my bed. I barely kicked my shoes off before my eyelids were drooping, and I was out like a light.

When I opened my eyes again, it was slightly dark in my room. I glanced at the clock and saw that it was seven-thirty.

"Shit..." I muttered to myself, sitting up and rubbing my eyes. I hoped my aunt wasn't offended that I missed her, but I dismissed that idea quick enough. She wasn't the type to be bothered by anything like that. She knew how hard I'd been working.

I noticed a piece of paper on my nightstand and picked it up, blinking over my groggy sleepy eyes to read what it said.

You were really out there, kiddo! Good for you. You deserve the rest. Relax and enjoy. You're done!

The pie is cooling on the stove, so help yourself. There's vanilla ice cream in the freezer, and whipped cream in the fridge, so go nuts! Well, no actual nuts because I know you're allergic.

I grinned and laughed to myself. My aunt was a hoot.

I'll be out late, so if I don't see you tonight, we'll catch up tomorrow. Love you! Proud of you!
-Auntie Jill

PS. A friend of yours stopped by looking for you. I told him you were sleeping and to give you a call later. I would've offered to let him wait in the house, but I didn't recognize him. He said he'd come back later.

I frowned and my forehead creased. *A friend? What friend?*

I stumbled over to my backpack and located my phone. There were no missed calls or texts from anyone, other than a group text with some friends from school who were all rambling on about how hard finals were and how stoked they were to be done. Then they mentioned going out later for a beer, but half of them were complaining about being tired, and collectively decided to postpone it to tomorrow... or next week.

I shrugged it off and went to the bathroom, hopping into the shower. I was in there for a while, savoring the feeling of the warm water, and relaxation, knowing that I had no more studying to do; no more books or papers or late nights force-feeding my mind. I was done until September. It was immensely satisfying.

I got out of the shower and threw on some sweatpants, then meandered into the kitchen. The pie was calling to me, like in those old cartoons where the steam formed the shape of a hand and started seductively luring you towards it.

I cut myself a huge piece with two giant scoops of ice cream and sat down at the kitchen table ready to devour the homemade deliciousness.

But before I could take a bite, there was a knock on the door.

I huffed and clenched my jaw. Whoever was interrupting me getting it on with this pie would be sorry. I was two seconds away from pulling a Jason Biggs and actually having sex with it.

Okay, maybe not... But still! I'm fucking hungry, dammit!

I reluctantly got up and unlocked the door, opening it slowly so I could peer into the hallway and see who was disturbing my meal.

Blue eyes locked on mine and my whole body froze. All the breath left my lungs in one long sweep.

Oh... my... God...

"Hey, kid," Ben's voice rung out in the hall, that sound so familiar, although I hadn't heard it in what felt like an eternity, slipping inside my ears, right into my brain. It was like everything I had done in the last six months suddenly disappeared and I was back where I belonged.

It was the most startling response to two words I had ever experienced.

My mouth opened, but I couldn't respond. I couldn't say *anything*.

I just stood there, staring through the cracked door, at the man I had loved. The man who destroyed me. The man I fled across the country to get away from.

Who was now here; In Boston, at my house. Standing in the hallway, gazing at me.

He looked almost exactly the same. His hair was grown out a little, but still styled the same effortlessly messy way I was used to; his stubble grown out a bit, lining that sculpted jaw. His blue eyes were so bright, though slightly tired, but he was still just so beautiful. Looking at him now brought every single feeling I had ever felt for him bounding back at me, like a swift kick in the chest.

I was still speechless. I couldn't move. I couldn't breathe. I don't even think my heart was beating. I may have been dead.

Just standing there in the doorway, staring at Benjamin freaking Lockwood, like *what the hell* is going on!?

"I'm uh... sorry to stop by like this..." he stuttered, finally breaking the silence. His face was so serious. He looked like he might throw up. "I came by earlier and met your aunt. She seems nice." He raised his brows.

This is tripping me the fuck out right now.

He was talking to me like everything was normal. Like we hadn't broken up. Like I hadn't blocked his number and moved across the United fucking States of fucking America to get away from him because I was in love with him and we could never be together.

I had no idea what was going on. I was seriously about to pass out.

"Kid, are you okay?" he asked softly. "You look really pale."

"I'm seeing a ghost..." my voice croaked from deep in my throat. "You're not really here. This is a mirage or something."

His bottom lip did this adorable little pout thing and my heart skipped in my chest.

Jesus Christ, what the fuck is wrong with you?! Did you forget everything that happened before you left?? Don't swoon over him! Yell at him! He's evil, remember?!

My body did the opposite of what my mind was suggesting.

"Sorry, I'm being so rude. Come in," I murmured, opening the door and stepping aside.

"Thank you," he strolled past me, inside the apartment. I caught a whiff of his smell and I was having heart palpitations.

I closed the door and turned to face him just in time to catch him checking me out, likely from my lack of shirt. It confused the shit out of me, as his entire presence was doing at the moment.

I raised my brows at him. "What the hell are you doing here? How did you find me? Did you come all the way from New Mexico? What do you want?"

I took a breath and closed my eyes, leaning my back against the door.

"Um... okay. Lots of questions," he nodded, running his hand along the back of his neck. "Understandable. So... I needed to see you. That's why I'm here. Don't be mad, but I finally weaseled some details out of Kayla..."

Kayla... God, I knew she'd be the first one to crack. She's too hypnotized by Ben's sexiness. It was inevitable.

"How the fuck..." I breathed, having an out-of-body experience. I felt like I was in a dream or something. There was no way this could be real.

"I've been bothering her every day since you left," he told me. "I have to hand it to her, she really gave nothing away for a while. But then she let it slip that you transferred to Suffolk. So I looked up Suffolk Law and found the one here in Boston. I remembered you saying you had an aunt who lived out here, and I figured it would be a perfect place to go... where you'd have seasons again." He paused, and I saw him swallow. "Anyway, I did some digging. It took a while... But eventually I found your aunt's info."

"So you just hopped on a plane and flew all the way across the country?" I snapped. He nodded slowly, looking guilty; fully prepared for me to yell at him. "Jesus, Ben, you could have just called me..."

"You still have me blocked," he grunted, apparently wounded by this fact.

"You could have used Jess's phone..." I muttered, internally accepting that I probably would have been just as annoyed if he had done that.

"I needed to see you..." he shrugged, pursing his lips at the floor.

"Why?" I huffed, stepping forward and crossing my arms over my chest. "Why would you need to see me now, after all this time?"

"Well, first off, I needed to see you the whole time you were gone," he said, shifting his weight back and forth, being his usual fidgety self. The sight of it made me want to smile, but I forced myself not to. "It just took me this long to find you. I mean... that and I wanted to give you some space..."

"This is giving me *space*?" I asked, unable to control the bite in my tone. "Chasing me across the country..."

"Yes. I gave you six months," he grumbled, that bossy control-freakishness finally showing itself again. It honestly gave me a strange sensation of excitement, like butterflies fluttering around in my esophagus. I couldn't believe I actually still missed him so bad. I didn't want to admit it to myself, but clearly six months wasn't enough time to erase my feelings for him.

"Ben, I just..." I rasped and shook my head. "I can't believe you're here."

His eyes softened, and he gave me the most intense look of longing I'd ever seen on a human being before. It tightened my chest and spread warmth throughout my entire body.

"Can I... hug you...?" he whispered, and I bit down hard on the inside of my cheek, trying to keep the tears in. "Please?"

"Fuck..." I whimpered, and I stomped up to him, closing the gap fast.

He wrapped his arms around me and squeezed me so tight I felt like I was being strangled to death. But in the best possible way. I held him back, nestling my face in the crook of his neck and just breathing him in.

I was whole again. I absolutely hated that fact that I had been missing this part of me since I left. I hated that he had control of my heart, still, even after months of trying to forget him.

I hated it, and yet I loved being with him now. I loved the feeling of his warm, hard body pressing against mine. I loved his big arms wrapping around me, holding me. I loved the sweet little breaths he was breathing by my ear. I loved feeling his heart beat steady on my chest.

I loved him. I fucking *loved* him.

His strong hands ran up my back, rubbing my shoulders briefly before he held my head, combing his fingers in my hair. I was coming undone.

I had no clue why I was doing this to myself, but it just felt so right. That was the problem with Ben and me. Even when it was wrong, it felt right. I couldn't convince myself it was bad when it felt so damn good.

Ben pulled back just enough to trail his lips gently along my jaw. My cock stiffened, but I closed my eyes and squeezed them shut, trying hard to pretend I didn't want him. A tear slipped out of my eye and I subtly wiped it on him.

His lips were still going, brushing my cheek, dangerously close to my mouth. I physically *needed* to kiss him. My body needed to remember how good it felt when our lips touched. I was like a smoker who had quit for years and was going in for that one cigarette. The one that would break me.

Or maybe just a quick peck... Like a nicotine patch. A quick fix to ease my mind and body...

No, stop it, Harper. This is very bad. Look how far you've come? And you're just going to go right back, just like that?? You're stronger than this!

"Ben..." I hummed, my voice barely scraping from inside my dry throat. "Don't..."

"Don't what...?" he spoke a soft breath, his hand finding my jaw so he could hold me in place.

"We can't..." I commanded my body to stay still and not grab his face and make him fucking mine like I wanted to.

"Just a little..." he whimpered, his perfectly curved lips moving on my face when he spoke, inching closer and closer to where we both wanted them. "Please..."

Fuck... I love when he begs. He's such a damn control freak, when he says please I just want every part of him all over me.

"Don't say that..." my lips trembled, and I could feel his erection as he pressed his hips into mine. "You know it makes me crazy when you beg..."

"Baby, I've missed you so bad, though," he admitted softly with a shiver. "Just one kiss, *please*, baby. I'm dying for it..."

"Fuck me..." I panted as he slowly and gently brushed his lips over mine. He moaned, and my dick throbbed against his.

My cock was rock-solid already and for some reason it made me angry.

He had to know how much he had hurt me; how much I had been suffering without him. I didn't doubt that he was suffering, too. Especially after the way I left things on Christmas Eve. But it was his fault. He should have been suffering. I gave him my heart, offered it up on a silver platter, and he turned me down. He needed to feel that pain; the repercussions of his actions.

I tugged away from him and he opened his eyes, giving me a look of rejection and sorrow.

"Ben, you can't just come waltzing back into my life after everything that happened and think we're just going to..." I waved my hand in the air between us, and he took a visible breath, nodding slowly.

"I'm sorry..." he murmured, biting his lip, glancing at his shoes. Then he looked back up at me, his eyes becoming much more severe. "Ryan, I know I apologized to you already. But I'll apologize a million more times if that's what it takes. I fucked up... I fucked up royally, but you have to forgive me."

"I *have to?*" I gasped, astounded by what he was saying.

"Yea... yes," he nodded. "You have to. Because I was scared. I'm human, Ryan. Humans make mistakes. You can't hold it against me forever. And I know, you moved here to get a fresh start and find yourself and figure it all out, but I know you're miserable without me and Jess. Because we're miserable without you."

He paused and stared at me, his chest moving up and down with nervous breaths. He watched my face closely, likely to see if I would fight him, or if I wanted him to keep going.

And just that one look made me fall even more in love with him than I knew I could.

He was changing, for me. He wasn't trying to control me anymore. He didn't want to *have* me; he wanted to be *with* me.

My eyes sparkled a little, and I gave him a subtle nod. Just enough to let him know to keep going.

"Ryan, I can't wait to hear all about what you've been doing here," he murmured. "I'm sure it's been fun and exciting and new. You're so perfect, and anywhere you go will be perfect. But, baby, we need you. I need you... Jess needs you..."

His voice trailed off, and he took my hand, our fingers instinctively threading together. It just happened naturally, and it felt phenomenal.

"There's another reason I came to see you..." he whispered, and all my muscles tensed. He looked so serious, it was freaking me out. "I need to tell you something. And it's going to completely change everything. So before I do, I need..."

He stopped talking again and this time his brow furrowed, and he looked almost pained. I was praying, down to my core, that everything was okay. That there wasn't something wrong with him... Or Jess.

Oh God, please let them be okay. If they're like, sick or something, I won't be able to handle it.

The impending seriousness of whatever he had to say lit a fire inside me. I needed him to know that whatever he was about to say, I was there. That I would always love him, no matter what.

I grasped his jaw with my fingers and tugged his lips to mine, kissing him soft and impatient. We both groaned into each other's mouths, and Ben instantly parted his lips, sliding his tongue inside to meet mine.

"Fuck, Ben..." I whimpered, kissing him over and over, tugging him by his hair.

"Ryan..." he panted, running his hands over my chest and stomach, gripping my waist. "I... Mmm... baby, I..."

"I'm here, Ben," I breathed, sucking his tasty pouted bottom lip while he struggled for the courage to say what I knew he wanted to say. "Tell me..."

"I love you," he said and then he groaned, his whole body trembling, like he'd just been freed from some invisible chains. "Oh my God, I love you, Ryan."

My dick was so hard it had its own pulse. I pulled him as close to me as possible while I sucked his mouth everywhere, sweeping my tongue over his.

"I love you, Ben," I gasped, and he moaned again, grinding his hard body on mine. "You know I've loved you this whole time..."

"Yes... *yes*, I know," he mewled. "I have, too. I fell so in love with you Ryan... Baby, I'm so sorry I was afraid. I promise I'll never hurt you again. Just come home."

He was pleading with me, in his tone and he actions. He wanted me back so bad, I could feel it.

But it was getting so real so fast. I moved. I transferred schools, mid-semester, which was basically unheard of. I'd been doing great in Boston, and I liked it there. I couldn't just up and move back to New Mexico because he wanted me to. Just because he loved me.

Holy fuck, we're in love. Oh my God... I think I have a man again. And a woman!

Wait, what about Jess? Is she onboard with this, too? Why didn't she come with him?

No, this is crazy. I can't move back. I need to be here for the internship, and school. I need to finish what I started. I can't just flake out on everything because I'm in a relationship. Maybe we could do long-distance for a little bit... Just for another year until I pass the bar.

But wait, then I can only practice law in the state where I passed the bar. Maybe Ben and Jessica would move to Boston to be with me...?

No, Ben has his company out there. Plus, Hailey. Oh my God, this sucks. We just got back together and already we have to break-up again!

I think Ben could sense my sudden hesitations, and he forced himself to stop kissing me, though it was seriously like work, for both of us. I was so hot for him, I could barely breathe. My entire body was burning out of pent-up lust and sexual tension.

Sure, I'd hooked up with a few people since I'd been out there, but none of them even scratched the surface of what it was like with Ben, Jess and me. It wasn't even on my radar.

Ben rested his forehead on mine, running his fingers over my chest, tracing the curves of my muscles, slowly, tantalizingly; teasing my skin with his gentle touch.

"I fucking missed you so bad..." he whispered, cocking his head to the side as he watched my mouth.

"Me, too..." I breathed, the aggressive outline of my hard-on super visible through my gray sweatpants.

"I never stopped thinking about you," he went on, his tone so needy and full of desire. "Not for a minute. I dreamt about what would happen if I got you back..."

"Show me..." I begged, flicking my hips against his. Just that one touch of my hardened cock on his crotch sent a jolt of electricity across my body. "Fuck, baby I need you."

"Ryan..." he gulped, shaking his head slowly. "What I have to tell you... It's very serious. It's going to be intense. I need to know that you're ready..."

The fear set my teeth on edge. I was so scared; I didn't know how to react. I pulled back and watched his face for some inclination as to what he was getting at. But I couldn't read him.

His face was serious, but his eyes were still hooded with his obvious arousal. I breathed out hard and ran my hands through my hair.

"You're scaring the shit out of me..." I grumbled. He said nothing, just nodded. "This is already so overwhelming. I just need a second to think."

"Okay, baby. Take as much time as you need," he hummed. "I know I just barged in on you and shook everything up. I mean, it looks like you were about to eat..." He paused and glanced at my plate of mushy pie and melted ice cream. "Whatever that is..."

I laughed and shook my head. "It *was* homemade blueberry pie and ice cream, but now it's all melted."

He grinned wide and pulled out the chair. "Well, don't let me stop you. You're probably starving. Eat, baby. I can wait."

"You're being unnecessarily sweet," I grunted, sitting down in the chair. "It's freaking me out."

"Sorry," he smiled, a devastatingly gorgeous smile, and leaned up against the table. "You want me to be mean?"

"Mm... No. Not *mean*," I replied, digging my spoon into the pie and ice cream mixture, then slipping it into my mouth. Even all melted together it was completely delicious. "Just Bossy Ben. I love you exactly the way you are. All your flaws and imperfections and quirks that just make you so fucking perfect."

He pouted down at me. "I love you so much."

I took another bite, trying hard to stifle my out-of-control smile.

"I can't believe you're here," I told him. "I feel like I'm in a dream."

"Me, too," he crooned, watching me carefully. "Boston is beautiful. I wish I could spend more time here."

"How long are you staying?" I asked, a knot growing in my stomach, which was making it hard to enjoy my yummy treat.

He gazed at me for a moment before responding. "Until I convince you to come home."

"Ben, I just..." I shook my head. "I have a whole thing going on here. I can't just up and leave-"

"Hold that thought," he cut me off, moving closer to where I was sitting. Then he leaned in. "Can I try a bite?"

I gaped up at him with wide eyes, my pulse rocking inside me. I nodded slowly and scooped some pie and melted ice cream on the spoon, then lifted it to his lips. He kept his gaze on mine as he opened his mouth and took the bite, so slow, sucking the spoon before tugging his lips off.

"Mmm..." he murmured, licking his lips. "That's really good."

Okay... I think maybe the serious conversation can wait.

I stood up slowly before him and he eyed me, curious and wanting.

"You want more?" I raised my brow, and he hummed.

"Yes, please," he whispered, doing that pleading, submissive thing

I loved. It was like he knew the perfect combination of bossy Ben and needy Ben that could make me wild.

And I was ready. I had been waiting six long *hard* months for this moment, which I wasn't sure would ever happen again. I had never felt so wound-up in my whole life.

Ben grabbed my waist and turned me so I was leaning my butt up against the table. He took the spoon and dunked it into the melted vanilla ice cream, then stood before me, his big body in between my parted thighs, and ran the spoon quickly across my bottom lip.

I gasped, and he grinned, moving in slowly and extending his tongue, gliding it over my lip, licking off the ice cream. I hummed and couldn't help myself. I slipped my tongue out to graze his, tasting the sweetness.

"Baby..." he groaned then moved back, blinking slowly.

He dipped the spoon into the ice cream again, this time making a trail of vanilla down my throat, onto the top of my chest. My heart was hammering inside me as he leaned in and began licking, kissing and sucking the ice cream off my skin.

I was basically scorching, gripping the edge of the table with my hands as I watched him plant kisses all over my neck, grinding his crotch on mine so I could feel how hard he was.

The spoon went back in for more, and this time he slid it across my chest, on my pecs and over my nipples. Before continuing with his little game, he tugged his shirt over his head, tossing it onto the floor. Then his mouth was immediately on me, licking, his warm tongue lapping up the ice cream, covering my nipples with his lips and sucking on them nice and hard.

"Oh God, Ben..." I groaned, reaching out to hold his waist.

He did the ice cream thing again, this time running the spoon down my abs and my happy trail, onto my pelvis, right up to the waist of my pants. His mouth went to town, his soft lips all over me, making me weak, the anticipation building from his slow descent down my body.

He finally yanked my pants down–I was going commando–until my erection popped out, ready for action. He glanced up at me and raised his brow in that sexy, cocky Ben way that caused my dick to flinch in front of his face.

"Mmm... Ryan, you have no idea how badly I wanted this..." he murmured, and I bit my lip, watching him take a spoonful of melted ice cream and drizzle it all over my solid flesh.

The ice cream ran down the sides of my shaft and he quickly caught it with his tongue, licking up and down, sucking and kissing on my throbbing cock.

"Ben," I gasped, and he teased under the head of my dick with his tongue until I flinched. "I missed your mouth..."

"I missed sucking your big juicy dick," he growled, sealing his lips over me as he worked me over, slowly at first, then picking up the pace.

I moaned, holding his jaw while he moved his mouth up and down, sucking me down his throat. His eyes stayed on mine the whole time while he blew me until I could barely stand up anymore. I had gotten head a couple times over the last six months, but Ben completely destroyed anyone whose mouth had ever worked on my cock. He was so fucking perfect at everything he did to me. And I knew it was because I loved him.

And he loved me.

The thought had my orgasm coming on, so I stopped him fast, though he didn't seem to want to stop. I stood him up and undid his pants, spinning him so he was leaning on the table. And then I shoved him back until he was sitting on the edge, legs spread with me in between.

"My turn," I whispered, giving him a fully devious look. He swallowed visibly, and I was so ready to play with my man.

I used the ice cream to get him worked up, like he did to me, dripping it all over his gloriously muscular body, kissing him everywhere I could reach, while grinding my cock on him, the friction threatening to unravel me.

When we were both panting and sticky, I took his pants and boxers off, then fully removed my sweatpants and pushed him further up on the table. He gasped and leaned back, allowing me to spread his legs and suck his dick.

I savored every single second he was in my mouth; every inch of him pushing down my throat until I couldn't breathe. I sucked hard, up and down his length, relaxing my jaw to fit his girth. It was unbelievable how much bigger he seemed since I hadn't been with him in six months. It was like his dick grew by inches in length and width while we were apart, which I knew wasn't true. But I had just missed him so bad. I missed his perfect cock, in all its glory.

I moved my kisses onto his balls, and he shuddered before me, his broad chest heaving up and down as he panted out my name. Then I went for his ass.

"Uhh... Ryan... fuck yes, baby..." he trembled as I spread him open and licked him over and over. I shoved my tongue inside him and felt his dick flinching in my hand.

I grinned, kissing his cheeks. "You like that?"

"Yes..." he groaned, his balls tightening. "God, don't make me come yet. I want you inside me."

"Fuck..." I hissed, my dick twinging out some arousal. I stood up and stroked with the slickness, spreading his legs wider and pressing my head into him.

He looked up at me, so fucking gorgeous with his cheeks flushed and his eyelids drooping. I had never wanted anything as badly as I wanted to love his body with mine.

"Take me, Ryan," he gasped. "Make me yours."

"You are so mine, baby," I growled and forced my thick cock inside him.

He was tight as hell, obviously not having done this in a while, so I rubbed up on his ass and hips, watching as he visibly relaxed for me. Then I pushed again, and he let me in, the head of my cock bursting through his entrance.

"Ryan! Oh my... *God...*" he drawled, his eyes rolling back as I continued to thrust, feeding myself inside him, deeper and deeper.

I watched my dick disappear inside his ass and it was wholly fantastic. I couldn't even control my movements. I was like a machine, dedicated to reaching the furthest depths of him that no one else ever had.

I pulled back and drove in, more, deeper, harder; giving him all of me, fucking him on the kitchen table and not giving one single fuck about anything in the world but us.

I moved over his body, touching him everywhere, kissing his lips, his jaw, his neck, holding his hips, his waist, his hands. I just couldn't get enough. I wanted so much, and I was only one person.

I stroked my cock in between his legs, deep in his behind, pumping into him over and over, the table creaking beneath us. Ben was crying out all kinds of words and moans and grunts, fisting his hand around his massive erection while I fucked him with everything I had.

"Ben... I fucking love you, baby..." I told him, balls deep in his ass while we fucked like animals, hard and raw, sweating and growling out of pure pleasure.

"I love you, Ryan..." he drawled, his voice hoarse as he wrapped his long legs around me, holding me close. "You fuck me so fucking good..."

My hips were working overtime, thrusting into him with all my might, muscles constricting all over my body. I could feel the orgasm approaching, like I was standing at the edge, ready to fall.

"Fuck, baby... I'm gonna come in you..." I hummed, holding his face so I could watch him.

He groaned out loud, jerking his dick hard. "You're gonna make me come, Ryan..."

"Come for me, baby," I rasped, pounding into his ass, the sounds of us fucking bouncing off the walls.

"*Fuck...*" he cried, and I could feel him stiffening. He was right there with me.

"Baby, look at me," I commanded, and he forced his eyes open. "Let me see you."

He whimpered, pressing his lips together, struggling to keep his eyes open as he came, his big, thick cock shooting his climax all over his abs.

"Ryan!" he gasped, the look on his beautiful face pulling me with him. I let go and started coming, my cock exploding like a damn rocket, pouring my orgasm deep inside him.

"Ben... holy fuck, baby... Yes!" I tremored, holding him in my arms while our bodies rocked together, both of us panting and gasping for air.

"Oh fuck, I fucking love you..." Ben hummed, pulling my face to his, kissing my lips softly.

"I love you so fucking much, Ben," I croaked, sliding my tongue between his lips.

We kissed for a few minutes while we came down from our high, and I could barely even process what had just happened.

Ben was here. He came to get me, because he loved me.

He was mine, and I was his.

And we just fucked on my aunt's kitchen table.

Wow... Jesus. Sorry, Auntie. Remind me to clean this before someone eats here.

Ben started fidgeting, and I pulled out of him quick, then helped him get up.

"Ow, fuck," he grunted through a pained chuckle. "Don't you have a bed?" He asked, raising his brow.

I gave him an apologetic laugh. "I'm sorry, baby. I got swept up in the moment."

"Mmm... me, too," he grinned, kissing me softly.

"You wanna go take a shower?" I asked, and he nodded with enthusiasm.

"Yea, please. I have ice cream all over me," he smirked, wiggling his eyebrows.

"Remind me to always have our fridge stocked with ice cream," I murmured with a grin, but it slipped away when I realized what I'd said.

Ben's face grew serious, and he watched me closely.

"Baby, we need to talk," he breathed.

"Okay... let's just clean up first," I grumbled, deliberately ignoring the subject, and brought him into the bathroom.

We took our time showering. It was one of my favorite things to do with Ben. Ever since that first time, it had become our little ritual. I cherished these moments and had been fully aware of how much I missed them when I didn't have him.

We played around in the shower, washing each other's hair, kissing and touching and being so cute my heart was sure to burst. Then we finally got out and wrapped towels around our waists, stumbling around my room, completely love-drunk on one another.

"Did you even bring a bag or anything?" I asked him, pulling out some pajama pants for both of us.

"No," he scoffed. "How presumptuous would that be? I come to beg you to take me back, but I show up with an overnight bag..." He chuckled, and I laughed.

"You have a point, baby," I grinned, and he bit his lip.

Ben put on his pajamas and sat on the edge of my bed, watching me closely. When I looked over at him, he patted the mattress, signaling for me to sit next to him, which I did, even though my heart was now beating a mile a minute.

I knew he wanted to talk about whatever serious shit he needed to tell me, and I was dreading it. I didn't want to come down from this high, but I had a feeling whatever he was about to say would definitely do just that.

He turned to face me and took my hands in his.

"Baby, I'm going to tell you something," he whispered, his eyes stuck on mine. "I want you to process it first, and then we can talk, okay?"

"Ben, you are really just... terrifying me," I whimpered, my teeth almost chattering.

"It's sort of scary..." he nodded. "But just hear me out..."

I held my breath, and suddenly time slowed down around us. It was like we were under water or something.

Ben's blue irises shined into me, and I was so scared I couldn't move.

But then the corner of his mouth quirked up into a hesitant little smile, and my brow furrowed.

"Jess is pregnant."

My eyes were so wide as I stared at Ben. I don't think I had blinked in minutes.

He was gazing back at me, saying nothing, patiently waiting for me to process what he had just told me.

I was trying to process it... But I didn't know how.

I was completely bewildered; baffled, befuddled. God damn fucking *shocked.*

The first thing to move in the room, other than my heaving chest, was Ben's head. He cocked it to the side as he stared at me, raising his brows as if he wanted me to speak. But I still couldn't. I had no idea what to say.

After a few more moments of puzzled silence, I finally opened my mouth to respond. And it still took me a minute.

"Your wife is... pregnant...?" I huffed, my voice so quiet it was like a squeak from inside my throat.

Ben nodded, and an adorable, excited little grin showed up on his lips before he tugged the bottom between his teeth.

"Jessica is... *pregnant...*" I gasped the word again, taking a deep breath and holding it in.

"Mhm," he grunted, nodding once more. He was watching my face very carefully, giving me a look that I really couldn't place.

"Oh my God, Ben," I shook my head over and over, my wide eyes set on his. "Congratulations. That's... incredible."

He smiled big then squinted at me. "You think?"

"Yea! Of course," I cheered. "You wanted this, didn't you?"

He nodded slowly, his eyes sliding down to our joined hands as he ran his thumbs over my knuckles.

"It was a surprise," he whispered. "I mean, unexpected... We weren't planning it..."

The look on his face was one of the sweetest things I had ever witnessed. He was so obviously happy; nervous and excited. The look of a father-to-be. It was so cute, I wouldn't have been able to look away if I tried.

"Yea, but still..." I went on. "You always said you wanted another baby."

"It's not too late, is it?" he asked, his eyes landing on mine again as his forehead creased. "I'm not like... too old?"

I chuckled softly and shook my head, admonishing him with the movement.

"You can't be serious..." I scolded, and he grinned. "Ben, you're thirty-six. Thirty-six is not old. Some people have their first kid when they're forty."

He stared at me again for a while, saying nothing. The look on his face was making me slightly uneasy. I wasn't really sure why, but I felt like there was something else he needed to say.

A knot formed in my gut and I gulped. *Oh, fuck... I know what this is.*

How could we keep seeing each other when there was a baby in the picture? It wouldn't make any sense.

That was why he'd come here. To have one last amazing night with me before we had to say goodbye forever. My chest was already starting to ache all over again.

But then I paused. *Wait... Why would he have asked me to come home then? If he was telling me goodbye... Why would he go on about how he and Jess needed me?*

Ben obviously saw the wheels in my mind turning and he took a deep breath.

"Baby..." he spoke calmly, reaching out to brush my hair back with his fingers. "Do you understand what this means...?"

I gaped at him for a moment, then shook my head. I really didn't. *Maybe something to do with Hailey...? I wonder...*

"Does Hailey know yet?" I asked quietly, my mind racing.

He nodded. "Yes."

I am so confused.

"And... Jess is happy?" I asked carefully. He nodded again. "And healthy?"

"Yes," he smiled, that proud papa-to-be thing again that was making me swoon so hard, despite how lost I was. He was acting so strange. I just couldn't put my finger on it. "Healthy and happy... glowing. Craving an abundance of cheese and pickles. And doughnuts. My God, the doughnuts." He laughed softly and shook his head, which had me smiling. "I've never seen someone eat a whole half-dozen doughnuts by themselves in one sitting. It's wild."

I chuckled, a strange longing settling inside me. I had a sudden overwhelming urge to see Jess. I wanted to hug her and kiss her and touch her belly. I wanted to watch her waddle around and cry over nonsense. I felt so left out; it was making me uncomfortable.

"How far along is she?" I asked, my head swirling with all kinds of thoughts and feelings I couldn't gauge. It was always like this with us.

The blinding happiness and the severe depression. I was beginning to think there was no getting past it.

Ben swallowed visibly and gazed at me for a moment. He was very serious again. My stomach turned. *What the fuck is going on?!*

"Twenty-five weeks," he whispered.

I nodded then my head tilted to the side. *Wait...*

"Twenty-five...?" I squinted at him. He wasn't blinking.

"About six months..." he added, his voice so quiet. He raised his brows at me.

"She's six months pregnant already?" I huffed. "I can't believe you didn't tell me sooner..."

"We wanted to let you finish the semester," Ben replied, again so soft, it was like he was hesitating.

I froze, gaping at him like he had just sprouted two more heads.

"Why would you need to let me... finish the semester...?" I asked, my whole body suddenly trembling.

"Ryan, listen," Ben closed his eyes for a moment. "I know this is a surprise. And it's... confusing. I mean, that was the other reason we didn't tell you right away... Because we weren't sure what to think about it at first. But I mean, do the math, baby..."

He paused, squeezing my hand tight in his, those bright blue eyes shimmering at me.

I swallowed hard. *Do the math....?*

I started squirming around. Everything was moving in slow motion.

"Ben... please," I rumbled, quaking down to my core. "Just tell me what you're thinking..."

"What I'm thinking, Ryan, is that I'm going to be a father..." he whispered. "And so are you."

My heart thumped so hard it actually hurt. "Me...?"

Ben nodded, giving me an eager look.

"How? How the... What the...?" My breathing was unsteady.

"Baby, relax," he crooned, letting a little chuckle slip that was so sweet and so confusing, I felt like I might cry. "It's okay. I know it's scary."

"So you think..." I breathed, fumbling for words. "The baby could be mine?"

"Could be," he grinned, running his fingers along my jaw. "If you remember that week... It would be hard to know for sure without doing a paternity test. And you can't do that until after the baby is born. But Jess and I talked about it. And we agreed that we... don't really care. We don't want to know either way."

My head was spinning. I was definitely going to pass out.

"You don't?" I grunted.

"Nah," he shook his head. "We just want you to come home. Come back to where you belong. With us... and our baby."

At the rate my heart was beating, I would probably have a heart attack soon. I really needed to relax.

"Ben..." I huffed, "How the hell would that even work? I just don't see how..."

"Ryan, don't think about that right now," he stopped me, taking my face in his hands. "We'll figure it out. We'll find a way. What it all comes down to is that I love you, and Jess loves you. And you love us... right?"

I nodded. "Yes. I love you both so much."

"Good," he breathed out a sigh of relief and I laughed, feeling like a dam was about to burst. *Please don't cry. It'll be so embarrassing.* "So, what do you say? Will you come home? Come home and be a daddy..." He smiled so sweet, I was melting everywhere.

Without a single hesitation, I started nodding, repeatedly. Nonstop.

"Yes. Yes... oh my God... fuck, I'm gonna be a father," I whimpered, shaking all over.

Ben laughed softly and grabbed me hard, pulling me into his arms. "Yea, you are."

We hugged it out for a while. I honestly didn't even know how long we were just holding onto each other, breathing and reveling in the feelings; the excitement. My entire body was vibrating. This was such an insane moment.

I finally pulled back, gazing up at Ben while my thoughts whirled around all crazy and jumbled in my brain.

"Shit... The baby will be due right when I'm supposed to start school..." I whispered.

Ben chewed on his lower lip for a minute. Then I shook my head.

"Doesn't matter," I huffed. "I'll figure it out. I'm sure I can be a few days late, if it's for the birth of my..." My voice trailed off. "Do we know if it's a girl or a boy?"

Ben grinned. "I do. Jess wants it to be a surprise. She said if I tell her she'll chop me up into little pieces and feed me to a crocodile." I laughed out loud, and he chuckled. "She's incredibly severe when she's pregnant, so... that's something to look forward to."

"I'll be careful," I hummed, smirking.

"So... Do you want to know?" he asked, raising his brow. I thought on it for a minute.

"Not yet," I sighed. "I'll let you know."

"Okay... if you say so," he sang, giving away nothing. I squinted at him.

"I can probably guess," I murmured, running my hand down his firm chest.

"Oh yea? You think so, do you?" he rasped, a smug look on his sexy face that made me want to pounce on him.

"Mhm... You're not as sneaky as you like to think you are," I leaned in to kiss his neck softly.

"Show me what you got, kid," he rumbled, breathy from the heat surrounding us.

"Mmm... boy," I peeked up at his face. His expression was blank, just a faint little smirk playing on his lips. "Girl...?" He chuckled, still not revealing anything. "Dammit! Just tell me!"

"You wanna know or not?" he laughed.

"No, I don't," I hummed, excitement and nervousness coursing through my body. "Jess and I will be surprised, while control-freak Ben has all the answers."

He giggled and bit his lip, falling backward on the bed, tugging me on top of him. I giggled, straddling his waist and taking his hands in mine, holding them down on the bed while I kissed him over and over.

"Wait!" I interrupted our little make-out session with a startled gasp.

"What?" he asked, breathlessly.

"Jess is alone?" I gaped at him, worry covering my face.

Ben relaxed and laughed softly, shaking his head. "She's fine. Her sister is staying over until we get back."

"You keep saying *we* like I'm just going to show up with you and move into your house so we can be a dysfunctional little family..." I was letting my doubts and insecurities consume me.

"*We* will," he said with confidence. "Look, I know you're scared. I am too. And so is Jess. Actually, she seems much less worried than either of us... But it's going to be okay, baby. We'll find a way, together. Whatever we have to do... We'll make it work."

I gazed at him in dazed wonder. I didn't understand how what he was saying could possibly be true. With our friends and family... and Hailey. How could we ever explain to them that we were together? Raising a baby as a trio... How would they ever understand and accept it?

"Don't worry about what other people might think," he went on, reading my mind in that way which made me feel so connected to him; like we were meant to be, from the beginning of time. "If they can't accept it, fuck 'em. We don't need anyone other than *us*."

"What about Hailey...?" I whispered. Ben's face wavered for a moment, his Adam's apple bobbing in his sexy throat, sheeted in that delicious stubble I wanted to run my lips over.

"It's going to be hard..." he answered, breathing out slowly. "No one's saying it won't be... difficult. But in the end, I know she'll just want us to be happy."

"How do you know...?" I asked, unable to allow the same confidence he had to overcome my skepticism. Not yet. It made me feel like an asshole for not having as much faith as he did. But I was still reeling from everything that had happened in the last couple hours.

"I just know," he murmured, providing me assurance with his eyes and his deep, emphatic tone. "In my heart. She's my daughter... She'll come around."

I nodded slowly and watched his blue eyes as they glowed up at me in the low light of my bedroom. I leaned in, keeping my eyes on his until the last second, kissing him soft, causing us both to gasp.

We kissed for a while, writhing around in my bed, grinding on each other and touching everywhere, letting the love flow between us. It was such an incredible feeling.

I was whole again. He'd healed my heart.

And I was going to be a father.

I still can't believe it.

Hours later and we were still lying in bed, naked, beneath my blankets, quiet and sated. My heart was full. And so was Ben's. I could feel it.

I was lying on his chest, listening to it beat, gradually slowing down from the aggressive thumping it did when he was inside me. Now it was nothing more than a faint murmur, rapping gently against my face, which was resting on his firm pectoral muscle.

Ben's fingers were in my hair, toiling around while mine traced the divots in his abs, trying hard to restrain myself from touching his ticklish spot. I had never felt more content in my entire life.

In between all the sex and cuddling, we talked a lot. Ben wanted to hear all about every single thing I had done since I left New Mexico, and I obliged him, recanting the tale of my journey to the opposite coast. I told him all about school, my friends and my aunt, leaving out no details. Even when I tried to glaze over something, he stopped me and made me get specific. I even told him about the people I'd hooked up with then consoled him when he got all jealous and sullen over it.

We agreed that I would go home with him tomorrow, back to New Mexico. Back to Jessica... Our pregnant wife. Well... Ben's wife. My girlfriend, I guess. We were still working out the terminology.

But Ben promised me we would be an equal partnership. No more jealousy, or animosity. No more controlling or hiding. It wasn't a married couple plus me anymore. We were a trio. A trilogy. The ultimate trifecta.

"Like the original Star Wars," Ben grinned, trailing his fingers along my back while we named famous trios.

"Or the Three Stooges?" I laughed, and he snickered. "The Three Musketeers."

"Snap, Crackle and Pop..." he mumbled and I gasped.

"Oh my God, we should totally name the baby Pop," I giggled.

"What about Crackle?" Ben teased, and I could hear him rolling his eyes, which made me laugh again.

"Oh yea, but once the baby is born, it'll be four of us," I pointed out. "Plus, Hailey..."

"Mmm... you're right," he sighed. "Five of us could be the Backstreet Boys." I laughed out loud and felt his body rumbling through his laughter.

"If you name all five Backstreet Boys right now, I'll give you a blowie," I turned my face up to him and smirked.

He squinted at me, seemingly deep in thought which made me giggle again.

"Nick, AJ... Brian...?" he grunted, really thinking hard. I nodded. "Um... fuck. Justin?"

"Nooo, Justin is from 'NSync," I shook my head and he pouted.

"Dammit! Jess totally would have gotten that," he huffed.

"Too bad. No blowie for you," I sneered, and he grinned, flicking his hips against mine.

"I'm sure I could get you to do it anyway..." he murmured, giving me a devious look.

"Is that so?" I moved up to kiss his neck, slow and soft, because he just smelled so damn good right there.

"Mhmmm... You are mine, after all."

"Am I yours, *Mr. Lockwood*?" I purred onto his sweet flesh.

"Oh yea." His voice was so deep and growly I could feel it on my lips. "All mine and Jess's."

"I don't see a ring on this finger," I teased, nipping his clavicle.

"We could fix that..." he whispered, and I paused, slowly pulling back to gaze up at him.

"Yea?" I raised my eyebrow. "Is that legal?"

He laughed out loud and bit his lip. That laugh, that smile... They were killing me softly, Lauren Hill style.

"Hmmm... not sure," he shrugged, holding my jaw with his long fingers. "But I don't need a government to tell me what's real and what's not. You could be Mr. Lockwood... if you want."

My stomach flipped. But then I narrowed my gaze at him. "Or you could be Mr. Harper..."

He laughed again. "Good point. Why don't you be Ryan Harper Lockwood, and I'll be Ben Lockwood Harper?"

I grinned at how fucking sweet he was. It was almost unbearable.

"And Jess could be Jessica Lockwood Harper, too?"

"Hell yea," he chirped, giving me a bright smile. "Why the fuck not?! We call the shots, baby. It's our world, we can do whatever we want."

I kissed his lips gently. "We need to start thinking of baby names..."

"Oh, Jess already has a list," he sighed. "She wants us all to sit down together to go over it." We both chuckled together.

"So I guess she was optimistic about me coming home with you...?" I asked, watching his eyes.

"She just really wants you back, baby," he replied, stroking my face tenderly. "We both do. And she knew once you found out about the baby you wouldn't want to miss a single moment."

"Well, yea. I already missed so much..." I huffed, slightly bummed by this. "Six months of doctor appointments and sonograms and Lamaze classes... Have you built any baby furniture yet?!"

Ben laughed softly and shook his head. "No. That's all you, Daddy."

My dick flinched against his waist. "My God, don't start that... We won't be leaving this bed anytime soon." He chuckled deviously and kissed my lips.

"Oh, and we haven't done any Lamaze classes yet," he told me, his breath warm on my mouth. "I think that's next month. Jess will give you the schedule."

I wasn't sure if he was kidding, but I hoped not. I wanted to do everything with them. I didn't want to miss one more second of this pregnancy.

A knock on my door startled me out of my baby-bubble, and I rolled off of Ben, scrambling to get my clothes.

"Kiddo, you alright in there?" my aunt called through the door.

I started dressing frantically while Ben laughed at me, giving me a look like I was insane.

"Yea! I'm fine, I just... have a friend over," I shouted my response then cringed and shook my head. "Why is that what I would choose to say?" I muttered to Ben who shrugged, still laughing.

"Are you allowed to have *friends* over?" he snickered, lying back, looking all hot and sexy and fucking beautiful, naked in my bed with the blanket just barely covering his worn-out dick.

"Yea, of course," I ran my fingers through my hair. "I just have to tell her I'm leaving... I'm nervous."

Ben got up slowly, stretching his arms behind his back. "I'll help you."

"Thanks, baby."

We finished getting dressed and straightening ourselves up. I took a deep breath before opening my bedroom door, mentally preparing myself for what I was sure would be an awkward conversation.

Ben and I shuffled out of the room and down the hall toward where my aunt was sitting, on the living room couch, smoking a cigarette. Her eyes flicked between Ben and me, and it was clear she was trying to remain impassive, but her head looked like it might explode.

"Hey, kiddo," she rasped, taking another drag of her cigarette, her eyes now stuck on Ben. "You doin okay?"

"Mhm," I nodded quickly, swallowing hard. "Um... Auntie, this is Ben." I waved my hand in front of Ben like a fucking magician or something, then glanced at him. "Ben, this is my aunt Jill."

Ben smiled politely, looking every bit the delicious stud-muffin he was.

"Nice to meet you... again," he placed his hand on my shoulder, squeezing it gently.

My aunt's face was still frozen.

"Ben's from back home..." I muttered, trying to figure out how to explain what the hell was going on. "New Mexico. He came to see me..."

"Came all the way across the country?" Jill asked, raising her brows to the heavens. "Must have been important."

"It was," Ben nodded, his tone soft and sweet. "I had to come get my man back."

He smiled at me and I felt my heart skip in my chest. But then I immediately peeked over at my aunt, waiting for her to start asking me how long I'd been gay. I knew it was coming. *Any second now...*

"Well... excuse me if it's not any of my business, but you are in my house," Jill started, puffing on her cigarette once more. "I can see that wedding ring on your finger... I just hope you're not getting my nephew mixed up in anything he shouldn't be. He's a good boy, as I'm sure you know."

My mouth dropped open as I stared at my aunt. She was being protective. I was a little shocked. I hadn't expected that.

"Um, yea... So, I am married," Ben started, fumbling for his words. "It's sort of an... interesting situation..." He shot me a look and raised his brows, silently asking if I wanted to tell my aunt about our relationship status.

I shrugged and nodded. No better time than the present.

I'll have to get used to this, anyway...

"Oh, I'm sure it's complicated," Jill rolled her eyes. "That's what all married men say."

"No, Auntie, it's not like that," I stepped over and sat down next to her on the couch. "Look, I need to tell you something." I glanced down at my lap and took a deep breath. "I'm going to be a father."

My eyes slid back up to my aunt's and she looked thoroughly baffled.

"A father...?" she asked, her brows raised so high they were a part of her hairline.

"Yea," I smiled at Ben and nodded him over. He strolled casually to the couch and took a seat next to me, grabbing my hand in his. "We're having a baby."

Jill was silent for a moment, staring at me with her jaw agape. She finally blinked a few times and shook her head.

"Correct me if I'm wrong, but last I checked neither of you have the proper parts to do that," she grunted, gaping at us like we were insane. "Unless... oh boy. I'm so sorry. Are you one of them transgenders?" She looked at Ben with apologetic regret all over her face. "If so, I have to say, you've done a hell of a job. You look all man to me."

I turned my head slowly, wide eyes giving Ben a look while he laughed under his breath.

"No... Auntie..." I giggled, shaking my head. "Ben's not a woman. I mean... neither of us are." I paused to laugh some more.

"Oh..." she sighed and shook her head. "Okay. So you're gonna adopt then? Doesn't that take a while?"

Ben was still chuckling to my left, and it was so cute it was making this horribly uncomfortable conversation much easier to bear.

"Nope... not quite that either," I huffed and shifted in my seat. "Auntie, Ben's married to a woman. Her name is Jessica... and *she's* pregnant.*" I paused and let her absorb this, yet kept on with my explanation before she could throw anymore crazy premature theories at me. "You see, Jessica, Ben and me... we've been... together. The three of us."

I raised my brows at her, waiting for her to process what I was saying. She still looked pretty confused, but she nodded slowly.

"We had a falling out, and that's why I moved here," I kept going, "But now that Jess is pregnant, I have to go home. I need to be with my family... and our baby."

"Wow, kiddo..." Jill breathed, flopping back in her chair. I glanced at her cigarette, which had a really long ash, like those old ladies at casinos. She put it out in the ashtray, then gazed at me. "You're sure this is what you want?"

"Yea," I nodded, looking to Ben for a moment, smiling and squeezing his hand. "I'm in love with them, Auntie. I have been for a while. And I so appreciate you letting me move out here and paying for everything... You've been a saint. You have helped me more than my own mother ever has..."

I stopped before I could get choked up, and I felt Ben's hand gently caressing my back. I loved having him there, supporting me. It finally felt like we were in a *real* relationship. Talking to people, out in the open. Comforting each other and backing each other up. This was all I had been dreaming about since I moved away; all I had been trying like hell to convince myself I didn't want, though it was no use. There was no lying to my heart.

"Ryan, I love you," Jill said, running her fingers along my cheek. "You're like the son I never had, you know that. All I want is for you to be happy. And if being with this guy and his wife, raising a baby with them will do that, then I say go for it."

I breathed out hard and smiled, showing her just how appreciative I was with my eyes. I felt Ben relax by my side, and I thought it was so sweet that he was actually nervous about this. It wasn't like he was meeting my parents or anything... *Though I suppose, in a way, it kind of is.*

"Now, I want you to promise you'll stay in school, though," Jill demanded, giving me a stern look. "Or at the very least, follow your dreams. Relationships are all well and good. And yes, kids can take up a lot of time. But you need to have something else to keep you determined. Something else to fill your cup. Don't let your happiness rely on other people."

Wow... That's wise.

I nodded slowly, giving my aunt a loving smile. She was right. Whatever ended up happening, I needed to find what truly made me happy, outside of my relationship with Ben and Jess, and our baby. If it was being a lawyer, I could transfer back to UNM, although they might hate me a little for all this back and forth.

And if it wasn't meant to be, then maybe I could find something else...

But I knew my aunt was right. And so was Ben. The world was definitely ours. Whatever I wanted to do, I could make it happen. Finally, my heart was restored. I felt invincible.

"That's some great advice, Jill," Ben's voice rasped from beside me and I glanced over at him. He smiled, and I couldn't resist. I just had to kiss him.

My lips locked with my man's until I suddenly flinched and pulled back.

Oh fuck, the table...

"Um, Auntie, you weren't at the kitchen table at all when you came home, were you?" I asked nervously, standing up quick.

"No... not yet," she replied, hesitantly, narrowing her gaze at me in suspicion. "But I was about to have some of that pie..."

"Oh okay! No, that's great!" I stuttered, scampering toward the kitchen, ransacking the cabinets for Lysol. "I just need to um... fix... something. Do we have any cleaning spray?"

I heard Ben laugh out loud, and I bit my lip.

Ben and I were sitting at the airport, by our gate, waiting for the flight to New Mexico to be called.

It was official. I was moving back home.

Well, not *exactly*.

I wouldn't be going back to Albuquerque. I was moving into my *new* home. Ben and Jess's house in Tularosa.

We still weren't sure exactly how everything would work out. The home I was moving into was Hailey's home, too. And she still didn't know that I was dating her parents. And that I would be a co-parent to her new little baby brother or sister.

Hailey had her own apartment by school-she wasn't living in the dorms-so she never moved home for summer break. But still... If she wanted to come home to see her pregnant mother, which was a likely possibility, then she would be coming home to a big surprise.

The whole situation was still very overwhelming and complicated. My mind had been running like crazy since Ben showed up yesterday and told me I was going to be a father.

And he still didn't have answers to half my questions, but I couldn't be mad at him. I was just so damn happy to be back with him. I was nervous, and more scared than I had been in as long as I could remember.

But I was also excited. I was happy and looking forward to the future.

We had called Jess last night, while packing up my stuff. She was so excited to hear from me-to find out I was coming home-that she burst into tears on the phone. I'd be lying if I said I didn't tear up a little myself. And so did Ben.

It was just such a wonderful, amazing, perfect time for the three of us. Just hearing her voice had reaffirmed all the feelings in my gut.

I needed to be home with her. I needed to be a part of her pregnancy. *And I need to build some baby furniture, dammit!*

Ben was on his phone, reading something while gripping my hand, methodically stroking his thumb over my knuckles. I was both calm and anxious at the same time. I always got a little nervous before flying. But mostly I just couldn't wait to get home to our woman. I was imagining what she looked like... how big her belly was; how much she would be glowing. I was so impatient; I was ready to run down onto the tarmac and help them get the plane ready myself.

"Ryan," Ben's firm, deep voice rumbled at me. I lifted my head in his direction. "Relax, baby. I can feel you shaking." He looked up from his phone and raised his brows at me in that sexy way that always made my stomach clench.

I breathed out hard and nodded quickly. "Sorry. I'm just... ready to get the fuck home. Like, how long does it take to fill a plane with gas or whatever they're doing out there??"

My knee was bouncing rapidly as I tapped my fingers on my bag. Ben chuckled and cocked his head to the side, giving me an adorable look.

"What?" I asked, my forehead creasing as I stared back at him.

"Do you know how much I love you?" he breathed, blinking at me slowly. A small smile tugged at my lips.

"I think so..." I murmured, my face heating a little out of timidity, and the fact that I wasn't exactly sure how much he loved me... Although, I liked to think I was starting to get it, since he'd flown all the way across the country to get me back.

Ben turned in his seat, tucking his phone into his pocket. He took both of my hands in his, those bright blue eyes set on mine, holding me in place. And suddenly, I wasn't moving anymore. I had fully stopped fidgeting and was completely still; hypnotized by the man of my dreams, who was gazing at me with a look I would have never expected was real until I experienced it for myself.

"You've changed my entire life, baby," he whispered, fully focused on me, and nothing else. "I used to think I had everything in the world figured out. I was in full control of my life... My marriage, my daughter, my house, my job... It was all perfectly structured and ordinary. And I thought it fit... which I guess it did. But deep inside my heart, tucked away in a place I would never let myself think about, I knew something was missing."

He paused and took a breath, watching me closely. I blinked at him.

"And then I met you. I didn't understand my feelings for you at first. They were so new, and different. So... unexpected. But after you left that first weekend, I realized it wasn't just an attraction, or some secret fantasy or whatever. I missed you... You, as a man. Not the sex, or your awesome body that makes me so hard I can't even think straight," he grinned, and I chuckled, biting my lip. "I missed being *with* you. And the way you made me feel just by being next to me. When you came to the hotel that night, in your car... I had never felt that before. I never knew that I had been missing something until I was back with you, and you were making me *whole.*"

He exhaled a sharp breath and finally broke our eye contact, glancing down at our joined hands.

"The guilt tripped me up for a while..." he murmured, swallowing visibly. "The guilt from lying to and betraying Hailey, and from sneaking around on Jess. That was the only thing that made me so confused. My feelings for you were always there, since the first day we met. You were a part of me, already. And I knew I had to do something so we could be together."

He stopped again, his eyes sliding back to meet mine. "My love for you is so... different than my love for Jessica. It's hard to explain. It's just a feeling, in my heart. Jess is like my rock. She grounds me and keeps me going. She's like my lifeline. If I didn't have her, I'm sure I wouldn't survive. She's a part of me. But *you*... you're the other part. The part that's so real, it's almost like we were made from the same stuff. The first time I kissed you, I felt like my soul was on fire. I've never felt something so strong before... shy of maybe the first time I held Hailey in my arms."

I nodded slowly at what he was saying. My heart was thumping so hard in my chest, I could feel it everywhere. I could barely believe what I was hearing... That someone loved me so much, and truly *felt* what I felt, down to his core.

"I can't wait to raise a child with you," Ben kept going, giving me the *love eyes*, so deep and full of everything I had ever wanted. "I can't wait to explore the world with you, and Jess. The three of us have something so special together, it's almost terrifying, because if anything ever took you two away from me, I'm sure I would die. You both are my heart and soul. That's how much I love you, Ryan Harper. You've made me... complete."

I sucked in a sharp breath and held onto it, afraid that I would really pass out this time.

Ben's face was so serious, it was making me tremble all over again. But now for a whole different reason. I loved him so much; I had experienced nothing like it before. I couldn't even understand how I'd been lucky enough to find not one, but two whole incredible humans to share my life with.

And now they were giving me the greatest give of all... A baby.

Ben's words filled me with the most thrilling sense of hope I'd ever felt. I couldn't wait to raise our child with him and Jess. And who knows? Maybe we wouldn't stop at one...

I grinned and bit my lip, reaching for Ben's face, tugging his lips to me so I could kiss him so freaking good.

Our lips touched, and he groaned softly, allowing me to part his and slide my tongue between them.

"I love you just as much, Benjamin Lockwood," I whispered in his mouth and he smiled. "You're everything I've always dreamed being in love could feel like."

He chuckled softly, kissing me harder, not giving the tiniest fuck on Earth who was watching us. When we finally pulled apart, we were breathless. And they were calling for first-class to board. So we needed to get our sappy-asses up and on the damn plane. *I need to get home and see the mother of my unborn child!*

Ben grabbed my bag before I could get to it, carrying it for me as we boarded our flight. I couldn't stop grinning to myself. I felt like such a corny loser, but it didn't matter. I had someone who loved me so much it made everything else in the world fade away.

We took or seats in first class—*yes, my man even bought us first-class tickets home. Am I fucking spoiled or what?* Ben let me sit by the window while he took care of the carry-on, then nestled up by my side, kissing my neck and being all sweet and sexy and perfect.

By the time we were in the air, we were cuddled up, watching *Shameless* on my iPad, when Ben flagged the flight attendant and asked her to bring us two glasses of champagne.

"We're celebrating," he crooned, showing off that million-dollar smile that made me beam with pride over the fact that *he* was *mine*.

The flight attendant smiled, her cheeks visibly flushing from the general hotness the dude sitting next to me and rushed off to get us our drinks. When she returned, she handed us each a glass, opening the mini bottle.

"What's the occasion?" she asked while pouring.

"We're having a baby," Ben hummed, glancing at me, blue eyes sparkling. I grinned and bit my lip.

"Oh my God! Congratulations!" she squealed, doing a little jump. "Your first?"

"My first," I answered, running my fingers along Ben's strong arm.

"Well, I'm very happy for you both," the flight attendant gave us a broad smile, then scurried away.

Ben and I raised our glasses to each other, smiling in satisfaction.

"Cheers... to the next step," he said, and we clinked.

Cheers to forever.

BEN'S EPILOGUE

I STEPPED OUT THROUGH THE WIDE-OPEN DOORS, stretching my arms behind my back as I took in the gorgeous view before me.

My bare feet guided me outside, past the infinity pool, past the large array of tropical trees and flowers, down to the edge of the deck. I gazed out over the most beautiful scenery I could never have dreamt up in a million years. I actually blinked a few times to check that I wasn't dreaming.

I was, in fact, awake, staring at the bluest ocean I'd ever seen; white sand, and large mountains in the distance; the sounds of birds and the water rolling in and out. I took the deepest breath and held it in, closing my eyes as the sun warmed my skin.

This, right here... This was true bliss.

Thailand was completely breathtaking. I couldn't have imagined a better place to really relax.

I walked around the deck for a few minutes, dipping my toes in the warm water of the pool that stretched all along the entire exterior of our suite. The resort was lavish and luxurious; modern and truly impressive. We had never seen anything like it.

None of the online brochures when booking this trip did it justice. It was a genuinely remarkable place.

Something caught my eye, and I turned to see movement from

behind the billowing sheer curtains to the bedroom. I smirked to myself as I slowly wandered back toward the doorway, my heart rate increasing with every step.

The giant California King bed, covered in all white linens of the highest thread-count known to man, was currently housing two heated and salacious bodies. I reentered the room and watched for a moment, licking my lips at the sight before me.

My pregnant wife, splayed out and naked, her giant belly golden and glistening from days in the sun; huge swollen tits moving up and down with her rapid breaths. And my undeniably gorgeous man, also naked; his glorious tanned skin a contrast to the whiteness of the sheets; muscular body on full display while he tucked his face in between my wife's thighs.

Jessica was humming. I could all but see her vibrating from where I was standing. And she was moaning out some of the sexiest noises I had ever heard a human being make. My eyes glided all over her naked frame, really cherishing the look of her body like that. She was a miracle; carrying our unborn baby and still managing to be the most beautiful and sultry woman I'd ever laid eyes on.

Then I looked to Ryan, and all those rippling muscles in his arms, shoulders, back... His delicious ass; so round and firm. He was such a *man*. A significant distinction from how much of a woman Jess was. I had the best of both worlds.

Luckiest guy on Earth, right fucking here.

I strolled casually over to the bed and ran my eager hands down Ryan's hips, grabbing his ass hard, yet gentle at the same time, making him grunt. My dick was inflating, becoming full and thick between my legs as the blood rushed below my waist.

I could barely believe it was possible to have this much sex in one span of time. But I had come to realize it was just the effect that Ryan, Jess and I had on one another. We'd been on vacation for three days and I had already lost count of how many times, and in how many different ways, we'd gotten each other off.

We were on our own private secluded island. An island on an island. It was mesmerizing.

I crawled into the giant bed with them and we continued to play, the three of us touching and kissing, panting and groaning... really just loving each other so much and so *hard*, it was almost unbearable.

I trailed my lips all over Ryan's neck and shoulders while I pushed my cock inside him and he cried out my name, right into Jessica's pussy as she clenched her thighs around his head and erupted into a graceful, staggering climax. Then her lips wrapped around Ryan's long, immaculately hardened cock, sucking him slow while I fucked him deep, both of us coming together in joint-ecstasy.

Hours later, we were all still lying in bed, playing and laughing; enjoying every second together. The three of us... We were everything.

I had planned this little getaway in secret, the day after I brought Ryan home from Boston. Jessica had been so excited to have him back, she was basically a big ball of emotions. After everything that had happened in those seven months leading up to that point, I really felt like we all needed a break.

We needed a vacation. And it needed to be exciting and different. And we needed to do it while Jess was still able to travel.

I picked the Dream Resort in Phuket, Thailand after reading an article about it in some travel magazine. I started seeing all these incredible pictures on Instagram and I knew it would be the perfect spot for a special, unique trip before the baby came. Plus, I wanted to find a place where we could have privacy, but also everything we could need or want, all in one magnificent spot.

The resort was huge. And it really did have it all, which was good because we couldn't exactly go anywhere else. It wasn't safe for Jess to be out wandering around in Thailand, but at that point we didn't need to. Everything we desired was right there.

By day five, I realized that the vacation harmony wasn't going anywhere. The three of us were having so much fun together, fully cherishing our alone time, like we were on a honeymoon or something.

And that gave me an idea.

Ryan was laying by the pool in some very fitted swim trunks that made him look shockingly good. We were relaxing that day after the slew of exciting activities from the day before... Boat ride, snorkeling, jet skiing–for Ryan and me. Unfortunately, Jess couldn't partake in that one, although she swore up and down she didn't mind.

I had just come back from a walk down by the shore to look for coconuts. Jess had a hankering. I stepped over to Ryan and straddled his waist on his chaise lounge. I couldn't see his eyes through his Ray Bans, but his smile was downright lethal.

"Don't burn," I whispered, leaning in close to his face to press a soft kiss on his bottom lip.

"Already sun blocked twice, *sir*," he murmured, smirking at me as I gave him a warning look.

"Where's Jessica?" I asked gently while running my hands up his bronzed, glistening torso.

"In the bath," he purred, yanking my hips down to his. I laughed and pulled away, attempting to stand back up. "Stay and play with me..." he pleaded, grabbing the waist of my shorts.

"Mmm... I'll be back in a minute," I pouted, kissing a trail from his jaw down his neck, listening to his uneven breaths. "I'm going to check on my wife real quick."

"She's fine, Ben," he huffed, giving me a patronizing smile.

I ignored him and pressed a chaste kiss on his lips before jumping off him and stammering inside the suite. I located Jess inside the bathroom. She was soaking her beautiful pregnant self in a massive Jacuzzi tub that was almost as big as our walk-in closet at home.

I meandered over and sat down on the edge next to where her head was, smiling at the cucumber slices covering her eyes.

"Did you find coconuts?" she asked, somehow knowing it was me without looking.

"Yup. Haven't cracked them open yet..." I replied, sliding my hand over her belly just beneath the water. "Found a mango, too."

"Mmmm..." she hummed, licking her lips.

"I want to ask you something," I rasped, my pulse instantly increasing out of nerves.

"Shoot," she grinned.

"These past five days have been the best of my life..." I started, watching my hand move in the water. "And I know you feel the same. Because you're my soulmate, and I've known you since we were young, stupid kids."

"This isn't a question..." she smirked, and I huffed a small, nervous laugh.

"We're not young, stupid kids anymore," I went on. "We're adults, and we own our lives, and I think we should seize the day, and live in every moment..."

"I agree with you," she replied, her voice soft and oozing relaxation.

I took a deep breath. "I want to ask Ryan to marry us."

Jess scooted up in the tub and removed the cucumbers from her eyes. She stared at me, hard, her eyes wide and sparkling.

"Wow..." she breathed.

I nodded. "Yea."

"That's really what you want?" she asked, her face brightening even more than its usual glow.

"Only if you want it, too," I tilted my head to the side.

"Of course I do," she smiled, a sweet, shy, gorgeous little thing. "Ben... Oh my God. That would be so great."

"You think?" I grinned, my brows knitting together.

"Yea!" she squealed, quietly, glancing at the door. "But we would have to do it here."

I gaped at her for a moment. "You mean... get married here?"

She nodded quickly. "It's not exactly legal." She giggled, and I huffed a knowing laugh. "But it doesn't matter. We could have a small ceremony here. Just the three of us. Well, the four of us." She beamed, rubbing her belly.

"Okay," I nodded along, feeling all the butterflies in my stomach. "I can go find someone to perform the ceremony tomorrow. Oh, and I'll find some rings." I paused and wiggled my brows at her. "This is so exciting."

"Yea it is!" she chirped. "When are you going to ask him?"

"Why do I have to ask him?" I pursed my lips.

"Because, you're the romantic," she muttered, biting her lip. I crinkled my nose at her, and she laughed. "I'll cosign whatever you say, I promise."

"Alright, cool," I said, and my mind started racing. "I'll ask him tonight."

"Fuckin a..." she whispered, her smile all but breaking her beautiful face. My eyes widened in excitement, then I leaned in and kissed her lips, gentle and slow.

I got up fast and darted out of the room, hearing Jess giggle behind me.

I was on a mission.

Roughly seven hours later we had just finished dinner, and I was so anxious I felt like I could fall down. I remembered such feelings from the night I proposed to Jess. And we were seventeen when that happened. Now, almost twenty-years later and I was going through the exact same thing, with Jess pregnant again. It was crazy how this was all working out.

The universe was truly baffling sometimes.

"Let's take a walk," Jess suggested, shooting me a look, likely trying to help me out because I was hesitating. I was so nervous, and I wasn't sure why. I knew Ryan would say yes...

Right?

"Sure," Ryan replied, smiling at Jess, getting up fast to help her stand from her chair. She was top-heavy, and it was getting harder for her to stand up on her own.

The three of us made our way down to the shore, walking along the illustrious teal water. It was so warm, we just had to put our toes in it. None of us had worn shoes since we arrived at the resort.

"Wow!" Ryan gasped, grabbing my hand. "Look at that!"

His face was aimed up at the sky, so I looked up to see what he was seeing.

It was the stars. They were so bright; lighting up the night sky. And the moon was huge, glowing and reflecting off the calm surface of the ocean water. It was one of the most beautiful things I had ever seen.

Jess stepped over and wrapped her arm around my waist, resting her head against my side. She kissed my chest through my shirt, and I tried to steady my breathing.

"Ryan..." I croaked, my hands shaking a little. He glanced back down from the sky, his dark eyes locking on mine as he raised his brows, waiting for me to speak. "Um... there's something I need to... ask you."

I breathed in deep and swallowed hard, watching his face. I was so damn nervous. It was truly insane.

"What's that?" he asked, casually.

I hummed out a soft noise and just stared at his gorgeous face. He looked so amazingly good, beneath the moonlight; sun-kissed skin, dark hair all tousled around, stubble overgrown. He was sexy as fuck. But not only that... He was my man. The only man I'd ever loved.

I took his hand and laced our fingers. "Ryan, I love you so much. With all of my heart, and then some. You've meant so much to me, that simple words aren't enough... So, if you'll let me... I'd like to show you just how much I truly love you..."

Ryan's face froze, and he looked momentarily startled. "Ben... this isn't a question..."

Jess giggled next to me, and he glanced down at her, his forehead creasing.

"What's happening?" he asked through a shaky breath. "Why do I feel like I'm being left out of something...?"

I grinned and bit my lip. "Baby... will you please... marry us?" I squeezed his hand hard.

I heard Jess whimper at my side, and I looked down to see her balling her eyes out.

"He hasn't said anything yet," I whispered to her, kissing the top of her head. My eyes came back to Ryan, and he was still shocked speechless, his mouth hanging open.

"Are you being serious?" he grunted, his chest moving up and down rapidly.

I nodded slowly, then I ran my hand slowly up his shoulder, and neck, holding his jaw. I leaned in closer to his lips, my heart hammering inside me.

"Holy fuck..." he whispered.

"Marry me, baby..." I breathed. "Please?"

He nodded and chomped his lip to stop it from trembling. He glanced down at Jess, who was hysterically weeping.

"Marry me, too... please," she sniffled, tears streaming down her face.

Ryan smiled through an adorable pout, breathing out hard.

"Fuck me... yes..." he huffed, grabbing my neck and pulling my lips to his. "Yes, of course I will marry you. Both of you... oh my God..."

He kissed me over and over and I felt like fireworks were going off inside me. Then he moved down to Jessica, kissing her lips and her cheeks; kissing away her tears. The three of us huddled together, hugging and kissing, and really just loving each other. It was almost too much for my heart to handle.

"But... how are we going to get married...?" Ryan finally asked, subtly sniffling. His eyes darted back and forth between Jess and me.

"We have an idea," Jess grinned, wiping under her eyes.

"If you're on board..." I pushed his hair back with my fingers.

"Of course," he nodded. "I'm down for whatever, as long as I get to spend forever with both of you."

Jess squeaked again, and Ryan chuckled sympathetically.

"You'll have to stop being so sweet, or she'll never make it," I smirked.

"Sorry..." Jess chirped, and we both laughed.

Ryan agreed to let me surprise the two of them with my wedding plan, and then the three of us decided to call it an early night. We went back to our suite and spent the rest of the night with our bodies entwined in passion and lust. My wife and my fiancé... The night was pure magic.

The next day I was out for hours, arranging everything. I found someone to perform the ceremony, an altar and flowers, and three rings, one for each of us. I figured Ryan could wear his on the standard left hand, and Jess and I could wear ours on our right hands. It would be different, but we were making our own rules, and that was the most exciting part. I had never been more thrilled.

When the time came, I wasn't anywhere near as nervous as I had been to ask. It just felt so right. Everything about it was perfect.

They set up an altar on the beach, with all the flowers everywhere, smelling so good it was downright euphoric. The three of us dressed up; Ryan and I in shorts and button-downs with ties, and Jessica in a strapless white dress.

We stood beneath the altar as the sun set, and we got married.

Jess and I read our vows to Ryan, and he read his vows to us. We vowed to always cherish and support him; to guide him and to honor him; to love side-by-side, without jealousy or bitterness; to give him solace in his time of need. And he vowed the same to us. To remain faithful and true; honest and open; to dedicate his life, his heart and soul... to us. The priest blessed us, and just like that... We were man, and man, and wife.

It was the most perfect, beautiful, real and genuine thing we had ever done.

And that night, we had a true honeymoon.

The three of us made love beneath the stars. Married.

After ten-days in Thailand, we were finally home.

Everything looked the same, but it felt so completely different.

At first, we were excited. Still dazed and high from vacation; the wedding; all the sex and delicious food. It took a few days for us to get back into the swing of things.

Going back to work definitely helped with that. I couldn't walk around the job-site daydreaming about my husband and wife. Shit actually needed to get done. So I buckled down and focused, because this job was important, and I had a growing family to support. But I was all right with it. I enjoyed knowing that Ryan was at home taking care of Jess while I made the money. Though I knew he was itching to go back to work at some point.

He kept asking me about landscaping jobs, and I was dodging it a little. I really needed him home for now. We could work everything else out after the baby was born.

A week after we got home, the inevitable drama began. Our friends and family were harassing us. They hadn't heard from us in a while, and I guess they were worrying.

Between my brother, Jess's parents, Greg and Marie, Bill and Rachel, Alec and Kayla, it seemed as if everyone we knew was dying to find out exactly what we were doing. Apparently, we wouldn't be able to hide away forever...

Jacob was calling me nonstop. I had been ignoring his calls for a while, because I was still trying to figure out how to tell him about Ryan. No one knew about our relationship yet, but now that we were home, and everyone was speculating, it was time. We would have to tell people.

I figured I might as well start with my brother.

I invited him over for dinner one night while Jess and Ryan were out shopping. He immediately knew something was up.

"So, there's something I need to tell you..." I muttered while we sat in the living room eating pizza.

"Yea, I'm sure there is..." he replied. "I heard you went to Boston, and then you came back and flew to Thailand for ten days. What's with all the traveling while Jess is pregnant?"

I took a breath and dove right in. "I've been seeing someone..."

"Ryan?" he asked, and my eyes darted up to his. "Bro, I know you. Something was obviously up when Tate brought him over for Christmas Eve."

I nodded slowly and swallowed hard over my nerves.

"What about Jess?" he asked, shaking his head. "You guys have been together forever... She's pregnant, for fuck's sake."

"Jake, it's not like that," I explained. "Ryan is... with us. Me *and* Jess." I paused and glanced at him, making sure his head hadn't exploded. "It's been a long, complicated story, but basically... I went to Boston to bring him home. So he could raise the baby with us. His baby... I mean, *our* baby. The three of us."

My brother stayed quiet for a while, staring at me with wide eyes. I took another bite of my pizza.

"Jesus Christ..." he finally breathed, shaking his head again in disbelief. "I don't even know what to say..."

"Well, hold that thought," I chuckled, awkwardly running my hand along the back of my neck. "We got married in Thailand."

Jacob was sufficiently shocked. I tried explaining things the best I could, but it was understandably difficult for him to grasp all these new details. He remained supportive, but when he left, I felt exhausted. And I knew this was only the beginning...

The next day, Ryan talked to his friends. According to him, it went well. And then Jess called her parents. They were downright stunned. *Confused and slightly disturbed*, were the words Jess had used. And of course they blamed me. *Wouldn't have expected anything else.*

After that, Jess and I bit the bullet and invited Greg, Marie, Bill and Rachel over for dinner next week. We wanted to tell them all together. It would probably be a bit disastrous, but we had agreed that ripping it off like a Band-Aid was the best approach.

There were many people in our lives we would have to explain our relationship to. And sure, some of them would get it, and support us. And some wouldn't. It was just the nature of the whole thing.

But to me, none of that stuff mattered. Because I had my soulmates. The people who would love me and care for me until the day I died. That was all I needed.

The next day, Ryan was building some baby furniture in the guestroom, which we had converted into a nursery. I came in to help him, but found him lying on the floor, staring up at the ceiling.

I sat down next to him. "Baby... Is everything okay?"

"No..." he murmured, closing his eyes.

"What's wrong?" I asked softly, running my fingers over his hand.

"There's that Lamaze class next week..." he whispered.

"Okay... What's wrong with that?" I stared down at him.

"I want the three of us to go together... But I'm worried about it. Jess said she'll probably know people there. It's a small town, you know...?"

I nodded slowly. "Baby, I don't think Jess is worried about it. So why are you?"

He opened his eyes and gazed up at me. "What if someone tells Hailey?"

I gulped down my dread and took a long breath. I had no idea what to say. The fact that this whole thing was happening behind my daughter's back was never far in my mind. Out of all the people we needed to explain ourselves to, Hailey was the most important, and understandably the most complicated. I had been putting off talking to her, but we were running out of time.

"I couldn't stand to hurt her, Ben," he whispered. "She's one of my best friends."

"I know..." I grunted, rubbing my eyes. "I'm so sorry I did this to you..."

"Don't do that. It's not your fault," he admonished me.

"I can't let her find out from someone else," I huffed. "Jess and I will have to talk to her. We'll do it this weekend. We'll drive up there and see her..."

Ryan nodded. "It's for the best."

"You're right," I leaned down to kiss him.

"You think we'll be okay for Lamaze?" he asked, so sweet and worrisome it made me smile.

"We'll be fine. Everything will *always* be fine, as long as we have each other."

He nodded again, then tugged me on top of him. We kissed for a while. Then got up and built some baby furniture.

RYAN'S EPILOGUE

I WAS PACING AROUND THE EMPTY HOUSE. My heart was basically bursting out of my chest, and I needed to take a seat, before I had a heart attack.

Ben and Jess were in Albuquerque. They drove up that morning to see Hailey.

It was finally happening. They were telling her about us.

It was crazy to think we were voluntarily telling her now, after all the time spent sneaking around, hiding it on purpose. But Ben and Jessica decided that she needed to know, and I agreed. After all, Jess would be due in about six weeks. Hailey would come down and want to spend time with the baby...

And I fucking lived in her house. It was weird. I still almost couldn't believe I was married to my ex's parents. *There should be a reality show about this shit. Or a Lifetime movie.*

Suddenly my phone started ringing. I pulled it out of my pocket, expecting to see the picture of Ben I took in Thailand and set as my caller ID for him. It was a great picture...

He was lying on a chaise lounge by the pool, teal ocean in the background, wearing swim trunks that sat scandalously low on his hips, showing off his big, firm body; muscles everywhere. His gorgeous blue eyes slightly squinted from the sun, dirty blonde hair mussed up from my fingers, and skin pure golden perfection, like caramel that melted in my mouth.

He was so goddamned perfect, I couldn't even process it. Between him and Jessica-my queen and the mother of my unborn baby-I was the luckiest, happiest man on Earth. I had never felt such bliss. I hadn't thought it was possible.

Minus what was happening at the moment. Because my phone was ringing in my hand, and it wasn't Ben, or Jess's gorgeous pictures coming up on the screen.

It was Hailey's name.

"Fuck..." I muttered to myself and swiped to ignore the call. I quickly pulled up Ben's contact and pressed call, tapping my foot on the floor over and over again.

The phone rang a couple times before he finally answered, and my heart was in my throat.

"Hey, babe..." he sighed, sounding spent.

"What's going on?" I grunted, pacing again. "What happened? Hailey's calling me..." My phone started beeping in my ear and I pulled it away to check the screen. It was her again. *Fuck me.* "Shit! Why is she calling me? Is she going to yell at me??"

"Baby, she's not going to yell at you," Jess answered through the Bluetooth in Ben's car.

"She might..." Ben grumbled, and the mere seriousness of his voice was making me tremble.

"Jesus... what happened?" I asked again, frantically. There was still beeping in my ear. She wasn't going to stop until I answered the phone. "Where are you guys?"

"We're like two hours away from home," Jess replied. "You might as well just answer and see what she has to say. It can't possibly be worse than what she said to us..."

I swallowed hard, feeling horribly ill all of a sudden.

"She took it bad...?" I whispered.

"Not *bad...*" Ben sighed. "She was just... hurt. That we hid it from her. She's disappointed." I heard him grumble to himself, and I knew he was beyond pissed off.

Hailey was his baby girl. And Ben was a stern, controlling dad. I already knew that Hailey being disappointed in him would make him feel frustratingly out-of-control, which was not something Ben enjoyed. Not one bit.

"Baby," I hummed, trying to pacify him with my comforting tone. "It'll be okay."

"Ryan... she's my *daughter*," he whimpered. "I feel so terrible for what I've done to her."

"Ben, this isn't your fault," Jess and I both said at the same time. Normally something like that would have made the three of us giggle, but clearly no one was in the mood for laughter.

"You both say that, but I'm the one who started all of this behind Hailey's back," he croaked.

"No, I did..." I whispered, glancing down at the ringing phone in my hand. If anyone deserved Hailey's disappointment, it was me. "I'll call you back."

I disconnected the call with Ben and closed my eyes, taking in a deep breath before sliding my thumb to accept.

"Hello...?" I cringed, waiting for the screaming to begin.

"Hey, Ryan," Hailey muttered, sounding... regular. Not necessarily upset or anything. But she certainly didn't sound like her usual chipper self, which immediately twisted a knot in my gut.

"H-how's it going?" I stuttered, feeling so fucking stupid.

"Ryan, you don't have to act like you don't know why I'm calling..." she murmured. "I know you're in my house right now. Or should I say, *our* house..."

She didn't sound thrilled in the slightest. She sounded brooding and sullen. It was so unlike her.

"I'm not... I don't..." I fumbled for my words then gave up and sighed out hard. "I don't know what to say... Do you want me to leave?"

"Ryan, don't be stupid," she scoffed, and I could hear her rolling her eyes.

"I'm sorry, but I don't know what to do to make you not hate me!" I plopped down on to the couch and rubbed my eyes. "I'll do whatever you want me to do, Hailey, just tell me."

"Stop being such a fucking people-pleaser, Ryan!" she shouted at me over the phone. "Jesus Christ, you love my parents, don't you??"

"Yes," I gulped and nodded, though she couldn't see me.

"Then nothing in the entire world should ever come between that," she mumbled. "Not even me sulking over this weird-ass shit."

"Hailey, what are you saying...?" I asked.

"I'm saying that I'll be fine," she breathed, and my head shot up. "I mean... it's gonna take some time. This is... fucking *crazy*."

"Yea... it is. I won't argue with that one," I hummed, finally allowing myself to smile a little.

"I just wish they would have told me sooner..." she sighed. "It hurts to be lied to, you know? Especially by my dad..."

"Hailey, I'm not asking for any overnight miracles, but just try to give Ben a break, if you can..." I pleaded, my tone soft and slightly desperate. "He's been killing himself over this."

Hailey was quiet for a moment, hopefully considering my words.

"Of course you would stand up for him," she huffed, and I thought I heard a little chuckle slip through.

"I have to," I said.

"I know," she squeaked. "You're lucky I already love you so much..." She finally giggled, and I felt a wave of hallelujah crash over me. *She'll get there. Thank God!*

"I love you like crazy, Hales. I always will," I told her. "You're the family I've always wanted."

She was silent again, and I heard her sniffle. I didn't want her to cry, but I knew she had to feel it. It was the only way the four of us could move forward.

"I so knew there was something up when my dad punched Tate on Christmas Eve!" she squealed, and I chuckled, shaking my head.

"Yea, he wasn't exactly thinking clearly at that point..." I murmured.

"Is that why you left...?" she asked quietly. "Because of them?"

I breathed out slowly. "I left because... Because I couldn't have them. Your dad ended it to protect you, Hailey. He loves you more than he's ever loved anyone or anything. But I think ultimately, he realized that you love him just the same. There's so much love between all of us, you know? We can't be mad about it. We should be celebrating it..."

"You're right," she whimpered. And I stayed on the phone with her while she cried softly in my ear.

Twenty-minutes later I hung up with Hailey and called Ben right back. He answered on a half-ring.

"Well?" he gasped, so obviously torn up over all this. It was really sweet. "What did she say?"

"She'll be alright," I breathed, a hundred-pound weight lifting off my shoulders. It felt incredible to have everything in the open. It was the most freeing feeling... Like I was floating.

Ben let out a hard sigh of relief and I could picture Jess squeezing his hand over the center console. It made me smile so big.

"Now come home, please," I chuckled softly. "I miss my husband and wife."

The moment we stepped through the doors, I could tell this would be an experience unlike any other.

Ben, Jess, and I were attending our first Lamaze class. I was so excited to learn stuff about how to take care of my wife up until she went into labor. The due date was approaching fast, and it was taking a lot for me to keep from panicking.

It helped that Ben and Jess had been through this before. I hadn't been around too many pregnant ladies in my life, but our wife seemed to be quite calm. I couldn't even begin to imagine how she and Ben had done this when they were teenagers. There was so much work involved, and the baby wasn't even here yet.

Jess rolled out her yoga mat on the floor while Ben and I looked around. Naturally we were the only threesome there. The rest of the room was filled with only couples.

I could feel people's eyes on us right away and I already knew what they were thinking.

Gay couple with their surrogate.

We got that a lot. Most of the time we didn't bother correcting people, if we were out at the grocery store or Babies R Us. The opinions of strangers didn't matter to us in the slightest.

But seeing their confused faces when we were out at dinner or the movies was sort of funny. I guess gay couples rarely did that with their surrogates...

"Hello!" a female voice chimed to my left, and I glanced up to see a lady approaching us with a huge smile covering her face. "I'm Stacey, the instructor!"

"Hi, there!" Jess crooned, shaking her hand while the other rested on her lower back. She was so big. It was amazing. "I'm Jess, and this is Ben and Ryan." She smiled up at me and Ben.

"Nice to meet you," I grinned, politely shaking her hand before Ben did the same.

"Nice to meet the three of you!" Stacey replied in an overly enthusiastic tone. I could tell she was dying to ask about our situation but was forcing herself to remain professional.

She probably didn't get many gay couples in class. And I was willing to bet she'd never even *seen* a poly-trio before.

"Have a seat and let's get Mom comfortable," Stacey instructed. "We'll begin shortly."

We all nodded, Ben and I each taking one of Jess's hands, helping her sit slowly on the mat. We both sat down across from her, and I breathed out softly, unable to stop my eyes from darting all over the place.

"How many of them are staring?" Jess asked with a wicked smirk on her glowing face.

"All of them," Ben hummed, trailing his hand up and down my thigh. "Don't expect this to be very exciting, kid. It's mostly just breathing and staring at each other." He chuckled, and I smiled at him, taking his fidgety hand in mine.

"They teach you how to give a mean foot massage," Jess hummed, rubbing her belly in slow circles.

"I could teach that class, beautiful," Ben bragged, winking at her. She flushed and bit her lip.

"Where's my foot massage?" I grumbled, elbowing him in the side.

"Where's mine?" he teased, and I slapped him in the chest, then kissed his cheek while Jess giggled.

"Now they're *really* staring," he whispered, and I laughed out loud.

"Should we give them a show?"

Jess nodded and squealed, clapping her hands together in excitement. I shook my head at the two of them.

"Come on, guys. Be serious," I scolded them. "I haven't done this before. I want to learn."

Ben and Jess shared a look, stifling their giggles.

"He's such a student," Ben grinned, and Jess nodded, wiggling her eyebrows.

"Shhh!" I shushed them as Stacey started her introduction.

An hour later, the class was about done. It was pretty straightforward, but I appreciated the central theme which was remaining calm and keeping Mom happy, no matter what. There was zero room for stress in a pregnant lady's world, and apparently there were many ways for Ben and me to keep Jess relaxed and *Zen* at all times.

Ben was sitting behind Jess, rubbing her shoulders and nuzzling his face in her neck, while I was on the other side, massaging her feet. Since about five-minutes into class we had been getting some interesting looks. It seemed like people had figured out Jess wasn't our surrogate.

No one appeared uncomfortable with our trifecta of a relationship. In fact, we had somehow wound up the most popular group in class. Everyone wanted to get close to us, like we were celebrities or something. And Stacey had singled us out a few times, using us as an example for some breathing exercises, especially because Ben and Jess had done this once before.

Stacey announced that the class was done, and Jess slipped her Uggs back on, holding out her hands for us to help her stand up. Ben and I were both smiling and touching her belly, reveling in how much our baby was moving around at the moment when I realized we were being surrounded.

It took us twenty-five-minutes to get out of there. All the other couples wanted to introduce themselves to us, most of them giving us their numbers and inviting us over for dinners. By the time we were buckling up in the car and driving home, my head was spinning.

"Well, it's safe to say we're officially the talk of the town," Ben hummed, backing out of the parking space and driving us away.

"It seemed like they were all pretty supportive," Jess yawned, reclining her seat. I moved up to the back of it and ran my fingers through her hair, kissing her head and treasuring that sweet smell of jasmine and honeysuckle.

"I never thought being in a *thruple* would make me so popular," I chuckled, glancing up at Ben, who smiled.

"It feels really good not to hide anymore," he rasped. I ran my hand along his shoulder.

My phone started ringing, and I rustled it out of my pocket, my face falling.

"Who is it?" Ben asked, clearly noting the uneasy look on my face.

"It's my mom..." I whispered.

It was quiet inside the car, the only sound that of my ringtone.

"Are you gonna answer it, baby?" Jess asked, soft and inquisitive.

I hesitated for a second. I hadn't spoken with my mother since before I left Boston. She had no idea about the move back, Ben and Jess... the baby.

And I supposed there was no better time than the present to fill her in.

I took a deep breath and finally decided, swiping the screen.

"Hi, Mom," I greeted her, putting the phone on speaker.

We talked for the entire duration of our car ride home. I told my mom about my relationship with Hailey's parents, the baby, and our wedding in Thailand. Needless to say, she was completely shocked, like most other people who found out about our situation for the first time.

But my mother had an open-mind. She was accepting of whatever made me happy and ultimately I think this whole thing made her realize that she didn't talk to me anywhere near enough.

By the end of the call, we had planned a trip for her to come out and stay at the house for a couple days, before the baby was born. She was itching to meet Ben and Jessica. I could hear her excitement over the phone which made me so happy I felt like I could implode. Jess was already talking about going out to Denver after the baby came. The both of them really wanted to see my hometown, which was sweet.

Once we were home, securely settled inside, the three of us cuddled up in bed and watched a movie. It was my favorite place in the world... In bed with my husband and wife. I had never felt as safe and loved as I did when Ben was holding me against him with his strong arms, Jess on the other side, holding my hand on top of her pregnant belly. It was a level of comfort I had never experienced in my entire life.

This was love. Real, true, consuming love, deep in my bones.

It was everlasting. Written in time.

Ben, and Jessica, and Ryan. Together forever.

I felt like I might collapse at any moment.

But I couldn't. I had to stay upright. On my feet. I couldn't pass out. Not now...

Breathe. Don't fall down. Do. Not. Fall. Down.

There was a lot of noise happening around me. People were shuffling about. Nurses plugging things in, wheeling tray tables over, unwrapping items covered in plastic and handing them to each other.

My heart was ready to surge through my chest.

Fuck me.

I wiped my sweaty palms on my jeans.

"Ryan," Ben's voice called to me from my left and my head darted up. He was handing me scrubs to put on. My hands began to tremble.

Oh God. This is happening. It's real.

Jess made a noise, and I looked up from pulling on my new protective garments to see Ben holding her hand while a nurse injected her with the epidural. She squealed out in pain and I swallowed hard.

"You're doing great, baby," Ben whispered, kissing her moist temple. "The pain will be gone in a second."

I stepped over to the bed and Ben grabbed my hand, squeezing it tight. He looked so strong and in-control the whole time. But that one little gesture told me he was nervous. It made me want to burst into tears.

Jess was already three days past her due date. We were getting impatient when her water broke while we were out shopping. It was chaotic. Luckily, we were only a couple miles from the hospital. And of course we were always prepared, with her bags in the car at all times.

She was dilating fast. By the time we got to the hospital, she was ready to be moved upstairs to our *birthing suite*, which was basically just a room with our doctor in it.

Now that she had the epidural in her, it was almost time to push.

I was so fucking scared, but also more excited than I ever had been. I couldn't wait to meet my baby.

"I can't believe you guys still don't know if it's a boy or girl," Ben crooned, trying to lighten the mood which we both appreciated to no end. "I feel so powerful. I'm like the Wizard of Oz." He did the voice and Jess let a strained giggle slip through.

"I really want to know..." I whined, brushing Jess's hair back with my fingers. I pouted at her and she laughed, soft and lazy. The epidural must have kicked in.

"It seems like you're gonna know really soon," she cringed through a contraction, visibly squeezing Ben's hand hard. She groaned, and I couldn't help myself. I wrapped my arm around Ben's waist and pressed my face into his shoulder.

I was going to cry. It was going to happen any second. I couldn't hold back.

"Baby, it's okay," Ben spoke, firm and commanding. He turned slightly so that his eyes were on mine, holding me down with that powerful blue. "Everything is fine. Our baby is coming."

"Ben..." I whimpered, chomping on my lip to stop it from quivering. "I'm so nervous. What if I fuck this up? What if I'm a bad father?"

"Ryan... shut the fuck up," Ben grunted, giving me a pointed look which made me chuckle and swallow hard. "You will be the *best* fucking father. I know you will. You love so hard and so strong, baby. You will shower this kid with love, so stop worrying please."

"I love when you say *please*," I hummed, holding onto him tight.

He laughed softly and kissed me quick before turning back to Jess again. She looked pretty out of it, but still so damn beautiful. I had no idea how she pulled it off. She was the most gorgeous woman in labor ever; I was sure of it.

The whirlwind of emotions lasted only another few minutes, before the doctor was in the room, between Jess's legs, telling her to push.

After that, I think I blacked out.

I tried hard to remember all the stuff they taught us in Lamaze class, and everything I'd read in the numerous baby books, but some strange instincts kicked in, and I was just there for Jess. Ben and I were right by her side the whole time, holding her, whispering encouraging words and telling her how good she was doing. I had sympathy pangs for Jess. It was almost like I was giving birth alongside her. It wasn't unusual, given how connected the two of us were. I felt her pain, especially now.

But Jess was a pro. She didn't need us to tell her how awesome she was doing. You would have never known it had been almost twenty-years since the last time she did this. She was a rock. Ben was right... She definitely was there to take care of us all.

I was so anxious to meet my son or daughter, I couldn't even breathe. I made my way over to the doctor to see what was happening and was momentarily horrified. There was an actual human coming out of Jess's body. It was psychotic.

"Almost there, baby," Ben held our wife's hand tight, allowing her to basically fracture his bones. She was stronger than she looked.

"How much longer?" Jess whined, out of breath and panting. "I want to be done..."

Ben glanced at me, raising his brows, wanting me to tell them how far along the process was. I gulped and peeked down again.

"Shoulders..." I croaked, then blinked hard. *Jesus Christ... what the fuck am I watching right now?!?*

"See? Shoulders, babe! That's great!" Ben cheered. He was so good at this. *God, I fucking love him. He's so perfect. Such a hot dad.*

I looked once more and saw the baby coming out...

"Okay, the stomach is out... and... holy fuck..." I grunted, running my hand through my hair, tears pushing behind my eyes. "It's a boy."

I gaped up at Ben and he was grinning so wide, his brows knitting together as he looked like he was about to break down himself.

"A boy??" Jess squealed, tears flowing down her face. Then she screamed out one final time as our son emerged, ready and waiting to be greeted by his eager parents.

"A healthy baby boy!" the doctor cheered, and all the nurses whooped and wailed, quietly of course. "Congratulations!"

"Oh my God..." I whimpered, sniffling as Ben cuddled Jessica, kissing her head all over.

"Do you want to cut the umbilical cord, Mr. Lockwood?" one of the nurses asked, and when I glanced down at her, she was looking up at me, waiting for a response.

"Oh shit, you're talking to me," I breathed, and Ben and Jess giggled. "Sorry! No one's ever called me that before. It sounds great." I bit my lip and let her show me what to do, snipping our son's umbilical cord before they took him to get cleaned off.

I stumbled over to my husband and wife, eyes locked on my baby boy in the nurse's arms, making sure he was okay.

"He's not crying," I mumbled, leaning down and kissing Jess's sweaty forehead.

"He's quiet," the nurse responded from across the room, likely to pacify me and all my swirling thoughts.

"Hailey was the same. Until we got her home the next day," Jess sighed, taking my hand and squeezing it tight.

"Yea, then she turned into a wild animal," Ben added, kissing my cheek. "Get ready, Daddy."

I whimpered and hugged onto Jess as much as I could, while the two of them laughed at me. But we were all crying. It was such an amazing moment.

The nurse finally brought the baby over, wrapped in his little blanket, placing him gently in Jess's arms.

"He's so beautiful," she whispered, coddling her newborn, while Ben and I huddled over them, blinking back tears. Ben's arm was wrapped so tightly around me, it was like he was trying to make us one.

"He's perfect," Ben sighed at the small being, who was blinking his blue eyes right at Mommy.

"His eyes..." I murmured as my whole body radiated love and affection. "They're *incredible*."

"He has your eyes, Momma," Ben nudged Jess's shoulder, and she nodded, crying softly.

"So I guess this means we have a name..." she sniffled, blinking up at me and Ben.

We looked at each other and nodded.

"Ethan James Harper Lockwood," Ben rasped, and I bit my lip.

It was such a perfect name.

We named our baby after Ben's and my fathers. Ethan was Ben's dad, and James was mine.

I quickly swiped at a tear falling down my cheek.

"Jessica..." I hummed, shaking my head slowly. "I can never ever thank you enough... You've given me the best gift of my life. You made me a father." I started to falter. It was all too much... "I love you so hard, baby..."

I bent down and grasped her face gently, kissing her lips while she cried into my mouth. Then I kissed Ethan's soft little patch of light hair. When I pulled back, he was staring right at me.

I could feel it, in that moment, more than I ever knew I could...

Love, and dedication, unconditional.

I would protect this child as long as I was breathing. I would make sure he was happy, and safe at all times.

He was my son.

"I love the three of you..." I whispered, and Ben kissed my neck softly.

"I'm so glad you came into our lives, Ryan," Jess squeaked. "This is us. Our little family."

I chuckled through my tears and nodded.

After that, Ben took Ethan and sat down with him, holding him close, letting Ethan's tiny head rest on his bare chest to feel his heartbeat.

And then I did the same.

Holding my son in my arms, and watching my husband and wife do the same, was the greatest moment of my whole life. I would forever remember and cherish this feeling.

I had finally found my happy ending.

JESSICA'S EPILOGUE

"**B**EN! CAN YOU GET THE DOOR PLEASE?!**" I squealed, up to my elbows in chocolate frosting.

"Got it!" I heard Ben's voice bellow from down the hall, and I listened closely to determine who was there. *Early, I might add. The party doesn't start for another three hours!*

I sighed out my relief when I heard Bill and Rachel's voices. They wouldn't expect to be entertained, which was good. They had a baby who needed to be looked after, but I knew Ryan would take the reins on that. Him and Ben would watch the kids while Hailey and I finished decorating the cake.

"Hi!" my best friend cheered as she walked into the kitchen holding a huge wrapped gift and a separate gift bag.

"Hi, sweetie!" I smiled as she darted over to kiss me on the cheek.

"Oh, let me grab those," Hailey said, taking the gifts and bringing them to the dining room.

"Where's the birthday boy?" Rachel asked, gazing over the counter which was covered in cake decorating supplies.

"Ryan has him in the living room, I think," I answered. "Did you see balloons when you walked in? Ben was supposed to put them up."

"Yes, honey. Everything looks great," Rachel crooned. "All ready for a party."

"Mom, did you hear back from Grandma and Grampy yet?" Hailey asked, staggering over to us.

I paused and tensed for a moment. "Not yet."

"That's crazy if they don't show up," Rachel muttered, a disapproving look covering her face. "It's their grandson's first birthday. They need to be here."

Hailey nodded in agreement.

I sighed and shook my head. "Honestly, if they feel too weird about being here, then it's their loss. I can't be concerned with what other people are doing."

I put on a nonchalant face, but inside I was wavering.

My parents were still a little uncomfortable about Ben, Ryan, and my relationship. They claimed they were fine with it, but I could tell when they came up to visit after Ethan was first born that they were struggling to accept us as a trio, raising our baby together.

I really didn't understand what my mom's problem was. She herself had never done a paternity test to prove that my grandpa was actually her father, even though she was always complaining about the fact that allegedly my grandma told her when she was younger there was a possibility her real father was a former boyfriend of my grandma and grandpa. I guess they all used to fool around together before my grandmother got pregnant.

You would think this would make my mother more understanding to the fact that I had two husbands, and that Ethan had two fathers, but no. My mom acted like we were aliens or something.

It was very frustrating.

But I forced myself to push all these insecurities aside and focus on finishing Ethan's cake. It was his first birthday, and everything needed to be perfect.

"Oh yea! Look who we've got here!" Ben stalked into the kitchen with Rachel and Bill's son, William Jr., on his shoulders. "It's master William of the shire," Ben drawled in a terrible English accent that had me and Hailey giggling. "I am but a lowly peasant, sir. Allow me to whisk you around the court at your leisure."

He spun around the room, and William started laughing up a storm. It was pretty freaking adorable. William was almost two, and he loved his Uncle Ben to death. Mainly because Ben was huge, and he could put him up seven feet into the air and swing him around.

"Say hello to lady Jessica," Ben hummed, bringing William over and bending down so I could kiss his little cheek. William was giggling like crazy. "All right, now let's go find the man of the hour!"

Ben winked at me as he left the room, likely to go find Ryan with our son. We were keeping Ethan away from the cake, not that he would understand what it was. The surprise aspect was more for our benefit. But I knew even a one-year-old would be excited for his first taste of chocolate.

I finished frosting the cake, then Hailey took over decorating for a minute so I could go check on the boys. Also, my boobs were a little sore, and it was probably about time to pump.

I made my way to the living room and peeked around the corner in time to catch Ryan with Ethan on his stomach, play peek-a-boo. It was his favorite game to play with Daddy.

I grinned watching them, my ovaries shuddering at the sight. Ryan was such a wonderful father, it was almost unbelievable.

I pulled my phone out of the pocket of my sweater and started taking sneaky pictures. My phone was practically out of storage, but I just couldn't help it. I *loved* taking pictures of my husbands playing with our son. I was obsessed.

William was sitting comfortably on the rug next to Ryan's feet, playing with some flashy, light-up toy, while Ryan entertained Ethan. It was too sweet to see him with both kids. It made me want to get pregnant again, like *now*.

Ethan was such a perfect baby. He was quiet and calm. He barely ever cried, even when he was a newborn. Plus, he was the most adorable boy on the face of the Earth.

He had bright blue eyes, like Ben's, and his hair was a light chestnut brown. It was growing so fast, and I could already see that it wanted to curl a bit, like Ryan's. Looking at him made my chest ache with a desire to be near him all the damn time. To touch him and kiss his chubby cheeks; to smell his sweet scent, like if heaven had been bottled up as a fragrance. I couldn't stand being away from him for even a minute.

Fortunately for me, I really didn't have to. Ben worked and made enough money to support the whole family. And the best part was that I had Ryan at home with me, too.

Ryan dropped out of law school after Ethan was born. At the time, Ben and I were scared that we had derailed his career and caused him to waste years and tons of money. But Ryan assured us that his heart hadn't been in it for a while. That he'd been keeping it up because he felt like he had to. According to him, it wasn't his dream to be a lawyer anymore.

He spent the first six months at home with Ethan and me. And Ben's company pretty much ran itself, so he could stay home with us for a while, too. It was honestly the best time of my life; just hanging out with my boys. I felt so complete; it was almost scary.

Eventually, Ryan decided that he needed to do something. So Ben bought him an old Mustang to restore, which apparently had been an interest of Ryan's. Ben said they had talked about it a while back, and he had a feeling it would make Ryan happy. And he was totally right.

It was a bit of a learning curve. Ryan started taking some automotive classes at the local tech school, and he was learning a lot. We were so proud of how dedicated he was. He was an excellent learner. He picked things up so fast.

He was already almost done with the car. He said he wanted to sell it and use the money to buy another one, and if all went accordingly, possibly open his own shop one day. I could see it happening. He certainly had an eye for it, and was getting really good at the mechanical stuff. I was just glad he finally had found something to make him truly happy. A dream to follow.

Speaking of the car, I could hear Ben talking to Bill about it. He was most likely about to bring him out to the garage to show him Ryan's unfinished masterpiece. He was so proud of Ryan. It was super adorable.

The day went on, and the rest of the guests arrived, one after another. Ben's brother, his wife and the twins, my sister, Greg and Maxine, a couple friends with their kids. It was almost a full house, but I was lucky because I had not one, but two husbands to help entertain everyone, especially the children. Ryan was basically running a daycare at that point.

Everyone had some food, and we were getting the cake ready so we could sing to Ethan when the doorbell rang once more.

"I'll get it," Ryan darted off quickly to see who the late arrival could be. My heart was in my throat. I didn't want to admit it, but I was praying it was my parents. I really didn't want to accept that they were disapproving of my marriage.

Being with Ben and Ryan together came so easy to me. I wasn't sure why, or how, but as soon as Ryan came into our lives, I knew he was meant to be a part of it. The three of us just worked.

Sure, it was difficult sometimes. No marriage is perfect. We were still learning things about each other, and ourselves. And working out the feelings and emotions of two men at once was sometimes a challenge. But we were always honest and open with one another. We had to be.

Ben and Ryan had their own thing going on. And I respected that. Hell, I *loved* it. I absolutely adored how much they loved each other, and how drawn they were to one another. It was fascinating.

Ryan and I had something different, too. We were so connected, sometimes it was like we were the same person. And I knew Ben loved it. Ben was my best friend in the entire world. We had shared so much of our lives with one another. Bringing Ryan into the fold just amplified our feelings... And our love.

I so badly wanted all my friends and family to accept us for what we were. And it seemed like most of them had. Even Hailey was happy about it. It took her some time, as we all expected it would. But she was our daughter, and she loved us. She was mature and wonderful. And she loved Ryan, so that helped our cause a lot.

Ryan's mom had immediately welcomed Ben and I with open arms. She considered us family from the moment we met. It actually brought her and Ryan closer together, which was fantastic.

I wanted that with my own parents. But I had to be okay with the fact that it might never happen like that.

Ryan came traipsing into the room with a wide, beaming smile on his pretty face. I raised my brows at him.

"Look who's here..." he whispered, biting his lip.

And sure enough, there was my mother and father, following

behind him.

My bottom lip started to quiver as I stepped over to them.

"Sorry we're late, sweetheart," my dad said with a smile, kissing me on the cheek.

"I'm so glad you're here," I whimpered, launching myself at him, hugging tight.

"We wouldn't have missed it for the world, darling," my mother hummed, and I grabbed her for a giant hug.

My heart was so full it was overflowing.

"You're just in time," Ben rumbled, and I saw him smiling as he slipped his arm around Ryan's waist.

They're here. They do accept us. Thank God!

Everyone gathered around the dining room table, Ben, Ryan and me huddling around Ethan's high chair. Hailey dimmed the lights, and we all *oohed* and *ahhed* over the *one* candle, lit in the middle of Ethan's giant, fancy cake.

The whole room boomed as we sang *Happy Birthday* to my baby boy, and he looked, well, slightly startled at first. But eventually he warmed up when he saw the enthusiasm on his parents' faces.

"Alright, bud. You're gonna make a wish, and blow out the candle," Ben cheered softly.

"Like this," Ryan said then mimicked blowing air from his lips. Ethan giggled hysterically.

"Everything Daddy does is funny," Ben whispered to me and we laughed together.

"Make a wish, baby," I whispered, kissing his soft hair.

"One, two... three!" Ben gasped and the three of us blew on the candle for Ethan, the flame flickering out.

"Yay!" we cheered, and everyone clapped. Ethan was eating it up. He was bouncing around and throwing his hands in the air.

Ben, Ryan and I were laughing so hard tears were seeping out of our eyes. The kid was a freaking ham already.

Marie and Laura helped cut the cake, handing pieces to everyone. We gave Ethan a nice big piece, though he ended up wearing more than he got into his mouth. I just *had* to take more pictures of that, too.

"Give Poppa a bite," I giggled to Ethan, eyeing Ben with an evil smirk.

Ben licked his lips and leaned in, opening his mouth. Then Ethan smeared his chocolate-covered hand all over Ben's face. Ryan and I were dying. It was the cutest thing I had ever witnessed.

Hailey brought over present after present, and we helped Ethan open them, showing him all of his new toys and clothes. By the end of it all, he was wiped, in spite of all the sugar.

At the end of the night, we were all pretty spent. Our guests had left. My parents went to stay at my sister's, and Hailey was tucked away in her room. Ryan and Ben had just finished giving Ethan a bath, and the three of us put him to bed together. The kid was out like a light, the second we kissed him goodnight.

In our bedroom, baby monitor switched on, we could finally relax. I got undressed, slipping on one of Ben's t-shirts and slinking into bed so Ryan could rub my feet. Ben stammered in from the bathroom in only his boxers, and he immediately had our attention.

"What a great fucking day," he sighed, plopping down on the bed next to us, running his hand along Ryan's back.

"Seriously," Ryan scooted up and grabbed me by the waist. "We have the best family ever."

"We really do," I hummed, looking them over.

"I love you both so much. You know that, right?" Ben asked, blinking over his shimmering blue eyes.

"Yes," Ryan and I answered at the same time, like we always did.

"I love you two," I purred, staring at them like there were hearts floating around their beautiful heads.

They shared a look, then gazed back at me, and I truly felt how blessed I was. Just watching the two of them, watching me, reaffirmed what I had known all along: We were meant for this.

The chemistry between us was like a burning fire that would never die down.

Fate gave us a push, and it made us whole.

I licked my lips, cocking my head to the side at my two fine-as-hell husbands. The men of my dreams.

My insides tightened as they touched each other, anxiously awaiting me to join them.

"Ready, boys?" I whispered, and they nodded slowly. "Let's have some fun."

The End.

ACKNOWLEDGMENTS

Wow! That was crazy.

I just want to thank everyone who read this book. Because it's pretty intense. Honestly, it's not a book I ever thought I would publish, or show to anyone. The idea for this story slipped into my brain and took over my life. For a month straight, all I could think about was this story. I barely ate, barely slept. I lived and breathed Ben and Ryan, and Jess... And when I first started, the story looked very different than how it turned out.

But it came together beautifully, and I decided that theirs was a love story that needed to be shared.

This isn't necessarily a story about finding yourself or coming out as anything. It's just a story about love, following your heart, and how sometimes you fall for the person you never expected to. Love has no labels, or defaults. There's no standard operating procedure. We love who we love, and it should be celebrated. I can only hope that maybe reading this book will help to open some minds, or give consolation to those who may feel unsure. The world is too big for us to close ourselves into a box.

All the thanks in the world goes to my family and friends for supporting me. My wonderful beta readers, my editor, my formatter (Julesies, aka Julia Scott... you are a genius!) And my cover artist, Jada D'Lee, who continues to crush it by making such phenomenal works of art.

To the bloggers, bookstagrammers, and readers: You guys are

everything. Your support and enthusiasm is what makes this all worth it. Keep on reading and being incredible.

If you liked PUSH, or any of my other books, please consider leaving a review. It means the world to this new indie author.

Thank you, and happy reading!

Love love love,

Nyla K

ABOUT THE AUTHOR

Hi, guys! I'm Nyla K, otherwise known as Nylah Kourieh; an awkward sailor-mouthed lover of all things romance, existing in Brooklyn, New York with my fiance, who you can call PB, or Patty Banga, if you're nasty. When I'm not writing and reading, I'm exploring the city, working at my day job, eating lots of yummy food and fussing over my kitten (and no, that's not a euphemism). Did I mention I have a dirtier mind than probably everyone you know?

I like to admire hot guys (don't we all?) and book boyfriends, cake and ice cream are my kryptonite. I can recite every word that was ever uttered on Friends, Family Guy, and How I Met Your Mother, red Gatorade is my lifeblood, and I love to sing, although I've been told I do it in a Cher voice for some reason.

If you tell me you like my books, I'll give you whatever you want. My readers are my friends, and I welcome anyone to find me on social media any time you want to talk books or sexy dudes!

Get at me:
authorNylaK@gmail.com
Instagram: @authorNylaK
Facebook: Author Nyla K
Twitter: @MissNylah
Goodreads: Nyla K
BookBub: @AuthorNylaK

Flipping Hot Fiction

Made in the USA
Coppell, TX
23 August 2021